XX

Sharlie Converse lives a careful life. A life stamped FRAGILE: DO NOT TOUCH.

Sharlie Converse is twenty-six, courageous, and beautiful. Born with a heart defect that has defeated a battalion of specialists, she has lived her short years from moment to moment. Everything that matters most to her—color and excitement, adventure and romance—is forbidden except in the vivid imaginings and secret longings that she has long accepted will never be made real.

Until, on a crosstown bus crowded with Christmas shoppers, she falls into Brian Morgan's arms.

And Sharlie, whom love can kill, must make the agonizing choice: to risk her life by loving or never really to live at all.

CHANGE OF HEART

Sally Mandel

A DELL BOOK

Published by
Dell Publishing Co., Inc.
1 Dag Hammarskjold Plaza
New York, New York 10017

Dell ® TM 681510, Dell Publishing Co., Inc.

ISBN: 0-440-11355-5

Reprinted by arrangement with Delacorte Press
Printed in the United States of America
First Dell printing—May 1981

For Gloria,
who taught me how to fly

I feel enormous gratitude to many people for encouraging me to write, but in particular: Robert Cenedella; Ann Loring; Bridget Potter; my agent, Peter Lampack; my editor, Linda Grey; and Loring Mandel, without whom I cannot imagine having become a writer at all. My special thanks go also to Dr. Robert Lewy for his invaluable medical information and to my long-suffering friends and family, especially Barry.

CHANGE
OF
HEART

CHAPTER 1

The damp December chill penetrated Sharlie's sheepskin coat. Her gloves were too short, and she yanked at her sleeves trying to cover the chapped red circles around her wrists. The last bus in the uptown caravan had just hissed to a stop at the corner, but she resisted the impulse to run for it. That faint jingling sound she heard was probably the Salvation Army band over on Fifth Avenue, but since her attacks sometimes began with bells, she stood still, watching forlornly as the bus slammed shut its doors and roared up Madison Avenue.

One kneesock had slipped down inside her boot and rode painfully against her ankle. She bent over to fix it, sleet trickling down the back of her neck. Sharlie's mother despised kneesocks. After all, she said, a twenty-six-year-old woman isn't a cheerleader anymore, not that Sharlie ever could have been one.

Suddenly the cold and her own bleak exhaustion overwhelmed her. She was going to be late for dinner

anyway, and if there had to be a scene, she might as
well rest in preparation. She peered downtown past
the brightly decorated windows. It was hard to tell
without her glasses, but none of the blurry shapes appeared to be a bus. She picked up her soggy shopping
bags, hoping they'd hold together until she got home,
and entered the steamy warmth of a coffee shop on
the corner of Fifty-third Street. No coffee. No tea.
Too dangerous, all that caffeine upsetting the careful
balance of chemicals in her bloodstream. She ordered
a hot chocolate and settled the packages under the
counter, remembering her father's admonition about
leaving things behind in restaurants. She put one foot
on either side of the shopping bags and took mental
inventory of her purchases: a book on maritime art for
her father, which he would leaf through once and display in his office; a pair of opera glasses for her
mother (Sharlie had left the old ones on her seat after
La Bohème), and since these were really a replacement and not a gift, a long silk robe, rose and silver,
which would look wonderful on Mother. Everything
did, with her long, graceful body. For herself, she'd
bought a pair of furry slippers, hoping they'd ease
what she called the blue-feet syndrome. Cold feet,
warm heart. Sick heart.

The waitress brought the hot chocolate, and as
Sharlie cupped the mug with her hands, warming her
fingers and enjoying the rich, sweet steam in her face,
she tried to picture herself in her mother's new robe.
She grimaced, imagining her feet catching in the sil-
very folds to send her sprawling in an unladylike
heap on the Oriental rug. Mother, on the other hand,
would look chic in overalls and orthopedic shoes,
though of course she'd never be caught dead in such

things. And I, Sharlie thought, in the most expensive basic black little number somehow always end up ripping the dry-cleaner tag off my sleeve after an evening at the opera. Even so, it wasn't that she didn't have the proper lean lines. It was just that they bent in the wrong directions—elbows, knees, all the angles sticking out like those accordion measuring sticks that open into zigzags.

Sharlie sighed, took a sip of her hot chocolate, and wondered if the habit of losing things was an unconscious impulse to leave some kind of impression, a legacy that said, I Was Here Once.

Suddenly she looked up, startled, holding herself very still. There had been a sound, and this time it was definitely not the Salvation Army tambourines. A menacing, discordant jangling, all too familiar, clamored in her ears. She struggled against the rising panic, trying to quiet the uneven hammering in her chest. She exhaled slowly, leaning on her elbows and letting her body slump toward the counter. She gazed down into the soft swirls of warm chocolate, concentrating on them and excluding everything else from her mind. Hot chocolate. *What Hot Chocolate Means to Me, by Charlotte Converse. Hot chocolate means a warm drink before bed when the sheets are going to be cold. Hot chocolate means steamy comfort after a January outing of skating in the park.* . . . No, she thought. Forget the fiction, that's risky. No skating for Sharlie, never was, never will be, world without end, ah-ah-men, ah-ah-men. The color, concentrate on the color.

After a moment the frantic clatter under her rib cage quieted. She squinted at her watch and imagined her parents sitting like statues in the living room, martinis sticking out of their hands, the clocks ticking away inside their heads. Her father would be furious, she thought, but at least he wouldn't worry. *She's perfectly all right, Margaret. She's only lost track of time or gotten on the wrong bus. Why in God's name can't she take a cab? I always tell her . . .*

She says she likes the human contact, her mother would say with a shudder, imagining all those warm bodies pressed against one another.

And they did feel good, Sharlie thought, as ten minutes later she stood, crushed upright in the bus full of shoppers. Warm and secure, she swayed with the lurching stop-and-go motion, sweating in the stifling heat. She surveyed the other passengers, particularly enjoying the black lady with the ferocious face and the bush of hair that circled her head like an electrified halo. Sharlie imagined the feel of it, soft and yet assertive.

Suddenly there was blackness all around her. She closed her eyes, held her breath, and opened them again, but it was still there, the dark that wasn't really dark because it was so alive with bursting, brilliant flashes. No ambiguous ringing this time—instead the ominous thud from deep inside her chest. The sweat she'd relished as evidence of shared humanity betrayed her now, turning cold. The empty thump sounded again, as if some vital piece of machinery had malfunctioned, abandoning its corresponding cog to knock away all by itself, beating against nothing, altering its rhythm in a bewildered attempt to catch up with its fellow gears.

She shut her eyes, speculating about the useless gelatin that seemed to have replaced her legs, grateful for the force of the other bodies packed against her, supporting her. A man's voice, gentle and far away, spoke from somewhere way above her head.

"Hey, are you all right?"

Her eyes refused to open, but with an effort she whispered, "The door . . ."

Her body squeezed through the crowd, the calm voice propelling it.

"Air for this lady. Let us through. Ring the bell, somebody."

And as she was expelled out the door into the icy darkness, the ding of the bus bell grew louder until it blurred into a roar. She looked up at the face of the man who held her arm, tried to smile, murmured, "Sorry."

Then she fell, Christmas lights swirling around her.

She woke to the monotonous clicking of the cardiac monitor machine. No bells, no roar, just the reassuring tick of her heart. She kept her eyes closed, letting her sense of smell come back to life next. She inhaled tentatively and breathed in the familiar aromas—disinfectant, starched sheets, and, always, mashed potatoes and gravy. Saint Joe's. She moved her left hand gingerly, anticipating the stiff resistance of the IV tube.

Eyes still closed, she guessed she was on the eleventh floor, in either 1106 or 1108. Her father alway insisted she have a private room with a view of the park. The light on the left side of her face seemed stronger, warmer, indicating that the window was on her left—1108, she thought, and opened her eyes.

She looked around the room, taking sardonic pleasure in her accuracy. Only an expert could discriminate among these impersonal cubicles, even with eyes wide open. It's so damn *white* in here, she groaned to herself. In my next life hospital rooms will be papered with soft lilac prints. There'll be squishy furniture and heavy old brass lamps. The dinner trays will exude aromas of garlic and peppers, and there must be tea cozies. The ones that look like roosters maybe.

Sharlie shifted her body, taking inventory. With the tiny movement her head swam, and she recognized the drifting sensation of Demerol. She would float on her cloud of relief for a little while, but soon the crushing pain would drag her down for the cruel hours until they could shove the needle in her arm again.

She wondered now, as she had before she even knew the words to ask the question: Whatever did I do? Whom did I offend? She had been born this way, after all, so whatever the crime, it must have occurred *in utero*. Maybe there was a twin fetus in there and she'd strangled it with their umbilical cord. Prenatal fratricide? sororicide? Or maybe she'd explored her unfinished body a bit too adventurously, poking half-formed fingers into places they weren't supposed to know about.

But the voice at the back of her head, the place where she first felt prickles when deeply moved by beauty or tenderness (and horror, too) said, *Nothing, Sharlie. You did nothing to deserve this. You have been ill-treated.* And she supposed that the twisting she felt in her stomach and the heat around her temples could be described as disembodied apocalyptic rage.

The pain was very bad now, and she'd been breathing slowly and deeply for an hour already, trying to survive it. Through a long inhalation she heard a rhythmic swish of white-stockinged things marching toward her door, and with exhausted relief she exhaled and looked up into the pink face of Mary MacDonald.

"What's new, Sharlie?"

"Just the same dull story. How about you?"

The nurse took Sharlie's wrist and started timing the weak little taps, ignoring the monitor in favor of human contact. Sharlie smiled at her and thought that in her next life she'd be a hospital administrator or a floor supervisor like Mary. That sturdy, corseted body deflected germs and anxieties like an immense lady buffalo galloping through a field of butterflies.

"I didn't think we'd see you for a while," Mary said. "What'd you do, climb the World Trade Center?"

"What's the fun in that?" Sharlie said weakly. "Everybody's doing it."

And for the first time, she searched her memory for the events that had put her there. There were lots of lights, she thought, and it was hot. No, cold. She shook her head, remembering a man's voice, a tall, gentle presence.

Mary put Sharlie's wrist down and reached out to stroke her hair. The nurse's hand was warm and round and soft.

Sharlie closed her eyes. "Don't be nice to me, Mary, or I'll fall apart right now."

Instantly the hand stilled, lifted away, and with an abrupt pat on the arm, Mary said, "Okay, kiddo. I'll send Rodriguez in with your shot."

Sharlie squeezed her eyes shut tightly, then relaxed her facial muscles and thought about blue sky. No clouds, no smog. Blue sky that went on forever. Gradually she felt herself being drawn into it, and soon she was asleep.

CHAPTER 2

Margaret Converse stepped off the elevator onto the eleventh floor. She unbuttoned her trench coat and let it fall open, revealing a rich fur lining. In her arms she carried a large bouquet of yellow roses, and she glided down the hall, head high, like a well-rehearsed but aging Miss America.

Grace under duress, Margaret thought, conscious of shoulder aligned with hip, legs swinging relaxed, just as Miss Newhouse had trained them in that soft southern voice, 'way back when. Duress to Miss Newhouse, however, meant showing up at a benefit in the same gown as the hostess. Not this incessant confrontation with death.

Margaret's eyes, frightened shiny circles in the smooth face, darted here and there, seeking someone in authority. Heaven knows hospitals could be intimidating places, she thought, but thank God for Saint Joseph's. Of it all, she most dreaded the weeks when Sharlie recuperated at home where there was no one to make complicated on-the-spot decisions. Except for Walter, of course, but eventually he went off to the office and left her alone with his lists of instructions and the memory of his face filled with mistrust and apprehension.

She stood hesitating near the reception desk when Mary MacDonald suddenly appeared from a doorway down the hall and swished toward her, carrying an aluminum basin. She nodded curtly and marched past. Margaret's stomach muscles tightened with familiar reticence, but she gathered her courage and called after the nurse.

"Uh . . . Nurse MacDonald. I wonder . . . could you . . . ?"

Mary glanced over her shoulder, eyebrows raised in polite irritation.

"Charlotte . . ." Margaret stumbled on. "Which room this time? Has Dr. Diller . . . ?"

"Eleven-oh-eight. She's asleep, but you can go in and sit with her if you want."

Margaret nodded at the nurse's retreating back and walked obediently toward Sharlie's room.

She looked down at her white-faced daughter and was overcome with the familiar sensation of helplessness and exasperation. Why hadn't they fixed her? Was it so much to ask in these days of space exploration and test-tube babies?

She averted her eyes from Sharlie's bed, uncomfortable with her own resentment. There was no call for ingratitude, she thought guiltily. Everyone at Saint Joe's was so kind, always helpful and solicitous. Why, Sharlie felt more at home here than she did in her own townhouse on Seventy-fifth Street. Heaven knows she'd spent more time here than anywhere else, even including the trips abroad for rest cures.

She glanced at Sharlie again. That poor pinched face on the pillow. Margaret's jaw ached from clenching her teeth—where *was* Walter anyway?

She started hunting around the room for a vase, checking in the bedside cabinet for one of those lumpy cardboard containers that were supposed to pass for china. Sure enough, there it was. She busied herself arranging the roses, then shut the curtain against the late afternoon light that came pouring through the window all brazen and cheerful as if there weren't a sick person anywhere in the world.

"Please leave it open."

Margaret whirled, startled to see Sharlie regarding her with burning eyes. She had remarked to Walter once that their daughter's eyes must be like those of Joan of Arc or some other martyred religious fanatic. So strange—huge, an indefinable greenish gray, but very dark, and always gazing at you as if they knew something you didn't, something very important, like the origin of the universe. They made Margaret uncomfortable. Walter thought she was being ridiculous. Big eyes in a small face, he'd said.

Sharlie turned away now, but Margaret had seen the ripple in her forehead.

"Is there much pain now, darling?" she asked.

Sharlie nodded.

"How long until the next injection?"

"Don't know. I think it's only been an hour."

Margaret patted Sharlie's hand, and the two women were silent for a moment.

"How did Daddy take it?" Sharlie murmured finally.

Margaret drew her hand away and fussed nervously with her hair.

"Oh, fine. I mean, of course, he's *upset*."

"Furious."

"Of course not. He's concerned."

Sharlie's mouth twisted up at the corners, and she deepened her voice. " 'Why the hell didn't she take a goddamn cab?' "

Margaret looked down at her lap.

"Well, dear," she said quietly, "there's no reason to subject yourself to those wretched buses. It's intolerable for anybody, much less someone in your condition."

" 'And irresponsible, too,' " Sharlie said in the same hoarse parody.

She lay silent for a long time. Margaret thought she was asleep, and sat chastising herself for being harsh. But as she uncrossed her legs in preparation to get up, Sharlie whispered something. Margaret leaned down next to her daughter's face.

"What is it, darling?"

"I don't want to see him."

"Your father? How can I . . . " Margaret began, but Sharlie had closed her eyes. After a moment she rose and went out into the hall to look for Walter. Before she actually set eyes on him, his penetrating voice informed her that he had arrived and was holding forth around the corner, at the nurse's station.

" . . . you to page Diller," Walter was saying. "He's not in surgery. I've been trying to reach him since last night. He'd damn well better not be on the golf course in Dorado Beach."

There was silence for a moment, then the voice growled again. "I'll be here until eight. Find him."

Margaret stood out of sight behind the corner, wondering how on earth to keep the proprietor of that bellow out of Sharlie's room. An orderly emerged from a nearby doorway, and Margaret pretended to be fixing the clasp of her handbag. The man's curiosity embarrassed her, so finally she lifted her head and walked down the hall. Walter caught sight of her just as the loudspeaker cracked and intoned, "Dr. Diller . . . Dr. Carlton Diller."

He strode toward her, tall and massive, his large square face set in what Margaret described as his Challenge Expression (Sharlie called it the hard-hat look, but only to Margaret, of course). Whatever anybody might say about Walter Converse, she thought, he's a reassuring man to have around in a crisis. But how in the world was she going to keep that hulking two hundred pounds of authority away from his own daughter?

"Hello, Margaret," he said. He put his hand on her arm and, without slowing, propelled her toward Room 1108. "First day on the job, the kid at the desk."

"Uh, Walter . . . she's asleep, I think. Let's let her rest and come back in a little while."

Walter said, "Hmm," which meant that he hadn't heard her. "MacDonald around? Where the hell is everybody?"

Margaret stopped walking and plucked at his elbow. "I really need a cup of coffee."

"Go ahead, then," he said. "Take your time. I'll wait here for you."

And he barged right in with Margaret following, trying to avoid Sharlie's accusing stare. Sharlie rarely complained and absolutely never lost her temper. But her eyes—sometimes it seemed as if they would burn up the world with their blazing fury.

Walter sat down next to the bed and took Sharlie's hand.

"Hi, Chuck. You hanging in there?"

Sharlie nodded.

"I'm getting Diller up here, and we'll take care of this thing, okay?"

Sharlie closed her eyes wearily. "Oh, Daddy . . ."

Walter inspected the room as he spoke. "Now, let's not have a discouraging word around here. We have not yet begun to fight." He rose and walked to the window, closing the curtain with an emphatic whoosh. Margaret held out her hand in mute protest, but Walter sat down again, and neither Margaret nor Sharlie felt inclined to listen to his discourse on the evils of sunlight in the sickroom—all part of the Unstimulating Environment Theory, straight from the mouth of Walter's mother into his collection of proven scientific facts.

Two weeks ago Sharlie had dreamed that under all of that steely hair her father's head secreted a rectangular slot into which he could insert cassette tapes. The image pleased Sharlie, and she entertained herself by composing the tape library Walter would compile for himself—selections from such luminaries as John Wayne, Ernest Hemingway, Anita Bryant, Billy Graham, but most often contributions from the wisdom of Christine Converse.

In her father's face Sharlie saw the old woman's jaw, the straight line of her mouth, disapproving as always. Sharlie and her mother had always dreaded grandmother Converse's visits; though, despite her anxiety, Sharlie had secretly enjoyed watching Walter snap to attention, trembling with eagerness to please the old harridan and never quite succeeding.

Christine Converse died when Sharlie was about ten years old. Walter had been crushed with a silent, black grief that lasted for nearly a year. Once, to her astonishment, Sharlie had heard her father's muffled sobs through the heavy mahogany door of his study.

After that Walter's devotion to his dead mother's doctrines became family ritual, until Sharlie could recite them word for word—and often did, for Margaret's amusement. Sharlie's grandmother had been tryannical, bigoted, misinformed, but worst of all, terribly, excruciatingly boring. Sharlie found the resemblance between Christine and her only son a profoundly compelling argument against heredity.

Now Walter was gripping her hand, squeezing hard for emphasis. For a devotee of the Unstimulating Environment Theory, Sharlie agonized, this man could be ferociously stimulating.

". . . and no more screwing around with this chemical horseshit," he was saying. (Not the Billy Graham tape, Sharlie thought gratefully.) "We're going to whip you into surgery and finish this up once and for all."

"I don't want those tests again."

"Look, Chuck, nobody likes tests, but if you have to do it, you have to do it. It'll be worth it, because this time you're going to get well. And you do want to get well more than anything."

Margaret glanced at Sharlie's face and read the question there. *More than anything?*

Walter squeezed his daughter's hand again.

"If you're determined to get better, you *will* get better."

Norman Vincent Peale, Sharlie decided, trying to keep her face averted. Walter reached out, hooked his big square finger around her chin, and turned her face to his. Taking note of the damp eyelashes, he shook his head.

"You can do it, Chuck. We're all counting on that fighting spirit."

Margaret said softly, "She needs to rest, dear. There's been a lot of pain today."

Walter patted Sharlie's hand and rose.

"Okay. I'll just see if I can track Diller down, and we'll get the old team into action."

He and Margaret left the room, and Sharlie murmured bitterly to herself, "Rah rah rah. Sis boom bah." But the final "bah" was more of a sob than anything else. With her parents' departure, another familiar visitor had entered. Sharlie called him Agony Jones. Unlike the occasional uncle or aunt, he remained a faithful companion and seemed unimpressed by hospital visiting schedules. His powerful presence filled the room now like a malevolent fog, pressing down on her chest until she felt she must be forced right through the mattress onto the floor and mashed like one of those ephemeral silverfish that disintegrate into dust at the touch of a careless toe. The cold sweat prickled the space above her lip, but her arms throbbed so acutely that she couldn't raise them to wipe her face. *Pain, pain, go away, come again some other day.*

She lay very still, concentrating on blue sky, trying not to cry out like some animal in a trap, knowing that once she got started, the howling would never end.

CHAPTER 3

Walter Converse prowled the hallway outside the staff lounge. If there was one thing he despised, it was waiting, but he knew that Diller stopped in here a few times a day for a cup of coffee and an appreciative look at the nurses. So Walter stalked back and forth, always keeping one gloomy eye on the lounge doorway, and as he paced, he thought about his daughter.

It was the greatest disappointment of his life that Sharlie had been born malformed. Well, not malformed exactly, but defective, even if the defect was someplace where nobody could see it. If she'd emerged from Margaret's cold body missing an arm or a leg or with her face all twisted and grotesque like some of the children Walter had seen, well, he was a strong man, but he didn't know if he could have put up with that.

He'd been grateful she was a girl. Any child of his would end up extraordinary, he'd see to that, and an extraordinary woman was far more interesting than an extraordinary man. Look at his mother, for instance.

But when they told him about Sharlie's heart just an hour after the elation of her birth, Walter had been crushed. Then furious: furious with God—for which he'd later asked and been granted forgiveness—furious with the medical profession, furious with the poor frail infant herself, and particularly furious with Margaret. Could she never do anything right? The incredible incompetence of the woman. She had looked up at him from her hospital bed with such guilt, asking him with her eyes to forgive her for producing such a poor specimen of a baby. She had wanted to please him, he knew that. So he forced the anger back down inside, patted her hand, and pounded his rage out on the squash court and in his conferences with specialists in New York and Minnesota and Houston and just about every place in between.

Sure enough, in Walter's obsession to learn all there was to know about his baby's condition, he tracked down a genetic disorder in Margaret's family that no one had ever spoken about because no one in that tight-ass, hot-shot bunch ever talked about things that happened in the, God forbid, *body*. But what, he wanted to know, was the point of blue blood if it pumped in and out of a fucked-up heart?

So while Margaret languished, grief-stricken and guilty, Walter set about to cure his daughter, lavishing time and money on the project as if there were no Converse & Mackin and no stock market to occupy his active days.

Maybe she wasn't as lively as the other babies in the nursery, and maybe her skin had a slightly bluish tinge, but when he held the baby Charlotte, she seemed so beautiful to him, so soft and so perfect on the outside that you'd never know. When he held her like that, he made himself a fierce promise to give her the life he'd dreamed about during all those years of waiting for Margaret to produce.

His eyes snapped to the lounge doorway as someone in surgical gear went inside. But no, it wasn't Diller. Walter began his pacing again, but more slowly now. Suddenly he realized that he was beginning to get discouraged. Here was Sharlie, twenty-six years old and basically an invalid. There had been so many disappointments, so many failed techniques, some so esoteric they were probably illegal, like the one where they blew carbon dioxide gas into the heart chamber through a tube. But each new test confirmed what the last one had indicated: Corrective surgery might repair Sharlie's heart, but the risks were prohibitive.

After each new hope dissolved, Walter had always managed to replenish his superhuman store of energy and confidence. But today he felt the supply dwindling. As he looked toward the future, there was a kernel of dread mixed with the faith he'd kept alive all these years, and kept alive in his wife and daughter, too.

In the early days he'd pushed hard for surgery but couldn't find anybody courageous enough to try a triple valve replacement on Sharlie. Goddammit, he wanted to cut her open and perform the frigging operation himself. And now, with each day of increased suffering, he became more convinced that a heart transplant was the only possible solution. What were the alternatives? Watch Sharlie disintegrate week by week, her spirit shattered like her shattered heart?

Wait like Sharlie for the injection that came every now and then to ease the merciless, unremitting pain? Pretty soon the ever-narrowing slice of bearable time would disappear altogether, and that left only the choice of prolonging a tortured life or tossing out the pill bottles and letting her go.

He came to an abrupt halt in the middle of the sterile hall. God forgive me, he thought. Walter Converse considering the willful destruction of his own child. Mother, where are all your answers now?

CHAPTER 4

Margaret tried to keep the querulous tone out of her voice, knowing it was unattractive. One had to make allowances for sick people, but considering Sharlie's upbringing, it amazed her that sometimes she had to be pressed to do the correct thing.

"But he picked you up off the street, dear," she said. "After all, we've read about people who've been left bleeding on the pavement to die because nobody wanted to get involved."

Sharlie, propped up in bed today, hair combed, if not exactly clean, closed her eyes.

"All right. Ask them to put a phone in here, and I'll do it this afternoon."

Margaret nodded, restraining herself from thanking Sharlie when she was only doing what was right.

"I'm sure he'll be glad to hear from you. Such a thoughtful young man, calling so often to inquire how you are."

Sharlie didn't respond. After a moment Margaret rose.

"Well . . . I think I'll go see about that telephone."

She went out, and both women felt relieved to have some time apart. Sharlie was accustomed to abbreviated hospital visits and had often noticed callers, her own, back when she'd had some, and other people's, sneaking looks at their watches after twenty minutes in hopes that they'd stayed a respectable amount of time. Except for Agony Jones, of course, who hung around hour after hour, sitting on the beds and making a nuisance of himself.

She picked up a magazine from the bedside table. *Cosmopolitan*. Her mother had brought it as a kind of joke, since Sharlie would sometimes entertain them both by reading the advice columns out loud. "How to catch a man on the crosstown bus, by the water cooler, in Paley Park, in the coronary care unit, on the operating table. . . .

> Don't lose this made-in-heaven opportunity, girls. Those green hospital gowns can be so *appealing*, and all those *doctors*—hovering around for the sole purpose of taking care of poor frail delicate you. We suggest a little Poor-Circulation Blue eye shadow and Near-Death makeup base. Looks so *compelling* under the operating-room lights. And by all means, don't neglect your body. Here's your perfect chance to show off what you've got without a hint of exhibitionism (*subtle* is *sexy*), particularly if you're fortunate enough to undergo open-heart surgery. Do your own preop prep by toning those pectoral muscles (*see exercises on page fifty-four*), or, in the event of hysterectomy,

we recommend Clairol's new Pubic Down to make that forbidden fur shiny and kitten soft. . . ."

Sharlie wondered if it were possible to donate one's body to Madison Avenue instead of to some stuffy medical research center. She thought she might enjoy modeling for the full-page ad on the back of *The New York Times*—lying flat on a shiny aluminum table, draped with a sheet, her cold, dead face impeccably groomed. *If you want to reach me, you'll find me in the morgue. I guess you could say I'm that* Cosmopolitan *girl. . . .*

Sharlie shook her head and tried to free it of the macabre image.

"Hey, I got you a phone. A Princess for a princess." Nurse Ramón Rodriguez stood in the doorway. Sharlie smiled at him as he brought the telephone over to the bedside table and bent to plug it in. He glanced at the magazine on Sharlie's lap. The page was open to a picture of Martina Schiller, this year's notion of ideal beauty—a blinding array of white teeth and carefully tousled thick blond mane. Nurse Rodriguez looked at Sharlie's limp hair.

"Hey, Charlie, you wan' I give you a shampoo today?"

Sharlie smoothed a strand behind her ear, grimacing at the lank texture.

"I guess you'd better before the mice move in. Thanks."

Nurse Rodriguez picked up the receiver, listened for the dial tone, then nodded.

"It's okay. I be back later with my rollin' beauty store."

Sharlie glanced wistfully at Martina Schiller.

"Ahh," Ramón said, catching her at it. "You don'
wanna look like *that* chick, man. She's *ice*. You got
more woman in you *any* day."

Sharlie watched him walk to the door, his small
body jaunty, and, dressed in the sterile white uniform,
impertinent somehow. He waved at her, and she shut
her eyes, exhausted from the conversation and from
the meanderings of her own imagination. Agony Jones
had spread himself all over the room like a thick layer
of foul smoke. If only somebody would rearrange the
schedule so that for one day all six hours of drugged
relief came at a stretch. She'd gladly suffer the despised company of Agony Jones for the eighteen searing hours that would follow.

Nurse Rodriguez had washed her hair, and it fell all
shiny and soft to her shoulders. She'd had her injection and wouldn't be this comfortable again for another four hours. She glanced at the phone squatting
reproachfully on her bedside table. The time had
come.

She'd gotten so far as to put her hand on the receiver, even dailed a few digits. But then she panicked and hung up. What was he like anyway, this
Brian Morgan? She had vague memories of a quiet
voice and a long, lean arm, but there was no face.
He'd disappeared by the time her parents got to the
hospital that evening. Her mother said that over the
phone he sounded like "a fine young man." How does
one talk to a fine young man these days? It'd been a
long time since she'd talked with anyone other than
her parents and the staff at Saint Joe's except to say,
"Good morning," or "Rain again," to the occasional

cab driver. Maybe she'd better take a closer look at *Cosmo* before she dialed.

Coward, coward. She grabbed the phone, dialed fiercely, and listened to the ring, gripping the receiver until her hand ached.

A voice answered, the words rushing together in a barely coherent stream. "Barbara—Kaye's—office—good—afternoon."

Sharlie gave her name and asked for Mr. Morgan in her best imitation of a nonterrified person. The voice sang again, "What is this in regard to, please?"

With regard to, thought Sharlie, her face reddening and a menacing thump sounding in her chest. *Oh Lord, this is not good for me.*

"It's . . . uh . . . a personal matter," she stammered. *The guy saved my life. Is that personal enough for you, madam?*

"Hello."

That was the voice. Sharlie remembered it now.

"Is this the actual Charlotte Converse in person?"

"Yes," Sharlie answered. "I . . . uh . . ." Oh, damn, she thought, pull yourself together. "I called to thank you for saving my life."

Her voice sounded prissy even in her own ears, and she heard Brian Morgan laugh.

"Think nothing of it," he said. "When can I come see you?"

"What?" she said. *Oh, clever.*

"I've got something of yours. At least I think they fell out of your shopping bag. A pair of binoculars?"

"Oh, you mean the opera glasses," she said.

"That's what happens when you make snap judgments," he went on, and she could hear the amusement in his voice. "You passed out there on the side-

walk with these glasses by your hand, and I figured,
'Of course, a pregnant birdwatcher.'"

This time Sharlie laughed, an unfamiliar sensation,
like bubbles in her throat.

"It's a damn good thing I saw your cardiac alert
bracelet," he said, and then Sharlie heard an intercom
buzzer sound in the background. Brian's voice
changed tempo, speeding up.

"Listen, my appointment's here. What're your visiting
hours?"

"Noon until eight, but . . ."

"Fine, I'll stop by around six. 'Bye."

The phone clicked, and he was gone.

But, thought Sharlie. *But* . . .

She felt a familiar sense of powerlessness in the
presence of a personality stronger than her own. I'd
make a great candidate for torture, she thought. Some
guy in a leather jacket would stand over her and say
(firmly, of course), "All right, lady, you know the
names of all the spies in the Upper East Side network.
I want this information, and I'll get it from you one
way or the other," and she'd just give him a little
trembly smile and say, "Oh, well *sure* . . . if it means
that much to you. . . ."

Brian Morgan didn't sound like the leather jacket
type. Maybe he's a CPA, she thought. What could be
scary about a CPA? She imagined a soft, round face
perched atop a rather baggy three-piece suit.

Then suddenly the shadowy image twisted, like the
distorted reflection in a fun house mirror. The pain
had caught her unaware this time, and she moaned
aloud involuntarily. At least no one had heard
her. Maybe she was losing her discipline. She thought

of her father's description of T. E. Lawrence holding his hand in a flame and explaining that the trick wasn't in somehow avoiding the pain, it was in not minding it. Her father found this heroic, and she always thought she had, too, until she'd heard the story applied to Gordon Liddy. Where were the human idols to cling to for inspiration in the bad times? She'd long ago given up on God. Convinced by a couple of spectacular earthquakes and news photos of starving children, she'd decided that if he existed at all, he was either a pathetic, inept milksop or a raging sadist. In any case, he wasn't of any use to her.

The pain now burned and twisted like a spit plunged through her chest, and she was turning, turning. Sweat spilled down her forehead, rushing in hot rivers into her hair and ears. She lay there, silent and tormented, for half an hour, her pillow growing soggy beneath her head.

Nurse Rodriguez's blurred face appeared above her left shoulder. She heard his voice now, disembodied.

"Oh, Charlie . . ." He was gone, but soon reappeared.

"It's early, sweetheart, but I won' tell nobody if you don'." The tiny prick of the needle released from Sharlie a cry that was so deep it seemed to rise up from underground, far below the deepest level of the hospital, a cry of archetypal protest, and in its presence, Rodriguez felt the impulse to kneel and cross himself. He watched her, transfixed. After a moment the struggle ceased and her face, masklike, stilled.

Sharlie woke up disoriented, but with the pain subdued and murmuring like muddled voices in a far-

away room. She looked at the clock with fuzzy awareness of an important assignment ahead of her.
Suddenly she remembered Brian Morgan. If he
showed up as threatened, he'd be in this very room in
half an hour. After a bad session with pain, Sharlie
felt like a piece of damp gray string and supposed she
was just about as attractive. She reached for the mirror to check the damage.

Not too bad, she thought, relieved. Her hair, silky
and almost black ("fireplace soot," she called it), ha-
loed her face and neck in soft dark shadows. Her skin,
always pale and fine-grained, seemed almost translucent now. And the eyes stared back at her, dark stars.
She put the mirror down quickly, avoiding the reflection of that secret part of her that sometimes gazed
back from the glass.

There was a rattling and clinking at the door, and a
nurse's aide appeared, pushing the dinner trolly. No
matter what lurked beneath those aluminum tins, the
odor was always the same: mashed potatoes and
gravy—that prosaic, sturdy, comforting smell. Sharlie
was surprised to discover that she was hungry, and
started on her veal loaf. She wanted to finish before
Brian Morgan arrived, embarrassed to be caught eating in front of him, a stranger, the business of chewing and swallowing seeming crass somehow, like
going to the bathroom.

But after three bites she was exhausted. She set
down her fork and leaned back against the pillow,
wishing someone would offer to feed her. When Brian
Morgan arrives, she thought, I'll ask him to cut up my
meat and mush my sherbet for me. He'd shown his
chivalrous bent. Maybe he'd enjoy playing Florence
Nightingale in drag.

She tried to relax and set about inhaling the fragrance from her dinner, hoping she'd soak in some of its nutritional value that way. When she opened her eyes, a young man stood in the doorway.

CHAPTER 5

He was tall, with very thick curly brown hair. He wore a soggy trench coat, and from across the room Sharlie could smell the damp cold air he'd brought inside with him. His face was flushed from the sudden hospital heat, and he looked wonderfully healthy and strong.

"I'm disturbing your dinner," he said, hesitating in the doorway.

"Oh . . . no, I'm finished," Sharlie said, smiling at him timidly and wishing he'd come closer so she could drink in the clean smell of him. "Why don't you hang up your coat and let it dry out a little?" Good Lord, she thought, don't I sound casual, just as if I'm visited every day by beautiful young men like you.

Brian removed his coat and made a tent with it over the back of a chair. He propped his umbrella in the corner, pulled another chair next to the bed, and settled into it as if he fully intended to stay. He wore a

three-piece tweed suit, warm and brown and coarse
like his hair.

"It's funny," Sharlie said. "A lot of days go by without my knowing whether they were sunny or rainy."

Brian glanced at the window, and Sharlie thought,
He doesn't think it's funny. It's *not* funny. He thinks
I'm whining.

She began again, lamely. "I guess I just forget to
look," and she reddened, thinking about the article
she could write for *Cosmo*: how to make an ass of
yourself when meeting the attractive man who saved
you life.

Brian was looking at her with such intensity and curiosity that her blush deepened. She cursed her pale
skin, that made a blush so obviously a blush. No way
to pretend the crimson cheeks were all because of
"this dreadful cough, *hack, hack*" or "isn't it *warm* in
here, I'd better remove my sweater."

"What exactly is wrong with you?" he asked.

Sharlie started, but he was looking at her with such
open interest that she found herself responding.

"Something I was born with—valvular heart disease."

"I thought they put plastic ones in now."

She nodded. "Teflon. But I've got three out of four
that won't cooperate. It gets a little sticky. Even for
Teflon."

He smiled. "Well, then, what are they doing for
you?"

"Pumping me full of digitalis and anticoagulants.
And lots of Demerol," she replied. He looked at her,
waiting for more. She smiled. "It's not so bad, really. I
get waited on hand and foot, and every now and then

they let me out for a walk . . . which is how I happened to pass out on your shoes the other day."

"You mean you live here?"

"Not all the time, no. My parents' house is pretty well equipped, actually. We've got shelves full of magic potions for this symptom and science fiction machinery for that symptom. I guess we're all medical technologists by now."

"When are you getting out?"

She shrugged. "I don't know. Last time it was a couple of months, and I'd only been allowed out of the house a week before I got on that bus. Then again, I might not get out of here at all." Oh damn, she thought, did I have to say that?

Brian leaned forward, resting his arms on his knees. His face was contemplative. Finally he looked up at her earnestly. "You're telling me you're not going to get well."

She nodded. "I didn't exactly mean to tell you that."

He was staring at her with eyes so wistful that finally, flustered, she blurted out a question about his job.

"I'm a lawyer," he said.

"That's very . . . nice," Sharlie said, and they both laughed.

"Right now I wish I were a doctor."

Lord, Sharlie thought. What was she supposed to say to that? "Are you in court a lot?" she asked finally.

"All day today. The judge read *The Wall Street Journal*."

"While you were doing your case?"

Brian smiled. "While the other guy was doing *his* case. I was much too interesting."

"Isn't that illegal or something?"

"His honor's got a lot of money invested in coffee beans."

"They're not all like that, are they?"

He shook his head. "Sometimes they listen, and sometimes they make remarkably sensible decisions."

"Did you win?"

"Yes," he said.

"Who's Bob Rackey?" Sharlie asked. Brian looked puzzled. "When I called you at your office, the secretary said—"

"Oh." Brian laughed. "Barbara Kaye. That's who runs me . . . my firm, rather."

"Is she your partner?" Sharlie was beginning to feel as if she were pumping him.

"I used to work for Legal Aid. Barbara snatched me out of civil court one day four years ago, and I've been with her ever since."

There was affection and respect in his voice, and Sharlie wondered whether Barbara Kaye was attractive.

But Brian was still talking. "She's shown me what the law can be, what it can do. I was drowning down there, all that bureaucratic bullshit, excuse me. She's probably the best civil rights litigator in the East."

But is she pretty? Sharlie thought. Brian suddenly stopped and grinned at her.

"You're a good listener."

"I get awfully bored listening to the inside of my own head. It's nice. How old a woman is she?"

He shook his head. "No. Your turn. Do you ever go out when you go out? On dates?"

"Good heavens, no," she said. "I couldn't inflict myself like that on anybody. Look what I did to you. You could have strained your back hauling me off the sidewalk. I pass out a lot."

"You aren't very heavy," Brian said.

Just at this moment the harried nurse's aide reappeared, lifted the aluminum cover from Sharlie's tray, and frowned.

"We don't have much appetite today, do we? We sure we're finished?"

Sharlie started to say yes, but saw Brian eyeing the rolls.

"Leave it for a while, okay? Maybe *we* can manage a bit more."

The aide shot Sharlie a suspicious glance but finally left the room. Sharlie nodded to Brian. "Go ahead."

He laughed and took a roll off the plate, swallowing it in two bites. Then he ate the other roll, the mashed potatoes, the string beans, and the Jell-O salad. He stirred the sherbet curiously.

"What's this?"

"It *was* orange sherbet," she said. His obvious disappointment that there was nothing more to eat made her smile.

"Not bad for what I've heard of hospital food," he said, washing everything down with a long swallow that drained the carton of skimmed milk. "Saves me the heartburn from corned beef on rye at the deli."

Sharlie thought, No wife? No little toddler and another on the way? Suddenly she was afraid he might get up and leave now that he'd finished her dinner. She said quickly, "Could you tell me what happened the other night?"

"You don't remember?"

Sharlie shook her head. "Just the bus. Then falling."

"I'd been watching you," he said, mischief in the

crinkles beside his eyes, "trying to figure out how I could get closer to you with all those fat ladies in the way."

Her face was thoughtful, but the voice inside her head shouted, Really? *Really?*

"You started to look sort of gray," he went on, "and when I saw you asking for air, I shoved you out the door. When I let go of you for a second to pick up your bags, crash, down you went."

He leaned back in the chair, folded his arms, and stretched his legs out in front of him. Sharlie thought she'd never seen anyone quite so graceful.

"As soon as I saw the bracelet, I flagged down a cab with some poor farm equipment salesman from Oklahoma in the back seat. He'd never been to New York before, and I explained that sometimes during the holidays there's a shortage of ambulances, and we have to depend on the good sportsmanship of people like him. Once he realized he could still make the curtain for *A Chorus Line*, he was very generous and paid for the whole trip. You had your head on his shoulder and looked so beautiful I think he kind of enjoyed himself. The driver said he was going to put it in his next book."

Sharlie shook her head, trying to absorb it all. It was difficult. Her brain resisted getting past Brian's words, the phrase playing over and over like a record stuck in a groove. You looked *so beautiful, so beautiful, so beautiful* . . .

"There are lots of slices out of my life," she said, "that other people remember and I don't." She supposed that sounded like self-pity, and when he got up right away, she was certain that she'd put him off.

But he only reached into his raincoat pocket for the

opera glasses. He put them to his eyes and peered out the window. "Nothing much going on in the park," he said.

"Fifth Avenue's more interesting once it gets dark."

He grinned at her. "Spoken like one who knows," he said, pushing up against the window so he could get a better view of the street below. "Hmm," he muttered.

He was silent for so long that Sharlie finally asked, "What is it? What's going on?"

Brian walked over and handed her the glasses. "Somebody in a fur coat and sunglasses got out of a limousine and practically broke her ankle sprinting to the front door."

"Aging starlet admitted for secret face-lift," Sharlie explained. Brian looked impressed. "Spoken like an incurable voyeur," she said sheepishly.

Brian waved toward the window. "You do a lot of that?"

Sharlie nodded. "Sometimes I've wondered . . . it's not illegal or anything, is it?"

He smiled. "As long as you don't open up a blackmail business."

"*I could,*" she said fervently.

"Oh? Tell me." He looked at her expectantly, but she shook her head, and he could see she was regretting her openness. "Sometime," he murmured, and looked at his watch.

Sharlie turned the opera glasses over in her hands. The voice inside was pleading, *Don't leave.*

"I guess I'd better get out before they throw me out," he said. He picked up his raincoat and umbrella and stood by the side of her bed. Sharlie's throat felt clogged with unspoken entreaties.

"Can I come see you again?" Brian asked.

What? thought Sharlie. But she couldn't get any words to come out at all.

"Tomorrow?" he urged.

She coughed, trying to clear her throat.

"I'm grateful to you," she said, and decided to allow herself the luxury of speaking his name aloud this once, "Brian . . ."

He smiled, "Then pay me back with some time."

"I can't." She felt wet heat building behind her eyes. Oh, for God's sake, Sharlie, she thought. You're not going to *cry*, are you?

"Listen, I don't want to hassle you." He took her hand, and she felt the rough, calloused warmth of him. He plays tennis, or squash, maybe, she thought, trying to memorize the texture of his palm.

"Thank you for everything," she said, with what she hoped was unmistakable finality. His face was sorrowful. Still holding her hand, he leaned down and kissed her gently. He didn't say good-bye, just let go of her and walked out. Sharlie lay exactly as he left her, a long time after the pain had begun to twist and writhe in her chest.

CHAPTER 6

Brian stepped out into a fierce January storm. The rain had turned to sleet, and the gray stone walls of the hospital formed a howling wind tunnel. He pushed against the gale, head down, deliberately choosing the struggle on foot to the crosstown bus. The wind would sweep through his brain, stinging, purging it of Charlotte Converse's mesmerizing face.

Her hands were pale, delicate as moths. She lay there fragile, exquisite, so close to death. And yet he sensed an energy beneath the frail surface. Once or twice she had forgotten how sick she was and how shy, and then the mellow light in her eyes had flickered with sudden heat.

He turned the corner and started walking up Third Avenue. The wind settled into irritated little gusts, and he relaxed, letting his legs carry him loosely. This is insane, he thought. He didn't know the woman. She hadn't said more than a hundred words to him, not that she'd had much of a chance with him running off at the mouth. Must be purely physical attraction. But she was dying. Could *that* be the turn-on? No, when he had seen her on the bus, he didn't know she was sick, not when he'd first fastened his eyes on her and decided he'd just as soon go on looking at the lovely face forever.

He imagined her lying there in her white bed back at the hospital, smiling at him, her eyes huge, dark, and frightened. And unmistakably hungry. He yearned to put his arms around her and protect her from any more hurt.

He belted his coat more tightly against the sharp, damp gusts. Maybe he'd stop off at Susan's apartment on the seventh floor. She was always game for an hour of tennis or an energetic roll in the sack. Her healthy vitality would do him good. But when he rounded the corner and caught sight of the white brick walls of his building, he felt reluctant to seek her out. He stood on the cold pavement, blaming his hesitation on a sudden craving for a beer. Instead of entering his lobby, he stepped into Crispin's, the bar next door.

Holiday trappings still hung from the ceiling, where they would droop until next March, when somebody would finally get around to taking them down. Three businessmen sat at the bar, but the tables were empty, their candles unlit.

Brian perched on a stool, loosened his coat, and stared at the blinking Christmas lights. The bartender appeared, and Brian regarded him gloomily.

"You know, Jim, there ought to be a law about Christmas decorations: all down by midnight, December twenty-sixth."

Jim grinned and poured Brian a beer. "Just trying

to prolong the festive holiday spirit." Brian reached for his glass. Jim watched him for a moment, then leaned on the bar. "You go to that hometown in the sticks for the holidays? Slimy Creek, PA?"

"Silver Creek."

"Whatever." He contemplated Brian. "What'd you do, lose that free-speech case today?"

Brian stared back into Jim's watchful face and took another long draw on his beer.

"You know, I bet you got more on your customers than the computers in Washington."

Jim shrugged. "All part of the job. Better'n pumping gas in Queens."

"You got a talent for this," Brian said, feeling the rhythm of his speech slip into synchronization with Jim's. He'd been unaware of the habit until Barbara Kaye pointed out that he did it with everybody. He'd felt like a chameleon and was embarrassed, until Barbara assured him it was a gift many attorneys worked years to acquire—an effective technique for gaining the confidence of clients and witnesses. Speak the same language—no condescension, no mockery, just a slight shift in style.

Jim went off to serve the businessmen, who were discussing the attributes of their secretaries in ever more intimate, ever more boisterous terms. Commuters, all of them, checking their watches to make sure they'd make the next train to Stamford.

Couldn't do it, Brian thought. New York streets, magnets on my feets. Terminal urbanitis, that's what I've got. And his mind leaped back to Sharlie. He'd never given any thought to the word *terminal*, not really, and here was somebody younger than he was, getting ready to terminate her life. His mother had died, but that was different. Quick. She was here, she was dead. There'd been no time to think it over.

Brian felt the impulse to call Jim over and say, "Hey, I've met this girl . . ."

Maybe it was just that after spending all day with legal briefs and people who think and talk in syllogisms, *whereas*'s, and *heretofore*'s, a dying woman was a nice change. He would just spend tonight thinking about her, trying to get her into some kind of sensible perspective so that he could put her to rest in his head and go on about his business.

Okay, he thought, I won't see her again anyway, and I'll just sit upstairs with a bottle of Scotch and figure the whole thing out. And that will be that.

CHAPTER 7

Sharlie stood in front of Goldberg's marine supply
store on West Forty-sixth Street. She had set her packages down on the sidewalk, waiting for a cab. But she
stood still, her coat open, relishing the damp smell of
February and the pale-blue sky. It was warm enough
to go out bare-headed, and the clean wind brushed
her hair back from her face. A few empty cabs passed,
and still she lingered, grateful for such a perfect first
day out. She smiled, thinking of the brass clock she'd
bought for her father's birthday. He'd be annoyed if
he knew it came from Goldberg's. Whoever heard of a
Jewish sailor? She'd read somewhere that Columbus
had been Jewish. Now, there was a real navigator for
you, she thought, not some navy desk-job landlubber
like Daddy. She liked the idea of her gift sitting,
triumphant and gleaming, in the center office of Converse & Mackin, bulwark of Waspiness, especially
since Walter's anti-Semitism had been particularly
rampant lately. A graduate student from Yeshiva Uni-

versity had won the squash racquet championship at the club last week, and Walter was outraged.

"Jesus Christ," he'd raved, gesturing menacingly with a martini. "It just encourages the rest of them. Next thing you know, we'll have Juan Gonzalez and Rufus Washington blasting their transistor radios in the locker room."

As he spoke, Sharlie remembered several years ago when Ned Wiederman first sauntered into New York's exclusive gentile squash clubs and walked off the winner in every tournament. Walter had been apoplectic, not only because Wiederman was a Jew, but because his sneakers didn't match. She must have smiled at the memory, because suddenly Walter had turned to her and asked her what he'd just said. She had shaken her head. He'd set down the martini, reached for the newspaper, rustling it crisply, righteous indignation radiating from his body like sparks. Sharlie had looked down at her blanketed knees, picking up her fantasy again. Against the blue folds she had visualized a squash court where, inside the frame of heavy glass walls, Ned Wiederman toyed ruthlessly with her father. Walter was dressed in what was once impeccable white, but now his shirt was stained dark with sweat. Wiederman wore a pair of cutoffs, a yellow T-shirt (half tucked in), and unmatched sneakers, one blue, one white. His socks weren't mates, the stripes along the top rims clashing. And *he* wasn't sweating one drop, just standing cool and relaxed at the line, stretching and leaning while her father ran back and forth, puffing, desperate to put his racquet on just one shot.

"Charlotte."

Her head snapped around toward the voice, and

there in the February sunshine stood Brian Morgan, grinning at her.

"I was worried for a second," he said. "Thought I might have to scrape you up off the sidewalk. But you look wonderful."

Sharlie gave him what she called her Howdy Doody smile, the submoronic one. Her feet told her she was in extreme conflict—one moved back and forth, trying to escape, while the other felt implanted in the cement. The effect was an awkward shift in balance. Brian reached for her elbow to steady her.

"Come have lunch with me."

She stared at him, flushed with pleasure and confusion. He leaned down and picked up her carton, still holding onto her as if he were afraid she might try to get away.

"Are you a sailor, too?"

Now she flashed him her remote-control smile, all mouth and no eyes—considered by Sharlie to be one small rung above the Howdy Doody—and nodded numbly as Brian steered her down toward Forty-second Street.

"We'll go to the Graduate Center cafeteria. So you'll think I'm very academic."

Sharlie was analyzing what was happening inside her chest. Panic, or elation, or both? Just this morning as she opened her eyes and looked out her window at the pale sky, she had decided she was finally beginning to erase the sight of Brian staring down at her as she lay in her hospital bed—warm face, so full of compassion and yet not pitying. He had *liked* her. He had scared her out of her wits and left her consumed with ardent adolescent longing. Still, the last few days she had thought she was gaining the upper hand in her censorship campaign against the memory of him. And now here she was, traipsing along after him like a groupie after a rock star.

He settled her at one of the quiet tables in the carpeted section of the dining room.

"I'll get you something healthy," he said, then looked at the package on the extra chair.

"Maybe I ought to haul that thing with me as collateral. You're not going to run off, are you?"

Sharlie shook her head again. Goddammit, she thought, I am struck mute by this man. If I try to say anything now, it'll only come out a croak.

Brian put his hands on her shoulders and pressed down lightly.

"Stay here."

Between mouthfuls Brian managed to tell her about his family back in Pennsylvania, the disconnected feeling of Christmas at home—as if he'd been cut loose from his childhood. His relationship with his brothers, Robert and Marcus, had evolved into one of wary respect. Worse, his father viewed Brian's renunciation of farming as a betrayal. Robert and Marcus, if uncomfortable, were at least friendly, but his father regarded him with sorrow and disappointment. Over Christmas dinner there had been an awkward discussion of Brian's life in the fleshpots of the big city. Marcus brought up the subject of his bachelorhood, and something in his father's face told Brian that John Morgan doubted his son's sexual preference.

His mother was dead, and Sharlie sensed, in his eagerness to get past the subject, that her departure had been very painful. But then he began talking about Barbara Kaye, and his face relaxed.

"She's going to retire early and write books on criminal procedure. And maybe a few pornographic novels to keep her in Lucky Strikes."

"She's an . . . older woman, then?" Sharlie asked, trying not to sound too hopeful.

"Not old enough," Brian answered through a mouthful of tomato salad. "She's promised her job to me when she quits, but I think I'll have to hire an army of guerrillas to get her out of there." Even muffled by the tomatoes, his voice was unmistakably affectionate. He smiled at Sharlie. "Barbara and I do not always see eye to eye." Sharlie was about to ask him what she looked like when he set his fork down emphatically. "I don't go on like this. Really."

Sharlie smiled at him.

"Your turn." He sat looking at her expectantly.

Finally Sharlie said, "You ate your cherry pie, and then my salad, and now another dessert. I never saw anybody do that before. Doesn't it clash?"

"You're cheating," he said, mouth full of chocolate mousse. He reached out and squeezed her hand briefly. "Try eating and talking at the same time. It's easier than you think. Come on. I've left you a few scraps."

She shook her head, and he scrutinized her pale face.

"You know, I appreciate a cheap date, but you're not going to get healthy on that diet."

Sharlie's chest ached, but not with the usual throbbing constriction. She felt as if she were swelling inside, the space under her breasts expanding with warm, unrelenting pressure, and that she must ventilate the volcano or explode into tiny pieces, making a mess of the quiet dining room. She started to talk, hesitating at first, but as she spoke, the feeling of imminent explosion dissipated and was replaced with a sensation of flying. It was scary but exhilarating. She seemed to be watching herself from the far corner of the room, recording her emotions on mental videotape so that she could replay them later when she was alone again. Now and then her eyes threatened to tear, but she was able to blink the mist away. Mainly, she felt free, dizzily and terrifyingly free. And once she got started, there didn't seem to be any way to stop.

She talked about her medical history, explaining it to Brian in minute detail because he asked her a thousand questions and seemed to need to have it all clearly visualized. She even made him a diagram of the human heart on a paper napkin.

She told him about the food supplements that compensated for her lack of appetite, about the precarious balance of chemicals in her bloodstream. He asked about pills and drugs. Sharlie smiled, opened her handbag, and showed him a dozen bottles crammed inside. His eyes widened, but then he grinned at her and told her to shut her bag, or they'd be arrested for making an illegal transaction over lunch.

"This is just the emergency stuff. There's lots more at home."

"Wouldn't it be easier to get a transplant and the hell with it?"

"That's not so easy," she replied slowly. He looked curious so she went on, still amazed at how the words kept brimming over and how powerless she was to stop them.

"After my last attack—not this one, the one before—Daddy took me to Houston, and I was there for six weeks waiting for a donor. Nobody ever turned up, and I finally got well enough to come home again. Thank goodness."

She played with the wrapper from her straw, making it into an accordion.

"I don't want it. I have really bad feelings about it. The whole idea gives me the creeps."

"But if it could help . . . Aren't there people who've been completely cured?"

"There were eighty-four alive last I knew."

Brain said, "So?" and waited, but Sharlie only shook her head and looked at him with haunted eyes. He sat quietly for a moment, thoughtful.

"Then what are the alternatives?"

"Nothing . . . at the moment."

Brian was startled at the flicker of fury in her eyes.

"See, I had this specialist who was a friend of Daddy's—my father's," Sharlie said, embarrassed at the childish epithet. "And he was the best." The last words sounded faintly ironic, but Brian couldn't be sure. "Dr. Nash convinced my parents that fixing me up wasn't surgically sensible. After he retired, I had another attack, and his successor told us I could have been helped. But by then there wasn't enough healthy tissue left to attach a prosthetic device to, and I needed at least two new valves, probably three." Her voice was matter-of-fact, as if she were reading him a moderately interesting newspaper article.

"How old were you then?" he asked.

"Fifteen."

"And did you sue this Nash character?"

She shook her head.

"He died shortly after he retired. Heart attack." She allowed herself a tiny smile at this and went on. "It turned out he wasn't much different from a lot of other prestigious surgeons. They don't want to operate on anybody risky for fear they'll mess up their track records."

"Jesus," Brian muttered, thinking he'd go kill somebody suitable right now and give her the heart in a hatbox. "I think I might have murdered the bastard."

Sharlie smiled at him and said, "I'm not supposed to get mad. It isn't good for me."

He shook his head. All our enlightened theories about self-expression—let it all hang out, open up, be straight, up front, rant and rage and let fly the great agonizing primal scream. And here was this frail creature with the ashen face and enormous burning eyes—silken butterfly impaled alive, with the specter of an early death to keep her company. For her, the release of rage forbidden. No such luxury as a hefty, piercing *Why me?!*

Brian had the sudden image of Sharlie as a young girl in a white dress, sitting on a wooden chair, hands folded primly in her lap, all the passions so exuberantly expressed in normal adolescence emerging from her in a quiet, ghostly smile—wings of the butterfly trembling, pinned—beautiful and crippled and doomed.

Then he looked at her across the table as she was now, a woman with flushed cheeks and eyes that looked at him with curiosity and hunger, whose breasts were outlined through the soft sweater, small nipples evident despite the restriction of underwear. The ethereal images of her faded in the presence of this warm, breathing woman, and he found himself blurting out, "But what about sex?"

Well, here it is, thought Sharlie, the heart of the matter, if you'll excuse the expression.

"Contraindicated," she replied.

"Have you ever been . . . involved?" he asked, the urgency to know overwhelming the reticence in her face.

"I had a crush on somebody once," she said, giving him a rueful smile. "He was a friend of Dad . . . my father's . . . and he kind of liked me, I guess. But he was so much older, and I figured we couldn't ever let things go too far for fear one of us would have a coronary . . . or maybe both of us, and there'd be nobody left to call the ambulance."

Brian reached out for her hand and held it between both of his.

"You know I'm attracted to you."

She nodded, struggling to hear his words through the sound of her heart pounding in her head.

"I want to see you again," he went on, and as she opened her mouth to object, he talked over her. "No. There's nothing I can do about it. I'm not going to let you get away from me. Forget it."

Sharlie's eyes were wide, but she didn't speak. Brian smiled at her.

"I'm going to quit cleaning your plate, and I'm going to take care of you and make you fat."

Sharlie felt the strange sensation of something light bubbling up her throat, and suddenly she was laughing—no ironic chuckle, no good-sport self-mockery, but delighted, joyful laughter.

"Wow," she said softly, and laughed some more.

Brian took her hand and pressed it to his mouth.

Well, she thought, maybe I'm going to die happy.

CHAPTER 8

Sex. Now there's a subject worthy of a girl's attention. Sharlie squirmed restlessly on her bed as the light from her window softened from white to pale gray. Tonight was her first actual date with Brian Morgan. Yesterday he had tucked her into a cab with Walter's clock, then poked his head through the door to pronounce, "Tomorrow we'll go to the movies." When she woke up this morning, the entire encounter seemed like last night's dream, but then the telephone rang, and Brian's voice said he was taking her to a revival of *Swept Away*.

Sharlie had informed her mother in a careful voice. At the mention of the film's title, Margaret's head shot up from her needlepoint. Have to give her credit, thought Sharlie, smiling up at the ceiling. Not one word.

Margaret disapproved of explicit sexuality. Sometimes during one of her speeches on the evils of pornography, Sharlie imagined her mother striding across

Forty-second Street in flowing Victorian skirts, slashing with blue pencil at the piles of lewd literature.

Still, Sharlie had struggled over the years to maintain an attitude of reserved curiosity toward sex. Her experiments with her own body had been of necessity abortive. As soon as her heart-beat sped up, she would force her fingers to some neutral location above the blankets and her thoughts to cooler topics. She'd lie in bed at night, her young body aching to be touched, and she'd think, Well, let's examine the plot structure of the nineteenth-century English novel. Safe enough.

But before she knew it, Darcy would be chasing a stark-naked, giggling Elizabeth Bennett across the immaculately groomed grounds of his estate, and Jane Eyre would stand in the firelight before Edward Rochester and, with smoldering eyes, slowly unbutton her shabby gray dress.

So she'd switch to nature. Think about trees, flowers, oogenesis—though that could get tricky, too. She had often wished she could adopt the attitude that there are worse ways to die than in midorgasm. It might be worth the risk to find out what orgasms were like. A heart attack making love to someone else seemed acceptable, but to die masturbating . . . She would shudder and try to concentrate on nuclear physics.

She could barely lie still in the quiet room, thinking about tonight. Perhaps the sight of naked flesh on the screen would send him into a frenzy. He'd rape her in the aisle, or maybe between the rows of seats on top of all the discarded chewing gum and used Kleenex. Just to be on the safe side, she'd better wear her old coat. The upholstery at the local Loew's was surely oozing with ejaculate and drool.

But there was no wild beast about Brian. She remembered the gentle pressure of his fingers on her arms and sighed. She was twenty-six years old, and except for several hundred members of the medical profession, she'd never felt the hands of a man on her naked body. The proximity of Brian Morgan made her flesh scream, "Hey! It's time already!"

Her reaction to his physical presence reminded her of those experiments at the Museum of Natural History in which someone would hold on to a source of electricity. As the current passed through his body, his hair would stand on end. Brian was her source, and if he passed anywhere near her, the tiny soft hairs on her skin would rise up in waves, following his path.

To be honest, Sharlie thought, if there were any raping to be done at Loew's East, she'd probably end up doing it herself.

They walked out of the theater at nine o'clock that evening.

"It's early," Brain said, steering her down Third Avenue. "Come on up to my apartment."

The air was sharp and cold, and he held her tightly against him as they walked. She watched the other night people approach and pass in the street, steam billowing rhythmically from each mouth—dozens of colorful locomotives chugging purposefully along invisible tracks. Little engines that could, she thought, remembering her father's all-time favorite children's story. He had read it to her regularly, all admiration for that simpering blue engine with the positive attitude: *I think I can, I think I can.* Well, *they* can, all these bustling Third Avenue engine-people with their pink cheeks and healthy turbine bodies. But what about me? Tell me what I'm supposed to do now, Daddy, with this gorgeous young man hauling me up to his apartment to see his etchings or his law journals or his whatever.

I cannot, I cannot, I cannot. *I cannot seem to say no.*

Brian propelled her into his building, nodding at the doorman, who leered suggestively, Sharlie thought, as they passed through the glass doors. In the elevator Brian pressed the button for 8, and still he didn't release her. He held her next to him, Siamese twins joined at the hip, and when they walked down the hall toward his apartment, his thigh moved against hers through all the layers of skirts and pants and coats. She glanced up at him. She had already learned enough about his face to detect the mischief there—a slight tension around his mouth, two or three tiny crinkles by the eyes. She thought, he's enjoying this, the rat fink.

Inside the apartment he snapped on a closet light, its indirect glow soothing after the glaring fluorescence of the hallway. He shrugged off his coat, then unbuttoned hers, slipping it off her shoulders. She felt as though he were undressing her.

Except for a few quick public kisses in the ticket line and some rather imaginative hand holding inside the theater, their physical contact had been negligible and always muffled by heavy winter clothing. Now, with his hands moving down her arms, which were covered only by a thin cashmere cardigan, it was as if he were caressing her skin just beneath its surface.

She must have made a sound, because suddenly Brian stopped and took a close look at her.

"Bad idea."

Sharlie stared up at him, dazed.

"What?"

He put his hands just above her hips, holding her away from him.

"I have no business doing this."

Sharlie was thinking about how he could easily encircle her waist with his fingers, and she had to fight hard to understand the remark. Finally it occurred to her that he was expressing concern for her health.

"Oh, *that*," she said, a little drunkenly. "Hey, Brian, really, I know my own heart."

Then she giggled, listening to her own words.

"I *mean* . . ."

He smiled.

"I've got this built-in stethoscope," she stammered, "and really, so far, so good. It's my knees. They've gone all . . . insubstantial."

He led her to the couch, but he sat very still, his hands on his thighs. Sensing the tension in his body, Sharlie put her arms around his neck and held him, her head nestled in the space between his shoulder and his ear. She sighed.

"It's nice without all the insulation."

Then she shifted her body, facing him so that more of her met more of him. She felt his shoulder relax, and soon his hands began to move up and down her back, gently, molding her to the hard contours of his body. Her heart clattered noisily, but the voice in her head responded with a defiant *I don't care!*

She imagined she was being dropped from a plane into a free fall, and while she speculated momentarily

about the parachute, mainly there was the sky rushing
past and the conviction that death doesn't mean a
thing in the face of such exhilaration.

She lifted her head so that she could study his
face—the strong cheekbones softened by slightly
rounded padding. Smile muscles, she thought.

With her finger, she traced the line of his jaw. Except for short stubble at the chin, his face was quite
smooth. She touched his mouth, running her finger
along his lower lip, a long straight line that lifted
slightly at each end, just enough to hint at the humor
lurking there.

His hand slipped underneath her sweater, the palm
rough and warm against her bare skin. She pressed
into him and put her mouth on his. Letting her body
guide her, she arched her back, wondering at the simultaneous tensing and relaxing of various pieces of
her—breasts stretched tight, pulling, and yet her arms
dropped weakly to her sides as if the muscles there had
simply melted away. She pulled back from him, put
her hand at the top of her sweater and, staring at him
with eyes immense and glistening, began to undo the
buttons.

When she'd finished, Brian slipped it off her shoulders. Naked, her skin shone in the soft light like pale
marble. His fingers were gentle, slowly exploring all
the curves and shadows. After a moment Sharlie
looked down at his hands as they covered her breasts,
and she shook her head.

"What?" he said softly.

"I thought I must be glowing in the dark," she whispered.

He pulled her against him, and she heard him murmur, "You are."

* * *

Sharlie insisted that he send her home in a cab rather than deliver her in person. She wasn't ready for the convergence of Brian and her parents. As she let herself in the front door, she wondered if she would ever feel prepared for that particular moment of reckoning.

Maybe if she stalled long enough, Walter would disappear or something. She couldn't bring herself to wish him dead, and anyway, if anybody were going to die, it would be Sharlie. They'd all have to meet sooner or later, she supposed, but for God's sake, let it be later. Especially not tonight, when the outline of Brian's hands was surely gleaming from her breasts as if traced in Day-Glo paint. Through her sweater, through her coat, two phosphorescent imprints as clear as the cement hands on the sidewalk in front of that Chinese theater in Hollywood: Brian Morgan Was Here.

She called out a noncommittal hello and rushed past the doorway of the living room, where she knew Walter and Margaret were waiting with set, silent faces for an account of this important night.

Once inside her room with the door shut, she took a long look at herself in the mirror, smiling at the rosy reflection she saw there, grinning at the smile, laughing at the grin. Finally she sobered up enough to realize how exhausted she was, and she undressed, taking her time, examining her body in the mirror as if she hadn't seen it before.

Always she had glared at her image resentfully, regarding her body as the traitor, the villain of the piece. Now she tried to view herself as Brian evidently did.

She heard the sounds of her parents preparing for bed and sighed thankfully. How much simpler to keep Brian stashed away someplace where they couldn't get at him and mar the perfection of their hours together, clomping brutally across their tenderness, two sets of heel marks, little sharp ones and flat heavy ones, treading to the merciless rhythm of common sense and reality.

She looked forward to lying in bed in the dark, remembering tonight, relishing it all as if it were some precious treasure to hold cupped in her hands, to turn over and over and examine from all sides.

She pulled her favorite long white nightgown over her head and took one more appraising look in the mirror. Anemic, she thought, but her dark hair mingled softly with the creamy frills at her neck, and her eyes were filled with light. She crawled into bed, and before she'd replayed the memory of herself walking out of the theater with Brian onto Third Avenue, she was asleep.

It must have been about four o'clock in the morning. She awoke startled, the cold pain gripping her hard across the chest. The sweat-soaked nightgown weighed heavily on her legs, and her pillow was clammy under her head. She reached for the brass bell on her night table and rang it sharply. With the movement, something through the center of her arm twisted as if it were being wrung by giant hands.

As she fell back to wait for Margaret to bring the medication, she thought that it had to happen this way. *Hubris.* That's what tonight was, and here came Agony Jones to tell her how he felt about her presumptuous expedition into the forbidden territory called love. She could almost hear him intoning, with words like thunder, "Thou shalt have no other gods before me!"

Okay, okay, Sharlie answered silently, I get the point. And lying there contorted with pain she raised a white fist to that deep resonant voice and thought, Agony Jones, you bastard, who the hell do you think you are—Charlton Heston?

CHAPTER 9

The phones jangled steadily, but Brian was deaf to them. In fact, sometimes in the night the absence of their ringing woke him from a restless sleep. Now, however, it was his intercom, buzzing at him like a gigantic enraged mosquito.

Oh, Jesus, not Mrs. Salvello, he thought with dismay as he heard the gravelly voice on the other end of the receiver. She'd brought the firm an age discrimination suit, an action Barbara believed would one day prove historic. In the meantime Brian endured regular doses of Mrs. Salvello's admiration.

"But, Mister Morgan, you know all those judges personally. You can get the date moved up, can't you? I mean, my nerves, I just can't take much more of this. And my daughter's mixed up with this man. She's only sixteen, and he's a junkie or a pimp, you should excuse me. Just this weekend she looked me straight in the eye, and you won't believe this, Mister Morgan, I mean, I've been a good mother, and I believe in dis-

cipline, I always have, it's not as if I spoiled her or let
her get away with anything when she was a kid, I
mean, Mr. Salvello didn't mind giving her a good
strapping when she deserved it. . . ."

Normally Brian could put his attention on hold and
go on working through the verbal deluge. Eventually
the client would run down and, in a voice choked
with gratitude, thank him for his understanding and
wisdom, which had consisted of a few well-placed
hmm's and *oh really*'s. Meanwhile, he would have
proofread a brief, signed his correspondence, and
skimmed the law journal. Mrs. Salvello paid one
hundred dollars an hour to talk about her daughter's
sexual digressions and then reported to all her friends
what a brilliant attorney she'd hired.

Today, however, her percussive narrative pounded
away inside Brian's head like thousands of tiny ham-
mers. He longed for an hour of peace to think about
Sharlie, and imagined himself saying, Hey, Mrs. Salvello, you think you got problems? There's this beautiful girl who's very sick and will probably never hit
twenty-seven and you sit there babbling about your
daughter, who's most likely brain-damaged because
dear old *Mr.* Salvello bashed her head in when she
was a kid for showing her little bottom to Anthony
down the block.

"Mrs. Salvello?"

The voice at the other end ran on for a few more
phrases just out of momentum, then came to a halt in
midsentence.

" . . . and you're such a . . . What?" she said, baffled.

"I've got to be in court in a few minutes. Could you

call back another time? Unless there's something urgent . . ."

"Well, I guess there's nothing *urgent*, I mean, I know you lawyers are very busy, and I'm sorry I bothered you about my daughter. I mean, someday when you're a parent . . . you don't have any kids, I can tell that. Well, you give me a call when you have some news for me, and I'll just wait. I'm a very patient person. Mr. Salvello always said . . . well, I guess you don't want to hear about it, with your appointments and all. . . ."

Finally she came to an abrupt halt and hung up. Brian stared at the phone in remorse. Poor lonely woman.

Half an hour later Barbara Kaye appeared at his door. Brian had been staring out the window, and he wondered how long she'd been watching him. He noted uneasily that she was wearing her "invincible suit," the navy-blue three-piece thing.

"I've just had a call from Salmonella."

Barbara's habit of distorting their clients' names had always disturbed Brian. He believed it encouraged an attitude of contempt toward the people they were supposed to be helping, but today he let it pass. His lack of response was not lost on Barbara. She leaned against his desk, her arms folded around an assortment of papers and files.

"What's all this bullshit about talking to me because she thinks a *woman* could understand her half-wit daughter? I thought you were going to keep her off my back."

"Sorry," Brian said vaguely.

Barbara watched his face, waiting for him to look

up at her. He did, finally, and she continued with quiet urgency.

"I want this case. She needs to have her hand held and she's getting billed for it. You're the one who told *me* she's a pathetic old lady with nobody to talk to."

"I'll call her later," Brian said with obvious lack of enthusiasm.

Barbara stood tall and handsome, head set in the no-compromise position so familiar to Brian and to the judges presiding at district court. She kept unsmiling eyes riveted on Brian's face until finally he threw his hands up in a gesture of concession. She shook her head, and he prepared himself for the full treatment.

"I do not read the usual level of human compassion in your face lately, and that scares me."

Brian smiled dubiously at her, thinking. Nothing scares you, dear Barbara.

"No, somebody around here has to bleed for our guys," she said. "I count on you for that. What the hell is going on?"

She waited, but Brian remained silent.

"You expending all your sympathy on this new girl?"

His eyes narrowed, and she shook her head.

"I can't lay off, Morgan. You bring it in here, and it's not private anymore."

He sighed at the rising heat in her voice and waited for the rest.

"You leave early every day and come trailing into court unprepared, and for all the work you accomplish when you do haul your ass in here, she might as well be standing over there in the corner doing a strip-tease."

She leaned over to tap his forehead with a long bright-red fingernail.

Brian said quietly, "You're right, Barbara. I'm sorry, okay?"

"What happened to the tennis freak?" Brian kept his face blank. "Susan. The one with the good legs."

"Nothing."

Barbara stared at him. "Nothing happened, or nothing's going on there?"

Brian only raised his eyebrows at her to let her know he'd heard the question and chose not to answer.

"You made a nice-looking couple."

"Do I ask you about your love life?" Brian snapped.

"No!" Barbara burst out, with a bitter laugh. She averted her eyes, staring out the window at the bright sky. Brian watched her pupils contract into tiny black specks. He was astonished to see that she was hurt. There had been harsher words between them over courtroom procedure and client relations, battles in which they attacked each other's basic competence and judgment. What had he said this time except a fairly restrained "butt out"?

He was about to make a bewildered apology when she turned to him and said quietly, "Her father's a real shit." Brian looked nonplussed, and she smiled. "Listen, I heard her name. I met Walter Converse at the McKaye examination before trial." Still Brian gazed at her in silence. "Don't you want to know the details?"

"Mildly," he said, and her smile widened at the curiosity in his face.

"Converse sits on the board at Hollins Communications."

"Wasn't McKaye the executive they canned for a juvenile offense?" Brian asked.

Barbara nodded. "He ripped off a baseball mitt

from the five-and-dime when he was fourteen. The other kids made it out the door, but Bill got caught."

"You got him a quarter of a million, didn't you?"

"Yeah, but he had a tough time finding another job. Hollins wanted him out, and I think it was Converse who dredged the whole thing up. He made these impassioned speeches about ethics and morality, and what amazed me was he really believed his own bullshit. It was like a crusade, for God's sake. Christ, I'd hate to be his kid." She hesitated. "How sick is she, anyway?"

"Very."

Barbara watched him carefully for another moment.

"You know something, Morgan? You're a soft touch for the suffering multitudes. That's one of the reasons I hired you, and also because you're also a shrewd lawyer and you can turn your compassion into logic. But you want to hear my theory?"

"Not particularly," he said, knowing she'd tell him anyway.

"Walter Converse's daughter is sick and helpless, and you absolutely cannot resist her. You're going to protect her and make her all better, except that if you did, I guarantee you that a bouncing, healthy Miss Converse would have nowhere near the same appeal."

Out of line, Brian thought. This was not his taste in ties she was complaining about. He felt none of the usual combative stimulation of his arguments with her, the productive contests of will that left them exhausted and smiling and proud of each other, no matter who won the point. He looked at her flushed face and tried to remember his gratitude.

"You're wrong," he said, carefully controlling his voice.

"I don't think so."

"In any case, you can keep your theories to yourself." He heard his voice quaver.

"That would be *nice*, I agree," she said. She slid off the corner of the desk and began to inspect her armful of files, leafing through the papers silently, methodically, giving him ample time to absorb her displeasure.

Oh God, he thought furiously. She's into her Supreme Court act.

Barbara dropped the files on his desk with a smack and faced him grimly. "You're screwing up around here, and *that* is my business."

Brian rose now, grateful for the extra three inches of height.

"Look, I'll leave it at home, all right?"

"That will be fine," Barbara said quietly. Brian strode toward the door. Suddenly she called out after him.

"Brian . . . about the Converse girl . . . hey!"

He didn't turn back, and when she followed him out of his office a few moments later, his secretary stared at her curiously. Barbara glared back until the girl reddened and started typing with rhythmic enthusiasm. Barbara rapped her fingernails on the desk, a machine-gun exclamation point, then marched briskly down the hallway.

CHAPTER 10

Walter had Sharlie by the elbow, propelling her up the narrow stairs to the crowded dining room on the second floor. A waiter with a heavy tray balanced overhead clattered up the stairs behind them, and Walter flung out an arm, pressing Sharlie and Margaret against the wall.

"Leave it to the Italians. Look at this, kitchen on one floor and dining room on the other."

Sharlie was silent, but Margaret looked downstairs anxiously, as if she expected a carving knife to come whizzing at them fresh from the hand of a Sicilian busboy.

Brian had chosen Pietro's for his debut, and Sharlie was prepared for vitriolic remarks from her father. There was inevitably something the matter with any restaurant, and Sharlie had often sat in humiliation while Walter refused the wine. In fact, the wine ritual had always signaled trouble. Sharlie was fully aware of her father's expertise in selecting the proper vin-

tage. Hadn't he stormed at Margaret for allowing a
new caterer to serve 1972 Lafite at their dinner party
for the sheikh and his entourage? Out with his family,
however, Walter felt free to expound on the idiocy of
spending eighteen dollars on "frog vino" when you
could get Blue Nun for six bucks.

Even with the cheap stuff he enjoyed making a ceremony of the first sip, serene under the contemptuous
eye of the wine steward. Once last fall he had stormed
out of an elegant Park Avenue establishment when
the manager protested that refusing Gallo Chablis
was like refusing Seven-Up. Sharlie remembered the
stares as she and her mother gathered up their hand-
bags and crept out behind him. She prayed that tonight Brian would disappear into the men's room
when the wine list arrived.

Margaret had offered to serve dinner at home tonight, but finally Sharlie opted for the restaurant, figuring they were better off luring Walter out for the
first meeting. In his castle the man was formidable,
but in the neutral territory of a strange restaurant,
perhaps Brian would stand a chance.

They sat over their drinks, waiting, while Walter
sighed heavily and Sharlie fidgeted. Margaret glanced
sympathetically at her daughter, giving her little nervous smiles of encouragement.

"Will you look at the grease spots on those glasses?"
Walter said, and Sharlie heard a faint click as the civil
servant cassette slid into the tape slot at the back of
her father's head. There were unlimited topics in this
category, aimed, among other things, toward the sani-
tizing of restaurant dining rooms, the erasure of graf-
fiti on public edifices, the reformation of derelicts.
Walter responded to each challenge with fervor, com-

plaining noisily that no one else had a community conscience anymore.

He made a great display of looking at his watch, and Sharlie squirmed. Where was Brian anyway?

Finally he appeared in the doorway, all ruddy-faced from the cold March night, bringing a roomful of fresh air with him just as he had that first evening at Saint Joe's.

He approached the table, smiling and relaxed. Sharlie thought, my God, he's not even *hurrying*. Walter stood up, extending his hand, and smiled a broad grin that was all teeth.

"I don't suppose you make your courtroom appearances with such casual disregard for time."

"No, sir," Brian replied. "Not if I can help it."

Turning to Margaret to shake her hand, he apologized briefly for the delay, offering no explanation. Then he leaned over and kissed Sharlie squarely, right on the mouth. Holy bananas, thought Sharlie. Daddy is going to take you apart limb from limb.

But Brian and Walter sat down, and Walter's stiff grin sat on his face, frozen there by shock. Sharlie gazed at her father, trying to pretend that his presence held no special significance—just some beefy stranger whose solid, emotionless expression reminded her of specimens on display at the Museum of Natural History. *Stuffed mogul*: Observe the beady, humorless eyes; the square face; and the small, ungenerous ears.

But the iced grin began to fade, and both Sharlie and Margaret noted with alarm the menacing shift of Walter's shoulders and a slight bulging of the muscles in his neck. Sharlie looked at Brian, her eyes fastening on him for comfort. How could he sit there so nonchalantly with his menu as if there were nothing else to think about but his empty stomach? Even Brian's monumental appetite must wither in the presence of such a man as Walter Converse.

When she was a little girl out to eat with her parents, Sharlie had gradually established a pattern of defensive techniques to sustain her through the ordeal. First she'd try to guess which course would provoke the collision between her father and the management. Next she'd turn her attention to the diners at nearby tables, manufacturing fantastic tales about them and their relationships. Loners and grim, silent couples challenged her imagination, and for them she invented implausibly happy outcomes for what appeared to be empty lives.

But tonight she wondered for the first time what other people might speculate about her own table. Middle-aged couple, quite comfortably wealthy (note woman's designer dress, man's initialed shirt), daughter in twenties (colorless young woman, obviously nervous, fidgeting with her napkin), and beautiful young man—not a brother to the young woman, see how she looks at him so hungrily. Her suitor? What could he possibly see in her? Must be the family jewels.

Sharlie glanced at the solid-looking woman regarding her placidly from a nearby table, jaws grinding away in relentless rhythm, a ruminating hippopotamus, then looked down at the mangled wreckage of the napkin that lay in her lap and decided that even a hippo would notice she was on the verge of a nervous breakdown. Twenty-six years old, she thought disgustedly, and here I sit, paralyzed with terror, waiting for Daddy to chop my man into neat, bite-sized morsels to consume with the antipasto. She watched enviously as Margaret sipped her Chianti. Must be nice to get pleasantly soused.

At this point she became aware of two opposing forces hovering on either side of her like uninvited guests. To the right, Parental Intimidation, an immense, dark, amorphous mass, who spilled over his imaginary chair onto Sharlie's lap, chilling her hands, and whose towering head inspected Brian menacingly, searching for some dire character flaw. The creature plucked at her sweater, pointing triumphantly at Brian's sloppily knotted tie. Sharlie twisted uneasily in her seat, protesting internally to the malignant shadow, What do I need you for when Daddy's here? And on her left, Young Love floated just above her shoulder, delicate and filmy as smoke. It curled itself in an aureole around Brian's head, whispering, This young god is yours. Just reach out and grab. . . .

Ill-behaved, these guest-ghosts, vying for her attention, tugging at her sleeves all through the appetizers. She tried to ignore them, but soon she was imagining Young Love wrapping its silken cloud around the bulging throat of Parental Intimidation, then pulling hard, harder, mercilessly. . . .

Walter harrumphed suddenly, and Sharlie glanced at him as he picked at his stuffed mushrooms. Searching for a trace of imported Neapolitan cockroach, no doubt, she thought. She felt Brian watching her, and turning to look at him, she saw the amusement in his eyes and made a surreptitious face at him. The phantom ghosts disintegrated and fell to the floor like soot.

They got through the first two courses without incident. Margaret and Brian discussed the advantages of growing up in the country, and Sharlie smiled as a hint of southern drawl crept into her mother's speech. Well, thought Sharlie, Mother's found for the defense. Easy victory. But the contest lies with His Honor, glowering away over there as if he just ate something rancid. She noticed suddenly that her father's face appeared decidedly reptilian. He sat, half crouched, chewing and watching Brian and Margaret with suspicious little eyes. A bullfrog on a lily pad, assessing his prospective dessert—Brian, of course. Brian, the beautiful *Callosamia promethea*. Without warning, the long, pointed tongue will flash, whipping around Brian's waist, snapping him inside, his unpolished shoes kicking feebly before disappearing forever between the gaping, dank jaws.

"In those days, life was so much *simplah*," said Margaret, sighing girlishly. Brian nodded at her, then reached out casually and took Sharlie's hand. Walter glared at their entwined fingers as if they were a pile of worms the chef was trying to pass off as spaghetti. Sharlie tried to slip her hand away, but Brian gripped it hard. She looked at him in surprise as he returned Walter's gaze.

"A lawyer, eh?" Walter said suddenly, the deep voice startling after his long, wary silence. Brian nodded. "I hear you specialize in bleeding hearts." Brian smiled pleasantly, but said nothing.

Undaunted, Walter poured the last of the wine for Margaret, Brian, and himself, then took two swallows from his glass. The silence seemed intolerable to Sharlie, and her eyes pleaded with Brian to say something. Anything. Finally Walter aimed his gaze at Brian again and said, "What about this legislation letting the gay boys into city government?"

"It'll be close."

"You think the fags'll win?"

"I hope so."

Walter glared into Brian's unwavering eyes. "You think it's just dandy for homosexuals to teach in the public school system?"

"I don't think the public school system is dandy for anybody," Brian said. He sat comfortably, his shoulders relaxed against the back of his chair, but Sharlie recognized the tension along his jaw. He never once took his eyes off her father, and she knew he was thinking, Enjoy yourself now, because one of these days, I'm going to get your ass.

Walter signaled to the waiter and listened impatiently to a translation of *zuppa inglese*. Finally Brian said, "Think you can scare up a piece of apple pie with a scoop of vanilla?"

The waiter looked pained and said he'd see what he could do. Walter called after the stiff retreating back.

"Make that two, will you?"

Sharlie gave Brian's foot a quick rap under the table. On the phone with him this afternoon, she'd agonized about Walter's restaurant behavior. No matter how elegant the cuisine, her father inevitably ordered apple pie for dessert. Walter's mutilation of foreign languages was legendary, and Sharlie suspected his mastery of the phrase *à la mode* made him feel dashingly continental.

Brian ignored the kick and said to Walter, "I understand you've met my boss."

Walter said, "Way back in the days when she was Barbara Krumberg."

"Kahanian," said Brian evenly.

"Yeah," said Walter. "Whatever. Very bright girl, but she's got a few wires loose." He looked at Brian for a response, but getting none, he continued. "She could be the first lady mayor of New York. I told her that myself."

"She'd make a good one."

Walter snorted. "Jesus Christ, we've got freaks up to our asses around here as it is. With that wild woman at the helm, they'd be air-dropping them in from the West Coast."

He stopped for breath, and Margaret remarked, "You're mixing your military metaphors, dear. *Helm* is naval. . . ."

Walter's eyes didn't waver from Brian's. "Why doesn't she try Los Angeles? California's got the greatest collection of loonies and misfits per square foot. She ought to win by a landslide."

He draped an arm over the back of his chair. Sharlie caught a glimpse of the damp stain at his armpit. Her fingers were beginning to ache from the pressure of Brian's grip, but she said lightly, "Well, Daddy, pretty soon the whole state's going to slide right into the Pacific Ocean."

Walter muttered dubiously, "No loss as far as I'm concerned."

"But what about San Clemente?" asked Margaret. "Isn't that somewhere—"

"Oh, Christ, Margaret. Sometimes you astound me."

"Well . . ." she began defensively, her eyes starting to water. "You sound so negative about California, and I *know* there are places out there . . . why, you adore Palm Springs."

To Sharlie, Walter's voice seemed a little sad. "It's all right, Margaret. I wasn't being literal."

Margaret said, "Oh," and looked down, embarrassed. There was a short silence while she collected herself enough to smile at Brian again. The southern drawl was no longer in evidence.

"Tell me, Brian," she said with effort. "You don't find it uncomfortable working for a woman?"

Oh, no, thought Sharlie, but Brian's response was thoughtful and courteous.

"She's never made an issue of it. I don't think her being a woman has ever gotten in the way."

"That's because she doesn't really qualify as one," Walter remarked.

Brian released Sharlie's hand suddenly. She noted the tight set of his mouth and thought, Here it comes. She looked down at her hands and prayed that it wouldn't be too awful.

"You know, Mr. Converse," Brian said quietly, "a lot of men attack Barbara's sex because they find her threatening. It's a nice cheap shot."

Sharlie held her breath. Walter smiled with forced amiability and began, "Your loyalty . . ."

But Brian held up his hand to stop him and went on in the same level voice.

"She gets a lot of crank letters, some of which have been traced to prominent members of the legal profession. They're pretty sick pieces of paper, and I'll spare you the details. But mostly they're an expression of protest from sore losers, who find a strong woman too humiliating for their own precarious masculinity."

He stopped, and the two men stared at each other. Both pairs of eyes icy cold. Sharlie's heart had stopped beating altogether, and Margaret wore a frantic smile as if to say, Aren't we all having such a fine time together with such spirited conversation?

Suddenly Walter cleared his throat and said, "I'd say you're getting decent training."

Sharlie watched Brian hesitate. After a moment he nodded, acknowledging Walter's compliment, and said, "I'm lucky."

Gracious winner, Sharlie thought, I love you.

Over coffee the two men debated recent rulings by the Supreme Court, always on opposite sides of the issue, wary but polite. Sharlie began to feel uncomfortable again, but this time as if she'd gotten on the wrong train and couldn't reconcile the landscape whizzing by the window with what she knew was supposed to be out there. Uneasily she listened to her father's questions about Brian's practice. This respectful person could not possibly be the same father whom she had so long ago learned to regard with fear. Was she going to have to shift her attitude at this late date?

She remembered business associates of Walter's commenting privately to her on his astute judgment, his uncanny insight, even—remarkably—his tact. She would nod and smile and label the speaker as the kind of person who would definitely buy a used car from Richard Nixon.

Eventually Brian excused himself to go the men's room. Sharlie and Margaret instinctively looked at Walter, their eyes questioning.

Not meeting their gaze, he said, "Too bad he's got himself tied up with that crazy female. Okay, she's a good lawyer. But she's definitely a dyke."

Ah, there's my Dad, thought Sharlie, surprised at her relief.

Outside the restaurant Brian got to the curb first and hailed a cab. He said he would walk home to work off his apple pie, but first held the door open for Sharlie. She slid inside, giving him a sickly smile. Margaret hesitated, then held out her hand and murmured how pleased she was to have met him. When she released his fingers and slipped into the taxi beside Sharlie, Brian turned to Walter, hand still extended. Walter brushed past him with a gruff good night, and Brian stuffed his hand into his pocket. The door slammed shut, and he stood at the curb watching the taillights recede, his breath forming an icy cloud around his face. Then he started off toward Third Avenue. His pace quickened gradually until soon he was practically running uptown.

CHAPTER 11

There was silence inside the cab from the moment the door slammed shut outside Pietro's. Margaret sat wedged between Sharlie and Walter, Walter's massive shoulder pressing hard against her. She felt the impulse to leap out of the taxi into the dark street where she could breathe. The remarks about Barbara Kaye, so uncalled for. So humiliating, especially in front of Sharlie's young man. And why was it that she always made a fool of herself whenever it was most important to make a good impression? When Margaret was a child, her mother had insisted that she take up painting: "All the Mackins are artistic. Of course you can paint, Margaret." But finally the tutor had gently set aside the little girl's muddy messes and explained to her disappointed mother that maybe they ought to try again when Margaret seemed a little more coordinated. There had been no more attempts at developing her artistic talents, but often, in Walter's presence, she remembered the splotchy efforts and wondered if that's what her brain looked like inside on nights like tonight, her thoughts all smeared and blurry when they came out of her mouth. Which only created more tension and made it all worse. When it didn't matter, when she was talking to the housekeeper or to Sharlie, well, then she had confidence. Then her thoughts and the words she used to express them felt sharp and clean. Sharlie had even told her once that she was witty.

The cab bounced painfully, and Margaret thought with resentment that Walter always chose the most beat-up-looking taxi with no springs or ball bearings or whatever it was that kept one's bones from being crunched into dust in the backseat. Oh, but Brian hailed this one, didn't he? She ran her hand across her forehead, trying to clear her brain of confusion. Then she scrutinized Walter's features as the lights from Madison Avenue flashed across his grim face. She wondered if she had missed something crucial with all her self-conscious anxiety at the restaurant. It had appeared to her that Walter had found Brian Morgan quite respectable. So why was he sitting next to her now like Mount Rushmore?

She stole a quick glance at Sharlie, whose expression was as rapturous as Walter's was dour. Margaret thought of those children's riddle books with the pages in which something was out of place—a tractor driving across the ocean or a carousel in the middle of a busy intersection. Sharlie gazed happily out the window, Walter glowered, and Margaret, looking at them both, thought uneasily, What's the matter with this picture?

Martha, the housekeeper, had already gone to bed, so they hung their own coats away in silence, Walter glaring and Sharlie oblivious. Margaret continued to watch them both with growing panic until finally Walter said tersely to Sharlie, "I want to speak to you."

Sharlie blinked her eyes dazedly as if he'd just awakened her from a sound sleep. He nodded his head toward the living room, and they all filed in, Margaret trailing behind, uncertain whether her presence was required and yearning for something soothing to put out the blaze in her solar plexus.

The living room was so still that their intrusion seemed an affront to its dignified paneled sanctity, the only sounds the shifting of coals in the fireplace as the ashes settled and the tiny clicking of the clock's gold pendulum. But Walter's heavy tread scraping against the Oriental rug as he paced back and forth and his careless slam of the door behind them offended Margaret. He had no respect for the ghosts of all those gracious people who'd once lived in this lovely old house.

Margaret, Walter, and Sharlie, shut up in the living room with Walter about to unleash some kind of tirade—well, thought Margaret, Sartre could do no better. She gazed with longing at the door, but Sharlie's frightened face held her there.

Suddenly Walter spun around, pointing a large square finger at his daughter. Margaret restrained the impulse to cover her ears.

"I'd just like to hear how you justify this thing."

Sharlie stared at her father uncomprehendingly, and Margaret thought her daughter looked very young, like a little girl groping for the response to a mysterious grown-up accusation.

"The boy is apeshit about you," Walter pronounced.

"I know," Sharlie said softly, and Margaret saw her search her father's face for clues.

"I want to know if you told him you can never have children."

Sharlie dropped her eyes and murmured something.

"What?" Walter bellowed.

"Yes, I told him that," Sharlie said, swallowing hard but meeting her father's eyes now.

Walter raised his arms and dropped them helplessly to his sides.

"Then he's more of a sucker than I thought." He made his words elaborately simple, as if he were speaking to a dull child. "Brian Morgan is not your friend. He is not some person who feels sorry for you or comes to see you because you are sick and he wants to make himself feel like a nice guy. Brian Morgan is infatuated. In-fa-tu-ated. He's got a great big hot lust for you. He wants your body. The poor sap probably wants to get married."

Sharlie's eyes flickered, and Walter exploded.

"He does, doesn't he? Are you crazy, or are you just monumentally selfish?"

Sharlie's face turned ashen, and Margaret felt her insides divide into two warring factions: concern for Sharlie versus terror of Walter. They thundered away, eroding the lining of her stomach.

"Did you ever stop to think what it would be like for a healthy fellow like that to be married to you? He's a real *man*, my girl, with guts and balls and . . ."

At this, like the summoning of reserves, Margaret's revulsion joined forces with her maternal instincts. She reached out a hand toward her husband, trying to restrain him.

"Walter, really, you're being very cruel."

He didn't hear her, or at least gave no indication that he had. He continued his diatribe as if Margaret were a piece of glass he could look right through.

"Think about his life," he was shouting. "If you have to trap a man, find yourself some pale, sweet thing, some interior decorator or that hairdresser of your mother's. Get yourself a nursemaid. Not a lover, for Christ's sake."

Walter turned abruptly toward the door, but before he got all the way across the room, he swung around again, his eyes all but invisible behind the bulging muscles of his cheeks and forehead.

"Brian Morgan may be a fool. But you," and he shook his finger at Sharlie again. "You . . ."

Without finishing his sentence, he waved his hand in disgust and dismissal and slammed out of the room.

Margaret put her head in her hands and began to cry. After a few minutes she looked up and saw Sharlie sitting quietly, staring in the direction of the door. Her face was so full of hatred that Margaret spun around to see if Walter was still standing there.

Finally Sharlie looked at her mother, her cheeks matching the stony white of the marble fireplace. With a thin, ghostly smile, she said, "Well, Mother, if I hadn't seen it with my own eyes, I wouldn't have thought it was possible for a person to clench his face."

CHAPTER 12

Walter sat in the lounge area of the Fifth Avenue Racquet Club. Behind the plate glass of the exhibition court two men hurtled back and forth, the hard ball slamming against the walls. Walter watched them dazedly, sweat trickling down his face in rivers, soaking his shirt. He sat on the edge of the couch so as not to dampen it. He had taken Freeman easily just now, three to one, and though his opponent had struggled hard over each point, he was barely damp under the armpits. And here I am, irrigating the rug, he thought, annoyed at the insubordination of his glands.

He wondered if Brian Morgan played squash. Good athletic body. Lean, probably quick, too. *How could she?*

He hunched his powerful shoulders, elbows on knees, hands hanging limp, and took two deep breaths, trying to cool off. He'd hoped a hard game with Freeman would work off some of his fury, but even now at the thought of young Morgan his jaw muscles began to ache. Good thing he had to be out of town the next few weeks. He didn't think he could bear looking at his daughter's face.

Walter knew he set his standards very high, knew that he extended his intolerance for weakness in himself to others. Humanity never seemed to measure up, leaving him with a constant nagging sense of disappointment. Except for Sharlie. Brave, uncomplaining, stoic Sharlie. How proud he felt when the medical staff remarked on her courage. Never whining, she faced the agonies of her condition with quiet fortitude.

An occasional lapse now and then, all right. A temper tantrum, a crying jag, some self-indulgence to let off steam. But to ensnare another person in her crippled life—a young man with lousy judgment, but obvious vitality. She wasn't deluding herself about his feelings for her, either—he was hooked. Walter saw in her face that they'd already begun discussing marriage. Marriage! Holy Christ! Hadn't she accepted long ago the unanimous prognosis concerning her life expectancy? And hadn't he explained to her himself that her capacity to function as a woman was negligible? Nonexistent, for all practical purposes—if you consider screwing a practical purpose—or childbearing.

He'd recently read an article about homosexuals that said you can't always tell. Sometimes they're married with kids, sometimes they're even pro ballplayers. Was Brian Morgan a fag? He shook his head, sending a shower of sweat onto the floor.

As Sharlie had approached puberty, Walter watched her carefully, taking note of the new softness in the lines of her body, her reluctance to undress for her doctors, her eyelash-shaded glances at his own body when he walked around in his underwear. Despising his own cowardice, he put off the job of enlightening her.

Finally one evening after dinner when Margaret had gone off to the opera, he marched Sharlie into the living room and sat her down at the couch. He explained to her what he knew she was beginning to feel, and he tried to be specific, realizing that her only sources of information, other than him, were books. Margaret would never discuss such things, and unless a kid went to school where there were other kids to exchange information with, there just wasn't any other way.

He told her about menstruation and that it might occur pretty soon, since she was twelve years old already. He asked her to tell him when it happened, and she nodded solemnly.

Then, pacing back and forth in front of the couch, he explained about sex—the part of it that went beyond reproduction. As tactfully as he could, he told her it could never be for her. That despite the warmth of her feelings, despite the yearnings of her young body, sexual expression was most definitely out.

Christ, how she had sat there, her eyes never leaving his face for a moment, looking at him as if his words came straight from the mouth of God. He'd felt as if he were pulling the wings off a butterfly.

When he was finished, she nodded slowly. Her hair reflected the light from the fire, and he watched it shimmer around her face.

"I didn't think I'd be able to get married or anything," she said thoughtfully. "But could I have a friend? A boy, I mean, if it was just like having a girl friend?"

Walter said yes, that was all right, and he saw her considering this, sorting it all through. He said he wanted her to come to him whenever she had a question or wanted to talk about it, and she had said she would. But except for telling him—reticently—just before Christmas that she had gotten her first period, she never mentioned the subject again. Sometimes he wondered if she'd understood what he'd told her, and then one night he studied her face during a romantic scene on television. The curiosity had disappeared, leaving behind a silent flash of pain and then a numb expressionlessness.

Pathetic joke of nature, he thought, that Sharlie had inherited his warm physical nature rather than Margaret's icy constraint. While Walter rejoiced in physical experience—sex, in particular—Margaret walked around in her high-necked dresses wishing that her too, too solid flesh would melt or something.

And Sharlie got stuck with his high blood. Mother Nature appeared to possess a rather warped sense of humor.

Suddenly the air-conditioned room seemed very cold, and he shifted his shoulders under his clammy shirt.

He rose stiffly, not noticing Freeman, fresh from the showers, wave at him on his way to the elevators. His feet had fallen asleep, and he shook them as he stared at the glass-enclosed court, now unlit and empty.

Fact is, no matter how tough it may be for Sharlie, she must accept reality. You don't take a young man's life and nail it in a coffin. Facts were facts, and she *would* be the courageous girl and give up this idiocy with poor besotted Brian Morgan before she destroyed his life the way . . . His mind halted abruptly. He shook his head and strode quickly to the locker room, hoping to shower away his sudden sensation of being particularly unclean.

CHAPTER 13

Sharlie and Margaret sat in the candlelit dining room trying to fill the silence with neutral conversation. Walter had left for London late that afternoon, and despite their relief at his absence, the table seemed lifeless without him. Their forks clicked against the china and echoed in the hollow corners of the room.

Sharlie's face glowed, pale and luminous. Her eyes glittered as if they were the only source of light in the room, the candles merely reflections of their brilliance. With Walter away, Margaret had hoped it would be easier to talk, but now it seemed as if the girl were more remote than ever. Each time Margaret had approached her daughter recently, she seemed to slip around a corner or behind a closed door, out of reach into some world her mother couldn't share.

Margaret set her fork down emphatically. The jarring sound brought Sharlie's eyes up, and Margaret folded her hands in her lap.

"I've been looking forward to speaking with you alone, dear," she said ceremoniously.

Sharlie's face held the resentment of someone yanked too early from a warm, happy sleep. Margaret smiled apologetically and forged ahead, the words sounding rehearsed in her ears.

"I think it's time we talk about this young man of yours."

Sharlie's face said, I think not, but Margaret went on. "As your mother, I have certain responsibilities to you."

Sharlie said quietly, "I think I've heard enough parental obligation from Daddy."

"Your father and I approach the matter differently."

"But you both end up in the same place," Sharlie said.

Margaret felt her stomach twist, wishing she could just drop the matter and ring for Martha to clear the table. But her conscience pressed heavily and forced her to continue.

"Your father's concern seems to be centered on your Brian. Not that he doesn't have a valid point, dear. You have to admit that."

Sharlie didn't seem about to admit anything, so Margaret stumbled on, feeling as though she were wading through great soggy heaps of mud, her thoughts turbid, her words sucking at her and pulling her down. Infuriating because only this morning, sitting in the kitchen over a cup of coffee, she had felt confident and clear about her anticipated conversation with Sharlie.

"I'm worried about *you*," she said, remembering that this was what she had intended to say. Sharlie's smile said, I'm all right, but Margaret shook her head.

"No, I mean especially worried. It's just not healthy for you to fall in love."

Sharlie burst out laughing, and Margaret sat bewildered and injured, waiting for her daughter's strange hilarity to dissipate. In a moment Sharlie was gazing at Margaret with open curiosity.

"What makes you think I'm falling in love?"

Margaret shook her head, puzzled.

"I mean how can you tell? Do I have symptoms or something?"

Margaret's memory flashed to Monday afternoon when she had come upon Sharlie standing by the mirror in the foyer. She was wearing her pale-pink sweater and gray slacks and was regarding herself with such intensity that Margaret's approach went unobserved. Sharlie had stared at the reflection of her own dark eyes, and at the same time her hands, beginning at her rib cage, moved down over the curves of her waist and hips, unselfconsciously and with undeniable pleasure. Margaret turned away quickly, but Sharlie's eyes caught her mother's movement in the mirror, and she spun around, face flaming. They stood looking at one another, embarrassed, until finally Sharlie moved her shoulders in a tiny shrug and smiled. It was a smug gesture, and Margaret responded to it with unspoken rage. She smiled back at her daughter with thin lips and said quietly, "Mirror, mirror, on the wall." Before Sharlie turned to walk down the hallway, Margaret had detected a look of triumph in the flushed face.

Now Sharlie's voice, insistent, brought Margaret back to the dining room again.

"Really, Mother, I want to know. What does somebody in love look like?"

Margaret said primly, "All right, maybe *love* isn't the proper word for it. Let's just say 'attraction.'"

Sharlie said, "You're talking about sex."

Her last words were spoken just as Martha entered the room to clear the table, and Margaret shot her daughter a look that said, For heaven's sake, not in front of the servants. Martha grinned at Sharlie, obviously longing to stay, removing each plate slowly and methodically and then lingering by the sideboard. Margaret said icily, "The veal was delicious, Martha. I hope you'll make it again when Mr. Converse is home."

"I'm glad you liked it," Martha replied, then abandoned her delaying tactics as Margaret continued to stare at her in cold silence. She picked up the loaded tray, gave Sharlie a wink behind Margaret's back, and went out of the room.

"Maybe that's what love is, do you think? Physical attraction?"

"Oh, no," Margaret said emphatically. "Why, if that's all it was, your father and I . . ."

She stopped abruptly, twisting her napkin in her lap. She looked so stricken and confused that Sharlie reached across the table to touch Margaret's arm.

"Mother," Sharlie said softly, "I'm going to give him up. It just seems so important to know what it is I'm losing."

Margaret and Sharlie looked at each other, both close to tears.

"Don't worry," Sharlie went on. "I'll work it out."

Margaret nodded. "Of course you will, dear."

Sharlie stood up and leaned over the table to blow out the candles.

"Come on. Daddy's away. Let's go sit by the fire

and play Scrabble and listen to *Don Giovanni*. Loud."

Margaret got up, head high, and started out of the dining room. Sharlie followed, marveling again at how pleasing it was to watch her mother's motion.

CHAPTER 14

The next morning Sharlie stayed in bed late, staring at the ceiling and concluding that it was all over with Brian. Well, she thought, tracing a hairline crack in the plaster with her eyes, that's the first time I've gotten so far as to admit it to myself. Progress of a sort.

Dinner at Pietro's had whipped her feelings into a turmoil. She had expected Walter to reject Brian, instantly and violently, perhaps dragging his daughter out of the restaurant by the hair to lock her away in some remote seaside tower. But Walter had eaten his dinner, drunk his wine, and even uttered a few civil words. She looked back on it now and traced the progression of her feelings from terror to surprise to relief, and finally, to hope. Seductive, treacherous hope that so quickly burst into flame, a blazing retribution upon her head. It was as if Young Love, her gentle apparition at the restaurant table, had been suddenly set afire with a foul cigar, to disappear into tiny flakes of ashes around her icy feet.

Sharlie felt the pain begin to suck at her chest. She took three deep breaths, willing herself to unbend her clenched fists. Double betrayal, she thought. Not only does he forbid me my love, but he does it to protect my lover from his evil daughter! Thanks a *lot*, Pops.

She looked toward the window, a bright blue rectangle, wondering if her father were somewhere safe on the ground, where the violence of her hatred couldn't rip through space and shoot him down, twisting and burning, conscious through it all, until finally he'd hit the cold waters of the English Channel and, with one brief hiss, sink to the bottom like a hunk of black sludge.

She groaned and turned away from the daylight, despising herself. This will get us nowhere, she thought, hand against her clattering heart, except maybe Room 1108 at Saint Joe's. *Brian*. What to do about Brian?

She had worked out three scenarios so far, like that book she'd read where the author (in a rather cowardly fashion, she thought) provided several endings and let the reader make the decision.

Finale Number One: Sharlie and Brian at Brian's apartment. They make passionate love, Sharlie has a heart attack at the very moment of her first orgasm, and Brian is stuck with nude dead body, or perhaps *in* nude dead body, depending on how fast rigor mortis sets in.

Finale Number Two: Same scene, except Sharlie lives through it to get pregnant and die in childbirth, leaving Brian with (probably defective) child.

Finale Number Three: Sharlie and Brian meet in a neutral, well-lit coffee shop, shake hands across their cheese danishes and remain friends, close enough and chaste enough to enjoy an occasional game of Go Fish.

She had opted for Number Three, but as the crack in the ceiling took on the shape of Brian's long leg, she found the composition of the dialogue difficult.

"Brian, this is no good." Hackneyed.

"Brian, we can't go on this way." Melodrama.

"Brian, I don't love you anymore." Bullshit. And besides, she'd never told him she loved him anyway, so what was the point of telling him she didn't? *He* was always the one to bring up the subjects of love and marriage.

The fact remained that her involvement with Brian would mess up his life. Distasteful to find herself morally aligned with Walter, but there it was. Lying on her bed as noon approached and she still hadn't composed her speech, she thought, Okay, amazing as it continued to seem, she loved Brian more than she loved herself. Her happiness was temporary under the best of circumstances anyhow. Say, for instance, her heart managed to thump its way through another year or two. In which time she could so screw up Brian's life that he would probably never extricate himself from the swamp of it.

She had always thought self-denial for love was too altruistic to be believed, but perhaps it wasn't nobility at all. The feelings she had for Brian seemed no more to her credit than the fact that she had been blessed with pretty eyes instead of beady ones and round breasts instead of the banana-shaped ones that used to fascinate and repel her in the old issues of *National Geographic* that her parents collected.

It's not nobility of spirit, she thought, but something chemical and scientific. And now, since she'd already said good-bye in theory, it remained only to do it in fact.

She picked up the phone and dialed Brian's office.

An hour later she took a cab downtown to the Pierpont Morgan Library on Thirty-sixth Street. She was glad it was a bright day. Reality seemed so sharply in focus in the white light glaring off the stone buildings on Fifth Avenue. No room in this merciless sunshine for dreams.

Brian's voice had sounded apprehensive over the telephone. He listens to voices through that receiver all day long, Sharlie thought. He knows there's something. And he said he wanted to talk to *her*. Could it be that he was planning to break off with her? Oh, Lord, let it be true, she said to herself. I'll make him go first just in case.

He was already waiting on the steps in front of the elegant old building, and his arm felt tense as he helped her out of the cab. They walked into the gray light of the entrance hall.

"How're you doing?" he asked.

"Okay." But as she looked around at the graceful stone and wood surfaces, their lines soft in the shadows, her courage began to fail. She suddenly tugged at Brian's arm and pulled him back outside into the brilliant sunshine. She sat down on the steps and brushed off a place next to her.

"I think I'd rather stand," he said, his face rigid. "What's going on?"

She clutched her arms around her knees. "You said you had something *you* wanted to talk about."

Brian shook his head. "Drop it."

They stared at each other. Sharlie opened her

mouth to tell him, and finally she burst out, "We can't go on this way. Oh, *no* . . ."

She couldn't believe she had said it, and she began to laugh, making sounds halfway between giggles and chokes. She wiped her eyes and looked up at him to try again.

"I'm sorry. I always laugh at funerals. I can't help it."

"If this is a funeral, you've been talking to your father."

"No," she lied.

"You've been putting me off since Pietro's. I haven't had one second with you alone."

"I needed to digest it. Oh, damn. Not the pasta." She started to laugh nervously again.

He looked at her closely. "You are not in great shape."

She held up her hand in protest. "No. No, I'm okay. Really. I've just needed to think everything out." She was acutely aware of the long line of his leg near her shoulder. Just this one last time, she thought, let him be near me. "I'm getting a stiff neck," she said, stretching to look up at him.

He sat down and stared into her face with clear eyes that seemed to look straight through her skull. She swallowed hard.

"I think you impressed him," she said. "Even if you do work for Crazy Babs." She gave him a feeble smile, but his face was grim. Not doing so hot here, she thought, and took a deep breath, wondering what nonsense would possibly come out next.

"What I've been thinking about was us sitting there all domestic and cozy at Pietro's and how unrealistic that was and how we should all quit kidding ourselves. *I* should quit kidding myself."

"You're rambling, Sharlie."

"I *mean* that I'm not . . . long for this world, and any ideas you or I might be cooking up about long-range . . . Oh God, I did it again."

Brian put his hand on hers and said, "This is the most incredible bullshit."

Sharlie stared at his tie—a paisley print with lots of maroon that clashed with his pale-peach-colored shirt. She had asked him once how he picked out his clothes each day, and he said he just put on a favorite-colored shirt and a favorite-colored tie. If he liked both colors, it had to work, right? Sharlie had looked unconvinced, and he confessed that one day Barbara had stood him in front of her full-length office mirror and said, "There, look. Don't you hear anything?" He had shaken his head, and Barbara told him that his shirt and pants were screaming bloody murder where they met at his waistline. Sharlie had wanted to know what he was wearing, and he told her—his rust-colored suit and pink shirt. They looked fine to him.

"All right," Sharlie said, forcing her eyes off his tie and pulling herself up straight. "It all comes down to this. I'm sick. My relationship with you makes me sicker. I have to choose between you and a longer life. So I'm choosing life."

He stared at her.

"Emily Brontë would not have approved, but I can't help it."

He sat thinking for a moment, and finally he said, "If this is what you really believe, I can't blame you for taking a walk. But I'm telling you, you look better every day. You're stronger now than when you got out of the hospital."

"I have my good days. But there are things I haven't told you."

"Like what?"

"Like what happened the night we . . . the *Swept Away* night. It's not just virgin modesty that keeps me from your bed, Brian. It's fear."

"You got sick."

She nodded.

"So we won't mess around."

"Oh, Brian, don't be ridiculous. The instant I see you, I want to start peeling off my clothes. It's practically Pavlovian." He was silent. "As a matter of fact," she went on in a desperately chatty voice, "that's how I can tell you're around. Suddenly I get this compulsion to unbutton my dress, and I say, 'Hmm, Brian must be about to walk through the door.' It could be very embarrassing at a cocktail party."

"I want to show you something," he said, reaching into his jacket pocket. He pulled out a newspaper clipping and flattened it on her knees: A DECADE OF HEART TRANSPLANTS: THE FANFARE'S OVER BUT AT LEAST 85 LIVE.

A gray-uniformed guard sauntered over to them, his feet scraping abrasively. From her vantage point on the steps Sharlie noticed that his shoes were scuffed. One of the laces had broken and been knotted halfway up.

"Can't sit here."

"Why not?" Brian asked affably.

"Rules."

Brian said, "Can't you see the young lady is ill?"

The guard shook his head. "Looks fine to me."

Brian shot Sharlie a quick glance that said, See? But he went on to the guard in a firm voice, "If she *stands* up, she will *throw* up."

The guard thought this over, then scraped his feet back to the entrance and remarked sullenly, "Ten minutes."

"I might," Sharlie said.

"What?"

"Throw up."

He gave her a puzzled look and she held the article out to him.

"I've read this before. Makes my stomach go all revolted."

"I bet you feel the same way about having a tooth pulled."

She rolled her eyes at him.

"Look," he said, "we could go see somebody. At least find out about it."

"I already know about it."

"That was a long time ago. Techniques have changed. The odds have changed. Oh, come *on*, Sharlie, maybe you can have it all. Life. Me. Babies . . ."

She closed her eyes and held up her hand. "Stop. I don't want to hear about it."

"Just to find out? Where's your grit?"

"I've run out. I don't have any more. I used to keep it under my fingernails." She held out a hand to him, showing him her immaculate nails. "See? All gone."

Brian sighed and snatched the clipping from her. He muttered, "If it weren't so self-defeating, I'd take my own heart out and give it to you."

"I'm not noble, Brian. I won't have a transplant, not

even for you. I don't want to prolong my life one second if it means living with somebody else's heart inside me."

"Why not?"

"It's . . . against nature, that's why not."

"Ah, a fundamentalist. What about kidney transplants? Spleens? Pacemakers? Or let's get back to teeth for a minute. I know for a fact that you have one tooth . . ."

She interrupted him angrily. "It's irrational, all right? Upper plates and hearts are not the same thing."

He shook his head in exasperation, and she said quietly, "Listen, Brian, we've had enough memories to last a lifetime, easily. A long lifetime. Let's leave it at that."

"Stick with me a couple more months and make up your mind then. We'll have a whole other bunch of memories."

"You'll have a bunch of memories. I'll be six feet under."

"I'm not going to let you die."

His tenacity was beginning to wear her down, and she burst out in frustration, "You're a closet necrophiliac, that's what you are."

"I don't think that's very funny."

She glanced at the guard, who was staring at them resentfully. Then she looked into Brian's stubborn face. Okay, she thought, I am not convincing this man. Brutality is the only way.

"If I see you anymore, I will die." Brian started to interrupt, but she went on coldly, willing her eyes to stay dry. "You may not believe that, but I do. It may seem amazing that I would rather live another few months without you than expire next week in your loving arms, but it's a fact."

He was watching her very carefully, trying to look past her expressionless eyes. She saw him searching, asking himself if he believed her. She dug deep into the lifetime supply of self-control, the place where she found the will to sustain her through hours of grueling pain. *I will make it through the next couple of seconds*, she vowed to herself, *and then he will go away and I can have a good cry.*

She stared at him, calm, with just the right touch of compassion in her voice. "Believe it, Brian."

He nodded slowly. She kissed him once, putting her cheek next to his for a moment, grateful that he couldn't see the misery flooding her face. Then she got up with her eyes averted and walked quickly away from him.

CHAPTER 15

She had lived two whole weeks without seeing him. She marveled at the vast stretch of a minute, how the second hand on her watch crawled along like an overweight turtle, laboriously, ponderously, excruciatingly slow.

She had felt crushed at first, and the time went faster then. At least the anguish was interesting, and she spent long hours in bed wiping her nose and replaying the memories of her times with Brian. She thought and talked to herself and contemplated swallowing the whole contents of a bottle of Valium that sat temptingly near her bed. But Margaret must have anticipated that possibility and made off with all of her drugs, henceforth dispensing them personally.

Sharlie's conversations with herself seemed to follow a particular pattern, beginning with the concept that perhaps she should continue the relationship. But she always ended up in the same place, just as Walter did. And as she examined her feelings, she began to suspect that something else was operating here, simultaneous with her fierce impulse to protect Brian. She realized that she had never truly believed in a future for them. Even introducing him to her family at Pietro's, she could not imagine a permanent life with Brian. Maybe it was because she had long ago learned to keep her sights trimmed short. Tomorrow or the next day was all she could realistically expect, and she had absorbed the habit of thinking ahead in very modest stretches.

But after two long days of analyzing her thoughts, she came to the realization that she was scared. Brian terrified her. He was so alive, his commitment to life so vital. He demanded from her the same passionate thirst. No holding back.

Take the transplant issue, for instance. Brian saw the chance for a better life and reached right out for it, asking her to do the same, demanding that she ignore her dread. Irrational dread. Foolish, queasy reticence that stood in the way of a new life for them both. Or at least the possibility.

The very idea of another heart taking up residence under her rib cage made her skin creep with gooseflesh. I have enough trouble coping with my own soul, she protested. Don't ask me to sublet my insides to some stranger.

Why was she talking to him? she asked herself. He was gone, and she was back in her constrained little niche where she belonged, safe and comfortable, cocooned in a world of invalidism. What she was, she decided, was an emotional shut-in, and Brian's headlong leap into her existence made her dizzy.

But the acknowledgment of her own reluctance to participate in life did nothing to ease her grief. She resigned herself to three months of mourning, figuring that the pain would begin to fade by midsummer. But this past week she found herself watching the second hand creep around her watch face past infinitesimal bits of time.

This morning she had awakened at six, dismayed that she couldn't sleep away a few more hours. She dragged herself out of bed and went to stand in front of the mirror.

Sickly cheeks and dark blotches under the eyes—corpses look better, she thought. Remembering her crack to Brian about necrophilia, she suddenly felt that if she didn't see him again, she might just as well drop in at the local mortician. Frank E. Campbell's was right up the street. She could put on a white dress, pick up a bouquet of lilies from the florist across Madison Avenue, and take a flying leap into the plushest unoccupied coffin.

Brian smashed the ball as hard as he could. It slammed into the tape at the top of the net and dropped with a small plop onto his side of the court. He threw his racquet at the net and began pacing back and forth at the baseline.

Susan stared at him from the other side, wide-eyed and silent. After a minute Brian walked slowly to his racquet, picked it up, shook his head at Susan, and headed for the bench where he'd put his jacket and warm-up suit. She followed him off the court and gathered up her things.

"Sorry," he said as they started for the changing rooms.

"What's the matter?" she asked. He just shook his head. "Can I help?"

"Don't think so," he answered, but he put his arm around her shoulders.

They shared a cab uptown. Brian was silent the whole trip. Susan kept giving him surreptitious glances, but she finally realized he wasn't even aware of her presence and she could stare at him with impunity.

In the elevator she took a deep breath and said, "Brian, I want you to come home with me."

He looked at her with surprise, as if she'd jarred him out of a dream. "Thanks, but not tonight."

"I think it would be a very good idea."

He shook his head. The elevator stopped at the seventh floor, and she stood against the door, holding it open. She pulled at his arm. "Come on." She smiled at him. "Please. Keep me company."

He smiled back at her finally and nodded.

In bed he clung to her as if he were drowning. Susan found herself murmuring, "I've missed you. Brian, I've missed you." Their lovemaking was quick, desperate for them both. Afterward, Susan gazed at his profile in the shadows next to her. He stared up at the ceiling, and except for the glint of light from his eyes, he might as well have been made of stone. After a while he sat up on the edge of the bed and turned to look at her. His smile was full of apology and sorrow, and when he put his hand to her cheek, Susan swallowed hard to keep herself from crying.

"I'm sorry," he said softly, then got up, slipped his clothes on, and let himself out the front door.

The courtroom was almost devoid of spectators. One old man leaned against the wooden arm of his bench, sleeping. There were six children, about ten years old, with a middle-aged black woman. A field trip, perhaps—schoolchildren learning about the American system of justice.

The jurors sat quietly along the wall. Perhaps it was the first day of this particular trial, because they seemed slightly awed, and all their faces were attentive.

The judge, gray-haired and berobed, presided on the raised platform opposite his audience. He scribbled notes for a few moments, and when he looked up, his face seemed more businesslike than solemn.

Back and forth across the center of the room between the judge and the spectators strode the young man. His pacing was not restless, nor were his words impassioned, but he seemed to require the motion of his body in order to speak. His steps were steady, his sentences quiet and deliberate. He glanced often at the jury, directing his attention to them rather than to the tense, corpulent man in the witness stand. Every eye was riveted on him, every head tilted toward him slightly so as not to miss a word.

A slim figure stood in the doorway, half hidden. In the pale face were enormous dark eyes that gazed at the young man with sorrowful longing. The figure stood very still, watching, for a few moments. Then, with reluctance, the eyes dropped, the figure turned away, and just as the young man lifted his face, it slipped unseen into the hallway outside. He hesitated for a moment, as if he'd lost the thread of his thoughts, then began to walk again, and as he walked, the words continued in their quiet, steady flow.

That evening Brian sat in his apartment while it grew dark. He didn't bother turning on the lights, and although his mouth was very dry, he couldn't work up the energy to get himself a drink. It had been years since he'd allowed himself a moment devoted solely to self-pity—not since his mother died. Whenever he had felt lonely in the empty apartment, he went out and found himself some companionship or talked Susan into a game of tennis or a friendly hour or two in bed. When he had lost an important case, he immediately threw himself into the next one.

Not tonight, however. Nor the three weeks of nights preceding this one. So *many* hours of feeling sorry for himself. Again today his work had seemed meaningless. Then there was the late afternoon tennis match with another lawyer, who, for the first time, whipped Brian soundly and thought he'd been sent straight to heaven.

Last week he had removed everything of Sharlie's: the snapshots from the instant-photo booth in Woolworth's in which she was making faces just like, she had said, Marlene Dietrich; a barrette he'd found under a pillow on the couch; two paperback books (a collection of Yeats's poetry and a mystery story by Dick Francis that she thought he might like). He gathered everything into a small heap and stuffed it down the incinerator.

Barbara had asked him if he'd like to plan a two-week vacation somewhere. She hated his vacations and had always become surly before he took time away from the office, so he was touched that she made the gesture. But there was no place he wanted to go. And there was nothing that eased the paralyzing mixture of gloom, anger, helplessness, and overwhelming need. He kept telling himself he'd give up just one more hour to wallowing in misery and then maybe he'd get back to his life with some degree of efficiency.

Goddamn her, he thought. His eye caught the newspaper clipping he'd shown her, and he grabbed it from the desk, crumpled it furiously into a tiny angry wad, and tossed it at the wastebasket, smiling bitterly when it fell short of the rim.

Wasn't there something or someone to pin the blame on? Maybe Sharlie was right. Maybe it was an elaborate joke fabricated by her Great Creep in the Sky. The thought made him uneasy, and he asked God to excuse it. Somewhere in his head a remnant of Presbyterianism still lurked.

It was just that everybody seemed to desert him. First his mother, and even now it hurt as if it had happened last week. Maybe because of the guilt for not being there. Maybe because, from what he could make out, her death hadn't been necessary. She wasn't that sick at first, and it enraged him that nobody bothered to fix her up while it still would have done some good. His father's fault, nearsighted old bastard.

With whom rested desertion number two? Brian supposed it was a toss-up as to who walked out on whom, but God knew he worked very hard to get a response out of the man. Displeasure was simple enough, but Brian knew that pleasing his father meant to quit toting home academic honors and instead put on his hip boots and wade out into the manure with Robert and Marcus. If it hadn't been for his mother, maybe he would have, he was so damn eager to make his father happy. In retrospect, she must have had a tough time of it keeping his father off his back about school.

Brian used to watch his face when she handed him

his report card. He would have liked to hold a magnifying glass up to those stony eyes to see if there was maybe a flicker of pride there someplace. Nothing. Maybe a grunt. Brian had been shocked at graduation after his valedictory speech when his father shook his hand. There was water in the old man's eyes. Maybe it was the air conditioning.

But the granite cracked when his mother died. Not at the funeral, or even at the cemetery. Not until they all sat around afterward in the old farmhouse wondering where all the warmth had gone. Four grown men with their hands on their knees not knowing what to do with themselves without her standing in the middle dispensing smiles and lentil soup.

At first Brian had thought his father was choking on his pipe, that weird gagging noise, but then he had looked closely and seen that the man was crying. Didn't even bother to cover his face, just sat there with the tears dripping onto his lap. Robert and Marcus got up and left him to it, but Brian figured he'd just sit there with him even if he didn't know anyone was there.

The old man deserved to grieve, self-centered old piece of Pennsylvania slate rock. He should have saved her.

And now Sharlie. Brian never thought himself a masochist, but taking an objective view of the facts, he had to wonder. She told him she was going to die, but who ever *believed* that? Too goddamn melodramatic.

Somewhere he'd read that neurotics repeat destructive situations or traumatic events over and over again, helplessly reliving some tragic pattern in the vain hope that, okay, folks, this time you watch, it's gonna work out fine. And of course it never does. Did he choose Sharlie, knowing how ill she was, figuring he'd make her all better and relieve himself of the guilt he felt about his mother?

He reached out a long leg and kicked idly at the wastebasket.

Oh, for Christ's sake, he thought. I sound like Susan. Poor Susan with the quotations from her incessant assortment of Manhattan shrinks.

It all came down to the same thing, and that was that he couldn't stop wanting the girl. They were hooked up in some basic way, some psychic way, perhaps, as if when she took a step, his foot moved too. In the middle of the night when she rolled over in her bed on Seventy-fifth Street, his body must turn to face hers, his arms reaching out for her. Someone would have to explain to him how there could possibly be anything wrong inside a body so beautiful. And her eyes. And watching her come to life sexually. Oh, he'd been blessed, and if he never saw her again, that was something he wouldn't forget in his lifetime. Not if a thousand other women sat on his lap and took off their clothes.

If I never see her again . . .

The room had gone completely dark, but Brian remained immobilized in his chair. The word *intolerable* kept flashing in his head, so he continued repeating "never see her again," hoping that eventually the concept would entrench itself in that mental collection of unpleasant facts where his mother's death was now firmly embedded.

He looked down at his hands and flexed them, his fingers remembering the texture of her skin, the long, soft lines of her body. When he had held her, one hand on each side of her rib cage with the padded

area beneath his thumbs touching the round beginnings of her breasts . . . how the hell was he supposed to live like this? *She* was used to pain. She'd
transformed it into Agony Jones, someone as familiar
as a lifelong boarder. How could she leave him before
she'd taught him how?

It was past midnight when the doorbell rang. She
stood in the soft light of the hallway, and he stared at
her, unable to speak or move. She smiled a little,
shook her head, and said, "Consistency is the hobgoblin of little minds. Or something."

He reached out a hand and pulled her through the
door. He held her as gently as he could, mustering
barely enough control to keep from crushing her. She
buried her head in his shirt, and he could hear her
saying, "I can't do it anymore. I can't, I can't. . . ."

CHAPTER 16

Sharlie's face suddenly went frozen on him, and he knew she was thinking about her father's return tomorrow. They had crammed so much into these past two weeks, and both of them dreaded Walter Converse's reentry into their world.

The crosstown bus was packed with chattering children waving their *Ice Capades* program guides and the spinning toys that glowed in the dark. Sharlie had been fascinated with the spectacle when the lights went down in Madison Square Garden and all those whirling red circles began to dance in the darkness. She said it made her feel like the Statue of Liberty the night of the Bicentennial celebration when they surrounded the great monument with fireworks. He laughed and asked her where she kept her torch.

The bus lurched to a stop at Fifth Avenue, and the standees stumbled forward en masse, shrieking and giggling. Brian felt Sharlie looking at him and turned to smile at her.

"What're you thinking about, lady?" he asked. She shook her head. "You're smirking at me," he insisted, then looked at his shirt. "Lousy combination with these pants, is that it?" She grinned and shook her head again. He said, "Well? Well?"

"I love you," she said. Suddenly it seemed to Brian that her eyes had captured the crystal laughter of all the children on the bus and were beaming the joy back to him, transformed from sound into brilliant light. He leaned his face close to hers and said, "What was that again, Miss? Speak up, will you?"

Sharlie bellowed, "I *said* I *love* you!"

Everyone in the bus turned to stare at them, and Sharlie sat there, flushed and smiling and very proud of herself.

They picked up their dinner at the deli on the corner near Brian's building. So close to Walter's return, they both felt the unspoken need to be alone together without the intrusion of other people's eyes on them in a public restaurant. They spread their rolls and cold cuts and containers of potato salad on a blanket in the living room and drank soda from coffee mugs.

Sharlie didn't touch her sandwich, and when she got up and headed for the bathroom, Brian thought she might be ill.

"You okay?" he called after her.

She turned to give him a strange smile, almost conspiratorial. Her eyes were sparkling. "I'm fine," she said, and disappeared beyond the doorway.

After what seemed like a long time, Brian called "Hey!" He heard a muffled sound from his bedroom. Alarmed, he sprang up and ran to find her.

She was sitting on the edge of his bed, gazing up at him, a streak of ink on her chin and torn fragments of paper beside her on the bed. He was about to burst out at her in baffled relief when he suddenly noticed something pinned to her sweater over her right breast. It was the remains of her paper napkin cut into the shape of a heart. On it she had written, *Out of order. To be replaced.*

Brian's eyes snapped up to her face, staring closely to make sure there was no mistake. She was grinning at him.

"It's too late for Margaret Mead. I would have loved to get Margaret Mead's heart. You think they can find me one like hers?"

Brian toppled her over onto the bed and crushed her to him until she howled in protest.

Alone in her dark room she lay watching the red glow of the souvenir toy peering at her from the bookcase like a giant crimson eye. Brian had bought it secretly when he'd left his seat for the refreshment stand, and surprised her by slipping it into her coat pocket when he brought her home. He said it was for luck. God knows they needed it.

But she wasn't going to think about that. Now was the proper time to remember today before it faded, to go over its contours and impress them into her memory so she could always retrace them.

Why was it she cried during the show? She'd been embarrassed and told Brian her sinuses were bothering her, but the moment the skaters came gliding out onto the ice in their crazy, tacky, ludicrously sequined and beplumed finery, she choked up. Same thing with parades. No matter if it was the gnarled old codgers from the Ancient Order of Bison, straggling up Fifth Avenue in moth-eaten uniforms to the bleating of a dented trumpet. The tears came with the ceremony somehow. The Olympic Games were always worth a box of Kleenex—all that running around in body suits with eternal flames. What was it Yeats had said about ceremony? She'd have to look it up in the morning.

Odd that she'd never been to an ice show before. She enjoyed skating competitions on television and was familiar enough with the participants to discuss with her father the relative merits of Peggy Fleming or Dorothy Hamill or even Tenley Albright, whom she remembered because the name appealed to her. She never missed an old Sonja Henie movie on *The Late Show*. So why had she never gone to a real live performance?

She supposed she'd been afraid of the crowds. So many people in that huge stadium, so unlike the staid glamour of the concert hall. What if she got sick? How would she get out? She'd be trapped.

But with Brian she was safe. She smiled to herself in the darkness and thought that if he said, Hey, see that tightrope a hundred feet above the ground with no net that you've never been on in your life? Let's walk across it, it'll be fun, and don't worry, I won't let you fall, she'd nod her head and say, Of course, and go find herself a pair of spangled tights.

Which was approximately what she was doing, she thought ruefully, except that the odds of surviving a transplant probably weren't as favorable as taking a long stroll on a tightrope. Oh God, they'd better give her the heart of a Flying Wallenda or she wouldn't have the heart to go through with it, pardon the idiom. If they'd let her choose, she thought she could manage the whole thing with a little more aplomb—

I'd like the one with the sexy aorta and the jaunty beat, please. Just wrap it up, and I'll take it with me.

She fell asleep imagining a glass case in Bendel's lined with plush blue velvet, displaying gleaming kidneys, hearts, and eyes.

She was in a small room, dark except for a smoky red glow that vaguely outlined her figure. Brian appeared, but no words were spoken. He held out his hand for hers, and she began to fall out of reach. She tried to call to him, but her mouth opened soundlessly as she fell backward, slowly, slowly. The sight of his face and of his outstretched hand grew dim as she fell, the distance to the floor a descent through miles of hot, dark, suffocating space. Inside her head she screamed his name but knew he couldn't hear her, and soon even that inner voice blurred until, just as she reached the floor, all consciousness ended.

She awoke in terror, gasping, realizing that she'd been holding her breath in her sleep. Her sheets were clammy, her hair soaked, and she lay unmoving as her body chilled. After a while she turned her electric blanket up as high as it would go, but she did not get warm again.

CHAPTER 17

While Walter boarded the plane at Heathrow, Margaret was sitting in her quiet living room, the morning sun streaming in the window to warm the back of her neck as she labored over a baby sweater she'd been knitting. Margaret tried not to think about her husband's return and concentrated instead on the little baby, her only niece's child. Always a great-aunt and never a grandmother, she thought, her fingers working the thin yellow wool into an intricate pattern. She wished she had a little baby around again, a baby she could take care of herself, not like with Sharlie when they made her go away and leave the nursing to the experts. Walter always said she didn't hold her right. My Lord, such lovely pale skin she'd had, like porcelain. It was still the same. Except that lately it'd gotten quite pink and healthy looking. Obviously Sharlie was seeing her young man again. The girl was so oblivious to everybody else that watching her these days was like sitting behind a one-way mirror. Two weeks

ago she was so absorbed in grief, so gray and sickly it
was plain she'd broken off with him, just as she said
she would. Frightened by the pinched, ghostly face,
Margaret had become alarmed enough to hope for a
reunion.

Had the Concorde left the runway in London yet?

Her head still told her that the relationship between
Sharlie and Brian was impossible, and of course Margaret would never actively defy Walter's wishes. But if
somehow it were all beyond her control, if the children were to run off together in the middle of the
night . . .

Maybe Walter would be delayed, maybe he'd trans-
fer himself to the London office, maybe something
would happen to his plane. . . . Oh, Margaret,
shame, shame. And besides, how would she get along
without him? She couldn't possibly manage.

In her preoccupation she had somehow dropped a
stitch two rows back, leaving a noticeable gap in the
complicated pattern. She stared helplessly at the defect, then suddenly found herself ripping at the fine
wool, tearing out row after row, passing the site of her
mistake until she had destroyed the entire piece,
weeks of careful, painstaking work. She had begun to
cry, and she gathered up the tangled spaghettilike pile
to bury her face in its softness. After a few minutes
she took a deep breath, got up, and carried the chaotic remains of her handiwork into the kitchen,
dumped it into a paper bag, and stuffed it in the garbage can underneath this morning's coffee grounds.

CHAPTER 18

The flight from Heathrow had included a movie, a "fantasy," they called it, about a prizefighter who gave birth to twins. Walter had spent most of the trip listening to Muzak through his earphones to escape the laughter of people who obviously hadn't a grain of taste. Not that he didn't appreciate entertainment. He could never fathom anybody's subjecting himself to those highbrow Scandinavian "films" that looked like they were photographed in a swamp in the middle of the night. Or those Italian jobs with dwarves jumping into the sack with obese women sprouting two-hundred-pound breasts. Why pay for a freak show when you can get one for free by walking west on Forty-second Street?

Good to get back to New York. He was looking forward to it, despite the pleasures of being away. He always enjoyed his first glimpse of the skyline—gave him a funny knot in the larynx. All the gleaming power, a shimmer rising from the skyscrapers like en-

ergy from millions of people hustling below. They saw
you cut your life short a couple of years living in the
midst of it, but Christ, each day here was worth at
least ten in a town like Boston or Atlanta—or London.

In London he had met with the minister of state for
energy, a real gentleman, although, to be honest, they
all sounded like gentlemen with those accents. The
minister had arranged for Walter to be driven up
north to the dismal gray city where Transamco sat
quaking in anticipation of a dockworkers' strike.

The management greeted him with the fanfare due
a representative of the company's heaviest investors,
but despite the hospitality Walter had been dis-
pleased. One trip through the plant convinced him
that the American operation was already infected
with the slipshod habits of the British industrial community. Just two years ago Walter had personally
overseen the formation of the outfit, ensuring its efficiency and profitability. And now look at the place—
two-hour lunch breaks, card games in the lavatory.
Was all of England managed by incompetents?

Rhetorical question. Of course it was. The country
was washed up, the brilliance of its glorious past
eroded by the shuffling feet of strike lines, the shifting asses of men playing poker or whist or whatever
the English play. The U.S. government ought to send
every budding American hippy socialist to the British
Isles and let him try to negotiate the newly built dual
carriageways—why, in Christ's name, couldn't they
call them thruways?—that began crumbling from poor
workmanship the month they were laid down. What
about those overpriced tin cans they called cars? And,
my God, the *hamburgers*! Must grind up their stray-

dog population to produce those pale-orange gristly lumps.

Mind you, he wasn't one of those nationalist jerks who debarked at Heathrow waving flags and yelling about how we Yanks won the war for the Limeys. He'd fought side by side with them—well, not exactly in the foxholes, but he'd read the reports at his desk in Washington—and there wasn't a country on earth that could have defeated them, except for the crazy Krauts. Even without us, they might just have pulled it off. Stoic bastards they were then. Pathetic what a dose of communism can do in just a few years.

In the limousine on his way into Manhattan, he gazed out the window at the yellow-gray smog hanging over the city and worried about Sharlie's oxygen supply. These were her worst days; he'd seen her turn pale blue as her body fought for air. Poor crippled Sharlie with her hot longings for that young fellow. Her mother must wonder what it's all about. Margaret with the ice reaching down into her very bones. She never sweated, never belched, never had bad breath. Never laid a fart in her life.

He knew he should never have married her, but there was all that pressure from Mother, all the sensible advice about the Mackins and the benefits to his career. Which had paid off, undeniably. Margaret's credentials, like her underwear, were impeccable. God damn the woman, with her long, cool limbs. She was fifty-five years old, for Christ's sake. How the hell did she keep her shape? She never took more than two steps forward and three steps back, as far as he could tell. Certainly didn't get that glowing skin from a healthy romp in the sack once or twice a week, that's

for damn sure. Infuriating, he thought, that the sight
of her still aroused him after all these years.

That woman at the hotel in London—same thing
again. Right in the middle of a really good screw,
damned if she didn't begin to look like Margaret. Not
that it was a turn-off—on the contrary. He snorted,
wondering if the act with that broad in London would
be technically considered adultery if he could make it
only by imagining that she was his wife.

He hunched himself upright in the back seat of the
Mercedes as they drove across the Queensboro
Bridge. Women. Christ, what a bewildering species.

As the limousine neared Madison Avenue, he began
to wonder about Sharlie. How to make it easier for
her, that was the thing. Maybe another trip to the
Continent?

If he could only get her interested in something outside herself and her books and all that intellectual
crap that does nothing to expend sexual energy. Sharlie would have been an athlete, with those long legs
and her quick reflexes. As a little girl she'd dreamed
of joining the circus, and for a short while she became
a trampoline artist on her bed, an acrobat on the living room rug. She could take about thirty seconds of
it, with Walter's heart in his mouth as he watched, but
in those brief moments her expression was transformed from the pale wisdom of a tired old person to
the sparkling exuberance of a healthy child, reveling
in the activity of wild young limbs. Then suddenly
she'd lie still, pale again and frightened, as the knocking began in her little bony chest. He couldn't bear to
stop her joy when she had it, hated seeing it disappear
behind aged eyes. Once she'd cried when the pain began, but when she saw he was watching her, she had

surreptitiously dried her face on the back of her hand and given him a ghastly smile. He'd patted her on the head, saying something like, "Never mind, Chuck," when he really wanted to gather her up in his arms and weep with her. Or somehow strap her to him so that when he played his own rough physical games, she could share the exhilaration of it.

Put a defective heart into Margaret and nobody'd notice, he thought as the car pulled up. Not even Margaret.

Dinner was particularly quiet. None of the usual eager questioning from Sharlie about the places he'd seen. Come to think of it, while he'd stood inside the front door, sweaty and exhausted, Sharlie had shown up to give him a perfunctory welcome-home kiss and then disappeared into her room. Usually the day he got back from a long trip she'd sit on his bed as he unpacked and pry into the corners of his suitcase to see what he'd brought her. And Margaret, too. Those first nights home were often the friendliest times between them. Her face would glow with an animation that deadened as the hours passed and life resumed its old patterns of wariness. But tonight Margaret sat at the other end of the table with a tense face, avoiding his eyes.

Sharlie's seeing that young man. For a moment, he was astonished, but, looking at her more closely as she played with her napkin, it occurred to him that after all, she was his daughter, wasn't she? Therefore a spark of rebellion lurked in her character somewhere, misguided though it may be. Certainly she was seeing him. How myopic of him not to have realized it from the minute he stepped inside the door and looked into her face. He set down his fork and spoke into the strained silence.

"I forbid it, Sharlie."

Both women's eyes shot up. He watched his daughter swallow hard and force herself to face him steadily.

"I know," she said, but her voice was quivering.

"If you give a damn about him," said Walter, "you'll leave the poor sucker alone."

"We're getting married."

Margaret made a little choking noise at the other end of the table. Sharlie's face was now as white as the delicate bone china dinner plates, and there was a tiny moment when he felt himself weaken—perhaps if his words struck too hard, that porcelain face would crack into millions of tiny pieces. But in the space of one deep breath objectivity returned.

"What kind of feeling could you have for him if you're willing to cripple his life, too?"

Sharlie grabbed hold of the edge of the table and closed her eyes. Walter steeled himself to get it over with as mercifully as possible.

"What kind of love is it to deny a man his sex?"

Her eyes still closed, Sharlie said hoarsely, "We'll work it out."

"You going to hire a live-in mistress? Who gets to have his babies, the hired help?"

Sharlie stood up and held onto the back of her chair with stiff arms. Her skin had turned pale gray now, and she breathed unsteadily. But Walter couldn't stop.

"He thinks he cares for you. Well, don't delude yourself. Before you can say, 'Here comes the bride,' three times, he's going to hate your guts."

Margaret rose, reaching out her hand just as Sharlie

gave a little sigh and crumpled onto the floor. Walter bolted to his feet, but by the time he reached Sharlie's unconscious body, Margaret was kneeling beside her. As Walter leaned over to lift up his daughter, Margaret struck fiercely at his arm. Stunned, he recoiled, and she spat out at him, *"If . . . you . . . touch . . . her . . ."*

Walter stood for a moment, his massive head bent, his shoulders sagging, watching Margaret murmur softly, as she stroked Sharlie's masklike face. Then he strode to the telephone to call for the ambulance.

CHAPTER 19

Mary MacDonald picked up the cold wrist for the third time in twenty minutes. Goddamn Diller, son-ofabitch prima donna, she thought, as the taps beneath her fingers beat frantically—the panicked feet of millions of tiny lemmings scurrying to the cliffs by the sea.

Come on, MacDonald, come on, she chided herself, tucking the arm between the crisp sheets and smoothing her uniform. She stared down at the still, gray face.

"Sharlie, my sweet, you're in big trouble this time, aren't you? And where's that goddamn Diller?"

It had been two hours since the ambulance brought her in, and still the girl hadn't recovered consciousness. MacDonald hadn't even recognized her, the color was so bad. Features change as death approaches, and the subtle transformation had already begun by the time they hooked her up in ICU.

Another miracle for modern science, MacDonald

thought grimly. We doing you a favor, girl? She stroked the lank hair, placing it gently behind Sharlie's ears.

"What's her CVP?" said a calm voice next to her shoulder, and MacDonald wheeled around, embarrassed at being caught in such an attitude of unprofessional tenderness. Diller was running his eyes down Sharlie's chart.

"Fifteen," she replied, frowning at the young woman standing beside Diller. Different face, same body—immense breasts, slim hips, legs that began at the armpits. Diller caught the look.

"MacDonald, Miss Nobring," he said with elaborate formality. "Mac's the best diagnostician in Cardiology. If there's any conflict between her and X ray, trust Mac over the pictures."

Mary MacDonald ignored his frozen smile and nodded brusquely at Sharlie. "We're losing her," she said. *You exhibitionistic, egocentric medical-matinee-idol asshole.*

"Where're the parents?"

"Getting coffee."

"I want to see them the minute they show up."

"They're pretty eager to see you, too," Mary said acidly. *Where have you been while my Sharlie lies dying?*

Diller gave her a cool smile, taking Miss Nobring under the shapely arm. "I'll be in my office," he said, and ushered Miss Nobring out.

Yes, and you'll keep your door locked for half an hour, too, won't you, doctor? Mary thought. Let's just hope nobody needs you before you're finished.

She looked down at her patient again, the slim body insubstantial, as if there were no one in the bed at all, just a crease in the sheet. Nothing to be done, Mary thought with an unfamiliar sense of panic. Usually she felt resigned when losing a cardiac patient. In fact, her recent lack of sorrow had begun to concern her, and she had spoken about it with the priest. After twenty-eight years of hospital work, had she become cold-hearted at last, another Carlton Diller? Herd 'em off the ambulance, hook 'em up to the machines, stick a dozen needles in their veins, and if they make it, shake their hands and ship 'em out. If they don't, well, that's the breaks. I did what I could.

But when Charlotte Converse was born, Mary Mac-Donald was just beginning in Pediatrics. The young nurse had held the frail infant and prayed for her to survive. In those days she hadn't been cold-hearted. Too much the other way, in fact, so that sometimes her compassion got in the way of her judgment, so that one time . . .

. She shook her head to clear it of ugly memories. No use crying over spilled milk, not when there were living people in her charge.

Sharlie stirred and opened her eyes just a slit, wincing at the glaring light of ICU. Mary leaned over her.

"Eyelashes about half-mast. Not bad, but you can do better."

Sharlie tried to make a face at her, and Mary was nearly overcome by the urge to grab the girl's thin shoulders and hold her close to her own substantial breast. Instead, she said gruffly, "Cut the comedy, Converse. Save your strength for the second act."

"I hope a comedy," Sharlie whispered.

"Oh, for Christ's sake, girl, did we ever let you down?"

Sharlie shook her head and closed her eyes wearily. Mary picked up the thin wrist again, checking the monitor to confirm what her fingers told her. Then, as she started to place Sharlie's hand back under the sheet, she felt resistance, the fingers clinging. Mary bent down close to Sharlie's face.

"Let me go, Mary," Sharlie whispered.

Mary stiffened and stared into the face that seemed old and twisted by suffering. "Bullshit," she replied.

Sharlie moved her head weakly back and forth on the pillow. "No more."

Mary couldn't find words, so she smoothed Sharlie's hair, letting her hands linger on the hollow curve of her cheek. She waited until sleep came, then stalked out of ICU with clenched jaw. The aides who saw her marching down the hall were quick to move out of the way.

CHAPTER 20

Anderson Carlton Diller stood in his office, glaring at the X rays of Charlotte Converse's heart. They hadn't done the angiogram yet, but all preliminary tests indicated disaster. Goddammit, why couldn't she have some nice, neat little obstruction? He'd perform a triple bypass, impress the hell out of everybody, and get Walter Converse to finance his artificial-heart research unit. If he only had the facilities, he could perform every kind of operation right here instead of sending everybody off to Houston or California.

But *this*, he said to himself, snapping off the lightbox in disgust. What a mess.

He sat down behind his desk and stretched his feet out on top of the cluttered surface. He contemplated the soft leather of his new Italian loafers sourly. Scuff mark already.

Converse would be in here any second, breathing condescension, outrage, and potential hundred-dollar bills. How much longer could Diller keep that kid of

his alive? She'd outfoxed the statistics as it was. If he
could just convince the guy he'd done a superhuman
job on his little girl, then when she went, maybe he'd
fork over. In her memory, of course. They'd call it the
Charlotte Converse Memorial Heart Research Insti-
tute. Catchy.

The office door opened as the desk buzzer
sounded. Diller reached for his intercom, but Walter
was already halfway across the room. With some ceremony—just who the hell did Converse think he was
anyway, there could have been a consultation going
on in here—Diller elaborately replaced the receiver
and rose. The mousy Converse wife trailed behind.
Great body for a woman her age, and some class, but
as far as personality was concerned, a mere puff of
smoke from her husband's cigar.

"Diller . . ." Walter stuck out a hand, and the surgeon took it. Diller wondered how the huge square
fingers got so rough, like a farmer's. His own were
soft and smooth and pale. He lived in continual fear
of damaging them and wore gloves as often as he
thought he could get away with it. He'd read somewhere about a famous pianist who wore gloves all the
time, indoors and out. Diller sympathized—anything
to keep the artistry from leaking out—still the guy
went a little too far, wrapping himself up in scarves
like a madman.

Diller gestured for them to sit, and though Margaret plunked herself down immediately, Walter continued to stand. Diller decided the man had difficulty
compressing all his energy into a chair and thought
he'd better stay on his feet himself if he were to maintain a vestige of authority. He arranged his face into
an expression of guarded concern.

"It's not good this time," he said quietly.

Walter replied impatiently, "I know it's not good. Obviously it's not good. Question is, what do we do about it?"

Diller glanced briefly at Margaret, who sat stone-faced, not really focusing on anything. He wondered if perhaps she were in shock.

"We have to see the angiogram. Then we'll have a better idea what's going on."

Walter strode to the lightbox, snapped it on, and said tersely, "That hers?" Diller nodded. Walter stared at the picture in silence. Then he said, "What's an angiogram going to show that we don't know already?"

Diller and Margaret were silent, and Walter sat down, almost slumped into the chair. Diller, taking advantage of towering over Walter Converse, put his hands on his hips and pushed back his white jacket to reveal a tailored pale-blue shirt monogrammed with the initials *A.C.D.* "It'll show us the exact position of the blockage."

Walter snorted, and after a moment Diller said, "I can call in a couple of people, but I think they'll agree. I'm sorry."

There was another long silence.

"I think it's time we discuss the possibility of a heart transplant," Margaret said.

Both men gaped at her until finally Diller responded, "But your daughter won't give us permission."

"Probably not," said Margaret.

"She isn't a minor," Diller protested, and at this Walter exploded.

"You should have done it when she *was* a minor.

She'd be walking around with a halfway decent heart instead of that hunk of flab."

Diller forced himself to remember the architect's cost estimates for the projected artificial-heart laboratory and controlled his voice. "If you remember, the last time we discussed transplantation, you decided against it yourselves."

"With a lot of prodding from you and your chicken-shit buddies."

They all sat quietly another moment. Ceasefire, thought Diller, waiting with clenched teeth for the next outburst. But there was none.

Margaret Converse looked him full in the face and said, "I'll see to it that you get your permission." Then she turned to Walter. Her expression was polite and cold, and Diller found himself wondering what their sex life was like.

"Does that conform to your thinking, Walter?"

"What?" said Walter dully.

Margaret repeated, "The transplant. Do you agree we should do it?"

Walter nodded.

"Then you do whatever you have to do, Doctor Diller, and we'll do whatever we have to do."

"It's not that simple, Mrs. Converse. There's a lot of arranging—"

"Whatever's necessary," she interrupted crisply, then stood up and left the room without another word.

Well, I'll be damned, thought Diller.

Converse sauntered after his wife with an elaborately slow pace. Once he'd disappeared, the doctor went back to his X rays and stared at them balefully as if they were his mortal enemy.

*   *   *

Margaret and Walter sat downstairs in the hospital cafeteria. They were alone except for an oversized young woman in a print housedress with her two unruly children. Margaret watched her slap at their hands and wearily push her straggly blond hair behind her ears.

"How come you never listen to me, Buddy? How many times I gotta tell youse kids? Don't I speak English or what?"

"Close," Margaret murmured under her breath. Walter looked up from his coffee cup to stare at her with a puzzled expression. She ignored him, and pretty soon he slipped back into his preoccupied munching. My God, she thought, he looks like a shaved buffalo.

Margaret flashed back again to the scene that still clung to her consciousness, attaching itself to her memory like a dark, exotic creature with fierce little claws. It was a slow-motion scene, with Walter blasting away at one end of the dining room table and Sharlie standing pale and quivering, defying him with huge glistening eyes. And suddenly she'd crumbled. Not a heavy-bodied crash to the floor, but almost as if someone had pulled a vital plug and all the essence of the girl hissed out, leaving a loose pile of clothes in a heap beside the chair.

At that precise moment Margaret had heard an audible snap inside her head. A tightrope would give way like that, with a sharp, metallic retort, and like the lady in the tutu, she began to tumble, her pink, frilly parasol useless against the powerful force of gravity. On her way down, she found that she had no curiosity about a net—whether or not it was there. She had lived with such intense fear for so long that now, in the midst of the disaster she'd always dreaded, she no longer cared what happened to her. Only the fall itself mattered, and she felt a thrilling exhilaration all the way down.

She glanced at Walter again now, and felt the same excited pounding in her head. *If he had tried to touch her then, I would have picked up a steak knife and stabbed him through the heart.*

"What's the matter, Margaret? Your gut bothering you again?"

Margaret stared at him from far away, across the vast Formica surface of the cafeteria table. Goodness, she thought, how long has the man been losing his hair?

He saw her gaze fastened on the top of his head, and swiped at his hair curiously, wondering if there were a thread or speck of lint there. He shifted uncomfortably.

"Goddamn granite, these seats. Only fit for people with fat asses." He looked pointedly at the woman with the two children, strewing food and paper napkins in an ever-widening orbit around their table.

What the hell's gotten into Margaret anyway? he thought, inspecting her surreptitiously as she tipped her teacup and drained off the last drop, her little finger extended just slightly in a manner that he enjoyed mimicking. He could almost always get a smile out of her with the performance, but something told him not to try it today.

"I'm going back to the waiting room," she said. She got up abruptly, smoothed her soft gray skirt, and left him sitting there to stare after her. She stood very straight as she walked toward the cafeteria exit, and it seemed to him there was a more loose-limbed spring in her walk.

Just who the hell did she think she was, leaving him here without even a consultation about the next move? To hear her talk to Diller, you'd think she was the one who'd run the show all these years, who'd made all the agonizing decisions, who'd held his hand while *he* whimpered and whined and leaned on *her* for every little thing. Maybe the strain was finally too much—Sharlie's illness—and this time she'd had some kind of mental breakdown. Except that she looked so goddamn put together. Crazy people didn't function like that. Unless she'd turned into one of those nuts who thinks she's Queen Victoria.

The dreaded image flashed into his mind again—the two women, one unconscious on the rug, one crouched over the inert body like an animal protecting her wounded young, glaring at him in white-faced fury, ready to pounce at his slightest movement. He kept trying to force the memory away, but its impact became stronger as the hours passed. He found it impossible to sit still when the scenario recurred in his head. Bedeviling faces, one as white as death, the other a portrait of hatred.

He shook his head and looked up, hoping to distract himself with the sight of the slovenly family sitting nearby. But their table was empty—not one scrap of litter remained behind.

Suddenly he could no longer bear the idea that Margaret was upstairs, maybe learning some piece of news before he did. This time she hadn't consulted him about anything, much less the usual niggling details that used to drive him crazy—whether to raise or lower Sharlie's bed, and if so, how far; what magazines to bring her to read when she was up to it again;

or maybe she'd like a newspaper, but wouldn't that be too upsetting?

Imagine Margaret just getting up like that and leaving him down here. He'd have to speak to her about their joint responsibility and the need for communication. He'd bring it up as soon as she wasn't acting quite so flaky.

CHAPTER 21

Brian's fear catapulted him up Third Avenue as if he were a wad of paper shot out of a giant rubber band. Despite the almost wintry chill of the April afternoon, he arrived at Saint Joseph's with body steaming. He eyed the crowd waiting for the elevator as it descended haltingly to the ground floor. Certain that the crammed cubicle couldn't contain the anxiety exploding from his chest, he vaulted up the eleven flights to the Intensive Care Unit and raced down the hall to the waiting room.

The sight of Walter and Margaret sitting across the room from each other stopped him at the doorway as if the atmosphere on the other side of the threshold were a solid block of ice, impenetrable. The two gazed at him, white faces marooned on separate frozen islands of animosity and bitterness. Silently Brian's eyes absorbed Walter's sagging shoulders, the pale-blue shirt grimy and wrinkled, and Margaret's stiff posture, arms held tightly to her midsection, legs pressed together in a straight line. Their misery, unmitigated by sharing, seemed instead exaggerated by the other's presence.

Their fault. Whatever happened to Sharlie. Martha's voice on the telephone half an hour ago had replied noncommittally to Brian's urgent questions, but he had responded to the careful words with a violent and visceral hatred for Sharlie's parents, a hatred that distracted him from his fear for her. But the angry speeches that boiled inside him all the way uptown cooled into silence now as he looked at the two guilty ones, staring from their ice block. Rather than melt that barrier with his hot rage, he turned, wordless, and walked away from their frightened eyes.

Walter's and Margaret's images dissolved like puffs of cold winter breath as Brain stood gazing down at their daughter. It was Sharlie all right, but he imagined this was how she looked as a young girl, perhaps about twelve years old. Her eyelids had the translucent fragility of the very young, and her figure appeared diminished in the midst of all the wires and machinery. Her face was so still that the lines of her mouth seemed carved. There was no movement, even along the delicate curves of her nostrils. He glanced at the machines ticking steadily, marveling that somewhere in her body life continued.

Sharlie! Open your eyes and smile at me and say something ridiculous about this place you're in—what did you call it? The Incredibly Complicated Udder? Tell me about the mail-order heart you sent for from L. L. Bean—the down-filled one to make you extra warm-hearted. As if you needed that.

Someone touched his shoulder, and he swung around ferociously. The startled nurse motioned that it was time to leave. He walked out through the double swinging doors into the empty corridor, and when he couldn't think of anything else to do, he pulled back his right fist and slammed it into the wall.

Later, in Diller's office, he stared down at his hand, wrapped in a light plaster cast. A hairline fracture, they'd said down in X ray. Amazingly, the release of frustration seemed worth the pain and embarrassment, but he knew the relief was momentary. Every day another plaster cast, perhaps? Left hand tomorrow, feet next, then head—which took him to the weekend. He'd have to content himself with the walls in his own apartment so as not to find himself expelled from the hospital for malicious mischief.

He knew that Walter and Margaret would not have included him in the conference, so he had just barged in and sat down with them. But now he found it difficult to pay attention. Diller's voice droned on, something about Jason Lewis—the Santa Bel heart surgeon—tests, flight arrangements. Brian watched Walter's hands, moving in a restless, helpless rhythm, one on top of the other in his lap.

Then Diller was standing, so Brian rose with Margaret and Walter, and they filed out of the office in silence. Brian didn't feel like asking, but he got the impression that Sharlie was about to leave for California.

Sharlie swam through the pale-blue sea, only she knew it wasn't water, it was sky. She floated easily, turning with the slightest movement of her arms. She took a quick look over her shoulder, just to make absolutely sure there were no wings. It was peaceful up here, quiet except for the faint ticking sound above her—God's wristwatch, no doubt, she thought, and felt herself begin to giggle.

But then the light dimmed, and suddenly she began to shiver. So cold. She tried to work her arms faster, but they were pinioned to her sides, and she started to fall, hurtling through the cold darkness toward the ticking that, below her now, grew louder and louder. She fought against the restraints, trying to free her arms so that she could perhaps cling to something to break her fall, and in her struggle she roused herself and stared straight up into Brian's face. She gazed expressionlessly at him for a long moment, and finally, as if they were in midconversation and had been briefly interrupted by a cough or a sneeze, said in a clear voice, "Bastards won't let me out of here."

Brian began to laugh, and he grasped her hand. She smiled vaguely at him, wondering why he seemed so ecstatic when she was lying around with all these wretched wires sticking out of her.

"Where are my parents?" she asked.

"Down the hall. Want to see them now?"

She shook her head. "No. I'm going to sleep. Hold my hand until I go, all right?"

He nodded, and she fell asleep almost instantly.

The same nurse who had been on duty when Brian made his first visit to ICU stood behind him now, well out of reach of his remaining unbroken fist. "Time to go," she said warily, eyes focused on the plaster cast.

Brian moved reluctantly from the bedside, and the nurse backed off a bit, giving him a wide berth as he passed through the doors.

CHAPTER 22

Two days later they performed an angiogram. Sharlie lay on the table while Dr. Parkiss threaded the catheter up through an artery in her arm and down into her heart. He kept a close watch on the fluoroscopy screen as the procedure was videotaped. After a few minutes of conferring with the technicians, Parkiss, a short, swarthy man with so much hair that Sharlie thought he looked like an exotic tropical fern, said, "All right, Sharlie. You set?"

Sharlie said, "Can hardly wait." Then she closed her eyes.

"Okay, boys," Parkiss said. "This one's a pro, so you'd better do it right. You'll have the big guys on your ass if you screw up."

The heat, pleasantly soothing at first, flooded her shoulder, but soon the pressure became a throbbing, aching bulge. Parkiss stood with his hip pressed to her side, and she found his body warmth comforting.

The assistant with the iodine looked at the monitor and whistled under his breath. Sharlie felt Parkiss stiffen next to her.

"What is it?" she asked, and Parkiss, voice carefully neutral, murmured. "Don't pay any attention to Iodine Ike over there. He's just never seen a heart of gold before."

"I'm only listening to your hip, Doctor. You have a very eloquent hip."

Parkiss smiled down at her and shifted his weight slightly so that his body no longer came in contact with hers.

"I must teach my hip to maintain itself in a professional manner."

"Tell me about the left ventricle," she said.

Another dose of hot liquid flooded her shoulder. Parkiss watched the monitor. His voice was distracted.

"You let me worry about your left ventricle."

Sharlie waited until the team relaxed to make notations and said quietly, "Look, it's my heart you're gawking at. Can't I know what's happening?" Her dark eyes pleaded for honesty.

"There's enlargement."

Sharlie's eyes flickered briefly, then faced his steadily. "Scar tissue?" she asked.

"Yes."

She nodded. "Thank you."

Dr. Parkiss's helplessness showed in the deep lines around his mouth. Everyone was silent as they carefully removed the catheter and turned off the machines.

That afternoon Sharlie lay sleeping in her room. Number 1101 this time, with the sun brushing the right side of her face. She heard small clinking noises and awoke to find Ramón Rodriguez changing her IV tube. He smiled at her and winked.

"Pretty exciting news about you," he said, fiddling with the bottle so that it sat just right.

"What?" asked Sharlie sleepily.

"The transplant."

Sharlie didn't answer, and Rodriguez suddenly looked down at her in horror.

"Holy Jesus."

"Transplant . . ." Sharlie said, still only half awake, but Rodriguez watched the panic spread across her face.

"They should take my mouth and fill it with shit and dump me back in the garbage on Avenue D," Rodriguez said fervently, his face contorted with dismay.

"It's all right, Ramón," she said softly.

He seemed unable to move. His face was stricken. Sharlie tried to reassure him. "It's okay, honestly. I should know what's going on."

His body sagged a little with relief, and he said, "They called Santa Bel, and Diller said . . ."

Sharlie put her hands over her ears and shook her head vehemently. Rodriguez turned and almost ran out of the room.

"Nice flowers," Walter said. He picked the card from its perch on a twig of baby's breath and read it aloud: "'Some people have too-big mouths. Love from a friend.' What the hell is that?"

Sharlie said, "I have a secret admirer."

Walter looked at his daughter. She lay there as if

they were telling her she ought to have her temperature taken.

"You don't seem surprised," Brian was saying, and Sharlie replied, "I watched the monitor during the catheterization this morning."

There was silence as they all stared at her. Sharlie's face pleaded with Brian, and he said quietly, "Walter . . . Margaret . . . leave us a minute, all right?"

Sharlie's eyes widened as her parents got up.

"We'll have some coffee," Margaret said, and they left the room.

" 'Walter,' " Sharlie said in an awed voice. " 'Walter'?"

"Well, what do you want from me? Mister-Master-Sir-Your-Majesty?"

"I must have been dead a long time. You're all so congenial."

"Unity in battle."

"Who's the enemy?"

"I hope you're not," he said, watching her face closely.

She turned her eyes from him.

"You going to fight it?" he asked.

"I told you I wouldn't."

Brian's voice was gentle. "It's different now that it's for real," he said, remembering the look on her face as she sat on his bed, the paper-napkin heart pinned to her chest and her chin smudged with ink. She nodded. "I know it's scary," he went on. "But, honey, if you're not with us, you're against us."

She was quiet for a long time. Then said softly, "Everybody's holding out this carrot, and it's going to turn into a big fat turnip."

He smiled. "What've you got against turnips? A

sturdy, humble American plant, and don't they give them to you at Thanksgiving? Very apt."

"I *hate* turnips." She reached out for his right hand. He had kept it on his lap out of sight. Now she contemplated the cast and looked at him questioningly.

"A brief moment of irritation," he said.

"Did you take a swipe at my father?"

"Ah *ha*," he said, attempting a Viennese accent. "Classic fantasy, my dear."

"Maybe that's why he's so docile."

"The next time you take a stroll past ICU, there's this picture hanging in a rather peculiar spot—kind of rib level. An ocean sunset, very phosphorescent."

"You put your hand through the wall."

He nodded.

She said thoughtfully, "What a waste."

"Of energy?"

"No," she said, shaking her head. "You should have aimed at Walter."

"You know," he said, tracing her fingers where they lay on his cast. "You're a lot more fun when you're conscious. You'd be dynamite with a new heart."

"Will they let you come?"

He grinned. "I am now considered essential to your health. They'll pack me onto the plane along with your Valium."

"When do you think we'll have to go?" Her voice quavered a little.

"Depends on beds. Soon, though." Her lower lip began to tremble. "You going to marry me?" he asked.

"You're insane. Get off my back, Morgan."

"I'd rather be on your front."

"Brian, they'll cut me all up and stick somebody else's heart inside me, and you won't love me anymore, and goddammit, I'm going to cry, oh, damn, damn . . ."

Brian leaned over the bed and held her, stroking her hair with his one good hand.

CHAPTER 23

Walter told Sharlie that Diller was like a pig in shit, rushing around making arrangements and throwing his weight all over the place. He'd managed to get himself a leave of absence from Saint Joe's for "research" so that he could "supervise" the procedures in Santa Bel. Of course, Walter realized Diller was eager to check out the transplant center so that when he wormed the millions out of the Converse Trust, he could establish himself at the head of his own renowned medical warehouse in New York.

Sharlie lay back and gave herself over to the excitement and flurry of arrangements. Brian and her parents seemed relieved to be doing something finally, and they competed for every errand.

"I'll do it."

"No, *I'll* do it."

"No, I'll be in the area, it's simple for me. *I'll* do it."

Finally Sharlie would say, "Oh, for God's sake, I

don't have anything better to do. *I'll* do it." And she'd make as if she were about to spring from her bed.

They all laughed a lot, though Sharlie felt her own giggles rising perilously close to hysteria. Breathing had now become difficult for her, but the pain had all but disappeared. Diller couldn't understand exactly why this should be, and theorized about it with alternately hopeful and ominous speculations. Sharlie just closed her eyes and blessed the departure of Agony Jones even as she panted and gasped through the days, fighting for air with her slightest movement.

Today she had dozed away the morning because each time she tried to reach for her magazine, she began to feel like a fish expiring on a creek bank. She finally managed to dial Brian at his office and informed him she was attempting to make an obscene call.

"Are you *(gasp)* that lawyer *(gasp)* I read about in the *Times* who's *(gasp)* defending the fornication case *(gasp, gasp)*?"

Brian replied, "Why, yes, madam."

"Well I just *(gasp)* want to tell you that I'd *(gasp)* like to . . . *(gasp)*"

"Like to what, lady?"

" . . . to . . . *(gasp)* to get a look at your . . . *(gasp)* . . . fornicator."

He laughed and said, "That's supposed to be obscene?"

"Well, I've got this heart condition, see, mister *(puff, puff)*, and I can't let the fantasies get *(gasp)* out of hand. If you know what I mean."

"Tell you what. I'll stop by your place this afternoon and give you a quick glimpse."

"Okay," she said. They hung up. She couldn't seem to tell him how frightened she felt.

Finally he was sitting on her bed, and she was telling him about the obscene caller she'd had when she was eighteen.

"He was foreign or illiterate or both, and he said things like, 'Your teeths is good to eat, and I wan' it' or 'I see you lower part up to the window, and I get you wit' my things.'"

Brian laughed incredulously, and she said, "No, really. I couldn't bear to give him up, so I never reported it to the phone company."

"Does he still call?"

She shook her head. "He did it once when Daddy was home. . . ."

"Oh, Jesus," said Brian.

"Daddy picked up the downstairs extension and outobscened the poor man."

"I'll bet."

"Sad. I looked forward to it."

"Listen, honey," Brian said gruffly. "I'll give you some stuff to melt your ear right off your head. Matter of fact, I'm gonna give you a little treat right now and show you my fornicator."

He stood up and started to undo his belt. Sharlie whispered to him to stop, delighted.

"How you gonna know what I got to offer, doll? Gotta see da moichandize, right?"

Ramón Rodriguez poked his head through the door. "Need anything, Sharlie?"

Brian made a show of zipping up his pants, very cool and casual. Sharlie groaned, and the nurse nodded, gave them a conspiratorial grin, and backed quickly out of the room.

"Oh, Lord," Sharlie wailed. "He thinks we've been messing around on my *death*bed."

Brian looked at her as if his eyes could never get enough, then grabbed her and held her as hard as he dared.

They left the hospital amid great fanfare. Everyone on the eleventh floor gathered at the elevator to send Sharlie off in style. Someone had attached half a dozen balloons to her wheelchair and a sign that said, Send This Kid a Sexy Donor, crayoned across the back.

As they drove away from the front entrance in Walter's sleek silver car, they passed the open plaza where many of the hospital staff took coffee breaks or enjoyed a picnic lunch. Today was a shining May morning, and Sharlie looked out at the white-clad groups of nurses and interns and thought they looked like crocuses standing in the warm spring sun. She grabbed for Margaret's hand and squeezed it happily.

The flights to California were heavily booked, but Walter finally managed to reserve three first-class seats. The OPEC representatives were meeting in New York for two weeks, which meant Walter couldn't go to California. Brian and Margaret let him vent his frustration by making all their travel arrangements. They watched the man tackle obstacles as if the trip were a religious crusade and each impediment the devil's foot, set in his path to trip up the forces of justice and truth.

For Sharlie, the flight was enchanting. She had always loved excursions; even a ride in a taxi from her house to the opera was delicious—something about the sensation of moving, or surrendering herself to the driver's skill, of not knowing what view would speed past next outside the window. It gave her a sense of adventure.

"Have you ever been across the country?" she asked Brian, holding his hand tightly as the pilot announced that they were cleared for takeoff.

"Not when I could see anything," he said.

Margaret intoned sepulchrally, "I have." She sat across from Brian in the aisle seat, gripping her armrests to brace herself for their inevitable crash.

Sharlie smiled and told her mother to relax. Margaret nodded stiffly, as though each slight movement were a possible threat to the precarious balance of the wings.

After a moment the plane braked at the end of the runway and began to roar and shudder. Finally, just as Sharlie whispered, "Come on, go," the pilot released something, and the plane surged forward, howling and gathering speed. It lifted into the air, and all the rumbling, ferocious power turned to gentle grace, soft, purring sounds, arching of wings. Sharlie's face shone, and Brian watched her, smiling.

"It's so sexy," she said. Margaret stared with fixed eyes at a financial magazine, and Sharlie said to Brian, "Ask Mother if she thinks it's sexy."

Margaret glared across Brian at Sharlie's mischievous smile, and Sharlie felt sudden remorse. As she looked into her mother's sad, strained face, she imagined that she had experienced more physical joy in her aborted hours with Brian than her mother had known in a lifetime with her father.

CHAPTER 24

Walter looked out the window of his office and listened to Sharlie's clock chime six bells. The sound pleased him, although at first its brilliant ringing had disconcerted everyone on the thirty-ninth floor. But if he closed his eyes, he could imagine himself at the wheel of a mighty ship, pushing through the gray ocean swells, alone in command against the sea.

He'd always been attracted to the ocean and was mortified and disappointed when the navy rejected him for sea duty during the war. Instead, they'd dumped him in Washington at one of those agencies where everybody pushed little flags around on maps and boozed it up in the officers' lounge. Every time Walter spotted a sailor home on leave, he'd felt ashamed.

He looked down over the concrete shadows of Manhattan. Why was he so enamored of the water? He'd never lived near it except for those couple of summers up in Maine when he was, what, about six or seven.

When Father was still alive. He imagined that tall, dim figure, towering above him in the bright afternoon, his back to the sun so that the light outlined his body and his features were a hazy blur. He remembered still his sense of awe gazing up at the man—the rough shirt against Walter's bare legs as he was lifted up and set on the broad shoulders—smooth tree branches under his hard little bottom. Walter had dropped his pail on the way up, he remembered, and hadn't even cared if the sand he'd so carefully tamped down and soaked with saltwater got kicked over and crushed under his father's bare feet.

Where was Mother then? He had to strain to find her. Finally he caught a quick glimpse of her, smiling and wearing a pale flowered dress, of all things. Maybe memory lied. He couldn't imagine now that she'd really have worn such a fanciful thing, and the face he put with the summer memory was old and haggard and stern, and didn't belong with the soft folds of the full skirt anymore than the sunburned hands she held out to him, so young and full of whimsical motion. He knew that her fingers had become arthritic by the time she reached forty, and she always held them quietly in her lap, a twisted bouquet, gnarled memorial to her youth.

Eight bells already. He shook his head, trying to clear away the unproductive clutter of memories and daydreams. The sky outside his window was gray—no discrete clouds, just a shabby curtain that seemed to stretch across the entire universe. Hard to believe the sun was probably shining in California.

The plane should be landing just about now. God *damn*, to have to sit here until tomorrow while God knows what was going on in Santa Bel. For sure they were screwing it all up, getting the records confused, paying too much for housing near the hospital, renting the wrong kind of car. That Brian Morgan was in such a fog over Sharlie he could barely find his way out of the Midtown Tunnel.

Then he remembered Margaret. How peculiar that her image emerged so distinctly when she'd always seemed just another incidental detail to cope with, someone to invent harmless errands for so she'd be out from underfoot. But as he thought of her now, it was as if she'd changed color. She had always seemed beige or pale gray—a shadow, really, and sometimes less than that, a transparency. Today the word *Margaret* evoked a darker shape—not completely formed, the outline was changing, indefinite, but her color, he decided, was vivid enough—a splash of deep violet. What the hell was happening to the woman? Or was it happening to him?

The extraordinary thing of it was that once he got past the initial shock of her behavior, she didn't seem all that strange to him. As a matter of fact, she reminded him very much of his mother.

He grunted aloud in the empty office and forced himself to concentrate on Sharlie and the operation. He always preferred to plan ahead so that there'd be no surprises. Nothing wrong with his ability to think on his feet and make split-second decisions under fire, but here he was stuck with the frigging sheikh until tomorrow morning. He might as well try to put himself closer to Santa Bel by at least giving it some thought.

The odd thing was, the harder he tried to think about his daughter, the more he saw Margaret's face. The more he tried to blot it out, the sharper into focus came the image of Margaret bending over Sharlie's body on the dining room floor, thrusting his arm away when he tried to help. Amazing what a little bit of loathing can do to a person. Not that he ever thought that she was head-over-heels or anything, but hate he didn't expect. It really wasn't fair of her. He was only saying what had to be said. His mind veered away from the detested scenario, but the silent accusation of the rebellious Margaret, crouched over their daughter, confronted him stubbornly. He pressed the heels of his hands against his eyes. Margaret, he thought, I'm sick of your face. Go away already.

CHAPTER 25

California. Like landing on the moon, Sharlie thought, as they whirred silently down wide, flat streets in the ambulance. Brian and Margaret sat on either side of her, holding her hands, and they all stared out the window. To Sharlie, western flora seemed like prehistoric beasts—stubbly trees with knuckles where there should have been branches, nothing leafy except for scattered palm trees, long-necked creatures with frazzled clumps of green on top. The fearsome *Conconutus rex* and his vegetarian sidekick, *Palmetto dinosaurus*.

Even the ambulance attendants were alien. A young woman with a naturally streaked blond mane, and a young man—her brother, perhaps—with strawberry hair, freckles, and a cleft chin. Sharlie found herself expecting them to offer her a stick of Doublemint gum.

She gazed admiringly at the girl. "Do you surf?"

The attendant shook her head.

"Doesn't everybody in California surf?"

"Not around here," the young man said, flashing his white teeth at her. Sharlie stared at them, transfixed.

"What *do* you do around here?" Brian asked.

They both answered at once: She said, "Disco"; he said, "Movies." They laughed, and the girl said, "Oh, we just lie around our swimming pools with movie stars picking grapefruits off the trees."

"Have you ever been to New York?" Sharlie asked. The girl shook her head, grimacing a little. Sharlie thought, *Nobody* looks like that in New York. People from the West must come to the city. What happens to them? Do they get covered with soot and turn pale and pinched and anxiety-ridden on their way in from La Guardia?

They pulled into the emergency entrance of the Santa Bel Medical Center and removed Sharlie from the ambulance—a very smooth and efficient operation, not the usual Laurel and Hardy routine of the New York crew, with all the accompanying grunts and complaints: *Hey, schmuck, whadya tryna do with this here sick lady? Tryna shake her brains loose or what?*

Before she knew it, they were whisked through Admissions, leaving a businesslike Margaret to remain downstairs and cope with the paperwork. Sharlie was deposited in a bright room with pale-yellow walls and flowered drapes. Before the attendants had even left them, a nurse with a name tag that read, *Irene Wynick R.N.*, entered. She said, "Welcome, Miss Converse. Mister Morgan. How was the trip?"

Sharlie said, "Fine," in a cowed voice.

Nurse Wynick nodded. "This afternoon you will have a chest X ray and an EKG. We'll take some blood and urine samples, and that'll be it. Mainly we want you to rest. Tomorrow we'll begin the other tests. You can have a few more minutes, and then I'll have to ask Mr. Morgan to leave."

She tucked in a loose sheet at the bottom of Sharlie's bed. On her way out she turned to Brian and said, "Fifteen minutes."

Sharlie and Brian looked at each other in silence, then Sharlie breathed, "Boy, they don't mess around in California." Brian laughed. "It took me three trips to Saint Joe's before they got my name straight," she said, "and they still send me the wrong tray. I'm not used to this, I mean, these guys are *scary*."

"On my way out I'll see if I can arrange a little screw-up in the medication."

"I'd appreciate it." She fell silent again.

"Scared?" he asked.

"Yup." After a moment she said, "How many minutes have we got left?"

He looked at his watch. "Twelve. And a half."

"I bet they split them into centiminutes around here. Give me a hug and go, okay? I can't take the anticipation."

"Oh, honey," he said, leaning over her.

"Oh, shit," she said, and kissed him. He looked at her in mock horror at her use of the word. "Well, I've been associating with the wrong sort of people lately." She felt tears beginning at the tenderness in his face. "Go," she whispered, giving him a little shove.

He lifted himself away from her, and with a wave left her alone.

Sharlie listened to his footsteps disappear down the hallway toward the elevator—characteristic sound, no muted shuffling in hushed hospital corridors, but bold, loose-limbed strides. She remembered the first

time he'd come to see her at Saint Joe's, how she'd
been seized with identical panic at his leaving her.
What if she were a normal woman and they fell in
love just like anybody else? Barbie doll standing at
the front door waiting for a chaste kiss from Ken doll
before he set off for his job at the insurance company.
Would she still feel the same horrible tearing sensation
when he withdrew from her, would her insides bleed
all over her little white apron and cover adorable Ken
junior with blood and gore? Brian once said he felt
like diving head-first down her throat. How she'd love
to swallow him whole and let him live inside her.

Ken and Barbie must come from California, she decided, and closed her eyes. She heard the piping
voice at the back of her head, chanting,

> *You never could take parting lightly;*
> *Separation always grieves you.*
> *First a kiss and then a hug, but*
> *In the end he always leaves you.*

Whiner, she said to the voice. Shut up.

She fell asleep, and the next thing she knew, someone with blue-black hair and Indian features was
smiling at her and rolling up her sleeve. Sharlie gazed
into the brown face and murmured, "I'm glad you're
not a blonde."

CHAPTER 26

Dr. Elizabeth Rosen's office was on the ground floor,
overlooking an expanse of green lawn and, just outside the window, a gardenia tree. Sharlie sat in a
wheelchair next to Brian, twisting her hands in her
lap. They were icy cold. Shaking hands with the psychiatrist a moment ago, she had been ashamed of her
clammy fingers in Dr. Rosen's strong, warm ones.

They sat in silence as the doctor leafed through the
file on her desk. The pages fell, crackling. Each time,
the sound startled Sharlie. How was it possible to feel
so benumbed and yet raw enough so that a whisper or
a minute gesture made her want to leap up screaming
from the wheelchair? A hightly strung slab of concrete, perhaps?

"Charlotte," Dr. Rosen said. A statement, not a
question. Sharlie wondered if she were required to respond, but the doctor looked up at her and smiled.
"Lovely name."

"Thank you," Sharlie said with her cement lips.

"We all call her Sharlie," Brian offered. Sharlie felt something now, a prick of resentment, which was quickly swallowed up in a distracting reverie about her name—*perhaps it would be pleasant to be a Charlotte—Sharlie was a little girl's name, which was okay if you never made it to forty—but a middle-aged Sharlie? No maturity, no dignity, like their one-time chauffeur, the balding, paunchy Sonny—if he'd used his actual name, Frederick, maybe it would have been tougher for Walter to fire him. Maybe if Sharlie were a Charlotte, she'd feel more authoritative. . . .*

She started, realizing that Dr. Rosen's eyes were fixed on her. "It's always tense the first time," the doctor said quietly.

"We've never been to a psychiatrist before," Brian said, then laughed at the sound of his words.

Dr. Rosen watched the two pairs of eyes reach for each other and hold, dark-gray eyes lost in blue. She waited, reluctant to disturb the mysterious, intense communion. After a while she said, "Tell me your plans."

Brian blinked and said, "We're going to get married."

"We hope," Sharlie murmured.

"For sure," Brian said flatly.

Sharlie dropped her eyes.

"Do you want the transplant?" Dr. Rosen asked.

Sharlie waited for Brian to answer, but the doctor's green eyes were trained on her. Finally Sharlie said, "Sort of." Brian made a soft sound of dismay.

"Most people in your situation feel ambivalent," Dr. Rosen said.

Sharlie smiled. Oh, that's what you call this sensation? And all the time I thought it was terror.

"But basically she's positive about it," Brian said, then turned to Sharlie. "Aren't you?"

Sharlie nodded, but so halfheartedly that Brian looked stricken.

"We don't expect anybody to jump up on the operating table and say, 'Take me, I'm yours,'" the psychiatrist said.

"But she has to want it."

"There are always doubts."

Dr. Rosen and Brian stared at Sharlie expectantly. Her eyes looked trapped.

"I don't think I want to say anything," she choked.

"What do you think would happen to you if you went ahead and had the transplant?" Dr. Rosen asked.

Sharlie felt as if her words were coming from somewhere far away, muffled perhaps by the sensation of thick stone encasing her thoughts. "People do strange things afterward—run around naked, attack the nurses. Nice, gentle people."

"Oh, Sharlie," Brian said.

"She's right," Dr. Rosen interjected. Sharlie and Brian stared at her, Sharlie with gratitude and Brian surprised. "But post-operative psychosis can usually be avoided with therapy. That's one of the reasons you're here. Also let me reassure you that oftentimes that kind of bizarre reaction is a response to the drugs. It disappears within a few days."

Brian looked at Sharlie. "You wouldn't attack anybody."

Sharlie looked unconvinced, and Dr. Rosen continued, "Probably not. More often a man who receives a young girl's heart will become temporarily impotent. Things like that. Donor identification."

Sharlie's face tensed, and Dr. Rosen prodded, "You've been thinking about that?"

"Not *every* waking moment," Sharlie replied. They all laughed, and Sharlie felt her cement shroud crack a bit.

"What about the people who can't hack it?" Brian asked.

"We've made some mistakes," she answered.

Sharlie said, "I couldn't bear not handling it. All those other people waiting . . ."

"That's not your responsibility," Dr. Rosen said firmly. "We make the final judgment, and most of the time we guess right."

"It's only an operation," Brian said. "I mean, of course it's more complex, but do you go through this for kidneys?"

Dr. Rosen smiled. "Just think about the mythology, the language. 'You've stolen my kidney'? 'You've got to have kidney'?"

"In my heart of hearts, I want to get to the heart of the matter," Sharlie said.

"Yes," Dr. Rosen nodded. "It's quite a burden. Sometimes an exhausted heart patient is just too worn out. Unless there's a compelling reason to withstand the stress."

Brian smiled at Sharlie, stretching his hands out, palms up. *Here I am. Compelling enough?* He turned to Dr. Rosen. "When do you think she'll get off the pot?" He looked startled. "I mean, out of the hop . . . *hospital. Damn.*" Brian wasn't used to muddling his words.

Sharlie grinned at him now. Shit or get off the pot, huh? Well, she could hardly blame him for feeling that way. Dr. Rosen had put it together, too, and shot her a quick glance. Sharlie's cement cracked again, shuddered, and fell away, crumbling into nothing.

"I'm sorry, Bri," she said. "I want it, but I'm so scared." Tears spilled down her cheeks, and Dr. Rosen saw Brian's eyes begin to water, too.

"All right," the doctor said softly. "Tell me about your donor. Who's it going to be?"

Sharlie began to talk, choking through the tears at first, about Margaret Mead and Dorothy Hamill and Charles Manson and the Reverend Jim Jones and all the others, dead and alive, wonderful and dreadful, the parade that strutted and stomped and danced and hunched across the sterile air above her hospital bed. Her words tumbled out uninterrupted until at last she came to a halt, suddenly crushingly tired. Dr. Rosen stood up. She reached a hand across her desk and held Brian's briefly, then Sharlie's.

"All right, then, Sharlie. Or would you like me to call you Charlotte?"

Sharlie hesitated and then nodded shyly.

"I'll see you tomorrow, Charlotte. And Brian, thank you for coming."

Brian pushed Sharlie to the elevator in her wheelchair. They had been silent, but now Brian said, "Well, Charlotte, what did you think?"

"Oh, shut up," she whispered.

"Why not, if you like it better?"

"It sounds ridiculous coming from you. Charlotte's my . . . my stage name."

A nurse in the elevator shot them a curious look, and they moved out onto the eighth floor.

"*Now* look," Sharlie said, dismayed. "She thinks I'm a star."

"Why not? You're in California."

"You say 'why not' more than anybody I ever met."
Sharlie said as he pushed her into her room.

"Why . . . oh, shit," Brian said. Sharlie got out of
the wheelchair, walked the few steps to her bed, and
climbed in with Brian lifting her by the arms. Then
she settled back against her pillows, gave him a
weak smile, and fell instantly asleep.

He pulled a chair over next to her bed and sat
down. There were dark circles under her eyes, and
her skin seemed pasty. Even while she was asleep, her
breathing came in short little puffs. Brian took her
hand and stared down at the slender fingers. So he
said "why not" a lot. Well, at this very moment there
were nothing but *why*'s in his head.

Sharlie gasped a little in her sleep, and Brian
glanced at her anxiously, feeling his body stiffen. He
averted his eyes from her mouth, open slack against
the pillow. She seemed like a stranger, and all at once
he felt a rushing sensation inside his head, screaming
sirens. *Out. Let me out.* Of this room, this love, this
life that was attached inside him like a dying fetus,
clinging to his intestines. Where was his own life, all
the pieces that were his? His work, his clients, his
crazy, hectic days in court, his fierce dialogues with
Barbara, his tennis games with the vital, energetic
Susan? All squeezed into some dark, musty corner of
himself to make room for this disease of hers, this re-
morseless struggle that allowed no distractions. Her
disease was his disease, her battle his battle, her pain
his pain. *Out!*

He released her cold fingers and dropped his head
into his hands. Double contradictory shame—self-
disgust at the panicked impulse to abandon Sharlie,

and the more shadowy repulsion at his inability to flee, a certainty that his identity had become so intertwined with this tenuous life on the white bed that he could no longer free himself and stand alone.

He sat bent over his hands until self-loathing became a numbed exhaustion. Then he looked up at the sleeping figure again. She was breathing more easily now, with faint color under the pale cheeks. She stirred in her sleep, and he watched the outline of her legs slide apart under the sheet. He found himself remembering the last time they'd been together in his apartment. He'd felt the urgency of her body, arching toward him. Was she dreaming now, her legs open like that? He wanted her. Even now, in this sterile room with her so close to death. He wanted to be inside her, as far into the center of her as he could thrust himself. He wanted to reach out and touch her breasts as she lay there.

Feeling the sudden, hot obstruction between his legs, he thought, Christ, maybe Sharlie's right. I *am* a necrophiliac.

CHAPTER 27

The *E.* in the nameplace on Dr. Rosen's door did not prepare Walter for the red-haired woman who ushered them into the sunny office. He knew his face registered shock, and he turned to see Margaret smirking at him. He held out a chair for Margaret and waited until Dr. Rosen was seated behind her desk before he took a chair next to his wife.

"Isn't that a little underhanded, that *E. Rosen, M.D.* on your door?"

"Underhanded," she repeated. She was tired, and ran a weary hand through her hair. Walter noticed how the late afternoon sunshine glinted on the soft curls, making a golden halo around her face.

"How's anybody supposed to know you're a woman? *E. E* for *Edward, E* for *Englebert.*"

Dr. Rosen's smile stiffened. "I guess you put your full name on your door to warn people you're a man."

Walter sniffed but settled back in his chair. Dr. Rosen sifted through the file on her desk. She ran her finger down a page of medical history, then looked up, controlled and professional. She directed her first question to Margaret, figuring she'd let the husband get used to the sight of what was probably his first woman doctor, and by the look of him, his first psychiatrist.

"How do you feel about your daughter's operation?"

Margaret said quickly, "Fine. Fine. I mean, of course, I wish it weren't necessary, but if it's going to help her . . ."

"It appears from the records that she's lived at home with you all her life. Is that true?"

"Yes. Except for the times in the hospital."

"It must have been tough on you."

"Well, we didn't have any choice."

Walter interjected, "You do what you have to do."

"Of course," said Dr. Rosen, giving Walter a brief glance before turning back to Margaret. Walter felt himself resenting all the attention his wife was getting from this redhead, as if Margaret had done something besides wring her hands all these years. *He* had coped with Sharlie. Why didn't this headshrinker ask *him* a question?

"How do you think you'd feel if your daughter were to get well and become independent? Move out of your house? Live her own life?" Dr. Rosen asked Margaret.

"Hallelujah," Walter said, more loudly than he had intended.

Dr. Rosen turned to stare at him. "You'd be very glad, Mister Converse?"

"Well, I meant I'd be overjoyed if she got well enough. It would be a miracle, what we've been hoping for," he said, floundering in an attempt to rectify the harsh sound of his interruption. She thinks I'm a brutal bastard, he thought. Dammit, she's got me all twisted around, this lady with the tired green eyes. Who gives a shit what she thinks anyway?

He gave her his best commander-of-the-fleet look and said, "Is there some special way we can help?" He was forced to admit she didn't look overly impressed by the manly authority in his voice.

"You *are* helping," she said.

Was that a condescending smile, the bitch? he wondered.

"What we want to ascertain is what effect a heart transplant would have on your daughter emotionally. It's impossible to predict with total accuracy, of course, but we like to get a general impression of her life up to now, and what you envision for her after the operation, should it be successful."

"You already met with her, didn't you? And Brian Morgan," Walter asked. Dr. Rosen nodded. Walter meant to make the point that Sharlie's emotional condition should have been evident already, but somehow the words twisted away from his tongue. Instead he blurted, "What did they say about me?"

They all sat in silence while Dr. Rosen gazed at Walter. He felt his face redden and suddenly remembered the time he'd strayed into the midst of his mother's weekly bridge game to ask her what the word *menstruation* meant. He was six years old and curious about something he'd overheard at school, but Mother was not amused.

Dr. Rosen watched the embarrassment rise in his face. She let the query pass. After a moment Walter asked, "When can we see Dr. Lewis?"

"I've spoken with him already, dear," Margaret said quietly.

Walter forgot his recent embarrassment. "You did what?"

"While you had your conference call. I happened to pass his office as he was coming out. I introduced myself. He was very gracious and helpful."

Walter felt his jaw muscles clamp down against the molars in the back of his mouth. He glanced at Dr. Rosen and saw her watching him intently. She wants me to lose my cool, he thought, sitting there with her little pad and pencil waiting for me to go nuts. He turned to his wife. Okay, Margaret honey, I'll be oh, so civilized. But I'll get you later, I swear it. "Did you ask him for the statistics and the information about the procedure? We don't want any surprises," Walter said, trying to mute the petulance in his voice.

"I wrote it all down," Margaret explained. "We can go over it after dinner if you like. Whatever I didn't get, you can ask him yourself."

Walter brooded in silence. He might as well have stayed home and gotten all the news from Margaret over the telephone. He gave Dr. Rosen a sickly smile.

"I was delayed in New York, unfortunately, so I have to catch up with Margaret here."

"Yes, I see," Dr. Rosen said pleasantly.

I'll bet you do, thought Walter. He rubbed his jaw. Dr. Rosen closed her file and looked up at them.

"We can talk again soon when there's been more testing. But if you find you want to talk, don't wait for a formal appointment. Call my office anytime, and I'll clear an hour for you."

Margaret got up and held out a hand to Dr. Rosen.

"Thank you, Doctor. It's comforting to know you're available."

Dr. Rosen walked around her desk to show them to the door, and as he got out of his chair, Walter noticed the trim legs under the psychiatrist's soft pale-gray skirt. He felt the impulse to know all about her, whether she was married, whether she had kids, whether she liked sex, and if so, what kind of sex. She had firm breasts under that white jersey top. Not the big clunkers so many other men seemed to find attractive, but enough to know she was a woman, enough so that lying above her he would feel their soft pressure against his chest.

By the time he reached the door, he was sweating a little, and he surreptitiously wiped his hands on his jacket so that he could offer Dr. Rosen a dry palm on his way out.

In the elevator Walter and Margaret were silent. They walked to the parking lot without exchanging a word until finally Margaret coughed and said, "She seemed like a pleasant person. Intelligent."

Walter slid behind the wheel of their rented Chevy. Goddamn rental people didn't even have a Buick, for Christ's sake, and this thing felt like a Mack truck compared with his own comfortable Coupe de Ville. Every bump jolted him to his back teeth.

"Do you notice how bumpy this car feels? Maybe there's something wrong with it," Margaret said.

"You just don't have the proper padding on your ass," he replied. "The princess and the pea." He swerved to avoid another pit in the road.

Margaret didn't respond, and when he stole a look at her face, he saw the tight knot beside her mouth.

Lost her sense of humor, that's what. Well, under the circumstances he supposed it was understandable.

"You've done quite a job out here. I'm proud of you," he said, enjoying his magnanimity.

"Brian helped." Her voice was cold.

That was all, just "Brian helped." She came out here and plunged right ahead with all these plans, picked out a ludicrous-looking motel with pink walls—*pink,* for Christ's sake—and stuck their daughter in some room back in the boondocks at least four miles from the nearest elevator. Jesus, he'd never have stood for it, and here he complimented her on the fantastic job she had done without even so much as a small choke on his words, and what did he get for his effort? No pleased smile, no tender flush of delight at his praise, not even a polite "thank you." Come to think of it, she hadn't even kissed him when he got off the plane.

They stopped at a red light, and he turned to look at her, his face red with self-righteous anger.

She met his gaze. Her face was filled with wrath, too, but hers was tight-lipped and stony. Walter's jaw dropped, and his voice sounded more astonished than irate.

"Well, what the hell is the matter with *you?*"

Margaret's eyes narrowed. "A lot is the matter with *me,*" she said, mimicking him with heavy sarcasm. Horns started bleating behind him, and in his flustered state, he pressed down too hard on the acelerator and lurched forward, tires squealing.

"How impressive," she murmured.

"Now, *look,*" Walter said, "I've had about enough of this." He pulled the car off the road and onto a side street lined with jocular-looking palm trees with fat trunks. He switched off the motor and turned to glare at his wife. She was looking straight ahead, but he could see the crimson spot on her left cheek.

"Spit it out, Margaret," he said, and waited.

Finally she turned to him. "I don't like the way you talk to me. . . . I don't think you're respectful or polite, and you are most certainly not sympathetic."

He waited again. She was having a hard time, he could see that, stopping and starting between words and twisting the strap of her handbag.

"I try to be pleasant, and you always have some . . . remark. You are damn rude, that's what you are."

Damn? Did his Margaret say "damn"? Hell must be freezing over someplace in the universe if Margaret just said "damn."

She paused to pull herself together, but she was close to tears. He could see her chin quiver.

"What did I say?" he asked.

"*Everything* you say to me!" she wailed.

Walter was shocked at the passion in her voice. She began to cry, and between gasps she sputtered out something about the princess and the pea and her ass and the way he always humiliated her in front of other people with his smart remarks.

Finally, after a deep breath, she said, "I didn't mean to cry. I don't want to, and I'm going to stop. Right now."

Walter reached a hand out and laid it gently on her shoulder. He felt the muscles grow rigid at his touch. She looked at him now. Except for the red-rimmed eyes and the wet cheeks, you would never guess there'd been any emotion in that face for weeks, or months. Maybe ever.

"You should listen to yourself sometime," she said coolly.

He took his hand off her shoulder and started the car. "I'll try to watch it."

He pulled away from the curb, veered sharply to avoid a little towheaded boy on a skateboard, and moved out onto the highway again, driving fast.

CHAPTER 28

Sharlie sat in her wheelchair, gazing curiously at the psychiatrist. Rather than pull the curtains against the sparkling sunshine, Dr. Rosen leaned against a bookcase to the left of the window so her patient wouldn't be staring directly into the blinding light. Sharlie regarded the relaxed figure, wondering how old she was. In her midthirties, at least. An M.D. with a psychiatric specialty. And who knew what esoteric degree one needed to treat potential transplants—three years' internship with Dr. Jekyll and Mr. Hyde?

"What are you thinking over there?" asked Dr. Rosen with a smile.

"Nothing much." Sharlie looked out the window. She could hardly ask Dr. Rosen her age, nor could she admit to the curiosity. Far too personal. "I guess I was wondering what kind of preparation one needs for the kind of work you're in."

Dr. Rosen said, "Funny. You looked so sad and

young just now, I thought perhaps you were missing somebody."

Sharlie shook her head, but felt a sudden lump in her throat.

"Tell me about Brian," the doctor said.

Sharlie thought a moment, then said, "Well . . ." Nothing more came out. She said, "Well," again and started to laugh.

"What?" asked Dr. Rosen.

"It's as if you just asked me to explain the creation of the universe. I don't know where to begin."

"All right, let me be more specific. Or . . ." She swung around in her chair to face Sharlie more directly. "Let's try it this way: What's the first word you think of when you hear me say *Brian*?"

Sharlie sat still, her eyes flickered, and then she shook her head.

"I distinctly saw a word go past," the doctor said.

"*Brown*."

"*Brown*," Dr. Rosen repeated.

"Well, it isn't a very . . . romantic . . . word. I wanted to think of something like *clouds* or *roses*. But *brown*? How embarrassing."

"Why?"

"Well *brown* is, well . . . kind of disgusting."

"How disgusting?" the doctor prodded.

"Maybe it's his initials."

"*Brian Morgan*," Dr. Rosen said. "Okay."

Sharlie laughed. "It's absurd . . ." And then the words began to flow. "He's got that warm curly brown hair that feels so good. It's a safe word, too—reliable."

Dr. Rosen watched Sharlie's fingers curl around one another as she spoke of touching Brian's hair.

"He's always wearing brown wool clothes when I visualize him, like the first night I met him . . . the first conscious night, that is. The very first time I was unconscious, and he could have been wearing silver lamé for all I knew."

Dr. Rosen asked her about it, and Sharlie told her the whole story, from the taxi ride to Saint Joe's, right through to the California trip.

"And now he's here with me, and I haven't any idea what to do with him."

"You don't mention sex."

"Oh. Didn't I?" Sharlie knew she hadn't pulled off the casual response. She began to blush. Dr. Rosen continued to watch her, and Sharlie stammered, "Well, I can't say as it's exactly a platonic relationship . . . oh, God, that's ridiculous, I nearly raped him, to tell you the truth. I mean, if I'd had any idea how to go about it . . . but he jumped right in, and . . . oh, dear . . . I mean, he took over, and basically it was very . . . basic." She faltered to a stop, feeling like an adolescent fool. After a moment had passed and the doctor hadn't responded, Sharlie said, "You know, I don't think I'd be any use on those talk shows where women discuss their mastectomies or sexual fulfillment. I can't even talk about it with a psychiatrist all alone just the two of us."

"You think it's necessarily easier just us two?"

"No, I guess not."

"All right. There's no need to tell me all the details. But I'd like to know how you believe sex fits into your life, into your relationship with Brian. And how you think it will be after the operation."

"Sex is important. I would have said, to him, but I

know it's just as important to me. Maybe even more so, and I haven't even experienced . . . everything . . . yet."

"You mean orgasm."

Sharlie nodded, grateful for not having to say it herself. She felt stripped.

"Nice girls like it, too, Charlotte," Dr. Rosen said, and Sharlie thought immediately, What about you, doctor? Do you like it? Maybe you're a nymphomaniac or a lesbian. No, impossible. Psychiatrists, like parents, never do such dirty things. They reproduce out of a sense of duty, prolonging the species. Certainly never, never for gratification. Not lady psychiatrists, anyway.

"Do you feel inhibited by your illness?"

"Uh, yes," Sharlie said with difficulty, wishing they could move on to another topic. "But not as much as I would have thought. There's more a feeling of not caring what happens to me. My attraction to him is very . . . powerful."

"Do you think the holding back is more an emotional response than fear for your physical safety?"

"Yes," Sharlie said.

"Would the operation change that?"

"I don't know. I don't see how it could, unless I got the heart of a nymphomaniac or something."

The girl's skin had turned ashen all of a sudden. The sun's rays filtered through the gardenia branches and cast sinister shadows across her face.

Dr. Rosen got up. "I'm sorry we have to stop, but you need some rest." She came around behind Sharlie's wheelchair and put her hand on the thin shoulder.

"We'll get you fixed up, Charlotte," she said softly, then wheeled her out and called for the nurse's aide to take her back upstairs.

CHAPTER 29

Margaret lay by the pool in the hot midafternoon sun. She could hear cars whizzing past on the expressway and thought that the sound had become part of the inside of her head—the whirring rush of California. How unlike New York's din, the jolting stop and start, loud screechings of brakes, howls from irate drivers, obscenities and laughter and screams of terror and joy punctuating the daily ritual. She missed the excitement of it, but the steadiness of California's zipping pace was probably soothing under the circumstances. It wasn't every day one's daughter sat perched on the edge of a heart transplant.

It's really my doing, she thought. I encouraged it, I pushed her. Walter might have even dropped the whole thing and let Sharlie drift off into death. He'd fought so hard for her all these years—maybe he was finally just too tired.

But there was Brian, too, of course. She had a partner in guilt there, and that was comforting. Someone
else who refused to let Sharlie die in peace, who
nagged and prodded and cajoled until the poor girl
had to give in just for a few minutes' respite. Margaret
knew that while she lay there listening to the low
buzz of cars speeding past, Sharlie heard the hum of
voices—do it, do it, reach out—so you're tired, tired of
pain, tired of fighting, tired of trying. Force yourself
this one last time—have to, for me, for us, for mother,
for Brian, if you love us . . . Hummmmm.

Margaret was frightened. More terrified than she
had ever been in her whole life, but it was different
terror this time. She'd always been afraid. Afraid of
her father, afraid of Miss Newhouse, afraid of doctors
and servants and waiters and even children. Maybe
even especially children, because she always thought
that with their own special antennae they *knew* about
her. Nothing was hidden from the round, penetrating
eyes of a child. There was never any chance of hiding
from Sharlie, of course, but she was always a frighten-
ingly perceptive creature.

Margaret sighed and rolled over, enjoying the sudden heat baking her back. She pulled herself up on
her elbows and surveyed the pool area. One other person, a young man, a boy really, probably about sixteen years old, in one of those tiny bikini bathing suits
that shows every bulge.

He was cleaning the pool with an elongated
butterfly-net contraption, and as he slowly swept
along the surface of the water, the long muscles in his
arms rippled and his body glistened in the reflection

of the turquoise liquid. No hair on his body at all—or perhaps it was so blond it just didn't show.

The boy was intent on his work, and Margaret decided he wouldn't bother looking at a postmenopausal, decrepit old wreck like herself. So she loosened her bathing-suit straps carefully. Just as she tucked them between her breasts, she looked up to see the boy staring at her with hungry admiration. She was startled, she could only stare back at him foolishly while the whirring noise from the expressway intensified to a roar in her ears. Finally the boy dropped his eyes and walked back toward the motel. But as he turned, Margaret saw the minute rayon swimsuit straining with the boy's erection. For one moment she wondered how the young brown hands would feel on her breasts, if they would be soft and gentle.

Through her sun-baked sensations of guilt and sardonic self-contempt, Margaret realized she had never before allowed her waking imagination to consider a sexual encounter. After all, she was an old lady already. And yet . . . and yet . . . the boy had stared at her so ravenously. His bathing suit could barely contain all that youthful lust.

Suddenly the old anger surfaced like a silver blade, slicing up into her conscious mind. Walter had gradually killed that precious part of her over the years, with his heavy body suffocating her, trapping her beneath his pounding hips, all her tender dreams of romantic kisses ground into the sweaty sheets as his teeth pressed against her mouth and he crashed into her most secret, sensitive center, intruding with pain and scraping heat. She had known he wanted to please her. He always used to ask how it had been for her, and she would say, "Fine. It was fine." But after a while he didn't ask her anymore. He would come to her bed occasionally, an uninvited gate-crasher who had spoiled the party for her for the rest of her life.

Would those young brown hands feel cool on her burning skin?

CHAPTER 30

"Hey, Harvey, don't let me down," Diller said into the phone. "I've been everywhere except the zoo, and I'm going to raid the ape cage if I can't come up with something in a day or so." The voice at the other end grumbled in Diller's ears. "Harvey, I don't think you understand. Her father's good for a few mil, and if I pull a miracle, we might just have ourselves a research center."

The voice grumbled some more. Diller smiled. "Gotcha right in the old test tubes, hey buddy? See what you can do for me. Find me an organ full of piss and vinegar and I'll set you up in a nice quiet lab for the rest of your life."

He hung up the phone and passed his hand across his face, yawning. He'd been up until three last night with the Davis baby—four hours inside the heart of a two-month-old infant. He liked the challenge of working on babies. He still got a kick out of rebuilding a newborn child, giving it a chance for life—more so than some of the old farts he worked on who really ought to donate their money to medical research instead of tossing it away on expensive operations that only prolonged the agony for another few months. But after hours of rearranging valves the size of an ant's eyelash, he'd just as soon perform his next operation on a full-grown elephant.

What the hell was he going to do about her? She was fading in and out, and each day there were longer outs than ins. He'd gotten so desperate he'd even talked with Elizabeth Rosen about the girl's will to live, hoping that the psychiatrist would tell him she'd hang on a little longer. But Elizabeth was far from encouraging—as he'd already discovered was her tendency in several respects. She said she was beginning to question whether they should perform the surgery even if they found a donor—ambivalence toward heart transplantation, confusion about her future, guilt and despair toward the people she loved, all conspiring to sabotage a successful recovery.

Damn, damn, dammit. There just weren't all that many millionaire's kids who needed Diller's particular skills, and if he blew this one, there might never be another chance to finance the center.

He picked up the phone again and asked the operator to connect him with Dr. Vogel in Phoenix. Maybe Phil had found him a flat EEG since yesterday.

Brian ran down the hallway with legs that felt as if they were functioning in slow motion. His body ached from the desperate effort to push them faster. Letters formed words inside his head, as if from a typewriter: *Why is it you can never find a doctor when you need one?* No, that wasn't right. It was something else. A postman. A doorman. What?

After what seemed like hours of propelling himself through white emptiness, he slammed against the desk at the nurse's station. Nurse Wynick glanced at his face and, before Brian could open his mouth, took off at a run toward Sharlie's room. He kept pace alongside, and she snapped, "The button, man. Don't waste time coming to get me. Push the *button.*"

"Broken," he puffed, and they entered the room where Sharlie lay unconscious, gasping, as if she'd been the one doing all the dashing around, when she'd only sat up in bed to brush her hair. Her cheeks were pale blue, and her lips were filmed with froth.

Brian watched helplessly from the foot of the bed while Nurse Wynick hooked up the oxygen. After a moment he heard himself say, "Please, please . . ."

Nurse Wynick glanced at him, read the frustration in his face, and handed him the phone. "Get them to page Diller," she said.

Once again they all sat in the waiting room down the hall from ICU. Walter shoved jigsaw puzzle pieces around on the coffee table, but after five minutes of collecting the edges he said, "Oh, screw this," and scrambled everything together again. He glanced at Margaret, but she didn't look up from *Sense and Sensibility*. Brian was staring out the window, his face sorrowful—a young man turned middle-aged practically overnight. Walter had known it would happen. Didn't he tell them all? God damn women. God damn them all.

They get their hooks into you. What if Sharlie'd

been a son? First of all, no son of his would have gotten stuck with Margaret's weak genes. Probably a
strapper like young Brian over there. Poor Sharlie was
Walter and Margaret jumbled up and reborn in the
most unlucky amalgam.

Holy Christ. If he'd had a son, the kid might have
inherited Walter's healthy body and Margaret's sex-
lessness. Jesus, he might have been a raving *fag*.

Walter forced himself to begin arranging jigsaw
pieces again. He would not sit around and whine to
himself about what might have been. For all he knew,
it could have been worse.

But what could be worse than that beautiful little
girl lying in there unconscious? He felt an obstruction
in his throat and closed his eyes against the water
burning behind his lids. What's the matter with me?
he pleaded. Can't think anymore, can't plan anymore,
can't face the future. Suddenly I'm a heap of Jell-O—
no guts.

He tried to track down the exact moment of abdica-
tion. His memory fastened again on the dining room
scene, and he took a deep breath. This time he would
think it through instead of fleeing the images as fast
as his cerebral circuitry would take him.

It was his fault. That was the crux of the matter. It
was Walter's fault that Sharlie lay there waiting for
the ghouls to cut her open and stick some dripping
hunk of meat into her chest. . . .

At that moment Diller appeared in the doorway, his
expression solemn and weary. Walter sat staring up at
the surgeon, and it appeared to him that the doctor
spoke directly to him, the brilliant eyes piercing Walter's face with accusation.

"I think we'd better face some facts here."

Walter watched Margaret and Brian snap to attention.

"She's losing ground very quickly, and there's no donor. I have to tell you I think we've got one more day. If that. I'm sorry." He stood there for a long moment, the shadows in his face lending him the aura of a tragic figure from some ancient drama—the noble god brought down by hubris, still dignified in defeat. Except that the golden hair seemed slightly stringy, as if it could use a washing.

Diller left the room, and suddenly Walter started to choke and shudder. The tears came flooding down his face, spilling onto his clenched hands and splashing in puddles on the floor. He looked at Margaret's blurry image through the water, and his words came out in twisted, heaving bursts of sound.

"I'm sorry . . . she . . . Sharlie's . . . all my fault . . ."

Then Margaret was beside him, holding his hands. He put his arms around her, and they clung together, rocking back and forth.

Two hours later Margaret followed Diller into his office, ignoring the irritation on his face when he swung around to find her standing behind him. She'd waited for him to finish surgery, terrified that at any moment she'd be summoned to Sharlie's room for the last time. She wasn't about to waste one precious second explaining her way into his inner sanctum.

"No word, Mrs. Converse," he said. "I assure you, I'll let you know the moment—"

Margaret felt her own heart knocking inside her chest and wondered quickly if that was how Sharlie's felt, hammering away in a perpetual state of agitation.

"Doctor Diller, I want this conversation to be absolutely confidential. Now and always."

He nodded. He'd always pegged Margaret Converse as one of those cold, eastern bitches with no ass and no sex. He looked at her with interest now, noting the flushed face, the urgent quaver in her voice. He motioned for her to sit. Her hands trembled as she gripped the arms of her chair.

"I don't know if there's a precedent. I don't suppose so . . ." she began.

He nodded again, curious now, encouraging her to go on.

"Is there any way, I mean . . . I don't care if it's legal or not, Walter could always fix it later. I want to be my daughter's donor."

Well, here it is, Diller thought. He'd seen it on a dozen faces before, during the long, gruesome wait for a stranger to die in just the proper manner. He'd seen the guilt in faces that needed to make the gesture but never quite forced out the words. But this woman's fear, he could see, was only that he might turn her down.

"You're not serious," he said to her, knowing full well that she was.

Margaret looked at him silently.

"You're asking me to commit murder."

"No," she shook her head vehemently. "I realize that's impossible, and I don't want to jeopardize your career. All I ask is . . . well, guidance, in my own . . ."

"Suicide."

"I prefer to think of it as a gift. But I want her to get the maximum benefit from my heart. I would hate to . . . well, go through with it and bequeath her a damaged one."

The woman is crazy, Diller thought. Look at her sitting there as though she's discussing a birthday present for her kid—a new pair of earrings or something.

"Mrs. Converse, the strain . . ."

"No!" she interrupted him fiercely. "I mean to do this with or without your assistance. I'll find a way on my own if I have to. I've read what I could find, which isn't much, but I do know my tissue type is more likely to be compatible with hers than somebody outside the family." She crossed her arms against her stomach as if it hurt her. "The thing is, I don't like pain. I never have had much tolerance, not like my daughter. I'm not a brave person, Doctor Diller, and I was hoping . . . well, I didn't want it to be undignified. I don't want to be crying or screaming or any such thing."

Diller stared at her incredulously. He wanted to get on the phone with Elizabeth Rosen right now and find out what she had to say about this woman, but just then his intercom buzzed. He picked up the receiver.

His eyes flickered up at Margaret's face, but he quickly looked away from her intent gaze. His voice was noncommittal. "How soon? . . . No, get a commercial airline. Fogelsohn will tell you how to arrange it. . . . They'll give you a ballpark on the tissue match. . . . No, not soon enough. Push it. We're in trouble. . . . Thanks, Harve." He hung up the phone and faced Margaret in silence.

"A donor for Sharlie?" she asked.

He nodded. "Possibly. We won't know until we get the complete work-up, but the preliminary tests from New York are encouraging."

Margaret took a deep breath, then murmured, "New York . . . Sharlie would like that."

Diller smiled for the first time. "Come all the way out to California so you can find yourself a heart from Queens."

"Is it someone . . . young?" Margaret asked tentatively. Then, before he could answer, she cut in, "No. Don't tell me. I don't want to know anything about it."

"Mrs. Converse, please don't get your hopes up. Not until there's a lot more information. More often than not, these things are blind alleys."

Margaret nodded and rose stiffly. She held out her hand to Diller, and he took it. She remembered thinking it was a very soft, almost feminine hand . . . but of course he must protect them carefully.

"If the donor doesn't work out—" she began, but he interrupted quickly.

"We'll face that if we have to. For the moment, let's just forget our conversation."

They stared at each other, both thinking how impossible that would be. Then Margaret headed for the door, back straight, legs moving in perfectly controlled strides, not one step the slightest fraction longer than the last.

Brian had walked quietly out of the waiting room, closing the door on Walter and Margaret as they clung together. He moved automatically, like a sleepwalker, down the hallway to Sharlie's room, then sat down next to her bed.

He held the lifeless, clammy hand and stared at the mask on the pillow. He remembered his pleasure in watching her face change, feelings and dreams playing over her mouth and eyes like an assortment of clouds passing across the sky—white, fluffy, mischievous clouds; gray, sad, rainy clouds; and now and then just clear open sky and shining, sparkling sunshine. He had delighted in the rippling reflections of her moods and sometimes called her, teasingly, the Woman of a Thousand Faces. Sharlie responded by comparing herself to Lon Chaney, exasperated by the inability to conceal her feelings. And besides, she protested, how was she supposed to maintain an aura of mystery in their relationship if he could read her face like the menu in a fastfood restaurant?

He liked to sneak looks at her while she was watching television, how her face would take on the expression of whoever filled the screen. She protested that this only happened when she identified with a particularly compelling character, but there were times he pointed out to her she seemed to find *that* lady very compelling—the one in the advertisement there for underarm deodorant or toilet paper. She would stick out her tongue, throw a pillow in his direction, and pull her hair over her face so he couldn't watch.

But now the features were expressionless, a wax form belonging to some stranger. He had lost her so many times already, and once more they'd told him sorrowfully that she wasn't going to make it, not unless something awful happened to somebody else very soon, and even then . . .

Brian closed his eyes, asked his vague God for forgiveness, and prayed fervently for someone to crash into a tree outside the hospital and die a quick, painless death, brain instantly crushed and heart beautifully, perfectly intact.

CHAPTER 31

Sharlie was lying very still inside her body, listening to the hum. It was all darkness, there were no voices, no faces, no colors, just a black, suffocating, hot cloud. Again she tried to open her mouth, but there was no connection left between her will and her ability to exercise it. No speech. No possibility of communicating to the humming place that what she wanted now was to die. It wasn't pain exactly. More a sensation of drowning in heat, of being buried alive under a ton of boiling earth, like the citizens of Pompeii. Away, far above her, through the seething molten clay, the faint buzz of life went on, but her relationship to it seemed a feeble thread, about to snap under the weight of all that lava. Being even minimally conscious in the airless grave made her frantic, and she screamed, Brian! She howled through the oppressive layers, Brian! Help me die!

But she was powerless to move her mouth, and her

screams melted unheard into the hot·darkness inside
her head.

"How long will we have to wait?" Margaret asked
Dr. Diller. Her voice sounded calm, but she was gripping Walter's hand so hard that he finally uncurled
her fingers and showed her the bright-red crescents
she'd left in his flesh with her nails.

"Less than twenty-four hours," Diller replied.

The three of them sat lined up as usual in the chairs
in front of Diller's desk. Brian felt alert and relaxed now that something was happening. He'd
passed through the last few days like a shell-shock victim, his eyes vague and expressionless, his mind blank.
It was as if his central nervous system had been over-
loaded with stimuli and finally short-circuited. The
sensation, or rather the lack of sensation, made him
wonder if he'd been so completely burned-out by the
merciless waves of fear and hope and dread and loss,
that nothing could possibly rouse him anymore. But
now word had arrived from New York about a gun-
shot victim—brain death had occurred, but his heart
was strong. It only remained to obtain permission
from his mother to use his organs for transplantation.
She wanted to speak with her minister first, but Diller
had been assured that she was receptive.

"We need somebody in New York to take responsibility for getting the guy out here," Diller said.

"The whole guy?" Brian asked.

Diller nodded. "We can't keep the heart alive anywhere else except inside the donor."

"What about Dr. Parkiss?" asked Margaret.

"In Minneapolis for a convention."

"Figures," Walter said.

"How about Mary MacDonald?" Brian asked.

Diller looked at Brian thoughtfully.

"But she's only a nurse," Margaret protested. "Shouldn't it be somebody with a little more training?"

Walter said, "There isn't anybody more competent than MacDonald. I don't give a damn about training."

Brian said, "Think she'd do it? She runs the show on Eleven."

Diller picked up his phone and buzzed the secretary they'd provided for him during his "sabbatical." While they waited, Diller crossed his elegant hands on his desk and spoke quietly to them. "There's a lot that can go wrong between New York and the operating room."

They all stared back at him with stubborn faith in their faces. Diller thought, They think I'm Jesus Christ. He felt the headache begin to pulse behind his right eye. "I have very little control over what transpires at that end," he continued. "How they get the donor shipped, what condition he's in when he gets here. We'll do as many tests as possible beforehand. They can do blood work-ups, we can have tissue samples flown ahead for matching. But it's a long trip, and the equipment isn't foolproof."

Walter broke in, "We won't hold you responsible for screwups. Except the ones in OR."

Foxy bastard, Diller thought, giving Walter a forced smile. "I'll share with you the one fact I'm sure of, and that's if they get the donor here, and if we have a match and the heart's in good shape and your daughter is still alive, then there's not going to be any slip-up in the operating room. I'll make it work."

Brian resisted the impulse to say, "With a little help

from Jason Lewis, Super-surgeon." But Walter and
Margaret gazed at Diller with desperately hopeful
faces. Diller wearily accepted his habitual burden of
irrational, unquestioning trust. Even in the suspicious
face of Walter Converse the ferocious need was evident—to believe in the performance of a miracle.

CHAPTER 32

Mary MacDonald went straight to Jason Lewis's office and asked him if she could observe the operation. She had felt torn about it, thinking it might be the first time she'd humiliate herself by passing out in OR, but the idea of just sitting around wringing her hands with the relatives cinched it.

Lewis impressed her. Like most of the personnel at Saint Joseph's, Mary had followed the progress of the first heart transplant operations, somehow breaking away to watch the press briefings on the lounge television. Lewis was a distinguished-looking man, tall, with a full head of prematurely pure-white hair. He spoke dispassionately about his patients, answering the reporters' eager questions with calm detachment. But the third transplant was performed on a ten-year-old boy. It had been a particularly risky case—the desperate search for a suitable heart had produced only that of a middle-aged man whose tissue type was less than ideally matched. When it became apparent that the child was rejecting his new heart, Lewis had stood in front of the microphones and detailed in his quiet voice the circumstances of the boy's imminent death. The great surgeon let the tears roll down his cheeks without shame or apology as he talked, and Mary, when she spoke with him now, kept seeing his face as it was then, all wet and shiny in the glare of the television lights.

Mary's admiration was reciprocated. Lewis was impressed by the efficiency with which the donor was delivered to California, and correctly gave Mary the credit. He told her in his soft voice that he would be honored to have her observe.

The operating room looked like a very clean garage. There was an atmosphere of controlled chaos as the technicians bustled about, setting up their equipment. Machines hummed and clanked and ticked, and the nurses made nervous jokes. There hadn't been a heart transplant in nearly three months, and everyone was excited. Diller would assist, of course.

Mary watched the two men scrub together and listened with a wry smile as Diller complained about the ever-present reporters downstairs. Then she entered OR to watch the assistants prepare Sharlie, remembering, as she stood transfixed, the first time she had assisted in open-heart surgery—how, after the initial incision, the breastbone was opened with a saw and the ribs were separated with rib retractors. Mary had thought then that OR seemed like a body shop. This morning she listened to the hoarse buzz of the saw and swallowed hard, reminding herself that this was Sharlie's only chance.

Diller and Lewis entered now, and the team stood

hushed as the men stared down into Sharlie's open incision.

"Holy God," Lewis said. "How'd you keep her alive?"

Diller shook his head at the pale, flabby heart, so enlarged it seemed to bulge out of the chest cavity.

"Let's get that thing out of there," Lewis said softly, and began to free Sharlie's heart.

Soon she lay on the table, chest cavity empty, her life supported only by the electronic wizardry of the heart-lung machine.

Lewis said, "All right," and his nurse opened the door to the adjoining operating room. Mary caught a quick glimpse of a body, swathed in sheets, on the table.

Within seconds the nurse reappeared, carrying a stainless steel basin. Mary averted her eyes and found herself suddenly whispering a Hail Mary. After all the years of assisting in surgery, the impulse surprised her. She fought to remind herself that she was observing a medical procedure, that the object in the shiny basin was merely a hunk of human muscle, not some evil offering for a black-magic ceremony. Diller and Lewis, masked and solemn, were really just technicians, not satanic priests performing a mysterious, dark ritual.

As the surgeons began the tedious process of attaching vena cava to vena cava, aorta to aorta, of the hooking up of coronary arteries, Mary relaxed, responding to the comfortable familiarity of surgical activity. She shook her head, chiding herself for her foolish notions.

It was nearly two hours before Diller and Lewis finished off their minute sewing and straightened up to stretch cramped muscles. The healthy heart seemed tiny inside Sharlie's chest, a fist clenching and un-clenching within a vast empty hole. They all watched it in silence, delaying the moment when the new or-gan must be severed from the heart-lung machine. Fi-nally Lewis murmured, "Okay, let's go."

Someone switched off the machine. The first sec-ond seemed like a long, long time, but suddenly the little fist pulsed, then relaxed, then pulsed again. A jubilant shout rose up from the surgical team, and Mary laughed out loud. Lewis handed his instruments to his scrub nurse and left the room abruptly. Diller remained behind to close the incision and asked cas-ually if the news people were still hanging around outside. He wouldn't mind having a quick word with them.

The scrub nurse looked at Mary over her mask, and the two women smiled at each other with their eyes.

CHAPTER 33

They put her in special isolation and kept everyone out except the transplant staff. The immunosuppressive drugs helped deactivate her body's antigens, preventing them from attacking the alien tissue of the new heart. But as a result she was vulnerable to infection from every stray germ. Even the common cold virus could prove deadly during this critical period of her recovery. Along with the elaborate equipment in her room, someone from the transplant staff remained with her at all times.

She hadn't awakened from the anesthesia, but she could be watched through an observation window. Mary MacDonald stood next to Brian, peering at Sharlie's companion, who, at the moment, was Nurse Wynick.

"Goddamn cowboys, who the hell do they think they are?" Mary muttered, her substantial body quivering with indignation. "I ought to know something about isolation, for Christ's sake."

Brian put his arm around her waist, enjoying the bright-pink fury of her face and the muscular girth under his hand. Nurse Wynick glanced at them, frowning slightly.

"Bitch," Mary said, then sighed. "Ah, well, I suppose I'd do the same if they stuck their freckled California noses into Saint Joe's, be sure I would."

Brian leaned his forehead against the cold surface of the window. "I hope she never finds out about the donor," he whispered, as if Sharlie might hear him through the glass.

"We'll just have to make sure she doesn't," Mary said. "Come on, let's go get some coffee."

Sitting in the cafeteria, Brian said, "I barely recognized her. She looks so withered."

"Oh, you'll get your pretty girl back soon enough, if all goes well," Mary said, cupping her hands around the styrofoam mug. "It's a miracle what happens to some people when they get their new hearts. So much misery they've had, and suddenly they feel brand new."

"Let it happen to her," Brian said. Then he went on, guiltily, "Besides, I shouldn't give a damn what she looks like as long as she's okay."

"You going to get married?"

"She's been talking to the psychiatrist about it."

"They got the shrinks after her now, do they? Well, that'll screw her up for fair."

"Gee, thanks," Brian remarked morosely, and Mary laughed.

They sipped their coffee in companionable silence for a moment. Then Brian said, "Mary, have I told you how glad I am you're here?"

"Mmm," she replied. "You mentioned it."

"I wish you could have been around through the whole damn thing."

"What about the Converses?"

Brian just smiled at her, and suddenly Mary was sputtering again. "That woman, she's a cold fish if I ever saw one. I don't think she gives a flying frog if her daughter lives or dies. Just fancying around in her lah-dee-dah clothes and her false eyelashes—"

Brian interrupted delightedly. "She doesn't really wear false eyelashes, does she?"

Mary looked away. "Well, maybe she does and maybe she doesn't, but she's the type, all right. This California trip's a great excuse to go out and buy herself a whole new wardrobe."

"She cares about Sharlie," Brian said.

Mary sniffed into her paper cup.

Brian hesitated, then said slowly, "I'm going to tell you something you're going to find tough to believe."

Instantly Mary's eyes bored into Brian's face.

"You hang around hospitals long enough, you get to know people," Brian continued. "They start telling you things they probably shouldn't."

"Go on," she said impatiently.

"A couple of days ago, before they found the donor, Margaret Converse tried to persuade Diller to use her own heart for the transplant."

Mary's face didn't change, her stare just stiffened. "I *don't* believe it," she whispered.

He nodded. "True."

"Jesus Mary," she breathed at last, then, after another moment of thinking it over, muttered, "Well, all right, but she's still a cold fish."

* * *

Brian sent Mary back to her motel with an obliging nurse who was going off duty and would be driving that way. Then he went back upstairs to watch Sharlie some more. He waved at the nurse now on duty, a stranger, and leaned against the window to gaze at the lifeless figure amid the hardware—electronic ticking and whirring beside the dehumanized lump that was once his warm, beautiful girl. A shrunken face, an emaciated body with wires and tubes sticking out of her flesh like tentacles.

He had participated in her humiliation, urging his reluctant lover into this awful arena of pain and degradation. Couldn't he have let her die with her beauty and humor and humanity still intact?

He looked down at his hand, now wrapped lightly in an elastic bandage. How many more bones can I break? he wondered.

As he was about to turn away, Sharlie's head moved on the pillow, and she looked him full in the face. He stared back at her stupidly, not knowing what to do with his eyes to hide his dismay. She began to smile and then rolled her eyes at him, making a small grimace with her mouth in the familiar way that said, Can you believe what I've gotten myself into this time? And suddenly he was grinning like a fool, waving and laughing and calling for everybody to come and see.

Diller attended Sharlie with the same kind of protective paranoia he reserved for his hands. No one else, except Jason Lewis, of course, was allowed to interpret her tests. She was his consuming passion, and he hovered at her bedside, fidgeting and fussing.

Margaret watched him with curiosity and amusement. Over the years she had come to realize that the surgeon's special interest in Sharlie focused more on Walter's wallet than on Sharlie's chest cavity. But now his absorption had become personal. Margaret wondered if Diller was bewitched by his own instant celebrity.

Since the transplant the waiting room had been crowded with newspapermen and television cameras. Sharlie's plight had come to the attention of a reporter in New York soon after the donor's demise on a dismal street in Queens. The writer, an ambitious young woman, discovered that frantic arrangements were underfoot to ship the body to California. She sensed exploitability in the story and began a series of articles describing the beautiful young woman on the brink of death awaiting a donor. She wrote about Martin Udstrom, how he had spent his short life attempting to make a splash in New York's criminal underworld, and traced his journey from petty larceny to assault and finally his graduation into homicide with the brutal murder of a shopkeeper in Jackson Heights. The story captured national attention—the hardened heart of a criminal implanted in the chest of a fragile girl—and the public eagerly devoured every word. The media hordes, pencils poised and cameras whirring, gathered daily for Diller's news bulletins.

Today Margaret encountered Diller outside the waiting room where he generally held court. This morning he would be taped for national broadcast, and he muttered to Margaret that the press with all the cameras and paraphernalia was getting in his way and wasting his time. He was fed up with newsmen underfoot all day every day. But she noticed that before he stepped into the room, he was careful to straighten his tie and brush his thick, gold-streaked hair back with his hands.

Margaret watched from the doorway as a jaded Los Angeles reporter asked, "When do we get to see the patient?"

Diller allowed himself a cool smile and turned his best side toward the camera. "I can't tell you that now, gentlemen. She'll be in partial isolation until we're certain she's past any danger of infection."

"Is she conscious?"

"Yes," said Diller. "We hope to take her off IV today."

The New York reporter broke in, "What's the publicity doing to your career, Doctor? Do you see yourself becoming another Christiaan Barnard?"

Diller smiled at her ingratiatingly. "Oh, I'm not interested in notoriety. I just want to do my job."

"But I understand you're due for several television appearances and speaking tours. Those things have to . . ."

"I'm sure you understand," Diller interrupted, "that all I want is to continue the work I'm doing. However, I do feel that the public is entitled to information about the kinds of strides being made in coronary surgery, and despite the sacrifice of time away from my patients, I believe I'm obligated to enlighten people who may benefit from these advances."

Margaret heard suppressed snickers behind her and turned around. Three of the eighth-floor nurses were enjoying Diller's performance from the safety of the doorway across the hall. Diller, meanwhile, dismissed himself for the day, saying he was needed for follow-up on yesterday's surgical cases. He nodded his head graciously at the expressions of appreciation from the reporters and left the room. He touched Margaret's shoulder briefly, then stopped at the group of nurses who were red-faced with the effort to remain properly sober.

"Find out when they're showing that tape, will you?" he murmured, then went off down the hall. Margaret smiled at the nurses but then stared at Diller's retreating figure, wishing him, in her gratitude, a best-selling autobiography and a starring role opposite the actress of his choice.

CHAPTER 34

Nurse Wynick helped Brian on with his mask and gown and paper slippers. He stepped quickly through the glass doors and stood by Sharlie's bedside, wondering if today would be the day she would wake up and talk to him. She opened her eyes and smiled.

"Hello, lovely man. That's you under all those sheets, isn't it? Did they make me bionic?"

Brian's eyes smiled, and he said, "Hi." He couldn't seem to manage anything more.

"Give us a kiss," Sharlie whispered.

Brian shook his head. "Not yet. I've got too many germs."

"Oh, come on," she urged. She reached out a hand for him, and he backed away.

"Sharlie, I'm not supposed to touch you."

"Oh," she said, disappointed. She held up her hands as if she were grasping a hose and pretended to spray him from head to foot. "You're disinfected. Hey, I'm injected, you're disinfected. Pretty good," she giggled.

Brian glanced at the window where Nurse Wynick watched them. She raised her eyebrows questioningly, but he smiled and turned away so he'd be left alone with Sharlie a little while longer.

"How're you feeling?" he asked her.

"Honey," she said, grinning, "I am soo-per. Soo-perb. And you know the best thing?" He waited, and she said, "All suspense, lambie-love? Really, listen, the *best* thing is . . ." She poked her toes out from under the sheets and said, "Taa-dah!"

Brian stared at her feet, then gave her a blank look.

"Pink toes! Can you believe it? Did you ever? I mean, who would have thunk it? No more blue feet, no more cold feet. Feel 'em for yourself. They're roaster-toaster warm. Hot off the old ankle. Don't you just love 'em?"

"Sharlie, you're bombed," Brian said.

"Ho *ho*! Bombed, the man says. This Pearl Harbor Day?"

Brian started for the door, and Sharlie reached out to him. "Don't go away. Oh, please don't go away. I haven't told you the most important thing, the thing I came here to tell you, all the way from Seventy-fifth Street. All this way I tramped on my little pink toes, and you go away before I get to say my little speech, all polished and practice-perfect."

Brian stood at the foot of her bed.

"Okay, lush, let's hear it."

She waved her hands in an effort at fanfare, then pronounced ceremoniously, "You, Myron Borgan . . ." She started to giggle and tried again through the snickering. "I *mean*, you Byron Morgan . . . oh, dammit, dammit, it's no use . . ." She was laughing helplessly now, and Brian hurried outside.

He interrupted Nurse Wynick's conversation with the dietician. "She's drunk," he said. "Absolutely looped."

"Uh-oh," Wynick said, and ran off down the hall. Brian called after her, "Hey, is she okay?" But there was no response. He went back to the observation window and saw that Sharlie was sound asleep again.

It was Tuesday morning, and Carlton Diller looked forward to making rounds. The notoriety over the Converse transplant had attracted several prominent surgeons from out of state, one of whom worked with Michael De Bakey in Texas. Diller was eager to exhibit his prize patient, so including the entourage of students, there were more than a dozen people peering at Sharlie through the observation window at nine thirty. Diller strode to the head of the bed to stand next to the microphone. Sharlie watched her audience solemnly.

"The patient is twenty-six years old, has suffered since birth from congenital valvular heart disease. Six weeks ago she experienced a pulmonary embolus secondary to a thrombosis from the tricuspid valve. Cor pulmonale developed rapidly. Enlargement and necrosis were severe, and the patient, upon arrival at the center, was near death."

Sharlie stared at the disembodied heads in the window, the faces gawking at her with undisguised curiosity. She'd seen the same expressions last summer near Seventy-second Street where an old man had been run over by a taxi. He lay crushed and mangled while a mob of pedestrians gathered to watch him gasp out his last breath on the bloody pavement.

Diller leaned over to place his stethoscope against

Sharlie's chest. As he reached to pull back her gown, she said in a low voice, "Don't touch me."

Diller recoiled.

"What?" he said, stunned.

"I said, don't touch me."

The faces at the window began to quiver like excited insects. One of the spectators spoke into the intercom beside the door. "She's still on immunosuppressives?"

Diller nodded. Sharlie glared.

"Any evidence of postoperative psychosis?" asked the clinical voice.

"Oh, lots," Sharlie said into the microphone. "The patient is adjusting most lousily to having her heart cut out."

Diller arranged his face into an expression of sympathy and tried to put his hand on Sharlie's shoulder. She shuddered and slapped at it as if it were a poisonous snake. Diller said, "Heh, heh," with his mouth twisted into a grotesque smile.

Sharlie looked at her fascinated observers and choked out, "Go away."

The faces remained until Diller turned to wave them off. They disappeared reluctantly, and he put his hand over the microphone to hiss at her through tight lips, "Quite a show, Sharon. I assume you're proud of yourself."

"I'm not your prize freak, Doctor . . . *Dalton,*" she retorted.

"You don't have a speck of gratitude, do you?" he said contemptuously.

Sharlie felt the waves of rage rising until they towered inside like thunderheads.

"I'm a person, a *person*. Look what you did to me!" she wailed.

Before Diller could reach the call button, Nurse Wynick appeared with a hypodermic. Diller held Sharlie's flailing arms while the nurse plunged the needle in, and all the time Sharlie was howling, "Don't touch me, don't touch me, don't touch me!"

CHAPTER 35

Sharlie lay quietly in her bed reflecting on conflicting sensations of freedom and insecurity. She had been unhooked from her last wire today. She knew she was doing well because her father had left for New York yesterday morning, and in the afternoon they transferred her into a real room with a window to the sunshine instead of the oversized incubator she'd been inhabiting. Her head felt quite clear despite some giddiness, which she attributed to the elation of functioning free of machinery. She put her hands to her cheeks. They were puffy, and she gathered from the way people looked at her that she had changed. So far, she hadn't mustered the courage to confront herself in the mirror, even though Dr. Lewis warned her that the heavy dosage of cortisone would eventually make her face swell. But there could never have been enough preparation for the dismay in Brian's eyes as he sat by her bed and gave her his brave smile.

She'd lost ten pounds since her arrival in Santa Bel,

and barely required X rays to discern the skeleton under the thin layer of flesh. She sighed as her eyes
skimmed over the surface of her blanket, filling her
mind with the image of a pitiful scrawny body topped
by a pouting cantaloupe head. Pumpkin head. She
imagined herself climbing out of bed at night, slipping into her wheelchair, the mechanized horse, to ca-
reen through the hospital like a dreadful ghost from
Sleepy Hollow in search of some poor Ichabod Crane
in a room down the hall.

When she was six years old, she'd contracted a severe case of the mumps. They couldn't figure out
where she'd picked it up, since she was isolated from
other children. Nevertheless, one morning she had
awakened with her glands ballooning out from under
her ears. Margaret had held up a mirror, and her reflection made her laugh. She wore her hair short in
what was known as the Buster Brown style. The texture was so fine even then that there was nothing
much she could do with it except cut it in a straight
line and keep it shiny clean. But with her hair perched
on her bulging glands, it was as if her hairdresser had
used a far too shallow bowl to guide his scissors. Margaret reminded her that one could get mumps on only
one side; at least she was symmetrical.

Sharlie lifted her hands to her cheeks again and
thought perhaps they'd shrunk just a little since yesterday. She imagined Dr. Rosen sitting all night by
her bedside chanting paragraphs from psychiatric
textbooks to reduce the size of her swollen head. Perhaps she should give some consideration to the other
end of her anatomy in hopes of cheering herself. Her
feet—now there was a miracle for you.

Hands finally unhampered by IV tubes, she pulled

back the covers and gazed. Remarkable what a little healthy circulation could do for one's digits. Her toes glowed and twinkled, robust testimony to the magical fingers of Lewis and Diller. First thing out of the hospital, she'd buy a pair of sandals so that whenever she felt the urge, she could take a quick reassuring peek. She had worried about lying in bed with Brian, imagining his body tense beside hers in anticipation of the icy implantation of her foot on his leg. She had warned him that sleeping together would require her wearing socks to bed out of compassion for his central nervous system.

She'd read somewhere that a man achieved mystical sexual heights if ice were applied to his genitals at the moment of his climax. Opportunity lost—they could have used her feet.

She covered her toes and picked up the inventory, deciding to skip everything between ankles and navel, since those areas seemed basically unaffected. She couldn't recommend heart transplantation for sex therapy patients, at least not today. The idea of body contact sent tremors of agonized protest along her scar tissue. She hadn't yet braved looking at it, but with her fingers gently traced the track running from her neck to the middle of her abdomen. Which brought her stocktaking to the *piéce de résistance*— the heart of things, so to speak.

If, out of fear of alarming her, they had told her she'd undergone a gall bladder operation instead of a heart transplant, she'd known the truth despite their denials. She could almost hear the steady, efficient hum of valves meshing, the rhythmic click of an effortless pulse.

But the sense of loss astonished her. What had they

done with her poor old, incompetent, derelict, flabby,
wheezing heart? Certainly they snipped off a piece to
examine under their microscopes and marvel over. But
the rest? Did they chop it up and flush it down the
toilet? Did they stuff it into a bottle of formaldehyde
to repose on a dusty shelf with fellow rejects—lack-
luster livers, somnambulant spleens, careworn kidneys? If she'd had the foresight, she would have re-
quested that they feed it to the handsome Bengal tiger
Brian had reported seeing at the Santa Bel zoo. Surgical consent forms should include the patient's instructions for the destruction of offending organs.

The fact was, she missed it—pathetic, unserviceable
thing—and wondered how Cyrano de Bergerac would
react to a nose job. Certainly he'd rue the loss of his
grotesque protrusion even as he admired his sleek new
profile in the mirror.

Disposal seemed abhorrent, almost sacrilegious.
Poor heart, house of all her most intimate yearnings. She
wouldn't ask.

That decision made, at least temporarily, the ultimate dreaded topic flashed through her mind in
bright-red capital letters: DONOR.

Fear invaded her stomach and sat there like an indi-
gestible lump. She thought of Diller and her angry
outburst. She had never before lost control of herself
like that. But it wasn't only the surgeon. There had
been moments these last few weeks when she'd felt
the madness rising in her throat with the staff, with
her parents, even with Brian. She would clench her
teeth against it, trying to wait it out, feeling as if she
were engaged in a battle against an unfamiliar and
violent enemy, who had taken up residence inside her.

They wouldn't tell her that morning, when they'd

pieced together their final vital tests and rushed her, drugged and protesting, down to OR. In the elevator it suddenly seemed so crucial that she receive the heart of someone simpatico. Through her tranquilized fog, she'd begged to be taken back upstairs. She'd rip up the consent form she'd signed under the pleading eyes of Brian and her parents the night before.

Please, she'd joked. *Let it be someone who played the harpsichord. I've always wanted to play the harpsichord.* They mustn't give her a mortician. Or a child abuser. Or a schizophrenic—these things were chemical. A dream is a wish one's heart makes—so give her a heart that makes nice wishes. A gentle, sensitive, intelligent heart. She'd grasped the hand of the nurse as the elevator doors opened and they rolled her bed out of the door. "Please," she'd cried, "Don't let it be inharmonious. The rest of me . . ."

Then her bed became a silver and white ship that sailed upon a white sea. Her tongue grew fatter and fatter, and her brain turned to flannel, and there'd been no more protesting until she woke up in the ICU to finish her sentence: " . . . won't like it."

Today the operation sat in her mind like a dark, snaking question mark, and somewhere within its coils lurked the secret of her future. She felt sick and frightened. When Brian came later, she'd try out her courage again and perhaps ask him what she so desperately wanted-yet-didn't-want to know.

Perfect gambit for a new quiz show, she thought. They'll call it *Name Your Donor.* The master of ceremonies will introduce the recipient, offering a brief medical history, perhaps even including a film clip of his or her transplant operation. Then a curtain will rise, revealing four marble slabs upon which repose four dead bodies, each with an identical scar (three of them provided by skillful network makeup artists). Each "donor" is accompanied by his next of kin, who answers the recipient's questions: "How did Number Three pass away? . . . Number Two, when was brain death established? . . . Number Four, what legal process is necessary to permit donation of organs for transplantation?"

Finally the recipient is allowed to wander among the corpses, examining the scars for professionalism and originality, and is then given fifteen seconds to make the final judgment as to the identity of the real donor. During this moment the suspense mounts, with the frenzied studio audience shouting suggestions. Then the thinking-music stops, and the recipient announces his decision.

If he's correct, he wins an insurance policy that will cover his medical expenses for the remainder of his life. The donor's family gets a check for three thousand dollars and taxi fare to the nearest funeral home. However, if the recipient is persuaded to choose a fake donor, the dead person's next of kin wins the cost of a funeral complete with horse-drawn hearse, marching band from New Orleans, and burial at Forest Lawn.

Sharlie thought it was too bad Bela Lugosi wasn't around anymore. Maybe they could get Vincent Price as emcee.

She glanced at the clock above her head, crestfallen that the game-show idea had provided only five minutes' worth of diversion. She wondered what she could possibly think about that wasn't going to send her anxiety level shooting sky-high, past the meters on her monitor—no more distinguishable clicks, just the blur of frantic heartbeats in one alarming buzz.

When Brian suddenly appeared, she nearly leaped out of her bed. He laughed at her startled expression. "Don't you recognize me without my Klan attire?"

"I recognize you," she said quietly. "That's more than I can say for me."

Brian looked quickly at the door, and said in mock horror, "Good God! They sent me to the wrong room." He started to get up, and she tugged at his hand.

"Hey, don't leave me, whoever I am."

He stared at her for a second. "Dr. Rosen's coming to see you tomorrow," he said finally. Sharlie's eyes veered away. "The mood swings are not entirely chemical, you know," he said softly.

"I was awful to Dr. Diller," Sharlie said.

"He'll survive." She kept her eyes averted from him. "Sharlie, why can't I look at you?"

"I'm ugly."

"That's no excuse." He hooked a finger under her chin and turned her face to his.

"Amazing you managed to find anything to hang on to," she muttered.

"Is that all this is? The temporary cherub look? I think you're pretty cute."

She was silent.

"Come on," he said. "What is it really?"

Her eyes widened with fear. "I want to know who it was. *Don't tell me!*" The last words came out an urgent plea.

He ran his finger along her shoulder and down one arm. "You don't ever have to know about it. It's not important. Just rejoice in those rosy pink toes and forget about where they came from, okay?"

She was quiet a moment. "I can't," she said finally. "I've got somebody else's heart in here. I should at least write a thank-you note to the next of kin, don't you think? It's a pretty extravagant present, some-body's dear-one's insides."

"Hey, listen, Sharlie, most of the time the patient doesn't even know who the donor is. Like adoption—"

She interrupted him. "But this time everybody knows who it was. Except for me. There's something special about this one."

"Not particularly," he said blandly.

"Brian, some nurse was in here and started talking about all the reporters in the waiting room and got all clutched when I started asking questions."

"I think you should speak to Dr. Rosen about it."

"It was somebody famous, wasn't it?"

"No, not really."

"Was it a man or a woman?"

"Look, do you really want me to tell you?"

"No. Yes."

Brian waited.

"Just tell me how come everybody knows all about it this time."

"Talk to Dr. Rosen about it, and if she says it's okay, I'll tell you all about it. Or she will."

Sharlie's eyes were enormous. He looked at her and shook his head. "It's a hunk of flesh, a pump, an organ like a liver or a kidney. All that matters is that it's a healthy one, even if the donor was Adolf Hitler."

Sharlie's eyes dropped. "That bad, huh?"

"You just talk with Dr. Rosen."

"Chicken," she said.

"Look, do you want to know or don't you want to know?" he asked, exasperated.

She swallowed hard and then murmured, "Don't."

He nodded and started talking about a phone call he'd had from Barbara Kaye this morning mercilessly relating the recent woes of Mrs. Salvello. Brian repeated it all to Sharlie, with some embellishment, until she began to laugh again.

CHAPTER 36

Brian went downstairs for a cup of coffee. When he returned to the room, Sharlie was lying very still, staring up at the ceiling. Her body was stiff, and all the color had drained out of her face.

"Hey," Brian said. "You okay?"

She blinked her eyes, but didn't look at him. Suddenly he noticed the newspaper on her bedside table. It was folded open to the headline CRIME FIGURE DEAD IN GUNFIGHT DONATES HEART TO GIRL. He grabbed the paper and whispered hoarsely, "Where did you get this?"

Still, she didn't answer him. "Sharlie, tell me. Where did this come from?"

She turned her head slowly on the pillow. "You shouldn't have let them do it, Brian. How could you let them do that to me?"

"The guy saved your life."

She grabbed the newspaper from his hand and,

with a howl of pain and rage, threw it at his chest. It fluttered to the floor at his feet.

"Go away!" she screamed. "Just leave me alone!"

Brian hurried out to find someone who could give her a sedative and make sure she was all right. Once Nurse Wynick was on her way to Sharlie's room, he telephoned Dr. Rosen's office, but the psychiatrist was out of town until the next morning. Then he took the stairs eight flights down and stepped out into the warm breeze. He felt calmer after he'd walked the length of the grounds a few times, so he went back inside again. At the nurse's station he was told that Sharlie was asleep and wouldn't wake up until morning. He might as well go back to his motel.

He was dreaming about Walter and Mrs. Salvello when his telephone rang at two A.M. He groped for it, and Margaret's anxious voice said, "Brian? Is that you?"

"What's happened?" he murmured, alarmed through his grogginess.

"Sharlie's rejecting. They think you should come."

"I'll be there in fifteen minutes."

By the time he got to the eighth floor, a confrontation was in progress outside Sharlie's door.

Tiny, wiry Nurse Wynick was putting up a mighty struggle to bar Mary MacDonald from Sharlie's room, and Mary was responding to Nurse Wynick's defensive posture in her characteristic straightforward manner.

"Out of the way, you monkey-faced bitch, or I'll shove your ass all the way to Hawaii." She gave a push that sent Nurse Wynick sprawling against the wall.

"I'll have your license. You're a madwoman!" Nurse Wynick cried, her forehead above the gauze mask mottled with fury. A young nurse's aide stood by, staring at her superior in horror and delight. Nurse Wynick brushed herself off and shrieked at the girl. "Don't just stand there like an imbecile! Call Security. And page Dr. Lewis."

Meanwhile Mary had slipped into Sharlie's room. When Nurse Wynick tried to open the door, she found it locked. "Don't you touch that patient!" she shouted through the crack.

The response from inside was unintelligible, but its intent was clear. Nurse Wynick tore off her mask and stomped down the hall with a flaming face.

Brian tapped on the door. "Hey, Mary. It's me."

In a moment the door opened a crack, and he slid inside. Mary quickly fastened a mask over his face.

"Know what that crazy Nazi was going to do? Spike her IV with Vibramycin. These hotshots may be able to do fancy footwork in OR, but when it comes to common sense, they're a bunch of yo-yos."

"What's the matter with Vibramycin?" Brian asked.

"She's allergic to it."

"Oh," he said, impressed. "Is she okay?"

Mary settled down next to Sharlie's bed as if she intended to remain there throughout eternity. "Trying to murder my girl, they are, and her on foreign soil," she muttered.

"Mary, this isn't Borneo, it's California. Is she going to be all right?" he repeated.

"She's holding her own."

"What about the rejection?"

"They upped her prednisone to a hundred milli-

grams. She's responding, but we're just going to have
to wait."

"But shouldn't somebody be here? I mean from the
staff?"

"Not when they don't know their nostrils from their
assholes."

"Isn't Margaret around somewhere? How did you
beat me here anyway?"

"I didn't like the way she looked at nine, so I stuck
around. Her mother's on the phone with Converse in
New York trying to decide whether he could come out
again."

"Should he?"

Mary shook her head slightly, but Brian hadn't
taken his eyes off Sharlie for a moment. Mary went on
indignantly. "I'm just glad I didn't get on that plane
home this morning. They'd have killed her for sure. I
want you and Mrs. Converse to talk them into sending
her back to New York, where she can get the proper
care."

This last was said very loudly for the benefit of
Nurse Wynick, who had just arrived with a security
man in tow. The women eyed one another malevolently, then Mary rose with great dignity, brushed imaginary lint off her skirt, and said to the security man,
"I assume you have come to escort me, sir." She
crooked her elbow, which the baffled guard took, and
sailed out the door.

Nurse Wynick stared after her with narrowed eyes.
Finally she muttered, "Who does she think she is,
Queen Elizabeth?"

"Wouldn't be surprised," Brian replied proudly.
Nurse Wynick glowered and turned her attention to

Sharlie, or rather to Sharlie's bedclothes. She fussed over them busily, tucking in loose corners until Brian finally objected, "She can't even wiggle her toes in there."

This was too much for the vanquished nurse. She started to cry, her words punctuated by deep sniffs of mortification and indignation. "You people . . . you all think you know what's right. . . . New York people . . . always the same, throwing your weight around. . . . There are other places in this universe besides New York City, you know."

Brian made some expression of sympathy, which only unleashed another flood of anguish. Her fresh mask was soaked with tears, and all the time, she fidgeted with the sheets, checked IV tubes, rearranged items on the bedside table.

"I've been in the hospital fifteen years, and I know as much about transplants as anybody, and I won't have a bunch of ignorant . . . busybodies . . . coming in here and messing up my work and telling me how to do my job. I mean, if you people thought you knew so much, why didn't you just stay where you belong instead of coming all the way out here? I won't have this . . . importation of personnel on my floor. . . ."

Brian tried to interrupt with an explanation of Mary's deep involvement with Sharlie, how she'd been caring for her since birth. But Nurse Wynick immediately seized on it as proof of Mary's lack of professionalism.

"Just keep that woman out of my sight until Miss Converse is discharged. If I see her on my floor again, I'll . . ."

Brian waited curiously for the dreadful plans Nurse
Wynick had in mind for Mary.

". . . I'll anesthetize her and slap her into surgery
and transplant her insides with that ugly old orangu-
tan we've got downstairs in the lab."

With this she left the room, but not until she'd
looked at Brian's face to make sure he was impressed
with her threat. He was, and she marched out with
her spirits somewhat restored.

Brian sighed. If only one could harness the energy
of those two veterans—it would cure the common
cold, wipe out cancer, maybe even establish order in
the chaotic tangle of the hospital accounting department. But now, left alone with Sharlie, no battling ladies of mercy to distract him, Brian panicked. He
looked in every direction except at the neat bed with
the crease up the middle that was supposed to repre-
sent the woman he loved. Finally he forced himself to
focus on her. She was staring at him, wide awake, her
eyes liquid and haunting in the middle of her distorted face.

"Brian," she whispered, "tell me what's happening."

He did, not coming too close, despite his mask and
gown, for fear of infecting her.

She considered what he'd told her, and after a minute said, "If I make it through this one, Bri, and if you
still want me with my big fat face, I'll marry you."

She talked with effort, so he just smiled, squeezed
her hand quickly and stayed near the bed until she
fell asleep. A cardiologist and two residents arrived,
and he left the room, guilty at the enormity of his relief to walk out of the hospital and into the California
moonlight.

*   *   *

The next night he lay in bed listening to the murmur of voices through the thin wall between his room and Sharlie's parents'. In the beginning, except for an occasional expletive from Walter, there had been silence, as if the room were unoccupied. Tonight, however, the dark was punctuated by Walter's low rumble and the lighter response from Margaret. Brian strained his ears trying to catch pieces of these prolonged conversations. They hadn't had much to say to each other in public, and Brian found the hint of private, intimate communication tantalizing. He remembered lying awake in the creaky old farmhouse when he was a child on those nights that seemed undefinably scary. How curious he was to know exactly what was being said by his taciturn father. There was even an occasional burst of laughter, low-pitched and full of love for the woman who had inspired it with some unseen bit of mischief.

As if on cue, Walter chuckled from next door. He had arrived midafternoon on the first plane he could find, which meant a circuitous route through Atlanta and New Orleans. Now, after all this aggravation, it looked as though Sharlie were going to make it. Thank God, of course.

Brian stared up at his fake Spanish stucco ceiling and wondered if Walter and Margaret ever thought the horrible things he did, and if so, did they ever say them to each other?

Sharlie had caught him off guard in the early hours of the morning—was it only this morning? He had imagined that her reasons for refusing to get married would intensify with the augmented severity of her illness. Here she was, trembling on the brink of death, saying yes. Maybe she thought the end was imminent and wanted to make him feel that she was truly committed? No. He'd read in her face, swollen and unfamiliar as it was, the clear communication that she *wanted* to marry him. But Christ, how could they do it? That girl was no longer his Sharlie but some bizarre caricature, who now and then gave him a cruel, teasing glimpse of the person he had lost.

He'd marry her. He'd gotten himself so enmired that there was no way out now, not, at least, any way that would allow him to look in the mirror ever again. Her life would be short. His stomach heaved in self-disgust at the thought.

Anyway, by the time that happened, his career would be finished, at least with Barbara's firm. The generous leave of absence had long since run out, and her voice over the phone had become more and more remote, her conversation liberally laced with "Joe did this" and "Joe says that," Joe being the young man she'd hired to take Brian's place when Brian eventually took hers.

He turned over on his side, willing himself not to think about the cases he'd prepared so carefully, that still mattered despite the girl lying near death a couple of miles away. Joe could never invest the same emotional commitment into Brian's causes—he'd have causes of his own.

With the sense of resignation toward the future marriage to Sharlie came a new awareness of the element in his attachment to her that transcended even her deterioration—mysterious dovetailing of fates that felt so inevitable that Brian suddenly recognized that if he'd been born an aborigine in the outback of Australia, he'd nonetheless be lying here in this very bed tonight contemplating his marriage to Sharlie Converse.

Fnally, lulled by the monotonous murmuring from next door, he fell asleep and dreamed of Susan on the tennis court, serving him a ball that, as it whirled toward him, changed into a grinning jack-o'-latern.

CHAPTER 37

Margaret sat in the waiting room while Walter went into Sharlie's room alone. He came out a few moments later, and Margaret noticed with a shock how deeply the lines beside his mouth had eroded the square cheeks.

"She's . . ." he began, then lifted his hands helplessly. Margaret took his arm and drew him down the hall toward the elevators. "She's not our girl anymore, is she?" Walter said.

Margaret put her face against the rough wool of his sports jacket.

"We were wrong to do it," he went on.

"It didn't have to work out this way."

Walter shook his head numbly, and they walked into the evening heat of the parking lot. Margaret stopped him at the car and said, "Let me take you to a place I found." He gave her a puzzled look. "I'll tell you how to get there," she said, sliding into the passenger seat.

Soon they were driving along the rocky-coast road, which ran parallel to the Pacific about a mile inland. Here and there gnarled pine trees stood silhouetted against the darkening sky, their shadows like aged hands twisted by the wind off the sea. The twilight faded quickly, and by the time they turned left toward the sound of the ocean, it was dark and suddenly very windy. The road narrowed, barely wide enough now for one car. Long grass grew to the edge of the crumbling pavement, and it billowed wildly in the headlights' glare, scratching against the windows. In the tall weeds ahead, two small lights gleamed, and a cat flashed across the road, then disappeared into the grass so quickly that Walter wondered if it had been a shadow or some ghostly mirage. He glanced briefly at Margaret. She was staring straight ahead, and he found himself unwilling to break the silence.

The wind gusted so powerfully now that he struggled to keep on the narrow track. The sky had become a deep, murky black, but intermittently a beam flickered up ahead like heat lightning. The flashing intensified, and soon they emerged from the grass tunnel onto a flat, sandy expanse, dominated by the pale-gray shadow of a lighthouse. It loomed above them, casting its blazing circle into the night.

Walter stopped the car and looked at Margaret with awe in his face. Her eyes were shining. They got out and walked silently, arm in arm, toward the rush of the sea.

They watched the black waves curl into foam, smashing against the rocks. They were silent, hypnotized by the rhythmic recurrence of light against the darkness. After a long time Margaret began to shiver against Walter's shoulder, and they started back to the car.

Inside, Margaret smiled at him, a girlish, secret-sharing smile he'd long forgotten. Suddenly, before he had time to think, he blurted out, "I'm sorry, Margaret." Then he sat feeling foolish and confused. What was he apologizing for anyway?

Margaret picked up his hand where it lay tense and flat on the seat, and she pressed it hard against her wet cheek.

CHAPTER 38

Sharlie woke up at two o'clock in the morning feeling as if something deadly, a poisonous smog, had lifted from her body and floated out her window into the cool night. She put her hands to her cheeks and thought she could make out the lines of her cheekbones. She was flooded with memories of the scene in old movies where a kindly old doctor emerges from the sickroom to tell an anxious family that "the crisis has passed—little Jimmy will be all right." The compulsion to whoop with joy was tempered only by her awareness of the patients down the hall, whose tenuous grip on life might snap if they were to hear a great, victorious shout from Room 841. She reached for the phone instead.

It took a dozen rings before Brian's voice mumbled on the other end. She pictured his hair all pressed down against his forehead, making him look like a little boy. He had told her that he slept facedown, and imagining his head burrowed into his pillow, she marveled that he didn't suffocate in the night.

"What happens is this, Bri," she said into the phone. "You can sleep on your face because when the sun goes down, you grow gills and breathe through your armpits. I don't know why I didn't figure it out before."

"Ungh erm," said Brian groggily.

Sharlie went on in her wide-awake voice. "You even talk like something that lives underwater."

"Sharlie?" He was beginning to wake up.

She said, "Except that you do sleep in the daytime too, sometimes. Maybe it doesn't have anything to do with the sunset. Maybe it's your alpha waves that trigger the gill response. You think?"

"What time is it?" he murmured.

"I'm not going to tell you because you'll pull all my plugs. But you saved at least one life by picking up the phone."

"Yours?"

"No, the lady in 831, who would have died of fright when she heard me scream at the top of my lungs that I FEEL FANTASTIC!" Instantly she was whispering again. "But I had to tell somebody."

Brian asked, "Who's on the desk?"

"I don't know. Vinnie, I guess."

"I'm coming over."

"You can't. . . ."

But the phone clicked, and Sharlie lay there with the receiver buzzing, cradled against her cheek.

She must have fallen asleep for a few minutes, because it seemed as if she'd just gotten off the phone and now there was somebody crawling under her sheet.

"Brian!" she whispered. "How did you ever get in here at this hour?"

He kissed her to keep her quiet. It had been a long time since they'd really kissed each other, and once they got started, her curiosity about hospital security began to feel irrelevant. Brian ran his hands down her backbone and said, "You could use a pizza."

She moaned. "Oh, pizza . . ."

"You'll have one for breakfast," he said and kissed her again, murmuring something about oral gratification.

"They're going to catch us," she protested, as he moved his hand along her side and down her hip.

"The shame of it. Think they'll make us get married?"

"Oh, my," she said.

"Oh, your what?" he muttered, but he didn't let her answer.

Margaret and Walter held hands as they entered Sharlie's room. They stood beside her bed and waited for her to open her eyes, enjoying the sound of her easy breathing. Finally she looked up at them but then quickly turned her head aside to face the wall.

"What's the matter, Chuck?" Walter asked.

There was no response.

"Are you all right, darling?" Margaret pressed.

Silence. Margaret looked up at Walter in alarm and whispered, "We'd better call the nurse."

Sharlie turned her head to glare at them. "Don't," she said. "Just get out."

Walter made a shocked, choking sound that was almost a laugh. But Margaret heard the fury in her daughter's voice and began to move away from the

bed, pulling Walter by the hand. After they had left,
Sharlie stared at the center of her door where the image of their bewildered faces lingered, until finally
the rage in her eyes turned to fear, and she began to
cry.

Sharlie sat in her wheelchair looking out Dr. Rosen's window. Today the view behind the soft red hair
was blurred with rain. The tree limbs bowed under
the heavy downpour, and Sharlie felt warm and safe
in the cluttered room.

"Have the side effects of the medication disappeared?" Dr. Rosen was asking.

Sharlie nodded. The doctor watched the reflection
from the window wash waves of shadows across her
patient's face.

"Then how do you account for the episode?"

Sharlie sat withdrawn inside her clouded face.

"It's unusual for a postoperative reaction to occur at
this late date," Dr. Rosen pressed.

Sharlie nodded again but kept her face averted.

"What is it, Charlotte?"

Sharlie's eyes fastened on the doctor for a moment,
their dark light disturbing the pale fragility of her
face.

"If I told you, you'd lock me up," she answered
softly.

"I doubt it. Try me."

Sharlie opened her mouth, attempting unsuccess-
fully to speak, then smiled, embarrassed. "I *know* it's
ridiculous. But I can't persuade my head."

Dr. Rosen waited, and Sharlie faltered, "I think, I
mean, I *believe* that . . . that man is affecting what I
do."

"You mean the donor."

Sharlie nodded.

"How?"

"By being inside."

"No," said Dr. Rosen. "How affecting what you do?"

"I get this swelling feeling like I'm all hot and bursting and I can't control it. It's not just my parents. I was dreadful to poor Dr. Diller." Her face flamed with mortification. "My God, the man saved my life. He performed a miracle for me, and I humiliated him in front of all those people."

"What about throwing the newspaper at Brian? Was that you or the donor?"

"Him," Sharlie said firmly, then with a small, frightened smile. "I'm losing my grip, aren't I?" But her eyes weren't smiling, and Dr. Rosen recognized the terror in them. Sharlie didn't wait for an answer, just kept on talking now, the words pouring out and tumbling over one another like too many hatboxes when the closet door is finally opened.

"The rejection, I think I did that to myself. It seemed like I had to get rid of him or make some kind of compromise and accept him as part of me, and I couldn't do that, and my body knew, and even now I don't see how I can live with this. I mean, the man was a homicidal maniac, and how am I supposed to cope with that? Even when I didn't know for a fact I still had this creepy . . . communion. Oh, it sounds so ludicrous, I feel like a perfect asshole. . . ." She looked up at Dr. Rosen in surprise. "I never used that word in my life. Excuse me."

"How did it feel, saying it out loud?"

Sharlie gave her a shy smile, but instantly fear replaced it, darkening her face. "Where is this going to take me? That man was crazy."

Dr. Rosen's voice was soft. "Charlotte, most transplant patients have strong emotional responses to their operations. Some, like you, experience a feeling of identification with their donors. The adjustment takes time. Give yourself a chance to heal. Don't fight it. You can damage yourself."

Sharlie looked thoughtful. The rain had tapered off, and the shadow from the gardenia tree reached through the window to cast a dark web across the girl's face.

"Are you angry with your parents?" Dr. Rosen asked.

Sharlie's eyes were wet. "They've kept me alive. They've given up so much."

"But are you angry with them?"

"How could I be?" Sharlie whispered.

"Do you still plan to get married?" Sharlie's face lifted a little, and the psychiatrist smiled. "Well, then?"

Sharlie smiled back. "Well, then . . ."

The room seemed to be a kind of ballroom, an expanse of polished floor and a balcony along three walls suspended halfway to the lofty ceiling. Benches with red plush cushions were set in rows. Cologned, clean-shaven men sat beside women in flowered hats. At the front of the hall was a stage or altar, upon which, pushed to one side, stood a shiny black coffin. It was open, and she reclined inside it, head raised on a satin pillow so that she could watch the proceedings. Organ music played softly—Bach's "Sheep May Safely Graze"—and then it suddenly swelled, and all the guests rose, turning toward the entrance behind them. At first she didn't recognize the music, but then she realized it was the Wedding March, only distorted into a minor key and played very slowly.

Brain appeared in the doorway, and she sat up in the coffin, watching him approach her, straight and handsome, a young woman holding his arm and leaning against him. She was blond and suntanned and glowing, and instead of flowers, she carried a bouquet of diminutive tennis racquets.

When they reached the altar, Brian glanced at Sharlie, who gazed at him from her satin perch. His face was fond, as if to say, "I'm glad you're here to share my happiness, dear friend." Sharlie smiled back at him, her throat constricted with longing. Then Brian turned to his bride and kissed her.

Sharlie awoke into the semidarkness of her room and spent the rest of the night watching her window change from black to gray and finally to the reassuring clear blue of daylight.

CHAPTER 39

The prospect of a wedding sent the medical center into an upheaval unlike anything since Dr. Lewis's first successful transplant operation. Everyone wanted to get into the act, from the chief of surgery himself down to the people who cleaned garbage cans in the kitchen.

"It's like I'm royalty or something," Sharlie complained unconvincingly to Mary MacDonald. They were in the solarium leafing through *Bride* magazine. Mary stopped at a photograph of an emaciated mannequin in a severe white gown.

"This one looks like she could use a transplant herself," she muttered.

"Queen of Hearts," Sharlie said dreamily.

"Come on, concentrate," Mary said. "You're going to be walking down the aisle in your birthday suit at this rate."

"Brian would like that."

Sharlie stood and cinched her hospital gown at the waist, pirouetting. "Maybe I'll wear this. . . ."

"My ass you'll wear that," Mary grumbled.

"One would think you weren't enjoying this, Mary. Maybe I ought to elope."

"Just you try it, my girl," Mary said menacingly, and Sharlie grinned at her.

Vinnie arrived with a tray of medications for Sharlie. "Is it true we're all going to come?" The young nurse was seven months pregnant and moved awkwardly.

"They're going to work out a rotating schedule," Sharlie said, swallowing a blue capsule, "so everybody can stay for part of the ceremony. We're making it *extra* long."

"It's so wonderful," Vinnie chattered as she poured out another cup of water for Sharlie. "I bet they do your life story on television or something. I mean, it's so fantastic. I bet the guy's mother is really happy. It makes up a little for what he did. . . ."

Mary's head snapped up from the magazine, and she gave Vinnie a ferocious look.

"I'm sorry. I forgot. . . . I didn't mean—"

Mary broke in, "Give Miss Converse her medication and get out, please."

Vinnie seemed to be paralyzed, so Mary grabbed the pills and yelled, "*Move,* girl."

Sharlie swallowed automatically, her eyes wide. Vinnie rushed out. She tripped at the doorway, nearly spilling her tray. Mary and Sharlie sat absolutely still, like overgrown children playing statue. Neither looked at the other until finally Mary breathed a heavy sigh.

"I don't suppose we can forget that."

"Yes, let's," Sharlie said.

She still clutched her hospital gown at the waist, and now she released it, leaving soggy clumps of wrinkles where her hands had bunched the material. She sat down on the edge of the couch, and Mary began to clear away the piles of magazines that lay open on the coffee table. "I won't have you going all morbid on me," Mary said. "Not just before your wedding day. You just remember that what you got from that poor tortured creature was a hunk of muscle and nothing more."

She lifted Sharlie by the arm, and they walked to her room in silence. Then she helped her into bed. "You thank heaven for the gift of a healthy new heart and forget the package it came in."

She pulled the curtain, and the room turned soft gray. She stood in the doorway a moment, looking at Sharlie's face as she stared wide-eyed at the ceiling.

"You hear me?" Mary called. "Sharlie?"

Sharlie said, "Yes. Don't worry. I'll be all right." But she didn't move her eyes a fraction and never noticed when Mary finally shook her head and left, closing the door quietly behind her.

They now allowed Sharlie to stroll on the grounds, provided she wore a gauze mask and always kept someone with her. Occasionally she would spot another masked face and that made her feel less self-conscious.

This afternoon she had tired quickly, so Brian spread his jacket on the grass, and they sat while he told her about yesterday's trip to Los Angeles. Ordinarily Barbara would have refused the case, since it was destined for trial in California. But it involved a film producer's unauthorized use of material written by a young woman screenwriter, and with Brian in Santa Bel, Barbara was delighted to leap headfirst into the action. Brian was secretly grateful for the chance to get back to work and away from the oppressive atmosphere of the medical center.

"I stopped by at a supermarket in Beverly Hills," he was saying, "and there was this old lady by the cornflakes. She must have been eighty-five, with a shiny gold jump suit thing—skintight—and Plexiglas sandals, and she had all this blue-white varnished hair that looked stiff enough to hang coats from and these huge hairy false eyelashes. And, I'm not kidding, she was shuffling down the aisle between the cereal and the lettuce with a *walker*."

Sharlie giggled and leaned against him. "Can we go there for our honeymoon? I'll sew sequins all over my mask."

"How long are you going to have to wear that thing?" he asked.

"Don't know," she answered. "I think I'll hang on to it and maintain the mystery in our marriage, you know? The masked wife. You'll always wonder what's underneath—whether I've lost all my teeth, maybe I've grown a moustache . . ."

"No, really," he said. She reached up to unhook the mask, and he put his hand over hers to stop her.

"Brian," she said softly, "I'm never going to be very much like your everyday blushing bride."

"Thank God," he said. But his eyes looked past her to the hospital gate.

"Hey," she said, poking him lightly to get him to look at her. "We've got options. We can live together and see how it goes. We can *not* live together. We can

get married later. We can meet every Saturday night
at a singles bar. . . ." She was thankful for the gauze,
which she hoped would muffle the trembling in her
voice. He looked into the eyes that read his thoughts.
Then he cupped his hands around her face.

"Look, I've never gotten married before. Can't I
have a few standard prenuptial jitters?"

"Are you sure that's what they are?" She unhooked
her mask deliberately. "My germs are going to have to
learn to live with your germs." He kissed her, and her
body relaxed against him. Then he slipped the mask
back on and pulled her to her feet. As they walked
back toward the hospital entrance, he told her about
the shopping-bag lady he'd seen who drove around
Los Angeles in a beat-up Dodge crammed to the
rusted roof with tiny pieces of paper and old scraps of
rags, how, in California, even the crazies need wheels.
Sharlie listened to him happily and told herself she
didn't care what happened to her as long as she had
just a few days married to him.

Diller stood next to Sharlie's bed, listening to her
heart with his stethoscope. He watched her warily, as
if at any moment she might turn mad and stab him
with her letter opener. Sharlie saw his eyes linger on
the tapered instrument and smiled. It was sterling silver and elegantly monogrammed with the initials
CCM, a wedding gift from Barbara Kaye. Sharlie
hoped she'd get a chance to use it soon on something
other than envelopes marked "Occupant," since the
only letters she'd ever gotten were from Margaret,
sent from down the street, or postcards from Walter's
trips, to cheer her up when she'd been in Saint Joe's
too long.

Dr. Diller slid the silver disk under her left breast and dropped his head, concentrating on the thumps from inside her chest. Despite Sharlie's regret for embarrassing him, she was amused by the surgeon's cautious respect. Since her public outburst, he no longer brushed off her hesitant inquiries, and it was now easier to ask questions.

"What do you think? Is there going to be a wedding?"

Diller stood away from the bed and offered her a cool smile. "As far as I'm concerned, yes," he said. "I've told you the conditions."

"Will you come?"

Diller was a literal man who carefully memorized other people's jokes and used them in speeches at benefits. He had little patience with humor, but had learned through experience that Sharlie was not always entirely serious. He searched her pale face now and saw only entreaty there.

"Please come," she repeated.

She held out her hand to him, and finally he took it. For a moment Diller looked at the pretty girl on the bed and felt his life touched by hers. He gripped her hand tightly, and then suddenly she was Walter Converse's daughter again, valuable as a potential sponsor for his research program. Sharlie watched the detachment move into his face and change his eyes to ice again, but she remembered the brief thaw and was pleased.

After he'd left, it occurred to her that she had never seen Diller really smile. He could manage a tense curvature of the lips, but the stiff arc did nothing to light up his eyes or lift the other muscles of his face. She remembered the drawings she used to make as a child—round faces with great sad eyes and a straight line for the mouth. Margaret would take a look and say, "That's very nice, dear," in her automatic voice, but Walter invariably burst out, "Christ! Can't you put a smile on the thing? Looks like a goddamn mortician." After a while she began to put the curved mouth on her faces before Walter got to them. A few months ago she'd dug one of the childhood scribbles out of her mother's desk drawer, and the face seemed horrible to her—terrified eyes, anxious eyebrows, and the hideous crescent grin. So much like Diller—a cartoon face in which only the mouth changed positions, a mechanical twitch.

That's why he's so intimidating, she thought suddenly. That solemn expression always made her wonder what offense she'd committed: Had she forgotten her green pills? Sneak a nibble from somebody's banana cream pie?

Maybe if Sharlie did what he did all day, she wouldn't be able to smile either. Hands stuffed down into some poor slob's chest, holding the future quite literally in his fingers. She would make it her particular goal to see if she could persuade the stiff old thing to smile. Maybe at the wedding, if they pumped him full of champagne and surrounded him with a dozen adoring nurses.

Smiling was an admission of one's humanity, an acknowledgment of being touched by someone else, a response to the world. Diller made smiling seem like a weakness, other people's grinning faces contemptible and childish. There's nothing funny about science, he was saying with that sober expression, or about disease or the origin of the universe. Life is serious, this medical center is serious, and A. Carlton Diller is serious. Untouchable, inaccessible man—that's why she was always trying to entertain him, to charm him.

Well, what the hell, she smiled all too much anyway. How pleasing to just relax her facial muscles and frown to her heart's content. Excuse, please. To *his* heart's content. How much had her donor, poor Martin Udstrom, smiled in his lifetime, after all? Probably only in the midst of committing some heinous sadistic act.

She decided to try it out on the next person who walked into the room. Not one twitch of a smile, and she'd discover if she could suddenly become a figure of vast authority like Diller.

CHAPTER 40

Brian drove more slowly than usual. Barbara must be pacing the airport lobby, chain-smoking and glancing at her watch every thirty seconds with that quick gesture—arm stretched to push back the sleeve, then crooked back so she could see the large face of her watch, a man's size, so that she wouldn't have to put on the hated glasses to find out what time it was.

Sharlie's the same, he thought, stopping for an amber light, which he would ordinarily have sped through. He smiled at the improbability of any resemblance between them. But Sharlie, too, preferred to squint rather than submit to her own myopia. The first time he'd caught her in glasses was at the movies, when she'd been forced to surrender to the subtitles of *Swept Away*. She'd slipped them on surreptitiously and whipped them off again before the credits had finished. She responded to his teasing by maintaining that the world seemed more palatable just slightly blurred. And besides, she'd protested, indicating a nearby apartment house, wasn't it more tantalizing to read Superior Promises than Supt. on Premises?

Oh, yes, he thought, pulling into the parking area of the airport. Let's just sit here in the car and think about Sharlie. Maybe the boss missed her connection in Chicago.

But Barbara was standing by the telephones, exuding clouds of smoke from her Lucky Strikes. Brian, striding toward her, thought uncomfortably that she looked a lot like Mount Etna.

"Hello, dear," she said, reaching to give him a cool kiss on the cheek. "Traffic?"

He nodded, and decided he was better off not apologizing. "Good trip?" he asked, picking up her suitcase and leading her toward the glass doors.

"Shitty, thank you," she said. "Why do they assault us with those asinine occult films when there's no way to escape except by jumping out at thirty-five thousand feet? Really, I don't find prepubescents who use their brain waves to knock down walls and lop off their parents' extremities particularly diverting."

"You don't have to watch," Brian said.

"Oh, come on, with all those jerks oo-ing and ahh-ing up and down the aisle? Irresistible."

"First Amendment," Brian said, smiling and opening the car door for her. She rolled her eyes at him and slid into the passenger seat. They were silent until they got to the exit toll booth. A tall brown-skinned blond took Brian's ticket and told him he owed eighty-five cents. He paid, and as they pulled away, Barbara said, "Why is it everybody in the godforsaken state is so fucking wholesome?"

"You'll get used to it," Brian said.

"I won't be around long enough to get used to it."

They were silent again until finally Brian said, "Thanks for coming. I appreciate it."

Barbara lit another cigarette. "Don't mention it. Your father going to be here?" Brian shook his head, and she looked at him closely. "I guess if you're a farmer, it's tough to write off a trip to California as a business expense."

Brian was silent.

"You did tell him you were getting married," she said.

He didn't answer.

"Now that is unconscionable."

Brian heard the combativeness rising and cut her off quickly. "Hey, look, I'll send him a note in a couple of weeks."

She shifted in her seat, visibly working to restrain her displeasure. "Are you taking a honeymoon?"

"The weekend. We're not going anywhere."

"Oh," Barbara said. Brian heard the effort to sound indifferent.

"I hope to be back in the office within ten days," he said. "It depends on how she weathers the excitement."

"Oh," Barbara said again.

Brian laughed and said, "You know, I'm so glad to see you."

"You sound surprised."

"What I meant was, you should have canned me."

"I admit the thought has occurred to me now and then."

"I was wondering if maybe you had it in mind this trip," he said slowly.

"Don't be a schmuck."

"No, Barbara. I don't know what's going to happen."

She interrupted him again. "Shit, whoever knows what's going to happen to anybody? We'll manage."

They stopped at a traffic light, and he turned to her. "You have been, you *are* the most incredible—"

"Shut up," she said tersely. Brian accelerated as the light changed to green. Her last words had sounded genuinely angry, but after a moment she murmured disconsolately, "I was looking forward to getting a peek at your daddy. Who knows? I might have spent my twilight years with the old codger, out in the boondocks."

Brian laughed, imagining Barbara sloshing through the mud in her Guccis, pitchfork in one hand, cigarette in the other.

She peered at him. "That's the look of a happy groom. You *are* a happy groom?"

He nodded.

"Sure?" Her voice was soft and concerned. Brian swallowed against the sudden tight place in his throat.

"Hey, Morgan," she went on briskly, "I don't want to get you pissed off at me, but I did come three thousand miles, and that gives me a certain latitude. You doing this crazy thing for the right reasons?"

"Are there any?" he asked.

She shook her head and laid her hand on his arm. "Just want you to be a happy kid," she said lightly.

CHAPTER 41

The hospital chapel was spilling over with flowers. Walter had rounded up a hundred white roses, but the nurses thought the effect was too sterile and colorless. They raided the day's crop of incoming bouquets—a rose from this vase, a bird-of-paradise from that—and confiscated the leftovers from those patients who had checked out. The effect was startling, as if someone had joyously flung a wild assortment of color against the altar.

Spectators crammed the aisles. The hospital staff, dressed in white or green, far outnumbered friends and relatives, but some of the nurses had pinned flowers in their hair, and the doctors wore makeshift boutonnieres. Walter had chosen a pale-pink shirt, and when Sharlie touched his collar with pleasure, he smiled sheepishly, proud of his flamboyance. Margaret, preoccupied but stunning in a raw silk silver-gray suit, stared blankly down the hall away from the chapel entrance. Sharlie stood trembling in her white

dress, face feverish, eyes shining. Over the protesta-
tions of Mary MacDonald, she had chosen a very simple, long-sleeved, high-collared gown that fell in soft
folds to midcalf. She wore no veil, but gathered her
hair back and pinned it with a gardenia. She peered
through the chapel door, eyes widening at the sight of
so many people waiting to watch her march to the altar. She put her open palms against her cheeks and
started talking in long, compulsive streams.

"I hope they have an extra donor hanging around
OR. I don't think Udstrom's going to make it through
this. Oh, Lord, please don't let Mary play 'Here Comes
the Bride.' She *promised*, but I know she's gonna do
it, I just know it, and I pleaded with her for some nice
stately Bach. . . . Mother?"

She watched Margaret forcibly withdraw her gaze
from some far-off place.

"What *are* you thinking about, Mother?"

Margaret's smile was so remote that Sharlie just
shook her head and clutched at her bouquet. She'd
insisted on pink roses because too much white was
boring, and secretly she imagined the red ones looked
like a splotch of blood against her dress. When she'd
ordered the pink ones, that's when Walter had crept
out to the department store to buy his fancy pink
shirt. With French cuffs, no less, so he'd bought a pair
of gold cufflinks as well.

Mary had begun to play the preprocessional music
they'd agreed on. Sharlie, finally silent, stared up at
her father as he stepped closer to her to give her his
arm.

"Well, Chuck . . ." He was smiling. Sharlie felt the
tears beginning. She blinked hard, took her father's
arm with one hand, her mother's with the other. As

they passed through the doorway, the quiet music swelled into resounding chords. The guests stood and turned toward the rear of the chapel, and the strains of "Here Comes the Bride" bellowed forth from beneath the stubby fingers of Mary MacDonald. Sharlie groaned, and looked toward the altar. Without squinting, she could make out Brian's tall form, resplendent in his new dark-blue suit.

The ceremony was a blur, but she remembered a few isolated details—the honeybee that flew in the window and cheerfully dive-bombed the roses behind the minister; the curly brown hair at the collar of Brian's shirt, so reassuringly familiar; the warm glimmer of the rings, slipping easily onto fingers stretched toward one another, fingers that didn't seem to be attached to anyone she knew. There was an intensity to these images and yet a fuzziness overall, as if the event itself weren't really happening, only little pieces of it—bright, sparkling mosaics that didn't fit together cohesively but were beautiful and astonishing on their own.

After what seemed like both a moment and many hours it was all over, and they were striding down the aisle, laughing and elated, past the grinning faces of the crowd.

At the reception the fact that they were married began to come into focus (perhaps, Sharlie thought wryly, because she'd finally relented and put on her glasses). And so many people took her hand and congratulated her that after a while she began to believe something momentous had happened.

It was hot, but they had decided to forgo air conditioning in order to celebrate on the grounds outside the solarium. In the midst of the initial flurry Mary

MacDonald, her perspiring face glowing pink, pulled her aside and said, "I'm sorry, I tried. I did. But when the time came and I saw the doors open and your face there with your parents, well, I couldn't help it. It was sacrilegious to play anything else, and my fingers just . . ."

Sharlie implanted an enthusiastic kiss on the flushed cheek. "You were wonderful."

But Brian grabbed his new bride's arm and pulled her around to face Barbara Kaye.

"Very nice," the older woman said with an appraising smile.

Sharlie smiled back, not knowing exactly what Barbara thought was "very nice." "Brian's missed you," she blurted, and then looked helplessly at her husband. "I'm sorry, is what I mean," she went on. Barbara looked confused. "I mean, that I kept him away from the office. With all this . . ." Barbara took her hand, and Sharlie wondered how a person with normal circulation could possess such a cool, unsweaty palm on a day like this.

Meanwhile Brian, out of the corner of his eye, spied Walter approaching, holding two glasses of champagne. He was already at Brian's shoulder before he suddenly recognized Barbara and stopped in his tracks. But Barbara had seen him also. Brian watched her expression take on a familiar delighted pugnacity.

"Hello, Mister Converse," she said, her voice carefully respectful except for the slightest stress on the *mister*. Walter stuck his hand out automatically, forgetting about the champagne. It spilled out over Barbara's pale-beige skirt, leaving a dark stain in the expensive fabric.

"Oh, Christ," Walter said, handing Brian the other glass and swiping at the mess with his handkerchief.

"You make a habit of raining on my parade, don't you?" Barbara said.

"Send me the cleaning bill," Walter muttered, wadding up the handkerchief and stuffing it into his pocket.

"It doesn't matter, really," Barbara said. And to their astonishment she began to unzip the skirt and pull it down over her hips. The silken material folded into a neat little bundle, which she crammed in her handbag. She stood regarding Walter, triumphant in her tennis shorts.

"I've got a T-shirt under this," she said, lifting a corner of her elegant blouse. Walter snorted in admiration.

"Jason Lewis challenged me to a game after the reception. I hear this place has pretty decent courts."

"You any good?" Walter asked.

"I could make you run."

"I'll just bet you would," he said, smiling.

"I have a whole pile of prehistoric bones to pick with you," Barbara said.

Walter took her by the arm and nodded at Brian and Sharlie. "Excuse us. I owe this lady a glass of champagne."

They walked away, leaving the newlyweds openmouthed behind them.

Once the initial crush of well-wishers had dissipated, people began to settle into comfortable knots of three and four, some sitting barefoot on the grass with faces lifted to the sunshine. Brian and Sharlie, in

their first moment alone together, stood watching
them happily when Dr. Diller suddenly appeared,
champagne glass in one hand, the arm of a leggy redhead in the other.

"Back to work," he said to Sharlie. "Just wanted to
offer my congratulations in person."

"If it weren't for you, I wouldn't be standing here,
much less married."

Diller shook his head self-deprecatingly, aware of
the green eyes at his shoulder that never left his face
for an instant. He raised his glass.

"To Sharlene—long and healthy wedded bliss." He
drained his glass, showed them his dazzling teeth with
an automatic smile, and strode off toward the solarium, redhead in tow.

"Doesn't count," Sharlie murmured, but before
Brian could ask what she meant, two X-ray technicians descended upon them, offering their slightly
drunken felicitations.

Soon after that, Mary MacDonald reappeared.
Brian had gone off to see if he could dig up a beer,
leaving Sharlie with one of the nurses from ICU.
Without interrupting the conversation, Mary took
Sharlie's hand. Sharlie felt the pudgy fingers slip toward her wrist and knew that her old friend was making a quick pulse check.

"Honeymoon time," Mary said, looking around.
"Where's your husband?"

Sharlie echoed, "Husband . . ." as if the word
weren't part of her vocabulary.

"Sadie, Sadie, married lady," the ICU nurse said.
Sharlie smiled, her eyes searching the clusters of
guests until she located Brian's curly head.

As they drove through the gate, trailing a noisy assortment of tin cans and instrument trays from their rear bumper, Sharlie began to experience real panic. Severed from this place that had sustained her during so many crises, where she'd been nurtured by life-giving machines, attached by complex electronic umbilical cords, she was free, at least for the weekend. What on earth would they do if something happened to her so far away from the mysterious wizardry of the medical center?

She stared at Brian, and he took his eyes off the road for a moment to look back at her. His eyes reflected hers perfectly—dazed, bewildered, and terrified.

"Well, that makes two of us," she said, laughing.

The hotel was only just outside of town. Brian made Sharlie lie down on the bed as soon as the bellhop disappeared.

"To sleep," he said.

"Perchance to dream," she murmured groggily. "I couldn't possibly. I'm much too hyped up. . . ."

He sat on the edge of the bed and watched her eyelids droop.

"I'm going to squish my beautiful dress," she said, eyes closed. "Oh, well, maybe I'll just rest for a minute. . . ."

Brian stayed next to her for a long time. She looked to him like the lovely princess who slept under the glass dome until Prince Charming finally showed up. What was it, Snow White? As he looked down at her, it seemed as though the faint aroma of flowers rose from her body as she breathed. His gratitude at having her all to himself made him feel fierce, and he imagined himself roaring and beating his chest like some primitive jungle beast. *Mine. She's mine, and no visiting hours or resident or nurse or even death will snatch her away from me today.*

CHAPTER 42

She slept for two hours without moving, her face so still that Brian watched carefully to make sure she was breathing. Finally she stirred and opened her eyes.

She never seemed surprised to see him there beside her when she awoke, even after anesthesia or a long period of lying unconscious. As usual, she started talking as if they were in mid-conversation.

"I love you with all his heart," she said solemnly.

He laughed, and leaned down to kiss her.

She held his head near her face. "What was that lecture you got from Diller after the ceremony?"

"He said I shouldn't let the operation stand in the way of a normal sex life," Brian answered. "To be unintimidated, unabashed, unrestrained, et cetera, et cetera. That the only thing to fear was fear itself."

"How come he didn't tell *me* that?"

"Because you're the sweet young virgin bride."

"Uh huh," she said, pulling him down for another

kiss. After a moment she extricated herself from underneath him and disappeared into the bathroom. Suddenly Brian heard her cry out.

"Sharlie?" he called. She didn't respond, so he got up and opened the bathroom door. She was standing in front of the mirror in only her bikini pants, her dress in a heap around her ankles. She was sobbing into her hands, and when he tried to pry them away from her face, she held them there as tightly as she could, refusing to look at him.

After several minutes of gentle but unsuccessful prodding, he finally almost shouted at her. "Now cut it out and tell me what's the matter."

She dropped her arms and lifted her anguished face to him. "Look at me," she said, and her voice rose to a scream. "Look what they did to me!" She held her arms out. The livid scar sliced from her throat down to her abdomen.

Brian reached for her. "Honey . . ." he said softly, but she fell in a crouch to the floor, doubling over to hide her disfigurement. He stroked her back until she was quiet.

"Haven't you ever seen yourself before?"

She shook her head, face hidden.

"Well, I've seen you," he said. "More than once."

"I look like the Bride of Frankenstein," she said in a muffled voice.

He ran his finger down her spine. "Your battle scar is indelibly etched into my most tantalizing sexual fantasies."

He heard her choke. She muttered, "Don't make me laugh. I don't feel like laughing." Then she sniffed and said, "Hand me some toilet paper, will you? My nose is dripping on the floor."

"Postnasal drip does not qualify as a tantalizing sexual fantasy," he said, handing her the tissue.

She wiped her nose and looked up at him with a red face, eyelashes matted together with tears. "I think I'm stuck," she said, trying to unbend. Brian stood behind her and lifted her by the arms. She was very light.

"Okay. Let's look." He turned her around to face the mirror, and she stared at herself with revulsion. Then she pulled away from him and went into the bedroom to wrap herself up in a bathrobe.

In the middle of the night she woke him, talking in her sleep. She was thrashing back and forth and hit him sharply in the shoulder with her fist.

"How come they always, they always, always . . ." she was murmuring. Finally Brian shook her arm gently. For once, she woke up disoriented. She stared blankly at him in the dim light, and he could see the confusion in her eyes. The shadows made them look haunted and wild.

"Do you remember what it was?" he whispered.

She shook her head. "Not exactly. But it was about . . ." She hesitated. "Brian, would you mind turning on the light for a minute?"

He leaned over her and flicked on the lamp. They both blinked in the sudden glare, but some of the fright passed away from her face, and her rigid body began to relax under his hand.

"About what?" he asked again.

"Just crazy nightmares. It's probably the drugs."

Brian held her next to him. Her body was soft, and he began to run his hands along her back. He kissed her but she was stiff and unresponsive.

"I'm sorry," she said.

"Sharlie . . ." he began, then stopped, trying to silence his frustration.

"I'm not the same person I was before," she said.

"I'm telling you that you are the same. Exactly. Except that you've got warm feet and a ribbon down your front. And a future."

She had turned her face away. After a moment he said, "Goddammit," and got up to go to the bathroom. When he came back, the light was off, and she was curled into a little ball with her back to his side of the bed.

The next morning Sharlie woke up early. Last night's nightmare seemed unimportant now, and she was relaxed and drowsy and delighted to begin the morning in a nonhospital bed next to Brian. His hand moved against her breast in his sleep. She took his palm and moved it gently back and forth, feeling her nipples stiffen. Then she got out of bed and went to the bathroom to brush her teeth and swallow her six-A.M. medication.

When she crawled back into the warm spot beside him, he was beginning to wake up. She pressed herself to him, kissing him until he reached out an arm and encircled her.

"You smell wide awake," he murmured.

"Pepsodent," she said, pushing her tongue between his teeth.

He yawned. "I'd better go brush mine if I'm going to kiss you."

"No," she said, holding him down with a leg draped across his knees. He stroked her body, first along the hip and down the outside of her thigh, and then, gently prodding with his hand, felt the softness between her legs. The hair was silky and fine, like the hair on her head, but a paler color, ashy gray. He felt her flesh grow damp and swollen under his fingers, and her legs fell apart now without urging. She arched her back, reaching toward his hand with her hips. For a moment she opened her eyes to look at him. He smiled at her, and she whispered, "Oh, my goodness," and closed her eyes again.

Her breathing grew rapid, and Brian held his hand still, frightened by her gasps. But she moved against him and murmured, "Don't stop." Suddenly her body shuddered, and she cried out, "Bri . . ." never completing his name. She reached for him, curling against his chest in exhaustion. He stroked her hair, and after a while she said matter-of-factly, "Well, I'm not dead."

"No," he said fervently.

"Now I'm supposed to say I can give it all up and pass uncomplainingly into the great beyond. Now that I've had this experience."

"Oh, yeah?" he said.

"I think I'd just as soon stick around and try it again."

He laughed. Her knee rubbed up against his penis. It was hard, and she touched it tentatively with her fingers.

"There's somebody else in here with us," she whispered.

"I know."

"He's taking up practically the whole bed," she said, holding him in her hand.

"Flatterer," he said.

"You know, it's funny." She propped herself up on one elbow to look at his penis curiously. "I felt inside like you look outside. Do women get erections?"

"Hmm?" he said dreamily.

"Oh, do come in," she said, letting go of him and hooking her leg around his hips.

He swung around, holding himself over her with his arms for fear of crushing her. He entered her gently, watching her face. She seemed to grimace, so he stopped instantly.

"Am I hurting you?"

"No." She shifted her hips and grimaced again.

"You sure?"

"It's not pain. It's . . ." Her eyes began to fill with tears, and she smiled up at him. "Together. I'm so happy." She urged him further inside with her legs.

"Oh, God, Sharlie," he said softly, and found that he was crying, too, as they pressed against each other over and over again until they lay exhausted and sticky on the rumpled bed.

Diller had insisted that the honeymoon be local and brief and that Sharlie check back into the hospital in three days. By the time Tuesday morning arrived, both Brian and Sharlie were secretly ready for a respite from each other. Brian delivered her to the nurse's station on the eighth floor, and she gave him a kiss.

"Come and get me at dinnertime."

"You sure you don't want me to wait around?" he asked.

She shoved him toward the elevator. "Go," she said. "You'll find something to do."

Brian turned around just before he stepped into the elevator. She was watching him. She made a face, and the doors closed.

On his way down to the lobby Brian decided that the worst thing to do was analyze the situation. What's one weekend in a hotel room three thousand miles from home with somebody who just got out of the hospital? Hardly representative of his future married years. He had stared at Sharlie so intensely these past three days that now he could hardly imagine her face—like back in high school when he'd replayed a favorite record over and over again until eventually it became so ingrained that it lost its impact. He'd listened the song into meaninglessness just as he'd stared Sharlie into a mosaic of memorized lifeless features.

Some people stay married for fifty years. He'd thought of that this morning as he gazed at her sleeping face on the pillow. Was she going to be with him *all the time*?

He thought he'd seen relief on her face, too, when he dropped her off. Maybe it was like this at first for everybody.

He pulled the car out of the hospital lot and turned toward the beach road, figuring he'd spend the whole day as far from people and as close to the sea as he possibly could. Water and sky. Space.

What must she be feeling? She seemed preoccupied so much of the time, and he almost felt that she was listening to a voice he couldn't hear. He'd urge her to talk to Dr. Rosen.

The rest of the way to the beach he thought about the legal complexities of the Los Angeles case. He was supposed to go to L.A. at the end of the week for settlement discussions. Maybe he'd make the trip on his own. Oh, hell, he thought. Four days married, and I'm already plotting to run away.

He parked the car and slid down a rocky embankment to the narrow strip of beach. He would lie by the water and stare into the future so that whatever happened, he'd be prepared, or resigned, or maybe even pleased.

He took off his shoes and socks, burrowed his back into the warm sand, and stared up at the pale-aqua sky. And planned. He visualized the possibilities in outline form—cool, measured, logical:

A. Sharlie is pronounced well. Thus:
1. They would proceed to Los Angeles on Thursday. He would appear in court on Friday morning.
2. They would mess around L.A. on Saturday (maybe Disneyland; she'd like that).
3. Back to New York on Sunday. Unbelievable.

or:

B. Sharlie is pronounced unwell.

And here there were several ramifications, depending on the degree of unwell. Either (1) He would wait until she was better and got herself released; (2) He would return to New York without her, she to follow later; or (3) Unmentionable, ungraphable, except in the most shadowy fashion. Too many subcategories, too many overlapping emotional responses exploded by even the hint of it.

He took a deep breath and forced himself to enumerate: (1) unspeakable grief; (2) exhausted relief; (3) guilt; (4) freedom; (5) a future forever loveless.

He picked up a fistful of sand, letting it slowly dribble out onto the beach. Bullshit, he thought. Anticipating his response to her death was like trying to determine the intentions of God. Or what was beyond the end of the universe. Not to be found in the current *New York Civil Practice Law and Rules.*

The sun made him drowsy, and the sound of water washing against the shore was soothing. Soon his mind drifted to fantasies of Sharlie sharing his apartment on Third Avenue. He imagined her hairbrush on his dresser and was touched—tangible evidence of their future intimacy. Her underwear, her clothes, her toothpaste, all the assorted oddments of her daily routine tumbling into his lonely space like the brightly colored jewels of sunshine he glimpsed through the filter of his eyelashes.

And the thing was, if he were to express this to her, she'd understand—smile, take his hand. There would be no hint of contempt for his sentimentality, not from Sharlie. She ridiculed only her own feelings—the more intense the emotion, the more flippant her attack on herself. But *his* feelings she took very seriously.

Oh, God, he thought, stretching in the soft sand. What do I need the sun for when I've got Sharlie Converse Morgan?

CHAPTER 43

Sharlie stared at the viewer in Diller's office and marveled at the contours of her new heart. Before the operation she'd shuddered at her X rays, her heart's flabby bulges expanding malevolently with each new set of pictures until it seemed as though there could be no room left for any other vital organs. Udstrom's streamlined heart, no bigger than Walter's clenched fist, nestled comfortably in its compact niche.

Diller lifted the corners of his mouth just perceptibly, and Sharlie reminded herself that he was smiling.

"Marriage must agree with you. You're fine."

"Can I go?"

He nodded.

"How long?"

"Indefinitely."

"You mean I don't have to come back? Ever?"

"Make your reservations for New York."

She exhaled slowly, a long, trembling sigh.

"If it weren't for Saint Joe's, we'd never release you this early," he said.

"I know."

"You must check in twice a week without fail. They're all set up for you in Coronary."

She nodded.

"You have your medications?"

"All sixty-three of them."

"You're clear on the urine and stool measurements?"

"I've been carefully coached."

"Don't miss even one day of medication, or you'll end up right back in the hospital."

"I know, Doctor Diller." She smiled, recognizing his reluctance to let her go. "Are you coming back to New York?"

"Soon," he said.

"Well," she began, then shook her head helplessly and whispered, "Thanks." She held out her hand, and he grasped it briefly. His palm felt very soft. Sharlie's eyes were beginning to sting, so she turned and walked quickly out of the office.

Walter and Margaret had been waiting for her and approached her eagerly when she emerged.

"Well?" Margaret asked.

"I'm sprung."

"Marvelous." Her mother gave her a restrained hug.

"I don't see why we couldn't come in there with you," Walter grumbled.

"I just wanted to hear the verdict by myself," Sharlie said.

"Well, I knew you were okay. I can tell by looking at you. Your temperature is ninety-seven point eight or point nine, and your blood pressure is a hundred and ten over seventy."

Sharlie said, "Aren't you going to congratulate me?"

"Congratulations," he said irritably.

Sharlie glared at him and said, "Let's go." She led the way down the hall.

"Well, what's the matter with you, young lady?" Walter asked, catching up with her.

"You know something, Daddy?" Sharlie said, her voice quavering. "Sometimes I think you don't give a damn about *me*. All you care about was that I didn't let you come in with me and monopolize everything."

Walter gave Margaret an exasperated look, but she just shook her head at him as if to say, don't look at me—*I* don't know what's the matter with her.

Walter put his hand on Sharlie's elbow to bring her to a halt. "Keep your voice down," he said, nodding toward the nurse's station. A young couple stood nearby, watching them curiously.

Sharlie's voice rose another notch. "I'm not a piece of office equipment you've taken a lot of time and money to fix."

"Oh, Sharlie," Margaret said reproachfully.

Walter looked wounded. "So what do we do, your mother and I? We drive out to the airport and hop on a plane, and you'll call us once in a while, is that right?"

"Something like that," Sharlie said.

"Oh, I'll just pay the bills. Or should I send them to your husband now that you're no longer my responsibility?"

"That's . . . *awful*," Sharlie retorted. "You know he can't come up with that kind of money."

Walter prodded her into the elevator, grateful that for once, there was no one else inside. He looked at Margaret briefly, then took a deep breath and said, "Okay. I'm sorry. I don't know how we got into this."

"Well, I do—" Sharlie began.

He interrupted hurriedly. ". . . but let's drop it for now. You just walked out of Diller's office, and I just said, 'Hey, honey, that's great news.'" He tried to smile. "Okay?"

She dropped her eyes for fear he'd see the triumph there. "Okay," she said.

The elevator stopped at the ground floor, and Walter put his arm around his daughter. "I'll go get things straight with Admissions. Is that all right?"

Sharlie nodded, but found that she was unable to speak through the confusion of her conflicting emotions.

"We'll see you in New York, dear," Margaret said, giving Sharlie a kiss on the cheek.

"Mrs. Morgan," Walter said, patting her arm awkwardly.

For a moment Sharlie's eyes welled up, but then she said formally, "Have a good time in San Francisco." She raised her hand in a stiff wave good-bye and went outside to wait for Brian.

Walter and Margaret walked down the hallway in silence. Finally Margaret said, "I don't know, Walter. She's baffling."

"She wants me to butt out, I'll butt out." His face was furious and hurt in just about equal parts.

Margaret put her hand on his arm. "Look, we've all been through a lot."

He snorted.

"Once we get back home, we can start living like a normal family again," she continued.

"Oh, for Christ's sake, Margaret. She's married. We're not going to *have* a family anymore."

"Now, don't hurt *my* feelings, Walter. I'm family, too, you know."

He ran his hand across his forehead wearily. "Let's finish up and get the hell out of this godforsaken place."

When Brian pulled up by the gate, Sharlie was perched on the cement column by the entranceway.

"Going my way, lady?" he asked, leaning out the window.

She nodded and slid into the car. Her face was flushed, almost feverish.

"So?" he said.

"So let's pack."

He slammed the car into "Park" and grabbed her. Then he held her away from him so that he could look at her face. His eyes were puzzled.

"I just had a fight with my father," she explained. She held out her hand to show him the trembling fingers. "I'm an awful ungrateful daughter, but some-times . . . sometimes he's like the bully in the advertisements who runs around kicking sand at the skinny, runty guy."

"What was it all about?"

"It's not like me at all," she went on shakily. "I don't do this sort of thing." Brian smiled. "I mean I *didn't*," she said.

"I'm sure he deserved it," Brian remarked.

"Did *you*? The day I threw the newspaper at you? What is happening to me?"

Brian took her hand between his. "There is nothing wrong, unusual, bizarre, or neurotic about any of it," he said.

"Maybe not," she replied slowly. "But it isn't me."

"Well, whoever you are, I'd like you to come home to bed."

He started the car and looked at her questioningly. She raised the corners of her mouth with effort, and he shook his head, unconvinced. She took a deep breath, batted her eyelashes seductively, and flashed him her exaggerated version of the Hollywood starlet smile.

"Oh, beautiful," he said, grinning at her. Then he put the car in gear, and they drove off toward the motel.

CHAPTER 44

Margaret and Walter had taken a suite of rooms on the top floor of a fashionable old hotel in San Francisco. They planned to stay a week and would arrive back in New York soon after Sharlie and Brian.

Since that eerie night by the lighthouse, Walter and Margaret had circled around each other, cautiously exploring and testing out their new relationship. He often took her out to dinner away from the hospital now, and they began to discover each other across white tablecloths.

With his new tenderness, she began to relax and bloom. He noticed she left her blouse open by one more button and even went bare-legged when she wore sandals. The day before, when he'd found her sunbathing on the terrace of the motel back in Santa Bel, she didn't instantly grab her robe and pull it closed with her belt as if protecting herself against imminent rape. Instead, she sat with straps tucked between her breasts and talked with him about the young man at the pool who had given her a diving exhibition that afternoon and how beautiful it was.

The first night of their trip to San Francisco Walter had lifted his wineglass to Margaret and said, "To honeymoons." They had smiled at each other and taken the first sip. Then Margaret lifted her glass and said, "To middle age." She was delighted with herself, and he was charmed by her happiness, and the mutual toasting became a kind of private rite between them. And sometimes as they walked together, he put his arm around her very lightly.

Walter found his sexual appetite for her undiminished but shifting. He was stirred by her as always but no longer tormented by the urgent need to crush her, to conquer her, and too apprehensive of damaging the delicate infancy of this new marriage with Margaret to assert himself sexually with her.

The last evening in San Francisco Walter ordered omelets and champagne, and they sat on the terrace overlooking the bay, bundled in heavy sweaters against the cool summer evening. They talked for a long time and gradually sipped their way through most of the champagne. They discussed Sharlie and Brian at first, with Margaret remarking how strange it was not to be thinking of her daughter all the time—practically the whole day had passed without her giving Sharlie a thought. She felt guilty about it, and they discussed how wonderful it would be if they could begin to enjoy their parenthood even at this late date in the way that other people with healthy children seemed to. Then they began to reminisce about their own parents, and Margaret asked Walter about his father. He would never tell her much, and now that he seemed willing to talk, she took advantage of the moment.

But she talked, too, about her mother's cool beauty, her grace, and her contempt for her husband, whom Margaret adored.

Perhaps when they had first met thirty years ago, they had discussed these things, but it all seemed new to them tonight, long forgotten on the other side of years full of wounds and habitual resentment.

Finally Margaret stretched and said, "I'm tired."

"Go ahead. I'll sit a minute," Walter said.

But Margaret didn't get up. She sat staring at him, and when he looked at her, she dropped her eyes.

"Walter . . ." she began hesitantly.

"What is it?"

"If you come with me . . . to bed, I mean. Do you think we could . . . well . . . oh, dear . . ."

He was stunned to silence. After a moment he got up and stood behind her to pull out her chair. They went inside. Walter closed the glass door behind them, and then the curtains.

Margaret began to undress in silence. She slipped off her bra and panties and slid into bed under the covers. She lay there looking at him with frightened eyes.

He undressed and sat at the edge of the bed beside her. His penis was huge, and he felt embarrassed at the blatant enormity of his response to her.

"Margaret, listen," he began. "I don't want to screw things up between us. . . ."

He saw she was smiling, but he went on earnestly.

"It's obvious that I want you. But you've got to be happy with me now."

Margaret said quietly, "Let's go very slowly, and if I'm not . . . comfortable, I'll try to tell you."

She tilted her face up to be kissed, and he leaned over her, trying to hold back his heat. They had never spent much time with preliminaries, and now they lingered over each other's mouths, delaying and exploring. Finally he pulled back the covers and slid next to her. In the past, Margaret had always worn a nightgown, forcing him to pull it up to her breasts to get it out of the way. Now her naked shoulders seemed lovely and vulnerable, a statement of trust.

He held himself up on his arms when he entered her so that he wouldn't hurt her as he began to move with more intensity. She lay still and quiet at first, but after a few moments of his slowly moving in and out of her, she raised her hips toward him slightly, and he felt her gentle motion beneath him.

It was too much for him, her movement, and he came almost instantly, crying out against her shoulder. Then he lifted himself off her and lay next to her, his arm across the curve of her stomach.

"I'm sorry," he said after a while.

"For what?"

"I was too quick."

"No," she murmured, and he thought he heard tears in her voice. He propped himself up on his elbow to look at her in the dusky light and saw that she was crying.

"Margaret, what did I do?" he whispered, anguished.

She shook her head, smiling through the tears. "No. It was . . . it felt good. Really. I don't know why I'm crying."

She began to sob in earnest now. He put his arms

around her, and she clung to him, with her naked breasts pressed against him for the first time in their lives, and he stroked her long, soft back and said awkwardly, over and over, "There, there. There, there."

CHAPTER 45

Traffic into the city from Kennedy Airport was heavy. When they finally inched their way through the Midtown Tunnel, the cabdriver waved a disgusted hand at the bumper-to-bumper lineup and said, "Holy fucking Christ, will you look at this? First Avenue's a fucking parking lot." He craned his neck around and shouted at Brian through the open partition. "Hey, fella, you mind if I try Park?"

Brian nodded that it was okay, and with some hair-raising maneuvers and a few expletives aimed at fellow drivers, they lurched their way to Park Avenue.

"Goddamn politicians, that's what screws it up. Buncha assholes. Jesus, on a Friday night even. Everybody's supposed to be leaving."

He swung his face around again, keeping one hand on the wheel. "Ya know, Fire Island, Hamptons. Must be a fucking faggots' convention in the city this weekend."

Sharlie and Brian blinked at him silently, and he

faced forward in time to speed through a traffic light that had just turned red.

Sharlie smiled at Brian. "Home," she whispered.

"California it's not," he agreed.

She took a deep breath. The air seemed more like crisp September than July, but maybe it was just the difference between Los Angeles and the Northeast. She stared greedily out the window as they hurtled uptown. The awnings stretched out from the magnificent stone buildings, making her think of rich old snobs poking their tongues out at everybody else who couldn't afford Park Avenue rents. She snuggled happily against Brian's shoulder.

She had hoped he could spend the weekend at home with her while they settled in, but after his prolonged leave, he felt compelled to plunge back into his work first thing Saturday morning. She walked him to the front door, he pulled her by the sleeve to the elevator, both of them laughing at their reluctance to say good-bye. But once the doors closed and he had disappeared, she found herself enjoying the prospect of a day alone to poke around Brian's apartment and think of ways to make it theirs instead of his alone.

She poured herself a cup of tea and sat at Brian's desk, contemplating the accumulation of papers and bills, realizing that soon she would be familiar with all the mysterious cubbyholes of his days. She was tired and felt the need for quiet thought, for taking stock and assessing her new life and what she would do with herself now. Whoever thought there would be choices?

From long habit she cupped her hands around her

mug as if to warm them. A police car raced up Third Avenue, siren screaming, and she smiled.

Until yesterday she had not realized how alien California had felt to her. Perhaps it was the frontierlike atmosphere of the place, as if the East were the staid mother country and the West her rebellious colony. Sharlie wondered ruefully that if she had been a settler during the American Revolution, she might have sided with England and King George. People seemed so earnest in California. The comfortable, shabby, worn-out East drew her back like a slightly cynical but dear old friend.

Out of embarrassment she had never admitted aloud to her fear of earthquakes. No one else in Santa Bel ever seemed to worry about them, but sometimes she had awakened in the night to a deep rumble beneath her hospital bed. The vibration had terrified her, no matter how hard she worked at convincing herself that it was only the generator snoring in the dark.

The East had sat placidly on the edge of the Atlantic for centuries, its gentle hills battered smooth and round. California perched on the other side, its landscape either scraped flat or tormented into monumental sharp protuberances. Surely the entire coast would someday tear free of the mainland and sink into the Pacific, leaving a jagged scar along the shore, lined with millions of young people with sun-streaked hair and disappointed faces, surfboards under their arms, and nothing but churning foam to greet them.

The forgotten inch of tea remaining in Sharlie's cup had grown cold. She got up from Brian's desk and walked stiffly to the window to peer into the apartment across the courtyard. She smiled, remembering how Brian had insisted on pulling the shade when they made love this morning. She had tried to persuade him that no one could see inside during the day unless the lights were on. Or unless she and Brian pressed themselves to the window and made love against the glass. She'd reminded him of her opera glasses and how she knew from firsthand frustration how impossible it was to see past the black reflection of a sunlit window.

Brian, unconvinced, pulled the shade down anyway, but prodded her to elaborate on her Peeping Tom experiences. She told him that the only diverting event she witnessed that didn't emerge from the embellishments of her imagination was provided by a middle-aged couple who stood near their lighted window one evening, and, with a kind of ritual slowness, exchanged clothing with each other. When they had finished, the woman was wearing the man's vested suit and he her flowered blouse and skirt—and her bra as well, which he stuffed with her nylons. Then they undressed each other and moved away from the window. Sharlie knew they would make love. She only saw this happen once, and sometimes wondered if she'd made up the whole thing. But no, it had happened, and it seemed to Sharlie a beautiful ceremony and somehow very touching.

This morning there was no one home across Brian's tiny courtyard, and Sharlie chided herself for looking. The spectator impulse was deeply ingrained. She turned away from the window, stood in the center of the living room, and decided that today she would become a participant in life.

Bloomingdale's. She would go to Bloomingdale's.

Her mother had always sniffed at the place, considering it the epitome of ostentation. After all those years of sedate shopping in boring Bonwit's, she would strut down to Fifty-ninth Street and buy herself . . . what? As she scrambled out of her nightgown and into a skirt and sweater, she decided that one of the rules was not to foreclose any possibilities. Spontaneity, that was the theme of the day.

On her way out she wished the doorman a slightly embarrassed good morning, thinking he must know what she and Brian had been up to at seven A.M., newlyweds and all. When she was first learning about sex, she had been fascinated by pregnant women she'd pass on the street, staring at them and thinking, She *did* it. She had sexual intercourse with somebody, and there's no way she can deny it. Sometimes the lady in question seemed so austere that it seemed impossible. But there was the evidence before everyone's eyes in the extended belly and loose clothes. Some of those ladies *must* have been raped.

The main floor of Bloomingdale's looked like Fifth Avenue on Easter Sunday. Sharlie stood at the millinery counter, trying on one hat after the other. She watched the parade pass by, wondering if anyone actually bought anything here or whether they all simply stopped by to stare at everybody else. In the contest between fashion and comfort, fashion seemed to win out every time. Women tottered past in toe-crushing high heels, stiff-kneed in the effort to remain vertical. Men with tennis sweaters and pancake makeup eyed one another over the cosmetics counter. Didn't their mascara run during their singles matches?

Finally she wore out the supply of hats and rode the

escalator up to the third floor. She passed through the designers' section, heading straight for the blinking colored lights of a boutique called In the Wild, Secret Heart. An omen, she thought, I'll buy a new dress for my heart. For Udstrom's heart. She hoped he didn't mind becoming a transvestite.

Hanging amid suspended velvet, plastic, satin, Plexiglas, and aluminum hearts were items her mother would hardly describe as clothes. Everything was brocaded or tassled—not at all the tailored understatement of the wardrobe Margaret had chosen for herself and her daughter.

I'll look like my mother's dining room curtains, Sharlie thought, choosing a lacy white-fringed dress. But when she tried it on, she was surprised at how attractive it looked. Radical, certainly, but pretty. She pirouetted in front of the mirror, enjoying the contrast between the dark sheen of her hair and the milky lace bodice.

Heavens, I'll take it, she thought. Oh, God, Mother would hate it. She resisted the impulse to giggle and marched soberly back to the dressing room.

When Brian got home, she was standing in the kitchen with her hand on the portable mixer. She wore her new dress, and her face was flushed from the heat of the oven.

"Hi," he said, leaning over to give her a kiss. "What're you making?"

"Yorkshire pudding," she said, looking at him with a distracted smile.

He peered into the bowl, his hand around her waist. Then, feeling the ropy belt under his fingers, he stood back a little, looking at her from head to foot. "What's that, an apron or something?"

"No, it's not an apron or something, it's my trendy new dress from trendy Bloomingdale's."

"Oh," Brian said. "Well, I'll go change."

"You don't like it."

"Well, it's . . . interesting."

Sharlie looked up at him briefly, still mixing. "What's the matter with it?"

"I don't know if it's you, that's all," Brian answered.

"You only like me in my nice little tweedy stuff," she said, irritation building in her voice.

"Tell you what, why don't we shop together from now on, and we'll get something we *both* like."

"Hey, I'm a big girl now," she snapped. "I can pick out my own clothes." Her eyes were flashing.

Brian smiled at her. "What's all—" he began.

"Freedom," she interrupted. "Hey, look, I spent a lifetime trailing behind my mother in department stores, letting her put clothes on me as if I were her personal paper doll. I'm not going to start that all over again with you."

"Sharlie, for Christ's sake . . ." he said, staring toward her with his hand out placatingly. She backed away from him, unconsciously lifting the still-whirring mixer into the air like a weapon. The thin batter flew about the room, whirling and splattering against the walls, speckling their faces and clothes with pale-yellow droplets. They both stood paralyzed for a moment. Then they looked at each other and began to laugh. Sharlie, still holding the mixer with one hand, pointing at Brian with the other, barely able to breathe from laughing.

"You . . . you . . ." she said weakly.

"Turn off the mixer, you idiot," he shouted, but as he grabbed for it, she dipped it quickly into the batter again, reloading, and held it above her head where he couldn't reach. It splattered wildly, and he grabbed her around the waist, reaching behind her to pull the plug out of the wall. Then they collapsed against each other, laughing and smearing the mess into their clothes.

It wasn't until they sat down to dinner much later, after a chastened Sharlie had scrubbed the yellow drops off the walls, that she said, almost surprised, "That was a fight, wasn't it?"

"Gooiest argument I ever had," he said, finishing off a slice of roast lamb.

"No, I mean about my dress."

"Mmm, that was a fight," Brian said.

"Sometimes I think I'm going completely insane," she said. Brian suddenly looked up at her, wondering at the fear he thought he heard in her voice. "I was ready to kill," she went on. "Over a damn piece of material."

Brian reached out and took her hand. "There was Bunker Hill, then there was Gettysburg, and finally the Great Bloomingdale's Batter Battle." She smiled back at him, but he felt her fingers tremble.

She walked through a densely wooded area carrying a basket on her arm. It was an unfamiliar path, and she stopped to rest, sitting on a large rock that projected from a mossy bank. Suddenly she felt the rock begin to move beneath her. She stood up, startled, her basket falling to the ground, strewing flowers at her feet.

The granite surface shifted and writhed, gradually taking on the shape of a man's face. The eyes were deeply hollowed, almost like a skull, but they followed her wherever she moved. The mouth twisted until it became a cave, and from its depths howled a scream of outrage.

She stood rooted to the ground with fright, unable to tear her eyes from the shrieking, tormented face. Finally, carefully, she stooped to gather the flowers. She drew back in horror. The pansies and forget-me-nots had turned to lumps of oozing flesh. Her fingers were stained with blood, and the more she wiped the grass to clean them, the gorier they became. She turned her back on the rock and began to run, and she could hear the voice behind her crying, "Mine . . . you are mine . . ."

She woke up trembling and pressed herself against Brian's warm back. It took her nearly an hour to fall asleep again.

CHAPTER 46

Tuesday morning Sharlie waited for Brian to leave for work, and called Queens information for the telephone number of Mrs. M. Udstrom in Elmhurst. She sat for a long time trying to summon the courage to dial. She remembered lying in her hospital bed at Saint Joe's working herself up to call Brian to thank him for saving her life. There was no use speculating what would have happened if she had never made the call. Would the numbers under her fingers at this moment precipitate a comparable upheaval in her life? Unthinkable, change of any kind. And yet not to make the contact left her poised on the edge of something forever unresolved.

The voice at the other end sounded tremulous. Suddenly Sharlie's carefully prepared words fled. She gripped the phone hard and managed to stammer, "Mrs. Udstrom, I'm Charlotte Converse. I mean, Morgan." She laughed a little with embarrassment and nervousness.

"Yes. I know who you are," the voice said tonelessly.

"I would like to see you. Meet you," Sharlie went on.

"Why?" asked Mrs. Udstrom.

"Oh," Sharlie faltered. "Well, I think it would be nice. . . ." Oh, my God, she thought. The woman's son is dead, and I think it would be "nice." "What I mean is, I would like to thank you."

"Not necessary," said Mrs. Udstrom.

"Oh, but it is," Sharlie gushed, thankful that video-telephones were not yet the norm. Her face was so crimson and hot that she put her hand against her cheek to cool it down. She took a breath and tried again. "Mrs. Udstrom, I would really like to talk to you. In person. If you think it would be difficult for you, of course I won't impose. But it *is* important to me."

"All right," the flat voice replied. They arranged a time, or rather Sharlie arranged and Mrs. Udstrom agreed.

The shabby frame houses on Twenty-sixth Avenue seemed deserted to Sharlie as she walked along the cracked sidewalk. She was grateful that she'd worn a pair of slacks. She shuddered, imagining herself waltzing into one of these sad homes sporting a designer dress whose every thread shrieked "privilege."

She passed a clump of dusty gray trees surrounded at its base by a bouquet of litter. In front of Number 159, she stopped, staring anxiously at the peeling paint and the cellophane stretched over missing window panes.

Do I *really* want to do this? she asked herself. But Udstrom's heart thumped steadily in her ears. She

walked resolutely up the cinder block steps and
knocked.

Mrs. Udstrom opened the door so quickly that Sharlie wondered if the woman had been watching out the
window as she hesitated on the sidewalk. Sharlie tried
to smile, but Mrs. Udstrom's face was expressionless
as she stood aside and said, "Come in."

She led Sharlie to a tiny living room. A tea set had
been laid out on the coffee table. The older woman
took her seat on a stiff-backed chair and motioned to
Sharlie to sit on the couch. Sharlie noticed that Mrs.
Udstrom's cup was chipped along the rim.

"Thank you," Sharlie said, lifting her teacup. She
helped herself to sugar, but her fingers had begun to
shake, so she set the saucer down and folded her
hands in her lap.

"Mrs. Udstrom . . ." she began tentatively, "I appreciate your letting me come."

Mrs. Udstrom nodded. She wore a faded-blue
dress—to match her faded eyes and faded, peeling
house, Sharlie thought. Her face was lined and nearly
as gray as her hair. She was a lean, bony woman, and
Sharlie thought she must have been quite handsome
before poverty and misfortune had worn her down.

"I want to thank you . . . for your son's . . . for
your son . . ." Sharlie began to blush. This was much
more difficult than she had thought, probably a mistake altogether. How much of her impulse to come
here had been the need to express gratitude and how
much was a macabre curiosity about the mother of
the stranger who had become so significant to her?

Finally Mrs. Udstrom spoke. It was the monotonous, flat voice Sharlie recognized from the telephone.

"I done my Christian duty, that's all."

"It was a wonderful thing. You saved my life."

"I done what I had to."

The statement seemed so final that Sharlie thought she should probably get up and leave, but Mrs. Udstrom sat stirring her tea and regarding her with pale eyes that were filmed with something indefinable. Grief? Exhaustion?

"Could I trouble you for a glass of water, please?" Sharlie asked reluctantly.

Mrs. Udstrom got up without a word and returned a moment later with the drink. Sharlie opened her bag and took out the ten-A.M. medication she had prepared before leaving the apartment. With Mrs. Udstrom watching silently, she swallowed nine pills and capsules, crowding as many into her mouth as possible in order to avoid being forced to ask for more water. She set the glass down, and still Mrs. Udstrom stared at her with complete disinterest, as if Sharlie had merely inserted herself temporarily into the woman's sole line of vision.

"I'm sorry . . . about your son," Sharlie said finally.

"He got what was coming," the woman responded curtly. She saw the shock in Sharlie's face and went on. "Giving you his heart's the one decent thing he ever done, and that wasn't none of his doin', was it?"

"He was so troubled?"

Mrs. Udstrom's mouth twitched in what Sharlie presumed to be the bitter remnants of a smile.

"That's what they call it, do they, 'troubled'? Well, he troubled me all his life. And it wasn't that he didn't get nothin' at home. I sacrificed and worked, two, three jobs, day and night, housework, laundry, and

anything so's he got a clean shirt for school and some-
thin' for lunch in his bag. And to keep this place."

"His father?" Sharlie asked.

"Run off. Before Martin was born."

"Oh. I'm sorry." She hesitated, then asked. "If you
were working, what did you do with . . . your boy?"
She couldn't bring herself to say "Martin."

"When he wasn't in school, he come with me. Or
stayed here."

"By himself?"

"Now, who would I keep him with?" Her voice was
tired, resigned. "Anyway, he liked bein' alone. The
other kids use to torment him so's he'd shut himself up
in his room, and I'd have to whip him to get him to
school."

Sharlie looked stricken, and Mrs. Udstrom continued, still without a trace of emotion in her voice. "He
couldn't talk right. Had this stammer. Oh, he didn't
say much anyhow, but when he did, it come out all
stuttery. The other kids, they'd make fun."

"How cruel," Sharlie said.

Mrs. Udstrom shrugged. "That's kids."

She sat musing for a moment. "Martin, he went for
a whole summer once without sayin' more'n a word or
two, and them you couldn't hardly figure out."

Sharlie was beginning to feel ill. Her head ached,
and her stomach was queasy. She longed to get out of
this shabby room, away from this woman who said
such terrible things in a worn voice as if she were re-
citing her grocery list. Sharlie set her teacup down.

Mrs. Udstrom was gazing off into a dark corner.
"But I kept this place. I did that."

"Yes," Sharlie said, hoping her urgent compulsion to
leave wouldn't come bursting out in a scream. She

stood up, forcing her voice to remain level. "Well, thank you for seeing me. And for the tea."

Mrs. Udstrom rose also. There was nothing in her face to indicate that she cared whether her visitor stayed or left. Sharlie walked deliberately toward the front door, resisting the impulse to run. She stopped at the threshold and tried to smile.

"Well . . . thank you again," she said. Mrs. Udstrom nodded wordlessly, and after hesitating for another moment, Sharlie started down the steps. She heard the door click shut behind her and kept her stride under control just in case the woman was watching her. Then, safely around the corner, she began to run. She ran and ran, further and faster than she had ever been able to run in her life. A ten-year-old boy-shadow raced beside her, laughing and jeering and stammering her name.

Despite her exhaustion, she couldn't go straight home. She took a cab to the Metropolitan Museum and spent almost two hours looking at Renaissance paintings, comforting herself with their classic order and their declaration of the civilized nature of humanity. She began to feel less distraught, and was able to think calmly about her interview with Mrs. Udstrom.

One of the astonishing things, she thought, was that the woman had never once inquired how Sharlie was doing. One wouldn't necessarily expect solicitude, but certainly there would be a natural curiosity. After all, it was her own son's heart beating across the teapot. If Sharlie were his mother, she knew she'd be straining all her senses searching for some hint of her child's immortality in the recipient's body. Mrs. Udstrom was a hollow shell, all the color bleached from her life, all vitality abraded away by misery. For such a woman there seemed to be no such instinct as curiosity. Only acceptance, a dull, grinding tolerance of everything that fell into her path.

Sharlie walked slowly through the Medieval Court and sat down to rest in the chapel alcove, imagining the face of Mrs. Udstrom's tortured son against the shadows. She understood his childhood torment, felt their fates converge—her years of pain and his seemed to twist together into a pattern of shared anguish. Her heart, his heart, pounded, echoing in the dark chamber of the chapel room. She knew him now. This afternoon in that defeated house, she had stared into the past of a man whose heart she carried beyond death. She realized also that finding him had finally set her free. Udstrom's life was over. Hers was not.

Sadness mingled with her relief, and she felt her eyes sting. She gazed up at the stained-glass windows, the deep-blue light like glistening seawater through her tears.

CHAPTER 47

Diller had sent Sharlie home with a list of permissible foods—bland, dietetic items that she learned to detest. After three weeks of obedience she decided that in her new life—the resurrection, she had taken to calling it—she would allot one day every four weeks to consumption of contraband. At the beginning of each month she gleefully pinpointed the night of sin on her calendar and tantalized herself for days with fantasies of the forbidden delicacies she would devour.

Tonight was Wednesday, the twenty-first of August, and she and Brian met in front of Mario's Pizzeria on Second Avenue and Seventy-fourth Street.

"I hope it's really greasy," she said as they took a table by the window.

"Don't look at me when your voltage drops to ten," he warned.

"Don't nag me, Brian."

His head snapped up from the menu.

"Sorry," she said, but her face was tight. "If I had to

stick to that miserable glop, I might just as well be dead. I have to be normal every once in a while."

Brian nodded, but it wasn't until their pizza came that they began to talk again.

On their way up to the apartment an hour later, just as the elevator doors were closing, a frantic voice called, "Hold it!" from the lobby, and Susan, Brian's downstairs neighbor, slid through the opening. She was out of breath from running, and in her tennis dress she was tan and lean, exuding vitality from every bronzed square inch.

"Brian!" she cried delightedly. "Where the hell have you been?"

"California," he said, and before he could introduce Sharlie, she rushed on.

"They kept telling me 'out of town' at your office. God, I've been scrounging partners all over the city, but nobody can give me our kind of game. When, my dear, when?"

With an uncomfortable smile Brian said, "Susan, I'd like you to meet my wife, Sharlie."

Susan's jaw dropped. "Hi," she said to Sharlie finally, eyes very wide. They had arrived at the seventh floor, and Brian held the door open as she talked. "You're who was in California, huh? Well, lucky girl. I've been working on him ever since I moved in, but I finally decided I'd better be satisfied with a singles match once a week."

She stepped out of the elevator and turned to Brian with a weak grin. "Married. Well, listen, don't let me keep you. But I want a game. Sharlie won't mind. Will you?" She looked at Sharlie, and the great dark eyes stared back until Susan's smile faded. The doors shut, and they heard Susan's deflated voice call, "Best wishes . . ." as the elevator rose to the floor above.

They walked down the hallway in silence. Brian unlocked the door and turned to give Sharlie a mischievous look as they went inside, intending to tease her for what he assumed was jealousy. But her face was set hard.

"You've slept with her, haven't you?" she said.

Brian, taken aback, hesitated, and Sharlie burst out, "I knew it. I could tell. She didn't give a *shit*, did she, whose feelings she clomped on with her P.F. Flyer Superwoman sneakers."

Brian pointed to the floor in alarm. "Hey, calm down."

This only enraged her further. "No, I don't want to calm down. I'm sick of calming down. She's so goddamn healthy, I hate her."

She slammed into the bedroom, leaving Brian to stand in the middle of the rug, suspended halfway between laughter and fury. He stood still for a few moments and then decided the best course was to ignore the entire incident. He went into the kitchen, drank half a quart of milk, and settled himself by the television. He flipped past the special ballet performance and stopped the dial at *Charlie's Angels*.

God damn her, he thought, staring morosely at the screen. Let her stew in her own venom.

Half an hour later Sharlie crept out of the bedroom and sat down beside him, very prim and quiet, her slight body barely making a dent in the sofa. He looked at her solemnly, and she stared back with huge eyes.

"I'm sorry," she said softly.

He tried to keep his face stiff but finally looked away, attempting desperately to maintain his righteous exasperation.

"I'm really sorry," she repeated, her voice barely audible.

"Oh, shit," he said. He reached out for her, and she felt the ferocity in his arms.

"Do you think we'll burn up with it?" she murmured against him.

"Sometimes I think so," he said.

"You're going to turn me into a piece of ash," she whispered, holding him as tightly as she could. Then she tilted her head back to look up at him mischievously. "And that's with an *h*!"

CHAPTER 48

It was one of those reluctant Monday mornings when Brian couldn't bear to sever the companionship of the weekend by leaving for the office. They kept the shades drawn against the bright September sky and prolonged breakfast.

But eventually Brian picked up his briefcase and stood regarding Sharlie sorrowfully from the threshold. She gave him a kiss on the cheek and closed the door behind him. Brian pried open the peephole from the outside and muttered, "Bitch."

When he got to the office, there was a telephone message waiting for him: *Wife at 9:12. Please call.*

"Morgan's . . . uhh . . . Butcher Shop," Sharlie said into the receiver.

"Oh, yeah?" Brian responded. "You got any chickens there?"

"Oh, mister," she went on breathily. "Have I got a chicken for *you*."

"I'll take two breasts and two thighs."

"Okay," she said. "But only if I get your drumstick."

Brian laughed. "What happened to the sweet young thing I married?"

"My innate raunchiness is emerging," Sharlie said. "With your encouragement, I might add."

"My wife, the porno queen."

"You wish. Can you have lunch?"

Brian looked at his calendar. "A quick one. Early."

They hung up. He extracted the Foreman file from the heap of papers on his desk and walked down the hall to Barbara's office. Their clients were already sitting inside, Mr. and Mrs. Foreman with their daughter, Brenda, between them on Barbara's secretary's chair. She was twelve years old and had been barred from her school's soccer team. Both older brothers had excelled at the sport, but Brenda was a girl and hadn't been allowed to try out.

Brian admired the Foremans. Brenda was a charming, bright, pixilated, gutsy kid, and she wanted her rights. Her parents had responded to their daughter's outrage with positive action, and Brian was pleased that Brenda would not grow up feeling helpless in the face of injustice. This morning she wore a dress, and her light-brown hair was pulled back from her face with a barrette. She had apparently drawn the line at her shoes, however, because on her feet she wore the usual battered sneakers. Brian smiled as she poked at the thick carpet with one foot, swiveling her chair back and forth. Her face was solemn under the sprinkling of freckles.

"Brenda," Brian whispered through the adults' conversation. The girl looked up at him, bright-blue eyes alert and curious. "You can give it a real whirl if you want." She grinned and pushed off with her sneaker to set the chair spinning.

After the third trip around, Mrs. Foreman said, "Enough, dear," and Brenda went back to making subdued little twists. Every now and then she shot Brian an appreciative glance.

In the meantime Barbara and Mr. Foreman discussed the scheduling for pretrial discovery. Brian had been through it already, and found his mind wandering to the little girl he imagined Sharlie once was. How he wished she had been blessed with a sturdy body like Brenda's. The thought of the child Sharlie, pale and fragile, playing her solitary games in that austere old townhouse brought a lump to his throat. God, what a life. But he thought of their lunch date and smiled.

"Brian, you with us?" Barbara asked pointedly.

"Punitive damages not less than ten thousand dollars," Brian quoted, grateful for his ability to record conversations in his head while simultaneously thinking about something else altogether. All those years of listening in court to the monotonous litany of the opposition. If he hadn't trained himself to manage several levels of consciousness at once, he would have gone mad from boredom long ago.

Barbara shot him a suspicious look and went back to her conference with the Foremans. Soon Brian drifted away again, wondering if Brenda Foreman admired Barbara Kaye and would someday aspire to become a lawyer. What would Sharlie have aspired to if she had been well? He tried to imagine her a powerful, aggressive businesswoman. Impossible. Just how much of a traditionalist was he anyway? He couldn't visualize her wearing Barbara's "invincible blue suit,"

but she must find something to do. How suffocating
to just vegetate as she'd done all those years under the
iron-eagle wings of Walter Converse. Brian would
come home at night to talk to her as if she were a
plant one sang to to keep it from dying of loneliness.

He listened to Barbara harangue Mrs. Foreman on
the advantages of Brenda's presence at the pretrial
conference and thought, No, Sharlie wasn't that type,
and besides, she would always tire too easily for a regular job. Perhaps something creative—interior decorat-
ing, something in the arts. Maybe he could talk her
into organizing group therapy for transplant patients.
He smiled to himself, anticipating what she would do
with that idea: *Your local chapter of TA (Transplants
Anonymous) is holding a panel discussion entitled,
"Kidneys and Hearts: Your Organ is Your Own Best
Friend."*

Fact was, he didn't want to let her out. He wanted
to keep her safe inside their world where nobody
could get at her. Well, once upon a time, maybe he
could have pulled that off. But she had changed. Her
unpredictable flashes of temper had dismayed him at
first, angered him, made him wonder if married life
would always be like swooping through the days on
some kind of roller coaster. No, Sharlie would never
again submit to the life of the hothouse plant, and he
knew it. And he was glad of it, really. After blowing
off steam, she no longer stared at him with haunted
eyes as if her own feelings had exploded at her from
some mysterious place outside herself. Yesterday, after
they made love, he had put his hand on her left breast
and said, "How's that lucky guy who lives under
here?" and she had smiled at him and answered, "Oh,
I'm doing my best to show him a good time."

" . . . anything to add to that, Brian?" Barbara said.

He shook his head. "No, I agree that it'd be valuable having her brothers there."

Barbara's mouth twitched. She knew he wasn't really there but couldn't trap him. He smiled at her mischievously as she ushered the Foremans out. Brian put his hand on Brenda's shoulder, holding her in her seat. Then he gave her a mighty push. She pulled up her feet and shrieked with pleasure. As they walked out of Barbara's office together, Brian touched her hair and said, "If I was putting together a soccer team, you'd be the first person I'd choose."

Brenda grinned and marched off after her parents, but before Brian stepped into his office, she turned and flashed him a look of absolute adoration.

Sharlie slipped into the office without a sound. Brian was so involved with his work that he didn't notice her creeping around behind him until she had wrapped her arms around his neck and very delicately placed her tongue in his ear. She knew his left ear was particularly susceptible, and she felt him shiver. He swung his chair around and pulled her onto his lap to kiss her. After a minute Sharlie murmured against his mouth, and he released her.

"The door," she gasped, laughing.

Brian glanced at the office door. It was wide open, and he wondered if perhaps his secretary had stood there watching them. Or Barbara. Barbara wouldn't have blinked. She always accused Brian of pretending Sharlie was on his lap, so it should barely make a difference to her.

He tried to hold Sharlie still, but she slipped away

from him and closed the door. Then she came back and stood looking down at his pants. They were bulging conspicuously. She gave his penis a tentative poke, and said, "Hmm," as if she were checking the quality of a cucumber in the grocery store. Then she sat down on him demurely, smoothing her skirt over her knees.

"You know who I ran into on my way down here?" she asked. Her eyes were sparkling.

He shook his head.

"Mother."

"How nice," Brian said, moving his legs under her in delicious torment.

"Thank God she was in a hurry. I felt very odd talking to her."

"Why was that?"

"Because I don't have any underpants on," she said blandly.

He examined her expression, deadpan except for the dancing eyes. After a moment she got up and said, "It's getting very lumpy here." Facing him, she swung one leg over to straddle his lap. Her eyes seemed like prisms, each facet glittering intensely and each reflection unique—daring and humor, hunger, vulnerability, adoration. He was torn between the wish to stare into the burning eyes forever and the pressure of the bare softness beneath her skirt. She lowered her eyes finally and began unbuttoning her blouse. He slid his hands up the smooth skin of her thighs and around behind, pulling her against him. Before either of them had gotten their clothes off completely, he was inside her, and for them both, orgasm was almost immediate.

Sharlie leaned against him, then lifted her face to grin at him.

"What?" he said groggily.

"You look like a little kid."

"Mmm," he said, stroking her back under the open blouse. "I'm amazed the phone didn't ring."

Sharlie looked at the clock and giggled. "It was only about eight minutes, my love."

"Oh."

"Let's see," she went on. "An hour for lunch, that's sixty minutes. Eight into sixty is seven plus. We can do this seven times and still have four minutes left over for Chock Full O' Nuts?"

He laughed. "Good choice."

She looked puzzled.

"Chuck Full O' Nuts?"

He watched her eyes blink as she figured it out. "Oh," she said. "I just thought of the first place that had hot dogs."

He looked at her in disbelief, and she blinked again.

"Well, what do you want from me?" she protested. "I'm in my prime."

"You're also in my lap," he said. "And I don't think I'll ever walk again."

The intercom buzzer sounded. He picked up the phone and said, "Just a second," then whispered to Sharlie, "Get up. Barbara's coming in."

Brian zipped up his pants on his way to the door. Sharlie buttoned her blouse quickly and tucked it into her skirt. When Barbara walked into the room, they were both standing very stiff, faces flushed. Barbara, neat and cool as always, in a trim gray dress, passed her glance without comment over their wrinkled clothes and awkward smirks.

"Hello, Mrs. Morgan," she said to Sharlie. And to Brian, "Got the Foreman file for this afternoon?"

Brian nodded. "Yeah," he said, his voice a croak. He coughed elaborately.

"Dry in here," Barbara said. "You're looking well, Sharlie. Enjoy your lunch." Then she left.

Sharlie glanced at her watch and wailed. "She just used up our four minutes for food."

"Come on," he said, grasping her hand and pulling her toward the door. "I need sustenance to endure the greedy passions of my wife."

They started toward the park, munching hot dogs and enjoying the brisk air. The leaves were yellow against the deep blue of the sky. A cool breeze billowed under Sharlie's skirt as they walked up Fifth Avenue.

"I had to pick today for my liberation from underwear," Sharlie said. "I've got a gale force wind blowing up my skirt."

"Feel good?"

"A little vulnerable," she said. "But I think maybe I'd like it in summer."

As they entered the park at Fifty-ninth Street, the strong gusts sent thousands of leaves swirling through the air in a brilliant yellow blizzard. Sharlie stopped short, tugging on Brian's arm to look. They stood in silence, the golden storm eddying around them crazily.

After a moment the breeze died down, and they walked on, their feet making uneven trails through the leaves.

"Mother's weird, you know?" Sharlie said thoughtfully.

"Why do you say that?"

"I don't know. She's got this sort of sneaky gleam in

her eyes lately. She almost acts as if she's feeling guilty about something."

"Maybe she's got a boyfriend."

"Oh, Brian, don't be ridiculous," Sharlie said.

"Typical attitude of the child toward its parents' sex life. If you didn't have the evidence staring out at you from the mirror, you'd swear they never made love."

"They never did. Make love. They just screwed. Or *he* just screwed, and she lay there looking pained."

"How do you know? You ever catch them at it?"

"No. But I know."

"When you ran into her today, I'll bet she wasn't wearing underpants either." Sharlie burst out laughing. "That would explain the mysterious gleam in her eye," he said.

She socked him in the arm. "Pervert," she said cheerfully.

They entered a playground that was nearly deserted except for one small child and his nursemaid at the seesaw. The swings made a metallic screeching sound as they moved in the wind. A bottle sat in the middle of one of the swings, and Sharlie walked over to inspect it. Suddenly she recoiled, but though her face was pale with horror, she continued to look. Brian came up beside her, took her arm, and stared inside. The bottle was half-filled with what looked like sticky cola soda, and there were at least a dozen bees swimming frantically in the dark liquid, struggling to free themselves. Many had already died, and their bodies floated on top, crowding the frenzied survivors.

Sharlie's hand in Brian's was clammy. "Brian . . ." she pleaded. He picked up the bottle and with a flick of his wrist sent it flying into the underbrush. Then they walked back to Fifth Avenue in silence.

CHAPTER 49

Wednesday was a late night for Brian. At eight o'clock Sharlie fixed herself a "Diller sandwich"—water-packed tuna with almost no mayonnaise and lots of lettuce. Then she curled up on the couch to watch the American Ballet Theatre reproduced miscroscopically on the minute screen of Brian's televison set.

The telephone rang, and she reached for it, thinking it must be Brian. But as soon as she answered, a woman's voice, cheery and rehearsed, said, "Good evening. I'm pleased to inform you that you have been selected as the winner of a free gravesite at the Riverside Rest Cemetery in Yonkers, New York."

"Excuse me?" Sharlie said.

The voice went on, relentlessly chipper. "Are you married, madam?"

"Yes," Sharlie replied automatically, then instantly regretted answering at all.

"Is your husband home?"

"No," said Sharlie. "Could you tell me—?"

"Your gift includes basic funeral expenses, our moderately priced coffin, with a credit toward the deluxe model, of course—"

Sharlie interrupted, "How did you get my name?"

There was a short silence. "What?" said the voice finally.

"How did you get my name?" Sharlie repeated.

The woman's voice was wary. "We don't *know* your name, madam. Only your telephone number."

"But we're unlisted."

The voice was placating. "It's purely random selection. We're given the first three digits, and the rest we just make up ourselves."

"You didn't get my name from anybody?" Sharlie asked again, her voice rising now. "Not from the hospital or the newspapers?"

"I assure you, madam, we don't have any idea. . . ." The voice faltered. "You say your husband is not at home?"

"No, he's not." Sharlie said. "I don't see what that has to do with anything."

"Well, as a matter of fact, we prefer to make our offer to married people, and since you seem a little . . . well, I thought maybe I should talk to—"

"You mean if I wasn't married you'd take away my free gravesite?" Sharlie asked.

Again there was a short silence, but after a moment the voice resumed courageously. "It's all part of the package. My company will make available an adjoining site for your spouse at ten percent off the usual cost. . . ."

"I want to know why you picked on me," Sharlie interrupted.

"I explained already. We're given—"

But Sharlie rushed on in a trembling voice. "How do you know what you're doing to the person who answers the phone? I mean, it's really a very personal thing, don't you think, a person's death?"

"Oh, we don't talk about *that*."

"Well, Jesus Christ, what *are* you talking about, then? I'm not going to jump into my free burial plot while I'm bursting with vitality, am I?"

"Listen, lady," the voice said in an injured tone. "Our intention was to offer you an unprecedented value. There's no need to get into the area of . . . passing away."

"Well, how do you know a person doesn't have a brain tumor or terminal cancer or something and you're calling me up with this . . . what about my obituary? Don't I get a free obituary?"

"I take it you're refusing the offer," the voice said.

"Oh, my God."

There was a click, and Sharlie sat with the phone in her hand until the dial tone began again. The buzzing sound suddenly made her think of the soda bottle filled with dead and dying bees. She replaced the receiver carefully and sat huddled in a corner of the couch, her arms around her knees, staring blindly at the television set.

The next evening Sharlie sat on the floor by the fireplace watching her parents drink their coffee. How long, she wondered, have they been sharing one end of the couch like that? Their thighs were even touching.

"I've never heard much about the San Francisco trip," Sharlie remarked.

"Oh, that seems like a very long time ago," Margaret said.

"Did you enjoy it?"

Margaret glanced at Walter.

"Yeah, we did," Walter replied. Sharlie thought she detected an unfamiliar quality in her father's voice, almost a kind of carefulness.

Then Margaret began a recitation about the scenic spots they'd visited in the Bay Area. As her mother talked, Sharlie let her eyes wander about the room. Everything was as it had always been—the clock on the marble mantelpiece, the heavy leather-bound books that once belonged to Margaret's grandfather, the worn place on the Oriental rug beside the couch. Exactly the same as when the three-year-old Sharlie had sat on this floor and pointed out the shapes in the carpet, delighting her father when she named the hexagon.

The same, and yet all of a sudden so strange. The first time she'd come here to dinner with Brian, she'd felt the impulse to send her husband off with a goodnight kiss at the end of the evening and go upstairs to her very own bed that she'd slept in for twenty-six years. But tonight there was a museumlike quality about the place, the objects in the old house like relics from the past, reminders of another life she'd left behind forever.

"If he wasn't going to make it, I don't see why he didn't just pick up the phone," Walter said.

His voice jarred Sharlie out of her reverie. "He'll be here," she said.

"The man is chronically late," Walter grumbled.

"Is this going to be get-Brian time?" Sharlie asked.

Margaret quickly interceded, "I'm sure he'll be here

in a few minutes. His meeting must have gone on longer than he expected."

"Well, then, he could have called. It's ten o'clock already," Walter muttered.

"Why don't you just go to bed and stop worrying about it?" Sharlie said angrily.

Walter, his face flushed, had begun to get up when the doorbell rang. Margaret pulled at his sleeve.

"I'll get it," he said, and left the room.

"Let's have a nice time," Margaret pleaded. "We don't see each other that often."

"I *was* having a nice time," Sharlie said irritably.

Brian and Walter walked into the room, and Brian bent to kiss Sharlie. "Sorry. I got stuck," he said.

"Why didn't you call?" she asked.

"I couldn't get out."

"You couldn't excuse yourself for one second to pick up the phone?" Her voice was rising.

"Brian," Margaret said. "Can I get you some coffee?"

"Wait a minute, Mother. We're fighting."

"I can see that," Walter said.

"Help me up," Sharlie said to Brian, holding out her hand. He lifted her from the floor, and she faced him angrily. "If you'd been at home with me and had to interrupt *our* time together to call some client, you'd somehow manage to squeeze it in."

"I *said* I was sorry," Brian said, his voice low. "Let's discuss this later."

"Come on," Sharlie said, pulling him by the hand. "We'll go to the dining room."

They left, and in five minutes Brian returned to say that Sharlie was bringing him a cup of coffee and a sandwich. He hadn't had time to eat.

"Is everything all right?" Margaret asked.

Brian smiled. "Yes. I'm sorry to screw up your dinner. I hear I missed something special."

Walter rose abruptly and excused himself. Margaret watched him stride toward the door, his shoulders tensed combatively.

"I'm afraid there's going to be a little bit more temper tonight," Margaret said.

"What else did I miss, besides dinner?" Brian asked her.

Margaret shook her head. "Sometimes I think she gets more like her father every day. She was never so . . . temperamental," she said with a sigh.

"Yes," Brian replied. His voice was neutral, but his eyes twinkled at her. They sat in silence, wondering what was going on in the kitchen.

When Walter marched into the kitchen, Sharlie was spreading a thick layer of mayonnaise on a slice of bread.

"Hi," she said, giving him a brief smile.

"I want you to explain something to me, miss," Walter said. "Why is it you got up on your high horse when I merely pointed out that he was late, and the minute he walks in here, you let him have it for the very same thing. Explain that to me, will you, please?"

Sharlie's voice held a menacing quaver. "First of all, don't call me 'miss.' I'm not your 'miss.' And secondly, when you talk about my husband, you can call him Brian, not 'he' or 'that man.' He's got a name."

"Hey," Walter said, "I'm not crazy about your tone of—"

Sharlie interrupted him angrily. "And I'm not crazy about your complaining to me about my husband."

"But you said exactly the same thing to him the second—"

"That's different."

"Will you quit interrupting me? I don't like it. It's damn rude and disrespectful."

"I want you to get this straight, Daddy. It's one thing for me to have a disagreement with Brian. It's quite another for you to sit harping about him to me. It's not your business. I don't give a damn what you say when I'm not around, but I don't want you finding fault with him in my presence. Ever."

"Don't you threaten me, young lady," Walter said, his face crimson.

"I hadn't gotten to the threat part yet, but since you bring it up, here it is. If this happens again, you won't see us. And I mean that."

Walter was finally stunned to silence. The two stood glaring at each other. After a moment he said quietly, "All right. It won't happen again." Then he wheeled around and stalked out of the kitchen. When Sharlie brought Brian's tray into the living room, he was asking Brian about the sex discrimination case he'd been working on. He didn't meet his daughter's eyes the rest of the evening.

CHAPTER 50

Sharlie sat on a bench at the Wall Street tennis courts gazing up at the roof of the bubble ceiling. As the sea gulls flew past outside, darting and diving above the East River, their shadows flickered through the white canvas expanse. Brian's shout interrupted her, and she looked down to watch his body arch as he stretched for a lob. He crashed the ball down the line past Susan's feet on the other side of the net.

"Bastard!" Susan called with a grin. He tipped his racquet to her in mock salute.

Sharlie felt a sudden wave of nausea, and she bent her head to combat the dizziness that accompanied it. She held on tightly to the edge of the bench, lowering her head to keep herself from fainting.

She had felt the queasy discomfort all day, but blamed it on last night's dinner—the monthly rebellion. Spaghetti carbonara and a slice of garlic bread at a trattoria in Greenwich Village.

But her symptoms had gradually intensified, until

now she felt she couldn't possibly wait to get into bed.
The wooden seat seemed to pitch and roll beneath
her, and she clutched at its rough surface, hoping to
ride out the attack without alarming anyone. She
lifted her head carefully to see the white figures darting back and forth, long legs spinning and turning.
She felt herself falling as the bench rose on its side
and tossed her off onto the green surface of the court.

She woke up in the back of Susan's car, with Brian
holding her tightly against him. She could hear the
thumping of the pulse in his neck and smell the salty
heat of him under his damp tennis shirt. They were
hurtling up the FDR Drive, with Susan weaving the
car expertly through the heavy northbound traffic.
Sharlie tried to move her head so that she could look
at Brian, but he put his hand on her hair and held her
still against his shoulder.

"I'm sorry," she murmured.

"Shh," he said.

"I thought we were home free."

"How do you feel?" he asked.

"Weird. As if everything's far away."

"*I'm* not far away. You rest."

She must have fallen asleep or passed out again because the next thing she was aware of was being
helped from the car at Saint Joseph's emergency entrance. As Brian and Susan propped her up, Sharlie said
groggily to Brian, "*Déjà vu?*"

They put her on a flat table, and Brian sat next to
her, holding her hand. He said to Susan, "Do me a
favor and page Mary MacDonald. When you get her,
tell her we've got Sharlie down here."

Susan went off, grateful to be useful, and in a moment they heard Mary's name over the loudspeaker.

She arrived almost immediately. Sharlie opened her eyes and looked up at the familiar round face with relief. Mary picked up Sharlie's wrist. As she timed her pulse, she regarded Brian intently. "What happened?" she asked.

Brian shook his head. "She passed out."

"Swooned," Sharlie said drunkenly. "Your basic swoon dive onto the floor. Good form, poor recovery . . ."

"Hush," Mary said sharply. Then dropping Sharlie's wrist, she moved quickly about the Emergency Room issuing orders and enlisting a harassed attendant to wheel Sharlie upstairs to the eleventh floor. Brian tried to follow, but Mary put a firm hand on his chest.

"She's so out of it she won't miss you. Go get yourself a stiff drink and come back in a couple of hours."

Mary glanced at Susan, who was standing off to the side in her damp tennis dress trying to look unobtrusive. "And you ought to put some clothes on."

Susan smiled weakly, not sure whether the brusque nurse was commenting on her risk of contracting pneumonia or her immodesty.

"What is it, Mary?" Brian asked.

Mary shook her head. "Won't know until we run the tests."

"You don't think she's rejecting," he said.

Mary gave him a noncommittal look. "Won't know until we run the tests," she repeated.

Brian put his arm around her shoulder and gave her a squeeze. "Thanks for being around."

"Oh, I'm part of the equipment in this place."

"The best part," he said, releasing her. She bustled off down the hallway, and before he and Susan had gotten to the elevator, they heard Dr. Diller being paged.

Her voltage had dropped alarmingly, and all her tests indicated rejection. Diller conferred with Jason Lewis in California. The cautious consensus was that they had caught the problem just on the brink of the acute stage. They injected her with the painful ATG serum immediately, pumping the powerful vaccine into her thighs while she lay absolutely still with clenched teeth, the sweat pouring off her body.

But in forty-eight hours she was well enough to sit up in bed and talk to visitors. Sharlie had insisted that Brian not interrupt his work again. Who knew, after all, how many times this sort of thing would happen over the years, she'd told him. If he took any more days off, he'd forget all his *thereafter's* and *heretofore's*, and none of the judges would understand him anymore. He had acquiesced reluctantly, but Sharlie knew he needed the activity and involvement away from the hospital. He hated feeling helpless, and she would rather think of him occupied in court than pacing back and forth in the waiting room.

And besides, she was tired. She had never been so tired. She felt as if she'd been fighting the Hundred Years War and that she was just about out of reserves. As she lay in bed waiting for her mother, it struck her suddenly that she no longer felt like fighting. The thought made her swallow hard, with guilt more than fear. Not to struggle—the greatest sin of all, at least in the Gospel According to Walter Converse. Giving up was unthinkable, and until now Sharlie had quickly forced such ideas back into the morass of her subconscious.

Maybe also it was because finally, finally, she was happy. In the past there had been fleeting moments when she'd felt death would be preferable to the unmitigated suffering, but in general, it seemed unthinkable. How senseless to disappear from life after tasting only the misery, all those years of hurt and loneliness. She would hang on another hour, another day, in the desperate hope that she could go out saying she'd experienced a little of the good stuff, too. But now. In just a few months it was as if she had lived a thousand lifetimes. She had fought so hard—to last through one more attack, to endure another siege of searing pain—and now, after all the struggling, she could feel herself beginning to release her stubborn grip on survival. She looked out the window and stared into the pale-blue morning sky. Not so terrible to let go now, she thought.

Sharlie heard rustling at the door and turned to see her mother standing there watching her. Margaret walked to the bed and took her daughter's hand. "What were you thinking about just then?" she asked.

"Woolgathering, I guess," Sharlie answered.

"Looked like lofty thoughts to me."

Sharlie laughed. "I was probably wondering what's for lunch."

"That's a good sign," Margaret said and sat down. "I talked with Dr. Diller this morning. He's optimistic."

"What's he doing here? I thought he was going to stay out West and be a movie star."

Margaret smiled. "Jason Lewis casts a long shadow, I think." Sharlie giggled, and Margaret went on. "He says you'll be home by the end of the week if you keep on the way you're going."

Sharlie smiled vaguely, her eyes fastened on the window.

"You don't seem all that excited."

"Mother, I could be back here again a day after I get out."

"Don't you want to go home?" Margaret asked. Her voice had deepened abruptly, and Sharlie stared at her.

"What is that supposed to mean?"

Margaret looked away.

"Mother," Sharlie said, and waited until Margaret faced her reluctantly. "Tell me what you mean."

"Well, it's hard to put my finger on it exactly, but you seem very . . . tense."

Sharlie laughed, and Margaret began to look flustered. "I'm sorry," Sharlie said through her laughter, "but there's nothing like a heart transplant to make a person tense. Besides, what does that have to do with going home?"

Margaret looked down at her hands folded in a tight ball in her lap. "I meant the tension between you and Brian."

"Oh, for heaven's sake. Is all this because of dinner last week?"

Margaret gave her daughter a significant look, and Sharlie sighed. "There's nothing wrong with a good battle now and then. Don't worry about it."

Margaret's voice sounded injured. "I only wanted to help. After all, I've been married to your father for nearly thirty-five years."

"And you never fight with him, do you?"

"Some things are worth an argument. Most are not. A husband's career, for instance. For whatever reasons he's out late. Even if it's not strictly business—"

"Oh, Mother, don't insinuate. Just come out with it."

Margaret took a breath and faced Sharlie squarely. "All right. I just wanted to say that you shouldn't let it upset you if Brian has another woman."

"What?" Sharlie's outburst was half laughter, half shriek.

"You're not a normal woman, don't forget, despite the transplant. You can't blame him if he . . . strays. Men do, even under the best of circumstances."

Sharlie stared at her mother in horror. Margaret interpreted the look as attentiveness and felt encouraged to continue. "I don't want to get into a discussion about your father. That's neither relevant nor fair, but suffice it to say that I have had my suspicions. Certainties. And I had the sense, thank God, to remind myself that fidelity is not within the framework of a man's character. I wouldn't want you to hold Brian to any foolish notions. He's obviously devoted to you, no matter what he may do just for the release." She hesitated, finally realizing that her daughter's face contained more menace than gratitude.

"I never heard such crap in my life," Sharlie said.

Margaret shifted uncomfortably in her chair. "Don't be crude, dear," she said in a quavering voice.

But Sharlie went on. "I don't know about you and Daddy, and as a matter of fact, I'd just as soon keep it that way. I like sex, Mother, and so does Brian, and he even likes it with *me*. I intend to wear him out until the day I die—in fact, that would be a damn good way to leave this world, wrapped around the man I love instead of lying in some cold, sterile hospital bed thinking about the women he's screwing because he's such a wild animal he can't help himself and I'm too refined for such filthy goings-on."

Margaret's face was very red, and her eyes threatened tears. Sharlie took a deep, shuddering breath and softened her voice.

"I'm sorry about you and Daddy. But don't you pass the system on to me. I don't accept it."

Margaret's expression suddenly shifted. Along with the tears, there was heat behind the eyes, and secretiveness. "And don't you make assumptions about your father and me," she said quietly.

The memory of her parents sitting together on the living room couch flashed into Sharlie's head—her mother's hand touching her father's knee, the meeting of eyes in a communion that had excluded their daughter.

The two women looked at each other carefully until finally Sharlie began to smile. Margaret smiled back, and there was a flicker of intuitive shared joy between them. Then Margaret's eyes clouded, and the moment passed.

"Anyway, we have to get you well so you can go home to your husband, where you belong."

"Okay, Mother," Sharlie said softly. "Whatever you say."

After Margaret left, Sharlie lay awake for a long time. Something had lifted inside, and she felt lighter.

I do believe I just did something important, she thought. She felt strong enough to leap out of bed and perform a dozen pushups in the hallway.

Had she really stood so close to her mother that she was forced to view the world from the same narrow box that Margaret did?

Well, no more. She'd spent too long in that elevator, shuttling up and down between floors, with her mother, with her father, even with poor Udstrom. She had finally reached her stop, and a tiny bell sounded—a small, ordinary ding, and yet, when the doors slid open, she walked out free.

CHAPTER 51

Brian arrived that evening, exhausted after his day in court, with the sleepy, fuzzy look Sharlie loved—his beard was very light, and with a day's growth his face seemed almost frosted, the angular lines softened.

After he had kissed her and sat down on the bed, she smiled at him and said, "So, do I look different?"

He rubbed his eyes and gazed at her blearily. "Cute. Healthier."

"I'm a new woman," she said. Brian looked confused. "I've got this incredible feeling, Bri. It's like there's been a war raging in here." She put her hand to her chest. "And it's over. Or at least there's a truce. The troops took off their helmets and shook hands and went off for a beer together."

Brian stared at her as if she were demented. She laughed. "They did not raise my Valium dosage. I swear it."

"*Something* happened."

"Mother was here, and we had this discussion, and

all of a sudden I feel so terrific." She threw her arms apart. "What do you think? Am I born again or something?"

"I would say that you have more likely reached a new plateau of self-realization."

She stared at him, and he grinned.

"But I didn't think it happened in one fell swoop," she protested.

"It doesn't."

"Well, how come it feels that way? Oh, never mind. I think I know."

"Why?"

She lowered her eyes. He waited for an answer, and finally she said, "I've been saving up my delayed adolescence for all these years, and finally it just exploded all at once."

Brian leaned over to kiss her again and went to hunt for her dinner, which was already twenty minutes late. After he left, she lay back and watched the sky outside turn dark blue. What's happened, she thought, is that I'm in more of a hurry than other people. If I don't grow up today, I won't ever get the chance. Basically, I'm a dying person.

Sobering thought, no doubt about it. But along with today's new feeling of integration had come the realization that she had known the truth for some time. Maybe some unconscious part of her mind had absorbed that knowledge and was pressing her to achieve the kind of freedom she had finally begun to experience. She wanted to spend three days wide awake in her bed thinking it all over. In fact, it would be nice to stay permanently awake all the time from now on. A waste, sleeping.

Brian arrived with the dinner tray. Sharlie sat up on the edge of the bed as he produced two plates, one with broiled fish and one with pot roast and potatoes.

Sharlie stared enviously at Brian's dinner. "How did you manage that?"

"Marylou-the-dietician's a great friend of mine."

"Oh?"

"She had a problem with her kid, and I sent them to the ACLU. Worked out fine."

"What can *I* do to get pot roast?"

"Don't worry, one of these days they'll get the trays screwed up."

He plowed through his dinner quickly, but when the aide arrived to remove the dishes, Sharlie's plate was barely touched. She leaned back against her pillow, tired from sitting up so long.

"Brian."

He was holding a bare foot that stuck out from beneath her sheets. "Yeah?"

"When I get out of here, I want to go on a trip."

"Where to?"

"Pennsylvania."

"What for?"

"Silver Creek." Brian was silent. "I want to meet your father," she said.

"You're not missing anything."

"And see where you grew up."

"I don't want to do that."

"Please."

"Let's go to Florida. Or Delaware. I don't care, wherever you want."

"Except Silver Creek."

He nodded.

"Oh, Bri, what can he do to you now?" Brian shook his head. "I'll bet he doesn't even have any teeth left to bite you with." He didn't smile. "Not funny, huh?"

"Not particularly."

"Will you think about it?"

"Yeah."

"No, really. I mean *think* about it. I want to go."

He squeezed her foot. "All right."

"Give us a kiss," she said. He kissed her once, and she brought his face back down to hers for another, longer one. "Okay," she said. "Now go away. Go to the movies. I'll see you tomorrow."

He left. Now when she looked out her window, the sky was black, and there wasn't a star to be seen.

She woke up in a cold sweat, her limbs rigid. It was as if an icy wind had suddenly swept her empty inside. The sensation was so powerful that she had to hold tightly to the edge of her bed for fear of falling out. Dizzy, she closed her eyes to wait it out.

The wind passed through her, howling, and left by the window, sucking the substance of her with it. Instead of the flesh-and-blood Sharlie of a few moments ago, she felt vacuumed out, so light that it was as if she were merely a tiny slip of paper fluttering helplessly in a black and furious universe. She saw shadowed horizons curving endlessly before her and enormous orbs—dark, menacing red—revolving slowly: omnipotent, magnetic shapes drawing her weightless body into a suffocating, malevolent universe.

She clung desperately to her connection with humanity—details of her daily life, the people she knew and had touched: Brian, her parents, the staff at the hospital—but they, too, seemed ghostly paper figures, powerless against the forces looming around her. The only realities belonged to her dark vision—a grotesque parade of disease, torment, dying children, war, senseless suffering. Death, her death, lurked just outside the window, a swirling, twisting blackness that waited to slide inside and obliterate her. She reached deep within herself for the calm acceptance of this afternoon, but terror rose up in her throat, her screams emerging as whimpers. She groped for her call button.

A nurse she'd never seen before appeared in the doorway.

"Yes?"

"Where's Mary?" Sharlie choked out.

"At the desk."

"Can't she come?" Her own words felt as if they belonged to someone else, sounding far, far away.

"Better not. She's got a cold."

"Mary has a cold," Sharlie repeated numbly. Mary would never have a cold. Mary would never get sick.

Suddenly she was crying and pleading like a child. "I want Mary. Please. I want Mary."

Mary was beside her in less than a minute, masked, but with the familiar pink skin visible above the gauze. Her hand was soft on Sharlie's wrist. "Jesus God, you feel like you just ran the marathon."

"I'm scared. I'm scared," Sharlie whispered.

"Anything hurt?"

"Just my soul. Oh, Mary, I feel all used up."

"Let me give you something."

"Will you stay with me until it works?"

Mary nodded.

"You're sick. Are you all right?"

"A rotten cold, that's all," Mary answered, pouring Sharlie a glass of water from the pitcher beside her bed.

"You can't be sick, not you," Sharlie said, gulping the sleeping capsule.

Mary laughed. "Well, why the hell not, I'd like to know?"

"I wish you'd take it off, that mask."

"Oh, no, m'girl, I don't want you getting my germs."

"It doesn't matter." Sharlie's face had stilled. Mary took the slim hand between her own round ones.

"Remember what you asked me to do once upon a time?" Mary asked.

Sharlie nodded her head slightly, eyes closed.

"Are you glad I didn't do it?"

Sharlie nodded again. "Stay with me," she said groggily.

"As long as you want me, honey."

CHAPTER 52

The next day Sharlie began to pester the doctors to let her out. She made fervent promises about eating and taking care of herself and checking in every few days for tests. Mary MacDonald allied herself with Sharlie, and together they made such nuisances of themselves that Diller finally, reluctantly, allowed her to leave.

It was Saturday morning, and Brian came early to pick her up. Her body was so wasted now that he could lift her with one arm. She seemed calm and cheerful, though, and bursting with plans for the trip to Pennsylvania. In the cab home she told Brian she'd hole up in the apartment for a week and eat nonstop, storing up energy for the five-hour car ride.

"It's a harebrained idea, Sharlie," he said as they pulled up in front of their building.

"Is that when your brain gets all coated with fuzz?"

"No, no," he said, holding her under the elbow and steering her into the lobby. "*H-a-r-e*. Derivation early

Bugs Bunny. My God, you must weigh about seventy-two pounds."

"*Fritos,*" she moaned, tottering unsteadily out of the elevator. In reality, the thought of eating anything at all triggered her gag reflex, but she would force herself to gain a few pounds before the trip.

For six days she rested, took short walks, ate whatever she could choke down, and reveled in being back home with Brian.

She sent him off to work each morning, his face tense with worry. She would catch him looking at her fearfully, and when she smiled at him, he responded with a ghastly forced grin. He lingered at the doorway, not wanting to leave her, and she always ended up shoving him out with a laugh and instructions for what to bring home for dinner. Then she would fall exhausted on the bed.

She was not unhappy. The freedom and serenity she experienced after her conversation with Margaret remained with her for the most part, despite isolated moments of nightmare and grief. She was grateful to have emerged into a new awareness of herself before it was too late.

But Brian worried her. He refused to discuss the future. Every time she hinted at the possibility of her never recovering, his face became rigid. She longed to talk to him, needed to speak about what was happening to her. He would tell her she was just being morbid and should remember how many crises she had lived through, most of them worse than this. The avoidance disappointed and saddened her.

They would lie next to each other at night, her slim body curled next to his, and he would stroke her and hold her. But that was all. Brian was immobilized by

fear, and Sharlie was too exhausted to feel aroused.
He tired her out. Everyone tired her out.

But the afternoon they set out for Pennsylvania she
seemed more animated than she'd been in days. For a
while she sat watching Brian pack his suitcase, but
suddenly she got up and began to snatch things out
again. She grabbed a T-shirt and stood swaying her
hips provocatively, humming a torch tune. She put it
on over her blouse, reached into the suitcase, and extracted a sport shirt. She wriggled her eyebrows at
Brian, who was standing stock-still, staring at her. She
pulled the shirt on, sleeves dangling almost to her
knees, and fastened each button as she ran her tongue
over her lips seductively. Finally Brian sat down on
the edge of the bed and folded his arms, the better to
enjoy the show. By the time she was finished, she had
donned the T-shirt, the sport shirt, Brian's heavy Irish-
knit sweater, his jeans, his jogging shoes, and a trench
coat. She had all but disappeared under the layers but
was still humming. Like a precarious walking tepee,
she swayed over to Brian and leaned down to whisper
in his ear.

"Hey, big boy, come on backstage and I'll show you
a good time."

Brian pulled her down onto his lap and kissed her.
They both laughed until Brian held her a little too
long and a little too fiercely. She scrambled away
from him and hopped into the suitcase, perching in
the midst of his underwear.

"You might as well just pack me."

"Why bother with the suitcase? Stick a toothbrush
in your ear and we're off."

* * *

The trip seemed very short to Brian, maybe because they talked so much on the way, and maybe because he wasn't really anxious to get there, the familiar landmarks of Devon County appearing all too quickly. But they had a good time, chatting together in a lazy fashion both had found difficult lately.

Sharlie confessed a one-time preoccupation with celebrities. "Every time I went out for a walk, I'd see somebody who was somebody. I got an enormous thrill out of it."

"I never noticed you do that," he said, watching the sky grow cloudy in the southwest, probably right over Silver Creek.

"I don't need the vicarious stuff anymore. I *married* a star."

He laughed. "How come *I* never see anybody?"

"Listen, my love," she said. "I have strolled with you up Madison Avenue and you have practically kissed Howard Cosell and Walter Matthau and you never noticed."

"Thank God," he said fervently.

"Howard Cosell's tough to spot because he's not half as repulsive as you'd think."

"Well, I'm glad to hear you've given it up. Who'd you see yesterday?"

"Greta Garbo and Dustin Hoffman."

He laughed and put his hand on her thigh. He squeezed very gently, feeling the bone under the thin layer of flesh.

"God, you're a pretty lady," he said. Her eyes were deep gray-green in the sunlight, and he found it difficult to drag his attention back to the road.

"I wouldn't look half so pretty with a telephone pole sticking out of my head."

"Nag," he said, both hands back on the wheel.

They stopped once for lunch and again at an overlook, where Sharlie exclaimed at the October landscape—neat brown-green hills, tidy farmhouses, some white, some stone, some red. She said she wished they'd brought their camera, and they sat down on a boulder to enjoy the view.

"We'll get the wedding movies back from your parents when we get home," Brian said. "I want to see them again."

Sharlie laughed. "Daddy probably edited out the bit where he's deep in conversation with Barbara. Somebody at his office might blackmail him."

"Or her."

"You should see the movies of my parents' wedding."

"I didn't think they had movies then," Brian said.

Sharlie looked out at the pale-gray sky. "It's crazy. When I think about anything that happened before about 1940, I visualize it in black-and-white. World War One, the Depression, people dancing the Turkey Trot, or whatever it was—no color at all, just like in the old movies."

"You're a victim of the communications media," Brian said. "What about the American Revolution?"

Sharlie thought this over. "Color. That's odd. And the Renaissance, too."

"From staring at paintings in the Metropolitan Museum."

She laughed. "You're right."

They rested a while longer until finally Sharlie began to shiver in her light jacket.

* * *

By the time they were within twenty miles of Silver Creek, it was dark. The moon, pale and round, had risen in the sky, and its face raced in and out of the clouds.

"He looks like I feel," Brian said pointing up at the white globe.

"How?" Sharlie said, leaning forward to peer out the window.

"Worried," Brian said. "Sure you don't want to turn around and go home?"

Despite Sharlie's prodding, Brian had steadfastly avoided discussing his father. But now, a few miles from his old home, he suddenly blurted, "You know, it's funny, he started getting these hard lumps under the skin on his thumbs, and they'd hurt him when he was working with a pitchfork. Finally he had to give in and see a doctor. Know what they told him?"

"What?"

"He's turning to stone. Calcifying."

"Are you serious?" Sharlie asked.

"I could have saved him the doctor's fee," Brian muttered.

She watched Brian's face in the headlights of an oncoming car. She could see the tough set of his mouth and his jaw muscle tensing. She felt wide awake, excitement keeping her alert and lending her a kind of surface energy. "I'm nervous, too," she said.

"Good. Let's go home."

"What if he hates me?"

"Don't be ridiculous."

"Well, not 'hate.' What if he . . . how do I make a verb out of *contempt*? Contempts me?"

"Holds you in contempt."

"No. That's not right," she said. "You think your father dislikes you, and if he dislikes you, he won't like me because I love you." She paused to catch her breath. "See what I mean?"

"You're just trying to distract me from my urge to make a giant U-turn."

Sharlie stared up at the moon, which did indeed look anxious, eyebrows knit, mouth pinched. "Mmm hmm," she said vaguely.

Brian sighed with resignation and turned off Route 13 onto a narrow road that wove through gentle hills. Sharlie rolled her window all the way down.

"It's positively deafening," she said, greedily inhaling the cold country air.

"The silence?"

"The crickets," she said. "I went to Vermont once when I was about ten, and I couldn't sleep with those damn things rubbing their legs together all night. Don't they ever go to bed?"

"That's how they snore."

"Oh," she said. "I married a naturalist."

"We're almost there."

"The voice of doom," she replied. "Is all this his?" She waved at the countryside.

"A lot of it, but don't be impressed. It's not worth much of a damn."

He pulled up in front of a rambling old building. In the moonlight, it appeared almost deserted except for a small square of light off the front porch.

"We're here?" she asked.

"We're here."

"Oh," Sharlie said. "Hey, let me sit here for a second and get myself together."

"Gladly." He switched off the motor and stretched his stiff arms.

Sharlie felt a sudden terror of entering that house.
She was weak and nauseated and afraid to stand up.
Finally after a few deep breaths she said shakily,
"This country air can kill you, you know. Too much
oxygen. Too rich a mixture."

Brian peered at her closely. "You okay?"

"Just babbling," she murmured.

"Ready?" he asked, staring at the orange window
waiting in the darkness.

"Charge," she said, opening the car door and step-
ping out into the cold night. She had to steady herself
by holding on to the door handle until Brian could get
to her. She tried to keep most of her weight off him,
just leaning enough to retain her balance. When they
reached the front porch and walked up the creaking
wooden steps, she straightened and gave Brian a desperate smile. He knocked on the door, and they heard
a muffled sound from inside. After what seemed like
a long time the porch lamp went on, spotlighting them
and sending a whirlwind of moths swirling above
their heads. Sharlie watched them dance around the
naked bulb, then looked down just in time to see
Brian and his father shaking hands formally.

"Sir," Brian said stiffly. He put his arm around
Sharlie. His father started to ask about the trip at the
same moment that Brian began to introduce her, so
they both broke off, leaving them all in silence again.

Finally Sharlie said, "I'm Sharlie, Mister Morgan.
I'm glad to meet you." She held out her hand and felt
the old man's callused fingers grip hers. She suddenly
remembered the first time she had felt Brian's touch,
back at Saint Joe's almost a year ago. The same sensation—rough, warm hands. She was moved, and looked

away shyly for fear he might see the emotion in her face and think her strange.

Then, with awkward heartiness, John Morgan ushered them into the house, the screen door slamming behind them. One of the little moths slipped inside, too. Sharlie found its company comforting, and watched it settle against the inside of the screen door. She turned and saw Brian and his father halfway down the hall toward the kitchen at the rear of the house. They passed a small sitting room on the right—the source of the glow they'd seen from the road.

"Thought I heard a car outside," the old man said when they reached the kitchen. He pulled out a chair for Sharlie. The table's red Formica surface had become so worn and been polished so many times that it was almost pink. Sharlie sat down carefully, thinking to herself, *Thank you, I'll sit down before I fall down.*

Brian started foraging in the refrigerator. He moved familiarly around the kitchen, finding a plate, a glass, utensils. John Morgan leaned against the counter and watched his son intently. Sharlie was grateful for the opportunity to inspect Brian's father with freedom. How fascinating to scrutinize someone related to the man she knew so intimately. She searched for the impulses behind Brian's well-memorized features and thought she could trace the familiar outline under the rugged, stubbly surface of the old farmer's face. The eyes were identical—blue chips of sky. Chips off the old block.

She must have smiled because John Morgan suddenly looked at her questioningly. "Your eyes, they're exactly like Brian's," she said.

The old man nodded. He didn't return her smile, but his voice was warm. "You hungry?" he asked.

Sharlie shook her head, and she saw his glance fasten briefly on her thin arms. "Good trip?" he asked.

She nodded. "There's a full moon. It was nice." Then they fell silent. Brian sat down, loaded with sandwich material. His father looked in Brian's general direction but didn't quite meet his eyes.

"You working hard at the lawyer business?"

"Yeah," Brian said, mouth full. "Busy time."

The old man nodded and stared down at his arms folded across his chest. Everyone was quiet for a while, until Sharlie began to grow uncomfortable.

"I've never been on a farm before," she said lamely.

"That a fact?" Brian's father muttered.

"It's . . . lovely."

"Hard to see much at night," he said.

Touché, Sharlie thought, and looked at Brian. *Despise*, that's the verb form of *contempt*.

"Well, got to be up at five A.M.," John Morgan said. He nodded to them both, said good night, and left the room abruptly. Sharlie could hear his steps receding up the stairway somewhere in the back of the house. She looked at Brian, trying to keep the dismay out of her face.

"Warm fellow," he said grimly, taking a swallow of beer.

"He's a little . . . shy," Sharlie said, and Brian hooted, nearly choking on his sandwich. Her voice rose a little in protest. "He has to be nice. He looks so much like *you*."

"Yeah, well, my brother looks like Dracula, and he's about the nicest kid on two feet," Brian said.

"Are we going to see them, you think?" Sharlie asked.

"Probably don't even know we're here." At Sharlie's

exclamation of disbelief, he went on, "Unless Dad happened to run into them out in the fields. And they happened to ask if he'd heard anything from me lately."

Suddenly she was overwhelmed by the excitement of the day, the long trip, meeting Brian's father at last. She thought she couldn't possibly hold herself upright at the table for one more second. She must have looked as feeble as she felt, because Brian set his sandwich down and said softly, "Where's your medication?"

"Suitcase," she answered.

He pushed back his wrought-iron chair with a scrape and went to fetch her pills. He returned with the special travel kit he had bought her for the trip, a square canvas case that held her bottles in neat compartments. Her instruction sheet was enclosed, and Brian read the directions under 10 P.M. She sat quietly while he sorted the drugs. Then she swallowed them down with a large glass of lukewarm water.

"I'm going to put you to bed," he said, helping her up.

She didn't protest, just leaned against him and let him lead her upstairs to Brian's and Marcus's old room. The two youngest boys had lived together until Brian left for college, and their beds were still there, neatly made up with plaid blankets. Sharlie sank down on the bed farthest from the door. Brian smiled at her.

"This was yours?" she asked. He nodded. "Don't you want it, then?"

"No, I like seeing you on it."

"I don't know if I can get undressed," she continued, smiling apologetically. He undid her buttons and draped her clothes across the cane chair by the window. Then he opened their suitcase, pulled out her nightgown, and put it over her head, lifting her arms through the sleeves. It hung loosely on her, and she knew that when she stood, it dragged on the floor a little now, as if she had shrunk in stature.

She kept her face averted for fear that he would see her tears, and said softly, to explain her hanging head, "Wow, I'm wiped out."

Brian went to get an extra blanket out of the closet, and when his back was turned, she quickly drew her sleeve across her cheeks. By the time he returned, she could show him a dry face. He snapped off the table lamp, and moonlight streamed in the high windows.

"Want me to pull the shade?" he asked, cupping her face with his hands as he stood over her.

"No," she said fervently. He bent down and kissed her on the top of her head.

"Sleep tight. See you in the morning."

She smiled, and he left her, closing the door quietly behind him. She tugged feebly at the blankets but didn't have the strength to pull them back far enough to crawl in. So she lay back on the rough wool and gazed out the window at the silver light.

She had thought sleep would be instantaneous, but she found her mind whirling with memories of the trip. Often after a special event she would spend the hour before sleep sorting through the day's images. The habit reminded her of the rainbow jukebox she'd seen when she was a child. Walter had shown her how to slip a quarter into the slot and choose three songs— J-6, K-5, M-11. The lights would flash, the machine's long arm stretching to select the favorite tune. Mechanical fingers laid the record precisely onto the turntable in full view of Sharlie's enchanted eyes. *Number J-6, as you wish, little girl.*

Today had added dozens of new selections to her collection. She would begin at A-1 and work her way through, relishing them one by one, playing them over and over if she chose, until she knew them all by heart.

This house. That was A-1. Despite her aching exhaustion, she could barely wait until morning to explore the rambling old place. So remarkable to think of Brian growing up here, playing on the floor in the kitchen under his mother's feet, reading by the fireplace in the sitting room, where, she imagined, his father had waited tonight, this bedroom with its ghosts of childhood and adolescence—the dreams and yearnings and heartbreaks suffered here by someone whose life had shaped hers so profoundly. Brian and Marcus murmuring back and forth in the dark with sleepy, conspiratorial voices—Brian, the little boy she could sense so vividly in the shadows of the old house.

The place touched her deeply, as if by visiting here she was in some way sharing the beginning of Brian's life. She imagined the child Brian, his small fingers exploring the worn books in the shelves between the beds. She heard his young voice, eager to please, calling out to his mother with some new discovery, smelled the odor of his boy's body as he tumbled on the floor, wrestling with his brothers. She felt her knowledge of him deepen and intensify.

Selection A-2: John Morgan. Astonishing to look into the face that Brian's would someday become. How grateful she was, because she knew she would never touch Brian's cheek when his face was carved and lined like his father's.

Same eyes, bright blue and deeply set, the father's shadowed with great bushy, grisled brows. She remembered her first glimpse of the man, framed by the front door, his shadow stiff, lean, a little bent, a figure cut out of black paper against the orange light of the hall.

She thought of Brian and his father, eyes averted from each other, formal and uncomfortable but each one needing the other's—what? Respect? Good opinion? No. It was care. Their caring was evident in the surreptitious glances each gave the other when there was no chance of being caught. The old man had asked about Brian's law office. Surely that was an overture after all the years of bitterness. But Brian remained rigid and wary, determined to barricade his father into some remote place where he could no longer wound.

The jukebox was blurring, colors fading from bright neon to pastel, the outlines wavering. She gazed once more at the moonlit window and drifted into sleep.

She woke up once in the middle of the night, tangled inside the blanket Brian had tucked around her when he came to bed. She looked over at him and could see his face quite clearly in the moonlight. Eerie how he almost seemed to have become a little boy again, the child she had sensed in this house—the outline of his face softened by sleep, his hand curled by his cheek.

She felt sorrow mingle with her tenderness. Only a few weeks ago Brian had slept either facedown or lying on his back, arms and legs flung out, totally open and vulnerable. Recently, however, she had noticed that he often lay clenched in the fetal position,

as he did tonight. It hurt her to watch him curl up
protectively, defending himself against injury. Against
me, she thought sadly. She resisted the impulse to
reach out and touch the curly head. Instead, she ran
her hand along the edge of her sheet. It felt curiously
dry and smooth for such a damp old house. She was
certainly awake for good now, she thought, but very
soon she slipped into a quiet sleep and didn't open her
eyes again until six thirty the next morning.

CHAPTER 53

The sound woke her with a start, an odd, jarring, daytime sound and somehow familiar. Suddenly she realized she was listening to a rooster. Crowing, just like in the movies, except that it wasn't exactly *cock-a-doodle-doo*, more like *aw-aw-aw-aw-AWW*. Same rhythm, same ridiculous self-proclamation. She rolled over to tell Brian, but he was sleeping so peacefully that she couldn't bear to wake him. He'd heard the damn thing so many times, she thought, it was probably like fire engine sirens for her, just subliminal background muttering. She got up, dressing quickly in the cold early morning air.

There wasn't anyone in the kitchen, so she helped herself to a cup of tea and, since she couldn't find a toaster anywhere, a slice of bread. The butter was delicious, so she shrugged away the disapproving specter of Dr. Diller and had another slice, surprised at how well she felt.

She let herself out the back door and strolled to-

ward the barn. John Morgan emerged, carrying two
large gleaming silver pails filled with what Sharlie
presumed was milk, although it was bluish white and
foamy, not like the creamy stuff that Brian consumed
by the carton at home in New York.

"Morning. You're up early," he said. He kept on
walking, the load heavy in his hands.

"Is it okay if I come with you?"

"Unh," he answered. Sharlie interpreted this to be
affirmative, and followed him into a shed where there
were large aluminum troughs into which he poured
the milk.

She asked him questions about what happened to
the milk next, and then followed him back to the barn
again. She watched him as he moved among the cows,
nudging them with his shoulder, comfortable with
their steamy bodies.

"The closest I ever got to a cow was the Children's
Zoo in Central Park. It was the raggediest-looking
thing I ever saw, not like these. It had great big bored
brown eyes. I think it must have died."

"City air probably killed her off," John Morgan said
gloomily, attaching a milking machine to the pink
udder by his knees.

"Do you ever do that by hand?"

"Nope," he said, then glanced briefly at her from
under the bushy eyebrows. "Except every once in a
while."

"It must be slower," she said. He either grimaced or
smiled, Sharlie wasn't sure which.

"Good—what do you call it—good therapy," he said.

Now Sharlie saw that his eyes were laughing—the
same way Brian's did, except that the rest of his face

didn't change at all. The man would be a whiz at poker, she thought.

"Yours or the cow's?" she asked, and he chuckled a little.

"Both, most likely. I get down in the mouth or mad and I get me and my stool and sit by this old lady here," he leaned against the side of the cow. "Takes the sting out of me after a while."

"I bet she likes your fingers better than those steel things." He didn't answer her, just watched the pail fill up at his feet.

"Mister Morgan," Sharlie said shyly.

He peered at her with such intensity that she almost lost her nerve.

"Will you . . . do you have time to teach me?"

His face broke into a grin. "Just let me get my stool," he said, and disappeared into a neighboring stall.

Brian stood in the doorway, peering into the dim light of the barn. The shadowy forms puzzled him. Marcus here now? But what was Dad doing? What were they both doing, hand-milking? He moved closer and stopped dead in his tracks as Sharlie and his father turned around to look at him. Sharlie's face was flushed from hard work and pleasure. His father looked embarrassed, but pleased as well.

"Brian, look at me!" Sharlie exclaimed. "Do you believe it? I learned *very* quickly."

His father nodded. "Better farmer already than you ever thought of being."

Sharlie flinched at this but then returned to her cow and said, "Why didn't you *tell* me this was so terrific?"

Brian stood watching as she became absorbed in her work. Then he left the barn to walk back to the house in confusion, his feelings a jumble of gratification, irritation, and a vague, disembodied jealousy. Mostly he felt he'd been manipulated into a position he wasn't sure he was prepared to accept. But he wasn't certain he was so angry about it, either.

He fixed himself some breakfast, toasting his bread on the stove burners as always. What did they have against electrical appliances in this place anyway? It had taken years to buy an electric iron finally instead of that cumbersome thing his mother had to heat every few seconds. Brian munched on his toast and thought about the scene in the barn. Every now and then he'd shake his head and smile.

After a while, they came clattering up the porch steps outside, Sharlie's voice happy and comfortable and his father chuckling. He hadn't heard that sound since long before his mother died.

They burst in, and Sharlie said, "Quick. Liquid refreshment. All that squirting . . ."

The old man pressed her into a chair and went to the refrigerator to pour her a huge glass of milk. When he cracked a raw egg into it, Brian began to protest, but Sharlie put her hand on his arm.

"Drink this. You'll get another one in a couple of hours."

Sharlie sipped and made a face. John Morgan took the glass from her and rummaged through the cupboards until he found the vanilla. He added a generous dollop to her milk, plus a tablespoon of sugar. Then he took a fork and stirred the mixture rapidly, his strong wrist whipping.

She took another sip, smiled at him, and swallowed

some more. He stood over her until she drank it all, then glanced at Brian with triumph. "She ought to have one of those with every meal. Fatten her up in no time. Damn, she's just a slip of a thing. Look at those arms."

"Your father says he'll come see us in New York," Sharlie said. Brian's eyes widened while John Morgan looked out the window. "If I can milk a cow," she continued, "your Dad can ride the subway. Right, Mister Morgan?"

"Guess so," he muttered.

Sharlie kept her voice neutral as she stood up, holding tightly to the edge of the table. "I'm kind of tired all of a sudden. I think I'll go rest awhile." She leaned over and gave Brian a kiss, then planted one on her father-in-law's cheek. He looked startled at first, then both men's expressions pleaded, *Don't leave us here alone together*. But Sharlie turned and walked out of the room.

She had to haul herself up the stairs by force of will. She was dizzy and weak, and had begun to feel the disorientation again, the sensation of being disconnected to the world and the people around her. It was as if she were watching everything from a distance.

She lay down on the bed and thought about the first time she'd felt it, during her most recent trip to the hospital. In the beginning she had been frightened and wondered if another undetected medical problem had arisen. Then the strange feeling faded, not completely, just enough to leave her with a slightly shifted perspective. It was as if she no longer stood in the center of her life, with the people she cared for revolving around her. Rather, she was edging slowly toward the circumference of the circle. At first the implication of her displacement seemed terrible, but gradually she acknowledged it as a merciful process. She knew that once she stood well outside the circle, it would be far less painful to turn and walk away from it.

She awoke to see Brian staring down at her solemnly.

"How long have you been here?" she murmured.

"Just a few minutes," he lied.

She turned her face away from the late afternoon glare streaming in the window. Brian went to pull down the shade. "You don't feel so hot, do you?" he asked her.

She shook her head. She could feel tears beginning behind her eyelids and kept them shut tight. *Two steps away from the center, one step back,* she thought. That must be the way it would happen.

"Tell me about your father," she said.

"Thanks for leaving me there like that, you witch."

The corners of her mouth twitched a little. "So?"

"So he says he's really coming. I don't know." He stopped to shake his head. "There's no way you could have made me believe it. He says he wants to see the agriculture exhibit."

"Didn't know there was one," she whispered, fighting the urge to go back to sleep.

"And also the Statue of Liberty."

They were silent a moment, Sharlie, through the mist, aware of a vague contentment.

Brian said slowly, "He's smitten with you."

She smiled at the word and opened her eyes. "He's not bad himself. Reports to the contrary notwithstanding. He tell you about the mortgage thing?"

Brian nodded. "I gave him some advice. Not that he had the guts to come out and ask for it."

"Oh, come on, Brian, have a heart."

He took her hand and held it to his face. "Anyway, he's full of helpful hints about what to feed you—all the stuff you're supposed to give an undernourished cow."

She laughed. "We're going to have to tell him about me, or he'll drown me in cholesterol."

Brian said, "He thinks you look ill."

"I am, honey," she said gently, but suddenly he wouldn't look at her. "Bri, would you do something for me?" she asked.

He nodded.

"Take me to the ocean." He looked at her in surprise. "Instead of staying here, we could go to the Jersey Shore, couldn't we? It's not that far."

"I thought you wanted to meet my brothers."

"Well, I do. But I've got this urge, and we only have another two days. Could we?"

"All right." His face was puzzled, but he didn't question her. Sharlie realized that his loathing to press her emerged from his fear of her answer.

"We'll go first thing in the morning," he said. He opened their suitcase and started piling clothes inside.

"Are you hungry?" he asked finally in a muffled voice.

"No."

"I'll bring something up," he said, still not looking at her.

"Bovine nutrients, please. On rye, and hold the mayo."

He didn't laugh, just continued packing in silence. His movements were clumsy, and he had to keep bending down to retrieve things that slipped off onto the floor.

After watching this for a few moments, Sharlie said softly, "Bri, I wish I could help."

"I'll manage. You rest."

"I didn't mean the packing."

He froze for a second, then continued working deliberately.

"Can we talk about it?" she asked.

"About what?"

"About me. My not getting better."

He turned around, and his face was fierce. "You've had a long trip. You're worn out. You'll be fine in a couple of days."

She watched sorrowfully as he muttered something about her dinner and bolted from the room.

Brian marched around the kitchen pulling things out of the refrigerator and slamming cabinet doors, hoping that if he moved fast enough and made enough of a racket, the sensation in his chest would disappear. His lungs seemed to be packed with dry ice, burning and yet frozen, the icy vapor making it difficult for him to catch his breath.

He imagined himself in the midst of a nightmare, running along the beach on a foggy winter morning. Behind him loomed a huge dark shape, cold, steady, invincible. The faster Brian pushed his legs, the deeper he sank into the sand until finally he was using every bit of energy just to free his feet from the heavy earth. And behind him the shadow grew, thundering, its breath like icicles piercing the back of his neck.

"What's for dinner?"

Brian started, dropped the glass he had been holding. It smashed on the floor. His father regarded him thoughtfully.

"Daydreaming," the older man said.

Brian bent to pick up the shards of glass.

"I still spend a lot of time doing that," Brian said bitterly. His father handed him the broom.

"Sharlie coming down?"

Brian shook his head.

"Still asleep?"

"No."

"Gotta eat."

"I'll take her something."

"She doesn't look so good."

"You've never seen her when she's bad. I have, and right now she looks just fine. Tired. Anybody'd be tired."

John Morgan looked steadily at his son. Brian swept furiously at the dark wood floor.

"She been real sick?"

"Yeah," Brian said. The old man put his hand on Brian's shoulder briefly, just long enough to stop the compulsive movement of the broom.

"Don't do what I did, son." His eyes bored into Brian's. "There's a lot of things I wish I'd of said to your mother. Too bad I was such a coward."

"You don't know she's going to . . . what's going to happen. You're not a doctor."

John Morgan just shook his head and took the broom from Brian. As he put it away, he spoke carefully into the dark mustiness of the broom closet. "Well, if you ever need anything . . . or her . . ." Then he shut the closet door and went outside in a hurry.

Brian watched at the window until his father's wiry

figure disappeared into the barn, then sat down at the table and put his head in his hands.

The next morning Brian packed everything up in the car before Sharlie even got out of bed. He took a tray to her and pressed her to eat, but she could only manage a swallow of orange juice.

He helped her dress, finally, and carried her down the stairs. "Don't you think we ought to go straight back to Saint Joseph's?" he asked.

"No," she said firmly. "I'm not sticking one toe inside any hospital."

"They could give you something."

"They can't do anything for me."

He started to protest, but saw by her pallor that he was tiring her.

In the rutted driveway outside he moved the front seat of the car back into its reclining position and stepped aside for her.

"Your dad," she said, supporting herself against the hood.

"You can say good-bye from there," he said, motioning to the seat.

"On my feet I will," she pronounced.

Brian gave her an exasperated look and went off to the barn. In a few minutes they emerged together, and as they approached the car, Sharlie noticed that they were conversing as they walked, both with their eyes on the ground but at least talking.

John Morgan stood in front of her, his blue eyes so clear and sharp that she experienced the same sensation she'd so often felt with Brian, that he was peering straight into the center of her head.

"Well, Sharlie," he said, his face somber.

"Well," she said, smiling up into his rough face. He held out his hand, and she took it, the skin leathery and warm around her fingers. She knew suddenly that her journey would be easier if she could only hold that hand right to the end.

"You've been good for my boy," he said quietly.

"I hope you're right." He nodded. "I worry about that," she said, looking at him with a question in her eyes.

"Don't. He'll be okay."

She nodded and reached up to kiss the sun-browned face. "I'm so glad," she murmured, and knew he shared her conviction that they would not see each other again. She held his arm as she slid into the car and lay back against the seat.

Brian shook hands with his father, said a gruff good-bye, and got in to start the car. John Morgan saw Sharlie's pale hand wave to him, a tiny white butterfly disappearing behind the trees. He stood watching until he couldn't see it any longer.

CHAPTER 54

"How long will it take us to get there?" she asked.

"Couple of hours. Three, maybe." He looked at her. "You in a hurry?"

"As a matter of fact . . ." Her voice was feeble. Then she seemed to slip off into sleep, or at least she kept her eyes closed. Her hair fell back from her face, and Brian could see the spot just under her left ear where her pulse surfaced. More than once he nearly drove off the road looking for the tiny beat.

Around noon Sharlie opened her eyes and lifted her head to look out the window.

"I smell salt air. Are we close?"

"We've been driving along the coast for about half an hour. It's just the other side of that rise."

She put on her glasses and strained to see over the low pine trees that fringed the empty highway. Brian turned off onto the shoulder of the road, got out, and raised the back of her seat. Before he could straighten up, she put her hand behind his neck, brought his

head down to her face, and kissed him. She felt him
press hard against her mouth for a moment, then pull
back.

"I don't want to hurt you," he said, with his face so
full of sorrow it was hard for her to look at him.

"If there's one thing I know in this world," she said,
running a finger down his cheek, "it's that you would
never hurt me if you could possibly avoid it."

He tried to stand up, but she kept her hands on his
shoulder, holding him.

"I wish I didn't have to hurt you, Bri."

He looked down at the folds of her dress. It was the
one she had bought at Bloomingdale's, the one that
initiated the Battle of the Batter. She had discovered
it looked attractive with a cowl-necked jersey underneath. But even with the addition of a bulky sweater,
it hung loose on her now.

He looked at her with pleading eyes. "Then don't."

She sighed and dropped her hands.

He said, "Please don't give up." She sat still, feeling
his fingers close around her arms. "I won't let you go.
I will not let you."

She looked down, her face shielded by a curtain of
soft dark hair. After a moment he saw drops splash
against the hands she had folded neatly in her lap like
a polite little girl at the dinner table.

"God . . ." Brian said in a strangled voice. He shut
her door firmly, got back in the car, and drove out
onto the highway again.

The trees along the roadside gradually thinned out,
and she could catch occasional glimpses of the sea beyond a long expanse of marsh. The tall green grass
moved with the wind, and she watched the breeze ap-

proach from far off, rippling the surface of the swamp. A fishing boat purred through the grass, pushing it aside and leaving a green wake behind. Here and there tiny wooden shacks rose on stilts above the water.

Her father had talked to her of the sea. How she had yearned to see it, and how eagerly she had listened to his descriptions. Her sudden urgency to visit the seaside now seemed like the need to complete a circle—the ending meeting the beginning. If the circle is complete, it can be set aside. Sorrowfully, but with a sense of appropriate finality.

She wanted to see the shore, to walk along it, or if she couldn't walk, then stand where the water rushed up against the sand. Then she could go home.

Brian insisted that they spend the night right there, and she was too weak to argue with him. Tourists were scarce so late in autumn, and they had no trouble finding a room that overlooked the deserted beach. Sharlie spent the afternoon in bed, staring out the window at the sea curling into froth against the sand. The colors pleased her—gray sea and sky, pale clouds, white-breaking waves, a foreground of soft gray-beige shore. Bright sunshine and brilliant colors had begun to disturb her. They jarred her like harsh noises, too loud, too discordant for the hushed, contemplative world she had entered.

When Brian went out to run along the beach, she saw him wave up toward her window, his lean body growing smaller, long denim legs disappearing against the sand. She fell into a kind of half sleep after that and didn't wake up until the middle of the night.

Brian had left the curtain open. He knew that she hated the darkness now and was comforted by the pale light that usually filtered through their window at home. But there was no moon tonight, and no street-lamps to brighten the sky. She woke up aching and disoriented, and in the heavy darkness she began to panic. She felt like a little girl, all alone in a terrible black world. She was sick, and there was no one to help her. She could cry for help, and nobody would hear her feeble child's voice through the oppressive weight of the night. She began to whimper quietly, trying to muffle the sound against her pillow.

After a moment a warm arm stretched across her chest, and curls brushed her shoulder. A sleepy voice murmured by her ear, "What is it, love?"

Suddenly she became a grown woman again, lying with the man who would hold her through her terror. He couldn't stay beside her the whole distance, but he could comfort her along the way.

She turned to him and burrowed into his body and let him stroke her back. Finally she fell asleep again and didn't wake up until soft daylight reflected off the wet sand.

Brian was already packed. He had run out for some rolls and fruit so that they could drive home without stopping for lunch.

The gray cast of her skin frightened him, and he hoped it was due to her restless night. He felt his helplessness as a crushing weight, almost a physical presence, dragging at him until it was barely possible to do anything at all, even put one foot in front of the other.

Outside Long Branch he was pretty certain she had lost consciousness, but just as he was about to pull off the road and look for a hospital, she revived enough to open her eyes. It was as if she had drifted into another level of awareness and was forcing herself back each time to take one more breath of the life they shared. Once he turned to find her staring at him. She smiled and said, "Hi," and closed her eyes again.

Pretty soon he was driving under the flight approach for the airport, and she murmured, "I smell Newark."

"Almost home," he said. "I think we'd better stop at Saint Joe's on the way."

"No."

He shook his head.

"Pull over a second, will you?" she asked.

"What's the matter?" he said, moving over into the slow lane.

"I'd like to sit up."

He got out of the car as trucks and cars whizzed past, some blasting their horns. He felt the breeze from their wakes. This time he lifted Sharlie's seat and bent to kiss her without prompting. Then he released her quickly and got back into the car.

"Do we have to go through a tunnel?" Sharlie asked.

"Why?"

"If it's not a hassle, I'd rather not. Is there a bridge somewhere?"

"The George Washington. It's north, but we can do it."

"Thanks."

He thought she had fallen asleep again, but after a moment she said groggily, "Wake me up for the bridge, okay?"

"Okay," he said and reached over to touch her knee. He left his hand there, and she covered it with hers—a cool, pale hand with slim fingers. So familiar, so tangible. *Don't*, he thought, the word a scream inside his head.

She awoke on her own when they started up the ramp. It was a bright day, the outline of Manhattan's skyline crisp and dramatic. The city seemed to glisten, the October air shimmering around it like heat rising from hot summer pavement. Everything was supervivid, the images so intense that Sharlie thought the sight must be etched forever into the horizon the way it felt seared into her memory.

"Realer than real," Brian murmured, and Sharlie gave his hand a squeeze. Uncanny how so often they shared the same perception. She missed that common vision in the shadows she now inhabited. She walked in places he couldn't follow her, but instead of listening hard for her footsteps in the gray light of that inner world, he grasped at her, yanking on her arm, trying to pull her back along the old paths.

She couldn't take him with her, but at least she could share some of her solitary voyage in words—if only he would listen.

She gazed at him now. The light from the window behind his face outlined his profile with the same vivid reality as it did the skyline. Sharlie sat quietly in her shadows, contemplating the blazing light all around her, not envious or bitter, just collecting the sight of it the way she had as a child when she had spent the last few moments before museum closing time, staring hungrily at a favorite watercolor. She had known that she must leave eventually but wanted to drink the beloved shapes and hues until the last moment.

Not that she hadn't been angry this time. She

looked back over the weeks since the operation and realized how violently she had struggled against what her instinct told her was inevitable. Everyone probably does it at one time or another—the right of every human being to shake his fist in rage at the final destiny. I just happen to know when and how, she thought, and had to speed things up by a few decades.

Not that it was an easy process. The anticipation of imminent and ultimate separation loomed before her in moments of agonizing grief. She was haunted by something she called the NTB's—the never-to-be's. Never to watch Brian growing older. Never to hold a child. Never to share the subtleties and infinite varieties of the long love she knew could have been hers.

The list was endless, but eventually she was always comforted by the realization that no one ever experiences it all. There would always be the longing for more—to live like an Eskimo, to set her foot down on every inch of the planet and then, of course, the moon and the solar system and the regions beyond. Hers was a universal resentment, she thought. There was always so much left to do. But how she had lived! Loving Brian had been an adventure of such intensity that each hour with him expanded within itself, a convoluted fan of many colors and folds, complex and mysterious, a discovery of themselves separately and of the two of them in the entity they called "us," which was so much more than the sum of the two parts.

They pulled up in front of the apartment building on Third Avenue. Brian got out, motioning to her to stay where she was. He handed their suitcase to the doorman and then reached in to lift Sharlie in his arms. She leaned against him, her cheek rubbing the nubbly texture of his heavy sweater.

He set her down while he unlocked the door, but once he'd shoved the suitcase inside the apartment, he picked her up again and swung her over the threshold. He stood holding her in the center of the room for a long while until finally he walked slowly into the bedroom and put her down on their bed.

She smiled up at him and whispered, "Home."

"Want me to call your parents?" he asked.

She nodded. "They should come tonight if they can, but tell them just for a few minutes."

He started out the door, and she called after him.

"And Brian . . ."

He turned around.

"Try to find Mary MacDonald."

"On the phone?"

"No. I want to see her. Soon. Okay?"

He nodded and almost ran out of the room.

CHAPTER 55

Sharlie's parents sat in chairs by the edge of the double bed. Margaret's eyes were wet, but her straight back told Sharlie she would discipline her grief. There would be no ululations from Margaret.

Walter was hunched in his seat, eyes dazed and bewildered, like a child about to receive punishment for some mysterious grown-up offense.

"Mother," Sharlie said, turning her huge dark eyes on Margaret. "I never thanked you."

"For what, darling?"

"For what you offered to do for me."

"I don't know what you mean."

Sharlie smiled. She had weakened to the point of needing to stop for rests between sentences. "You do know." She looked at Walter, but his face was puzzled. Sharlie said to him, "When they couldn't find me a donor, Mother wanted them to take her heart."

Walter gaped at his wife, and she dropped her eyes.

"How did you find out?" Margaret asked softly.

Sharlie shook her head.

Walter was still staring at Margaret. "You never told me," he said accusingly.

"Oh, Daddy," Sharlie said. "You would have had a fit."

Margaret took Sharlie's hand, warming it between her own.

"Are you two all right?" Sharlie asked.

"Of course we're all right," Margaret said.

"No," Sharlie protested, shaking her head weakly. "I mean *together* all right."

Walter and Margaret glanced at each other as their daughter went on. "People in my condition get to ask all kinds of impertinent questions." She watched her parents looking at each other. "Never mind," she said. "I think I can figure it out."

She closed her eyes.

"Do you want to sleep, Chuck?" Walter asked.

Sharlie nodded. After a moment she said, "Stay a few more minutes, and then I want you to go home."

Walter's shoulders had begun to shake. He clenched his teeth, trying to control the shuddering, but in a matter of seconds Sharlie was sound asleep, and he let the tears stream down his face. Margaret was crying, too. The first time she tried to remove her hand from Sharlie's, her fingers would not obey her, but finally she let go and stood. She and Walter walked out together, and didn't even notice Brian standing by the doorway. They looked old and bent like two aged trees leaning against each other for support.

Brian went into the bedroom and lay down on the bed, carefully, but so that his body touched hers lightly. Then he stared up at the ceiling and thought about Mary MacDonald.

She had arrived at the apartment half an hour after he had had her paged at Saint Joseph's. She went straight to Sharlie without asking Brian any questions except "Where is she?" The nurse did a quick examination, but before she could get to the phone to call an ambulance, Sharlie had asked Brian to leave her alone with Mary for a few minutes.

He left the room obediently, but once outside, he began to panic at being separated from her. What if something should happen and he wasn't with her? Any time away from her was a moment lost, irretrievable. Precious minutes now. He resented having to go to the bathroom, having to sleep—anything that drew him away from her for even a second.

He fought with himself constantly. She had told him in the beginning that she was going to die. She'd worn that wry smile and said, *Isn't the whole damn thing one big sick joke?* He didn't accept it then, and he couldn't accept it now. *They* do, he thought, her parents and Mary. And Sharlie. She got there before any of the rest of us. But then, she knew before we did.

He had felt a great heaving inside his body, as if everything within his rib cage were massing a protest against the travesty. He looked at the bedroom door, open just a sliver. Maybe she's already gone, he thought. His heart beat so fast he didn't think he could breathe. He started toward the room, and then he heard Sharlie's voice.

"I want them to use everything," she was saying.

"You sure?" Mary asked quietly.

"All of it. Eyes, lungs, kidneys. I don't suppose they can use poor old Udstrom anymore."

"It would be a first," Mary said.

"They can take what's left for medical school and burn everything else."

Mary must have turned away then, because her voice sounded very low. He retreated back to the living room and slumped onto the couch, sickened by what he had heard. Finally the nurse appeared. Her face was solemn, but she was dry-eyed and calm.

"Brian, you're being a pain in the ass," she said.

He looked at her with a stricken face.

"You want to make it tougher on her," she went on, "you're doing a great job."

Brian opened his mouth, but nothing came out. Mary sat down, shoving at him to make room for her broad backside.

"Listen, honey, it's a lousy thing," she said, and at the kind words his eyes began to tear. "But you've got to let go."

"You can't let them carve her up."

Mary's voice was sharp. "It's her body. It's her death. You'll have plenty of time for your own grief, but she doesn't have much. You're screwing up what's left."

"What should I do?" he asked hoarsely.

"Just be with her when she wants you there. If she wants to talk, fine. If she wants quiet, be quiet. But don't keep trying to hold her back."

"How the hell—?"

"I don't know how you're going to do it," she interrupted. "You're so crazy about her I figure you can at least try."

"We never had a chance . . ." he began, but she interrupted again.

"You sorry you got yourself into this?"

Brian waited a long moment before answering. Finally he shook his head.

"No. Not even now."

"I think she might like to know that," Mary said quietly. Then she told him to call her if there were anything she could do, gave him instructions about drugs, and let herself out, closing the front door firmly behind her.

That was over two hours ago, and he hadn't been alone with Sharlie since, except for a few minutes between Mary's departure and the visit from his in-laws.

Now he turned his head so that he could look at her face on the pillow next to him. She was so thin that her bones were clearly outlined under the pale silken skin. Her eyes, full of fire even now, were sunken and shadowed. She was so still and emaciated that he couldn't help but imagine that she was already dead lying on some stainless steel table, the body that had known so many intimate touches from his warm hands now laid open, desecrated—gloved fingers of strangers reaching in, removing mysterious pieces of her, maybe making jokes. . . . He stopped himself forcibly for fear he might begin to scream or to vomit.

A glint of light appeared under her long lashes, and she opened her eyes, turning her head painfully to look at him. "Hello," she said softly.

"How you doing?" Brian asked, reaching out to stroke her hair.

"Fantastic," she said with a little smile.

"What did Mary have to say?" he asked neutrally.

"Stay off the water skis and be a good girl."

"You know what?" Brian said.

She waited.

"I love you," he said, keeping his voice light.

"An old married lady like me. Fancy that."

"I *do* fancy that," he said. "I'm so fucking lucky I can't believe it," he whispered.

"That's onomatopoetic. Or something," she said.

"What?"

"Fucking lucking. I mean, fucky lucky."

"I never heard you say *fuck* before."

She closed her eyes. "Never too late." He was silent, just kept on stroking her hair. "Why lucky, Bri?"

"You. The one who passes out getting off the bus." She sniffed a little. "That was *luck*, huh?"

"I wouldn't have missed it."

He could see the tears collecting under her eyelashes. After a minute she said, "You mean that?"

"I do," he said firmly.

She sighed, in what sounded to him like great relief. Then two little trails of shiny water trickled down her cheeks.

"This is not exactly a breeze," she choked.

He wiped the tears away with his hand.

"Tell me how to help," he said.

"Just be with me, that's all."

"All right."

"But Bri . . . would you move over a little? Everything hurts."

He moved away so that his body no longer touched hers.

"You can hold my hand." She held hers out to him, and he took it gently.

"You want something for pain?"

She shook her head.

"When I fall asleep, you go make yourself a monster sandwich." She smiled a little through her drowsiness, and her body gradually began to relax. He lay back against the pillow, pleading inside, *Don't let it be this time. Not yet.*

Despite his battle to stay awake, he soon fell asleep himself and dreamed of California, and Sharlie making love to him with her gauze postoperative mask on.

I am approaching this thing ambivalently, Sharlie thought to herself. On the one hand, we all have to go sometime, and there's my conviction that I have lived more fully than most. Certainly inside my head I have. But on the other hand, there's the greed: more days; more Brian; children; growing middle-aged, getting wrinkles and silver hair and varicose veins. Seeing. Tasting. Making love in every possible position. I've only begun. And yet, on the other hand— how many hands do I have, anyway?— I've finished something, too. Not growing up, exactly. Nobody ever does that. But my life seems completed in some way, as if I've come full circle on my round-trip ticket.

Here I am lying next to Brian on the bed that's known so much joy. The air in this room must still be vibrating from the intensity of our lovemaking.

Here I am in the center of space that's so vividly alive, and very soon I won't be at all. That's when I start to get scared. What will I be? I cannot bring myself to believe in God. Even now, if he were to come sit on the end of this bed and say through his long white beard, *Charlotte, my child, here I am, in the flesh* (or in the spirit, as the case may be), I'd probably sock him right in the long Roman nose and tell him to go away and leave me to my hellfire and damnation, thank you very much.

Everybody's always so concerned about divine forgiveness. If there's somebody up there, how can *we* ever forgive *him*?

So that leaves the scientific approach. We are merely an ambulatory pile of chemicals, and when they malfunction, that's the end. Just black unconsciousness. Not so horrible, really, as long as there's not one iota, not one speck, not a whit of awareness. Total wipe-out.

However . . . what about the magic? There *is* magic in the human personality, something beyond mathematical equations, Pavlovian responses, Freudian impulses. Heredity plus environment plus chemicals do not quite equal Sharlie. Too simplistic. Too arrogant. Imagination seems more to me than mere electrical circuitry. But perhaps that's *my* arrogance.

It's all most confusing and troublesome, and I don't expect to have it worked out before I breathe my last. What a thought. It sends my heart pumping and probably brings that last inhalation even closer. Will there be a death rattle? I think there's always supposed to be one.

She cleared her throat, making a little rasping noise. Like that? she wondered.

If I had my druthers, I would simply go right on lying here next to this beautiful man. But druthers have been in short supply these days, and besides, I am so very tired.

Brian. Letting go of him is the supreme cruelty. It's probably easier to be the one who's going, not the one who's left behind, although I'm not sure of it. It's almost always been me who was abandoned, left alone in some hospital bed while everybody else went roller-skating or building snowmen or falling in love.

Separating. All my life I guess I've been trying to figure out how to do it, and I think I'm finally getting the hang of it. . . .

Brian rolled over in his sleep and came to rest against her shoulder. His warmth was worth the discomfort, and she didn't nudge him. As she looked toward the window, the blue light was fading, and she felt the shadows easing their way into the room. There was numbness in her body now, a curious sensation. First a slight tingling feeling, like faraway bells ringing a final farewell. Then nothing. It was not altogether unpleasant. How simple it would be to let go and slide away from everything in this gradual, merciful closing down of circuits.

No, she must not leave Brian that way. He was entitled to his completed circle, too, and waking up to find her lying cold and dead beside him simply would not do.

She gave him a little prod with her finger, wondering that she could get her hand to respond at all. There was no sensation of touching, but she saw the indentation of the fabric of his shirt as she poked at him. He turned his face to her, and it was the sleepy one that always made her smile. The creases from his pillow were etched in his flushed cheeks.

She opened her mouth to say his name, but nothing came out. She felt brief panic but then resolution. Well, she thought, that's gone already, is it? Good thing I woke him when I did.

He looked into her face, and with his father's eyes he saw inside her mind and read what she was silently telling him.

"What can I do?" he whispered.

She couldn't answer him, just watched him with hungry eyes. He propped himself up on one elbow so that she could see him without straining.

She had already begun to disappear from him, and he knew she woke him so that he could say good-bye. He lifted her hand from the bed and put it to his mouth.

"Thank you, Sharlie," he said. She gazed back at him wordlessly and soon the light began to leave her eyes. Then she closed them, and he knew that she was gone.

CHAPTER 56

Brian held a small ceremony in the apartment. There was no minister. He knew what Sharlie thought of funerals, could imagine her wry smile, the slight shake of her head.

"The funeral's for us," he said to Walter. "She would have thought we were nuts."

Brian's father arrived that afternoon. He gave his son a white china pitcher in the shape of a cow, intended as a wedding present that he thought would amuse Sharlie. Brian began to cry when he opened the gift.

"I'm sorry. I shouldn't have brought it," John Morgan said gruffly. "Better throw it away." He reached for it, but Brian held on to it tightly.

"No. I want it. Thank you." He smiled apologetically at his father and led him into the living room to be introduced.

There were only a few of them—Walter and Margaret and Mary MacDonald and Ramón Rodriguez

(Brian couldn't bring himself to invite Diller, or even Barbara Kaye). Brian read some of the poetry Sharlie had been particularly moved by—Yeats, John Donne, Emily Dickinson. For himself, he read Elizabeth Barrett Browning, all the time imagining Sharlie's amused face just behind his shoulder.

They drank wine and talked quietly together, and even laughed a little. Then everyone left, and Brian, surprised to find himself glad to be alone, sat among the dirty wineglasses and bouquets of carefully cheerful flowers and let the room go dark.